SONG

OF

RAMONA

A FAIRY TALE FOR PIRATES AND ROGUES

MEG MERRIET

This is a Zazie Books edition 2021.

Designer Credits
Cover Art by thecovercollection.com
Interior Design by Anna Zubrytskaya

Print: 978-1-62134-413-1
Mobi: 978-1-62134-414-8
E-pub: 978-1-62134-415-5

For gutter punks and street musicians.
And for Kurt, my fearless big brother.

ACKNOWLEDGMENTS

I am deeply indebted to all those brilliant minds who provided feedback on my early drafts, particularly Dmitry Feller, Rachel Poy, Andrew Wahlberg, Sara Stone and Kay Dominguez. Their insights and suggestions were instrumental in rounding out the spirit of this novel.

I am also indebted to my incredible cousin Sarah Toledo who has encouraged and supported my writing since I was twelve years old, offering critique on all my early manuscripts. When she read my first pirate novel, she was devastated by the violent death of a crewman named Thomas. To make amends for this egregious blunder, Thomas has been restored to life in Song of Ramona. Keep an eye out for him, coz.

TABLE OF CONTENTS

ARTICLES OF THE WASTREL

I. A man who disobeys orders in battle shall be thrown to the cloudsea.

II. A man who steals or withholds prizes from the crew shall be wind-hauled (bound in rope and flown under the gondola from bow to stern).

III. All quarrels must be settled at port. If any man does bodily harm to another in the crew while on the Wastrel, that man shall suffer such punishment as the majority of the crew sees fit.

IV. All men shall receive equal rations.

V. A woman discovered on board shall be quarantined in the Captain's Quarters until she and any who aided in her subterfuge are cast out at the nearest port.

VI. A man who shall smoke tobacco or hold any open flame aboard the Wastrel shall suffer the same punishment as in the former Article.

VII. A man who neglects to keep his weapons clean and ready shall be locked in the cargo hold overnight.

VIII. A man who forces amorous congress upon a woman without her consent shall be shot.

IX. A man who suffers amputation shall be discharged with one hundred gold pieces for every limb lost.

X. Musicians shall only play above deck, and never past the hour of midnight.

1

THE WASTREL

The noise of the sky was terrific, wind howling in my skull, the hum of the engines filling my ears. These sounds, along with the hiss of the hoses that pushed lift into our balloon, made it almost impossible to make out the commands of my superiors.

"Fledglings! Prepare the Hawks for the first wave!" called out our quartermaster Mr. Bentley as he charged down the center of the main deck.

Remembering all the terminology of an airship was challenging in its own right. I knew the business of locks and clocks quite thoroughly, but sky piracy was still a relatively new enterprise for me. I had been at it just under a year.

The Wastrel was a rigid airship of early design that employed many elements of naval engineering in her construction. Beneath her elongated balloon, she carried an enormous gondola suspended by steel cables. These were attached to the riveted framework. A pair of red membranous batwings extended from the ship's sides, catching the wind when we made our descent. If we needed to be more aerodynamic, they could be swept back with the maneuvering of a few ropes, but they usually remained open to stabilize us on the air. The Wastrel also had a rudder to help steer her trajectory. It did not work too well; it had been cracked by a bolt of lightning long before I ever joined the crew, and the captain saw no reason to pour man-hours into fixing it.

The ship had a sort of rugged beauty about her, with embellishments from a time when embellishment was all the rage. Her railings, doors, and archways boasted accents of crown molding and carved sirens. Though the paint was chipping away on these details, the men revered the Wastrel with romantic wonder and took pride in keeping her. She might have been an old bird, but for many of us, she was the only home we knew.

"Full speed ahead!" shouted Captain Dirk from the helm as we chased our prize. At the moment, I could not see the target through the clouds. Only a dim shadow loomed beyond the misty swells.

Our propellers shrieked as we heaved forward, rapidly ascending. Whenever we picked up speed or made a sudden maneuver, it was protocol to hold onto something. I grabbed the nearest rail, training my eye on the other ship as we gained on her.

"Fly the spade!" commanded Captain Dirk.

Every proper pirate had a notorious Jolly Roger, something unique to distinguish himself in the Cloudsea. People in Elsace knew the Roger of the white spade, knew the stories of gore in the clouds, of severed heads raining down from any ship that gave chase to Captain Alexander Dirk. When targets saw the black flag trail out just beneath the cracked rudder, they surrendered every time.

The Wastrel was equipped with twenty-five cannons, a ballista, and enough parachutes to save a hundred and fifty souls. They lined the rails and each and every day, I prayed to all my gods I would never have to use one.

Prayer was a useful thing to sky pirates. It helped us to cope with the unknown, which had become a constant in our lives on the air. We prayed to Ithicus, bird-god of the sky, for lift and smooth air. We prayed to Rheus of the sun and Camilla of the moon to light our way in the dark. The all-father, Throm, controlled the weather. To him, we prayed the most, for a single storm could rip an airship apart. As robust as our vessel appeared in the sky, it was made of only wood, cloth, and rubber. It was a fragile, man-made thing and its keeping to the air continued to amaze every one of us.

The Wastrel pitched starboard to show the Roger. As it did, I toppled off the bulwarks and rolled across the deck. Someone hoisted me up by my jacket collar, shoving me forward.

"Quit tossing about!" shouted Jasper. He was a stout, brown-bearded man with wide shoulders and stiff legs. His beard usually carried breadcrumbs or a stain of white flour. Of all the men on board, I found him the least hygienic. Naturally, he was the ship's cook.

I gave him a shove, and in a rasp, said, "I've told you before not to touch me." Though shorter than I was, his body proved too dense for me to knock back. The man hardly budged.

"Scrawny tosser. You're real intimidating, ain't yeh?"

"Leave me be, Jaz."

"Or what, Clikk?" He got up in my face, so close I could smell the garlic and onion on his breath. "Let's not forget who handles your meals. Not to mention the meals of your friends."

I had no time for this. As a Fledgling, I was squire to a Hawk and needed to prepare my raider for battle. Where was the man? I abandoned the quarrel and went with the rest of the crew to strap our grappling hooks to our forearms.

The grappling device rested above the wrist, secured by leather straps. Every snare was a claw made up of brass pincers, and it had a canister running up the forearm that held a tightly wound cable.

As I was tightening the belts on my forearm, I realized Jasper had followed me. He made a deliberate show of touching his thumb to my nose.

"Smell that?" he taunted.

I swiped at him with my brass claw. Jasper jumped back, chortling like a turkey as he dodged me by a hair's width.

Jonathan Pierce came up behind me and passed his arms beneath mine, encircling them behind my head and lifting me up on my toes. "Whoa, Fledgling!" he laughed. "Save it for the raid!"

"Put me down!" My shoulders reeled in pain as he tightened his hold, squeezing his folded hands against the back of my neck. It was enough to make my skin crawl, for now his body was pressed to mine. I became terrified, thinking he might feel that I was softer than most men, that I was slighter, and not as heavy. The ship articles ran through my head, Article V in particular. *A woman discovered on board shall be quarantined in the Captain's Quarters until she and any who aided in her subterfuge are cast out at the nearest port.*

"Why are you trying to whack poor Jaz?" asked Pierce.

"He put his filthy thumb in my face!"

"Did he really? Aye, that's not right. We all know where he likes to shove it," said Pierce. "Go on and kick him in the stones!"

Still holding me, he moved forward enough so that I was able to lash my boot at Jasper's groin. I'd nearly got him when the captain came marching over. Before he got any closer, Pierce relinquished me, and the three of us scrambled in three different directions.

"Get on, you useless curs!" Dirk shouted after us. "She may be a mercantile dig, but it's still a battle!"

Dirk was a compelling figure, tall and remarkably tan for a gent with ginger stubble. He had a strong square jaw, prominent cheekbones, and blue-green eyes that cut through a person like a jade dagger.

One could spot him in his stylish striped scarves and fitted patchwork britches, always with a flask on his hip, its supply seemingly endless. He wore a leather skullcap to hide his receding hairline and had a flair for brightly tinted goggles, which came in variant shades of red, yellow, or blue.

"Ease up on the thrust!" he bellowed at the helmsman.

The targeted ship, only slightly smaller than our own, was within range. A shine reflected off her silvery balloon. A rope ladder went up both sides of it. As we neared, I saw a man was climbing up the side. He looked out at us with a spyglass, and panicking as we speedily gained on them, he dropped it and slid down the ladder to land behind the bulwarks.

No-Nose Ned pulled a lever on the mounted switchboard and the Wastrel decelerated.

I would have loved to pilot someday, but the men who got that assignment always had prior experience. My skills would more likely land me in mechanics, which held nothing for me but greasy hands and the occasional electrocution.

"Veer port!" The wind's roar almost swallowed the captain's orders. I shaded my eyes and hopped up on the bulwarks to get a better view, holding myself steady by a frayed cable.

The mercantile ship had an open deck with a large ballista mounted aft. The mechanism moaned as its aim was directed at us. I silently condemned these merchants for not giving up their haul. Once they fired on us and missed—and they would miss—we would have to do battle and kill their captain.

A loud twang vibrated through the air as their ballista launched its shimmering harpoon.

The Wastrel pitched sideways, dodging the lance with room to spare. This time, I clung to the cables and held firm.

"Attack!" Dirk's command echoed down from the quarterdeck.

The Hawks were our first wave of offense, an elite team of twenty-five of Dirk's fiercest. They took formation along the rail, Pierce among them, and vaulted themselves across the divide, riding the wind and latching by hook to the target ship.

I lined up with the second wave along the Wastrel's flank. Securing my flight cap and lowering my goggles, I climbed over the railing with the rest of them and hung off with one arm, aiming for a sturdy beam. As the Wastrel floated beside the merchant vessel, I saw the black wood of her gondola.

"Gods keep me topside," I whispered, and with the rest of the men, fired my line.

My bones rattled as the grapple cinched the ladder of their quarterdeck. Without thinking, I retracted the line and vaulted across the open air.

The heights meant nothing to me now. What was death to an urchin with no one? My nose went numb against the windchill. Crinkling my face, I held my breath and braced for a hard landing.

I came zipping in so quick, I thought I'd splatter like pigeon shite across the deck. I turned my body to get my legs over the railing and landed with a shuffle into the chaos of steel and flintlocks.

2

BLOODSTAINED PAGES

Blood thrummed in my veins as I ducked under the slash of a machete. I freed my grappling hook and swung it like a flail. Round and round it flew, warding off my would-be assailants from the opposition. I retracted it into the apparatus on my forearm and drew my vicious little cutlass, a lightweight blade I had pilfered from the armory of a Dassanian warship.

These were the moments the world made sense. My brain shut off and I did not have to think about anything except self-preservation.

There were a hundred of us against less than fifty of them, and we were better armed by far. A proper pirate always had a sword on his hip, a dagger in his boot, and a pistol holstered over his heart. These merchants had naught but their swords. Their captain and his officers had pistols, but those had been spent. They were finished.

It was my experience, that in battle, time slowed, and I became more at peace than ever since before the revolution. Weapons collided and produced a rhythm like the ticking of machinery, punctuated by a cry that tore through the brain like an engine coming to life. I slashed and parried, spinning out of Death's reach whenever an attacker stole advantage. Every breath of gunpowder charged me with adrenalin and hurled me deeper into a flow of evasion.

As a child, I had known nothing of battle. All I needed back then were my threadbare boys' clothing to keep me safe. Each day, I rose early to ready my master's pawnbroker shop for business. Mr. Greyson had found me wandering the streets asking for work as a seamstress, the only trade I knew. My parents both died in the revolution. Had I not found the old pawnbroker, had he not made me a boy, I would have surely perished or been sold to a house of pleasure.

The little shop, tucked away up a side-street from the market square, dealt in secondhand treasures. Beside a velvet armchair, a clothing rack overburdened with coats sunk in the middle. A writing desk, a pipe organ, and a cider press lined one wall. Bookshelves, full to the brim, lined another. We stacked the books vertically, for there were too many to do otherwise. Beneath our glass counters, a thousand trinkets glittered, each with its own individual story, perhaps of the date a couple came to be married, of the rare gem's journey from Leridia, or of the lady who needed money to leave her husband. In the window, we showcased a singing automaton, one that I found frightening and uncanny with its unblinking and unseeing eyes.

I put the utmost care into my work for Mr. Greyson, for all I craved in the world was his approval. Even though it was often cold in the mornings, even though my fingertips would be numb through my torn-up mittens, I scrubbed every last smudge of oily residue from the windows until they sparkled clear as day.

I could still see it in my mind's eye. Mr. Greyson, a white-haired old man with skin like wrinkled parchment and a beard as wispy as raw cotton, waddled out of the shop with some porridge for me. He adjusted his black-rimmed spectacles and inspected my work.

"You're too ambitious for your own good, Clikk. I'm sure you imagine you'll own this shop the day I croak. Eh, boy?" With his cedar wood cane, the old grouse prodded my arm.

I turned my head down and rung the water out of my shammy. "No, sir. A girl cannot own property."

"What nonsense is this about girls? Go on and practice your letters, son. If you're to manage a business, you'll need to know how to read and write."

"Yes, sir!" I took up my bucket and scurried inside. The old man's chuckle bubbled up as he came in behind me. I loved the sound of that more than anything. He might have seemed cantankerous, but he had a soft heart, the sweet old bear.

I descended into the basement, where the old man let me sleep. My books were still lying open on a trunk.

I liked to read boys' adventure stories about pirates and treasure and bad-tempered captains. In fact, I was reading something about pirates the day Mr. Greyson died.

I'd heard the store bell clatter overhead, muffled through the floor, but sharp and violent.

Steel lightning crackled in my ears. I had to focus on the swords coming at me. I battled on, still swept up in the memory.

While I could block these merchants' steel and clubs, I could not block the images of that terrible day. I had been a little older. Fifteen. And my hair looked wretched. By then, Mr. Greyson's gout had turned him bitter, and he always gave me the worst haircuts he could devise. He could be a cruel, old bastard; he used to laugh at how ugly I looked and tell me I was lucky he made me a boy when he did.

I remembered reading about a young woman who stole her father's ship and crew, a woman pirate who proved more vicious than any man alive. And when she took a prize and cut down a ship captain, she would remove her bandana and let her long, golden hair dance on the wind. This image would flash through my head whenever I imagined my hair growing long. I never dreamed I could be as bold as that.

"Open the cash drawer!" I heard a man shout upstairs.

The drawer clanged. Heavy thuds on the glass counters rattled noisily. "Give me a moment!" shouted Mr. Greyson.

"Open it, or it's your life, old man!"

"It's jammed!"

A clatter of coins rang out as the register crashed against the floor. "Agh!"

Every soft part of my body ached at the sound of Mr. Greyson in anguish. The odious silence that followed was worse yet.

"Nuffin' but ten coppers in here," said the assailant.

Blood dripped down through the floorboards over my head, falling into the crease of my book.

"You..." Mr. Greyson's voice was fading, but I could hear him through the floor. "Bloody thief."

More red splotches bled the ink.

I was only a child, a child of the revolution no less. I should have been afraid and kept hidden. I should have at least known well enough to run, but in a rage, I jumped up, hands shaking. "Mr. Greyson!" I dashed upstairs.

There I found the brigand breaking the glass of the display cases and stuffing watches into his sack. He was no older than me, a kid with sallow cheeks, his head shaved bare, and his face darkened by soot. When he saw me, he drew a knife and backed away slowly. "Easy," he said. "Don't make the same mistake as the old man."

Crimson spread across the length of Mr. Greyson's white shirt above his belt. Blood flowed over the ridges in the floorboards, slipping in between the cracks.

"Look what you done to him!" I shrieked. "For coppers and cast-off jerries!"

"Shush now, Clikk," wheezed Mr. Greyson. "Let him go."

"It's not right what he done!"

"He's a kid. Like yourself. He's what you might have been without my charity. Go on, kid. Take the jerries and run back to your master."

The little thief fled through the front door.

I knelt to staunch Mr. Greyson's wound with my own hands. He just smiled, teeth pink and glittering. "My boy," he said, holding the side of my head. "It's no use."

"What do I do?"

"Nothing. He stuck me deep."

"I should have killed him for this. I will. I'll find out who he is and—"

"Stop that, Clikk. Stop it now. It's not his fault. He's a symptom of a greater evil. Now listen to me. Find someone to teach you how to fight, so you don't end up like me and your pa. This world has no place for gentle folk like us anymore. You stay a boy, or this world will eat you alive. You hear me?"

I didn't want to remember how I wept . After losing my mother and father in the war, I had been too much in shock to weep for them. I had been exhausted, starved, and wounded. I had to walk miles through lavender country before I found another villager still alive. And so the grief for my parents and my master came all at once, compelling me to spill bitter tears over the old man.

Mr. Greyson held my shoulder and said, "Stop that, child. Don't you shed a tear for me or any man—you hear me?" He swallowed hard, arching his back as he wheezed pitifully. "Not one tear."

I came out of the memory with a start as I watched one of my brothers sink his sword into a merchant's midsection. Blood slithered down the length of the blade. A soul-rending war cry erupted from a man who came running in our direction.

The pirate had killed someone's friend; the man was screaming the bloke's name—"Pete! Pete!—" his face red and shiny with tears. And he kept yelling it. "Pete!"

A loud thwack cut the air as the man's sword lifted my crewman's head from his shoulders. His eyes trained on me next. "Bloody thief," they seemed to say. Mr. Greyson's voice was loud in my head as I held a defensive stance.

I could barely focus as I deflected his sword twenty different ways. Was I any different from the boy who killed my master? What did it matter? I was going to die today. This man was older than me and experienced enough to have killed me three times over. Maybe I deserved it.

A cold sweat broke out on the back of my neck. I saw his blade trick mine into submission and I reeled back for a swift decapitation. Dread surged in my veins as I anticipated the fatal blow.

3

A Dangerous Friend

I perceived my attacker to be moving much like a man underwater. The priests of Throm tell us that when we die, our spirits go on an epic journey before they reach the World After. There is a maze, a trial, a loved one serving as a guide, and a fountain of black wine that one must drink to pass on. I was ready to embark. May the next world be kinder than this place of pain and fragile flesh.

I was nearly ready, when in a fraction of the second before my assailant could kill me, another sword point erupted out from his belly. He coughed up bloody spittle that dappled my face. Our eyes locked in the utmost mortification.

"Pete," he cried one last time before falling to his knees.

On the other end of that sword was my Hawk, Thomas Baker, and from his narrow-eyed sneer, I could tell he was pissed. Tossing his knot of dreadlocks over his shoulder, he moved the dying man aside.

"There's my bloody shadow," he muttered. He pressed his boot between the dead man's shoulder blades as he ripped out his sword, spraying blood across our shins. "I've told you a hundred times. Keep close; don't die. It's simple, Clikk."

An adept crewman with some savvy of piloting, Baker had taught me everything I knew about piracy. He was the third tallest brute on our ship, a good friend to have amongst pirates, especially for a scrawny creature like myself. He stayed swarthy, no matter how much sun he got, and he never wore his flight cap, but instead let the wind toss his dreadlocks.

All across the deck, our victims dropped their weapons and fell to their knees in surrender. We'd cut down enough of them. I stared at the man who had nearly been my demise. He lay just a few feet from his friend. Seeing them, I could not help but feel my heart swell with pity.

"Where were you?" asked Baker, sliding a red, silk scarf down the length of his blade. "I had to put on my own gear."

"Gods forbid."

"See what I've done in my grief." Opening his flight jacket, he showed me that instead of buckling the leather ends of his holsters, he had knotted them up.

"Sorry," I said. "Jasper and Pierce grabbed me, had a bit of fun."

"Trying to replace me already? I see how it is. You won't be a Fledgling much longer. Don't need me holding you back." He cracked a smile and tousled my flight cap askew. I liked it when he smiled, even when he vexed me. Baker's most distinguishing feature was a silver fang that glistened in the sun.

"Prig." I knocked his arm and fixed my cap.

"What's wrong with you, Clikk? Life flash before your eyes?"

"Them two were friends," I said, ticking my head to indicate the fallen. "Maybe even brothers by the looks of them."

Baker folded his arms, glancing between the two. "Could have been us," he returned bluntly. "Get back in your skin, Fledgling. They're dead. We're alive. That's all you need to think about."

He navigated through the crowd to get closer to the quarter-deck, where the two captains were engaged in a duel. No man alive could best our captain with a sword, but he certainly enjoyed letting them try. One feint and a pirouette later, Dirk had his blade pressed against the other captain's neck.

This was the part where he'd cut his throat, the part I didn't need to see. I could stand the sight of blood, guts, and brains, but something about the slitting of a man's throat made my whole body cringe.

I found an open water cask, dipped my cupped hands, and drank, rubbing the soot and gunpowder from my eyes.

Then came a sputtering cry. Dirk shoved their man overboard. Even though I didn't watch, the sound turned my stomach, and I could envision his neck opening up in the sky and spilling a trail of radiant, red blood.

I barely paid any mind to the rest of the raid. My job was done, so once we latched our ship to theirs with gangplanks and ropes, I hopped the rails and went about taking inventory with the rest of the Fledglings.

When we finished loading their cargo, we pulled in our planks and untied our lines. Their ship drifted out into the open sky. Our gunners used mounted artillery to put a leak in their balloon. The punctured envelope hissed, slowly deflating. A cold sweat formed along the edge of my scalp.

They would find a way to land. Probably. That hope went to Hell when their balloon caught fire. The blazing framework of their ship sank into a sea of black clouds.

"Could have been us," said No-Nose Ned as he caught me staring over the rail. "Had I not pitched when I did."

I nodded and used my crowbar to open a crate.

Like theirs, ours was a hydrogen ship. This highly combustible agent could result in a horrific end if the balloon's element came into contact with oxygen. Most airships used hydrogen, as it was cheaper and lighter than helium.

"Any Skye?" asked Ned.

I peered under the crate's lid and frowned. "Sorry, friend."

"Wine? Ale? Anything?"

"Only water, if you can stand to drink it."

"I'd sooner drink my own piss," he grumbled.

I went on organizing our new cargo. Another day, another ship of ruined lives. I tried not to think about it. Most days, I just did my work. I ate my rations, maintained the ship, or shadowed my Hawk in his duties.

As the Wastrel picked up speed and hurled us into the ever-blue horizon, Baker came toward me and stole my cap.

"Sing me a song, Clikk."

"Sod off."

I tried for my cap. Baker laughed and sang, "I wish all the oysters were pretty, young girls. I'd pry their lips open and fill 'em with pearls."

"The only oysters up here are the ones on the wall of the privy."

"Help me out here! You know I'm rubbish with lyrics." He went on smiling, his silver fang glinting like a spike of pale fire. "I expect you to have a song for me by nightfall," he said, returning my cap.

I hoisted a crate of vinegar bottles on top of another and sighed.

"What?" he said. He poked me in the side. "You got something to say? Speak up, Fledgling."

"It's nothing. Just… ain't nothing funny in opening a woman against her will."

Baker's humor evaporated. He stared at me, his eyes burrowing into my flesh. My pulse quickened. Did he see through the façade? I tilted my head down, pulled my scarf up over my nose, and rubbed my hands together, pretending to be chilled by the wind.

"I didn't mean nothing by it," he said.

"No, I know."

"I'd be the first man here to enforce the eighth article." He muttered something under his breath, something to the effect of, "Such crimes hit too close to home for me."

This statement intrigued me, especially coming from him. The first thing I ever learned about Baker was that his mother had been a whore and had raised him in a room she shared with three other prostitutes. Everyone on the ship knew it. He shared details of being a whoreson as if he enjoyed the disquiet it caused in his friends.

Generally, I made an effort not to discuss women with him. Most of the crew only talked about women in two contexts: as the shrews they'd abandoned or as the harlots they pined for. To be fair, I had all this time misrepresented my own opinions to match their standard of chauvinism. Who's to say my brothers of the Wastrel had not done the same? Perhaps they only offered half of every story. A boy could, after all, spit at his mother while loving her all the same. And while these men might mock a woman to tears, they would come to her aid if some ruffian gave her a clout.

Amidst the stolen cargo, I discovered a small luggage trunk filled with old, shoddy clothing. Laid on top was a book, which I took up and dusted. *The Ratcatcher of Locwyn* it was called. It would be lunchtime soon, and now I had something to read. I tucked the book into my jacket and carried it down to the mess.

The Ratcatcher of Locwyn turned out to be an autobiography chronicling the story of an orphan. The poor lad had been born to a ruined woman, who died of a fever when he was seven. He made his home on the streets of Locwyn, earning a living catching rats and turning out delicious pies. I read the first chapter aloud to Baker. He said he wished I hadn't, or that I had at least chosen a time when he wasn't shoving his face with ground pork.

I continued to read after our lunch hour was over. By the end of the book, which I skimmed while neglecting my other duties, the boy had built an empire that employed and supported a group of almost a hundred children, all catching rats, all baking pies, all making a fortune that eventually afforded them lodgings with a proper kitchen. They had their own little hole in the wall, frequented by the citizens of Locwyn. As their business grew, their quality of meat improved, luring new patrons and eventually investors.

The moral of his tale was that any urchin in the slums could make decent work for himself without resorting to thievery. All he needed was some ingenuity and a willingness to work hard. The novel's propagandist agenda left me unable to accept this orphan ever existed. Nobody got rich selling rat-meat pies.

The book offended me on a personal level. After Mr. Greyson died, I tried to live an honest life. A thief had killed him, after all. I should have rather loathed thieves. But despite my unique skills, knowledge, and musical talent, none of it had been enough to keep me fed and safe from the violence of the streets.

Fifteen years old and too frail to pass, I was scooped up from the streets by a fetching young thief named Mikhail. He made me his girl and taught me everything I needed to know to survive.

First, I learned the art of pickpocketing, practicing on our fellow thieves, and later joining them as they worked the early morning markets. From there, I graduated to burglary. When I turned sixteen, I had to assist with mercenary work. At first, this involved only a bit of skull-knocking, but then the day came when I had to carry out my first assassination.

My target was not a good man, but how many of us can claim to live without sin? He was a fence with an unsavory fetish for young boys. My boss wanted him dead for cheating us on our goods. So one day, as I passed the old bastard on a crowded street, I drove a dagger in his back. And I ran, my heart in my throat, until I reached Lake Street and slipped beneath some scaffolding. There I vomited into the water, trembling and thinking I would pass out every time I tried to stand.

In the end, the stabbing did not kill the man. My boss had to finish the job himself, and he told me I'd be spared future mercenary work since I was "just a girl, after all."

I found I did not care for brutality without cause, and eventually I left that world behind me. After months scraping by on my music without success, I got into the habit of drowning my sorrows in ale at the Bird and Cloud, a ramshackle tavern in the Aixenport slums. This was where I met Captain Dirk and came to call myself a sky pirate of the ship the Wastrel.

4

THE CRYPTEX

The barmaids of the Bird and Cloud catered specifically to sky pirates, the most despised criminals on the face of the earth. Something about air travel made people nervous by its very nature. Already one had to brave the heights, close quarters, a lack of control, and the possibility of burning alive in a fiery wreck. Throwing armed robbery in the mix just seemed cruel and untoward.

As a result of this prejudice, sky pirates congregated in numbers when they came to port, and many establishments took advantage of the trend. To name a few, there was the Aeronaut, a restaurant with walls painted like a tranquil sky, Lydia's Hall of Angels, an airman's brothel, and the Moon Balloon, a secret speakeasy in a hot-air balloon that lifted over the city once a month.

I could not afford to go to those establishments, but the Bird and Cloud suited me fine. Crews coming in from the mooring tower gathered around tables, playing daft games and grabbing at the women's skirts. The air was rife with the bilious odors of ale and vomit. I loved a spirited crowd such as this, and often came to get lost in it or to pinch some purses off the more inebriated patrons.

Sometimes, I would listen in on their conversations about life in the air. They would brag about skydiving from a raid gone sour or recount the time they had to crash land on water.

One night, I had nabbed myself an abandoned pint and was nursing it sip by sip, when the most impressive voice I ever heard bellowed beside me, "Damn that gypsy harlot!"

I did not know him then, but despite his reddening color, I saw that Captain Dirk was a striking, well-built man. He sat hunched over some kind of puzzle, twiddling with a row of brass letters that turned around a cylinder. As he tried to open it, he became increasingly enraged, finally slamming the thing into the table.

Seated around him were twelve other men, all wearing flight caps, except for one.

I studied Baker's dreadlocks, fascinated by their length and the trinkets woven in—an ivory bead here, a leather string there. Folding his burly arms, Baker laughed. "Never trust a woman who peddles opiates and old junk."

The men wore brown leather jackets lined in sheep's wool, some decorated with hand-painted patches depicting scenes of carnage and gore: fiery blimps, cannons, cracked skulls. One man had a row of bullet casings along his front laces. Another had an ace playing card sewn on the sleeve.

"What are you looking at?" remarked one of them.

My brain was too fatigued to remember my last scrap of meat. One swift punch could have knocked me out cold, so I didn't answer, just went back to my grog and pretended not to have heard him. As I eavesdropped, I learned the name of the gent with the cryptex, and that he was the captain of the Wastrel.

Leaning on the back legs of my chair, I raised my voice to speak to them. "Is that a cryptex?" I rasped.

The sky pirates eyed me warily. "Aye," said Dirk. "Bought it with the intention of keeping my gold pieces inside. Now it's jammed, and I can't get at my damn money."

The cryptex cylinder would only open for someone with a lettered code… or someone like me. Sliding my chair over, I said, "Give it here. I can open it."

"What's wrong with your voice?" asked one of the pirates, a young lad with a crooked underbite.

"What's wrong with your face?" I bit back.

The lad hid his face in his tankard, grumbling under his breath.

"What would you like as payment?" asked Dirk.

"How about you give me one of them taters?" I pointed to their plate of baked potatoes.

Dirk shrugged, and I seized the moment to devour one greedily. He nearly handed me the cryptex, but he hesitated. "If you run off with it, I will come after you. I'll find whatever hole you crawled out of and kill you and anyone else living there."

His eyes had an intensity suggesting he was not to be trifled with. Feigning nonchalance, I wiped my mouth on the back of my glove and nodded. "All right."

Dirk handed me the toy. "Damn gypsy said the code was *spectre*, but it's not working."

I went letter by letter, pulling at the release each time. If I lined up the correct letter, the lock would produce a gap, and each correct letter produced a little more of a gap until—click—the cryptex opened. As it turned out, the gypsy had not lied to him. She had simply used a variant spelling of *specter*.

The men were stunned by my speed, and they gawked as though I'd performed a magic trick. I was not sure which they found more amazing, that I had solved the code or that a street kid in Aixenport knew how to read.

The captain took my arm and gave me a firm handshake. "Name's Captain Alexander Dirk," he said.

"Clikk, at your service."

"How did you do that, Clikk?"

"Popped all kinds of locks when I apprenticed in a pawnbrokers' shop."

"Are you a pawnbroker?"

"Nah. Just your average brigand."

"Ah." He looked me over. I slouched forward, as I always did when anybody looked at me too closely. If he saw the girl, it meant trouble. "Then you've killed before?"

"I used to be Kindred." That was enough for him to understand that I had.

"Ordrick's crew?" Dirk blinked, evidently impressed. "There's a nasty bunch."

"Them the devils who jumped Garrett last year," said one of the crew. "Left him with a broken jaw."

"But you're not Kindred anymore?" said Dirk.

"No. Had a falling out... over a girl."

"I see," He ran his thumb over the patch of his reddish-brown goatee. "Ever consider sky piracy?"

"Course I have. I've heard sky pirates are the bane of the Duskmen."

"Occasionally, our paths cross."

"Every last Duskman is a pawn of the usurper's corruption. Does your ship have the artillery to take them on?"

Dirk surveyed the faces of his men before chuckling softly. "Their authority remains tenuous across Elsace. Nearer the capital, one might have to worry about coming up against an imperial warship, but we do not hunt anywhere close to Locwyn."

"But when you find Duskies, you kill them, do you not?"

"They don't exactly give us a choice."

"Then my sword is yours, if you'll have me."

"If you are to join us, you should know the risks. Good men die up there, drilled by bullets, blown up, maimed. It's not pretty. But we eat well, we die well, and every man gets an equal share."

There was something off about this sky captain. The way he spoke was more eloquent than any pirate or thief I'd ever met before. From his vocabulary alone, I could tell he was a well-read individual, a rarity amongst our lot.

"One thing worries me," he said. "Sky piracy demands a powerful physique."

"Get some food in me, and in a week or two, I'll be bigger than him." I pointed to Baker. The men laughed heartily at this, but I went on, "I've many skills, sir. You've seen I can pop locks. I can also appraise jewelry, manage a sword, play fiddle—"

"Fiddle, you say?" The captain had the slightest tell of intrigue in his blue-green eyes.

I nodded. "I know all the sky shanties."

Turning back to his men, Dirk asked, "What do you think, Baker? You need a new Fledgling. And this lad needs a job."

"I don't know." Baker folded his arms and leaned back with his knees apart. "I like his scar."

I adjusted my scarf to cover the fibrous tissue running across my throat.

"What I wonder is, can he keep the boys and me entertained? Aixenport is rife with kids who can fight, but what about a kid who can boost morale with a song? What do you say, boy? Got a song for me?"

I shrugged. "Sure."

"It's got to be fresh. I'm tired of the same old shite. You've got to show me you can think on your feet. Sing me something about sky pirates."

I took a moment to think. "All right," I said. "I can do that. Wait a tick." I went to the bar and asked Gretta for my fiddle. The young wench went in back and returned holding the case.

As I returned to the table of sky pirates, a few of them nodded approvingly at the sight of my instrument. She was old and scratched, but as I tuned the strings, they could hear her voice had the most soothing, resonant quality. I took a deep breath and stumbled my way through a ditty that lent itself to improvised verses:

I know a girl whose old man is away,
She's pretty as pie and will do as she may,
She works at a shop fixing watches and clocks,
If we handle her sprockets, she'll handle our cocks.

My verse did not play particularly well. One of the men cracked a smile, but the rest of them offered me only vacant stares.

"Come on. You can do better than that!" Baker shouted. He joined in on the next chorus, knocking the tempo into the table.

I frantically formulated a new verse for them:

I know it ain't easy to live in the sky,
Without wenches or doxies to help pass the time,
I'd never admit to be missing the land,
But it's just my first week, and I'm sick of my hand.

A better, though admittedly mixed, reaction lifted off the crewmen. Some laughed while others muttered derisive comments. Baker, at the very least, was laughing under his breath.

"Ain't it the truth!" he cried, and his praise bolstered my confidence enough to contrive the next verse:

Our ship has a baker, he's big, and he's tough,
On the roughest of skies, he kneads dough in the buff,

When he comes to port, all the girlies will dread,
How their little bread boxes can't fit all his bread.

Captain Dirk patted Baker on the shoulder as the man buried his face in his hands. He came up for air, laughing so hard he was almost crying. I played a rapid succession of notes, drilling my fiddle with a fervor that at last won the attention of the tavern's other patrons. When I finished, a much larger crowd applauded.

After the noise had died down, Baker said to the captain, "Yeah, all right. I'll take him."

"Welcome aboard, Fledgling," said Captain Dirk.

One of the men jumped up from his chair, came up behind me, and tried to pull down my trousers. I leapt away from him, knocking several empty tankards from the table as I did. Baker chugged the rest of his ale, grabbed his brother by the jacket and shoved him against the wall.

"Nobody hazes Fledglings in front of me!" he growled.

"I was skylarking."

"The lark'll be when I soapsock you in the dead of night."

"Baker," said Dirk. "Weren't you, just a month ago, caught dangling a Fledgling over the stern?"

"He said something about my mum. You're not going to say nothing about my mum, are you, Clikk?"

"No, sir. I'm sure your mother was a very nice woman."

"She wasn't. And don't call me *sir*. Baker's fine. This ain't the soddin' Sky Force."

"Got it."

I never forgot how much his smile surprised me after that churlish performance. In that moment, I knew there was something different about these men, something good in them. I had spent a great deal of time in the company of black-hearted thieves and mercenaries. Now, the mist lifted, unveiling a new layer above my gloomy little domain of Aixenport. These new opportunities held the promise of a better life for me. I had a future with these men. The sky was waiting.

5

—

SOMETHING IN BETWEEN

"Get your head out of your arse, Clikk!" Mr. Bentley snatched my book away and cracked me over the head with it. I had considered myself entirely hidden away behind the stacks of luggage and cargo, but now I saw most of it had been dissembled and cataloged, leaving me exposed.

"Sorry, Mr. Bentley! I was appraising it. Turned out to be a harder task than I thought."

"Oh really? What's it worth?"

"Upon further inspection, nothing, I realize."

"Turn it into privy papers. Now get to work on those padlocks, boy. You should have been done ages ago."

The dead captain's steamer lay before me with padlocks across four latches. I stuck my betties in the locks, tripping them, one by one. Baker came by to watch me work.

He said, "What great treasure do you think Dirk's got in his cabin for the emperor? I'm thinking it might be the original crown jewels of the dead king."

In addition to our raids, we were to sell some precious heirloom to our nation's hateful usurper, an heirloom so precious, the man was willing to negotiate with pirates to get it. Captain Dirk had not provided us with any details, but Mr. Bentley assured us the deal was sound.

"Could be anything," I said, struggling to focus with Baker in my ear. "Only thing I'd ever give the emperor is a dagger in his gut."

"Treasonous thoughts, Clikk."

"We got reason for treason."

"Regicide, though?"

"He ain't no king! He's a usurping mongrel."

A smile tugged at the corner of Baker's mouth as he shook his head at me. He nudged me. "What you plan to do with your share?"

A bitter feeling stewed in my gut as I thought of accepting the emperor's coin. It would be one thing to steal it, but trading with him was enough to make my blood boil. I did not want to get into any of that, so I shrugged and said, "I don't know. Got any ideas yourself?"

"The usual. Wine, women, cards, a hot bath. And if I'm not dead after the first week, I'm going to gather all my girls in Amaranthia and set them up in brownstones as kept women."

"Really?"

"Really. Then I'll take some mansion on a city block and host a séance twice a month."

I laughed outright at him. "I never took you for a spiritualist."

"I ain't one, but I've always wanted to be one of them eccentric aristocrat types. I'll walk with an ivory cane, even though I don't need one. My home will be decked with priceless artifacts, a fireplace in every room, a pantry fully stocked with Skye and the finest cricket fudge in the world."

"Cricket fudge?" I trembled with a mixture of humor and utter revulsion.

"Have you never had it? It's the best."

I covered my mouth, sure I would be sick. "That's foul, Baker."

"Don't rag on something you never tried. They sell it on the street in Locwyn. Taste of home, that is."

I popped the last padlock and slid it from the latch, opening the steamer. A musty odor lifted as I unloaded it. I was pulling out velvet frockcoats and tailored shirts when a spider the size of a cat slipped out and crawled up my arm. I flung it away, shrieking.

"Don't hurt yourself, Fledgling!" jeered one of the cousins as they both passed me. I hated the cousins. The cousins were the only men on the ship related by blood, and one could always count on them to make scornful comments at every opportunity. Whatever one of them said, the other would laugh.

"Don't mind them," said Baker, scooping up the tarantula and cradling it in his palms. "Everybody's afraid of something."

"I'm not," I said. "It surprised me is all."

"Not afraid of anything? Not afraid of lightning? Fire? Falling?" He spoke softly as if he worried the fates might hear him and get ideas. He offered me the tarantula. "Do you want to hold it?"

"I'm fine, thanks." In the bottom of the steamer, I found a paper bag. I opened it, and inside were a bunch of dead crickets caked in powder. "Look, Baker. A snack for you."

"I think this spider might have been the captain's pet."

I started packing up the steamer. "What kind of person keeps a spider as a pet?"

Baker frowned, turning his hand as the creeper crawled over his fingers. I could tell he was considering it.

"Oh, no, Bakes. That thing ain't coming in the sleeping quarters. Toss it overboard."

"We can't. It's too beautiful. I'll give it to my girl in Briarton."

Seeing him so enamored, I gave in. Baker had been my first real friend, one I held dear to my heart. My life had been filled with fatherly types, allies, acquaintances, and one truly reprobate lover, but never before had I known a friend.

Sometimes I would feel a twinge of guilt for perpetuating the great lie of my sex. But it pleased me how, even as time went on, Baker was never the wiser to my ruse. People generally assessed gender based on one's silhouette. My natural silhouette being boxy, broad-shouldered and narrow-hipped, I had an easy time standing in as a boy. And once the framework of masculinity was established, men never suspected I was anything else.

I stood quite tall for a girl, tall enough to meet the eye of most men, even to look down on others. At sixteen, I considered the widening of my hips to be the greatest of my body's betrayals, but life was always hard, food always scarce, so this development turned out to be somewhat stunted.

One of my greatest advantages, which I suspected was a result of malnutrition, was bleeding only once every four to six months, and for no longer than a day or two. My lover Mikhail told me this was unnatural for a girl. He said a girl should bleed every single month, and if she didn't, it meant she was in trouble.

I still remembered going with Mikhail that first time to the midwife to have her take a look at me. She laughed at us and sent us away with a lambskin.

"You aren't with child, dearie. And thank your lucky stars for that. With those hips, you would likely die a violent and miserable death."

"So why don't I get my monthlies?" I asked.

"Your humors are imbalanced. Too much bile in your gut. Eat more fruit. But don't get yourself up the duff." Her laugh was shrill and jarring. It rang in my memory.

A boy without a pillar and a girl without her monthlies, I was not one or the other, but rather something in between. I accepted it and got on with my life. But when I played the boy to join Dirk's crew, it hardly seemed a lie. I could say with pride that I was not a girl—and to do anything like one was humiliating.

I continued to study men, the way they rolled their cigarettes, the way they spit, adjusted their trousers, or occupied space with confidence. And I could laugh with all the rest at girls' expenses; women and their hysterics, their silliness, their squeaky voices and little minds. And yet each time I laughed, I hurt inside, thinking of my mother and how much I still missed her.

She wanted so many things for me when she was alive. She used to speak of weddings and lineage. *This dress will be yours someday, Mona; but perhaps you will want your own wedding gown.*

"Everything all right?" Baker asked me, noticing that I had been staring at the ledger of goods for several minutes.

"Yeah, I'm fine."

"Thinking about a girl or something?"

"Or something."

"Get your head out of the clouds, mate."

He tugged the strap of my flight cap and wandered off toward the bow. It was then I noticed a dark shape suspended just beyond the veil of cloudsea to the North.

The sight of her jarred me out of my thoughts. I stood erect and called her out to my brothers. "Ship! Passenger vessel!" My call echoed across the deck as others saw her too.

She was no ordinary ship. She hung motionless in the air, as still as a speck of black mold. To see such a thing in the sky gave me a chill.

"Approach with caution!" commanded Dirk. "Prepare to shoot her down if she makes trouble."

His voice could not conceal a layer of concern. A feeling of deep foreboding stewed in my gut as we neared that menacing shadow.

6

—

THE WITCH

An odd sort of buzzing screeched in the distance, a noise that was high in pitch like an insect's wings. The bird was unlike any sky ship I'd ever seen: a copper-plated sphere crowned in red fins, with glass doors on its sides, and a façade shaped like a beak. Heavy winds blew down from a single high-speed propeller fixed to its top.

"On your guard, men," said Dirk.

Mr. Bentley asked, "Should we engage?"

"No. I know this vessel. It belongs to a powerful witch. We'll invite her to board, but keep the men on high alert."

Merely the use of the word "witch" would usually send a chill across my back and shoulders. The prospect of one boarding our vessel brought on a cold sweat. I had never seen a witch before, just heard of them in passing, and hoped never to meet one. A witch was a rare commodity, scarcer than a crimson diamond, for they only emerged in society every ten years or so. Generally, they served the elite class: kings, queens, and emperors. The Wastrel slowed as we drew near. The other ship hovered, its propeller scattering a powerful wind across our deck. It landed far back on the forecastle deck, which had ample room behind our long balloon.

We climbed up and surrounded the vessel as its propeller slowed and gradually came to a halt. A figure could be seen in the fuselage, a pale woman dressed all in black. An aircraft operated by a woman was unheard of in the sky. Women were bad luck, started fires, caused fights.

With a hiss of pressure, a side door slid up on two mechanized arms.

Every man drew pistol, sword, or dagger at once. When I noticed their weapons were trembling in their feeble grips, my own sword began to feel like it weighed ten pounds more than it did.

The witch stepped out onto our deck. Her fingers brushed her collarbone as she emitted a girlish snicker. Strings of black pearls twined around her neck in many rows. For all the black and gray around her deep-set eyes, her face looked much like a skull. Two streaks of purplish rouge accentuated the gauntness of her cheeks. Black feathers trimmed her neckline, licking at her jaw. She could not have been younger than thirty, but she was beautiful.

"Well, well, well, Lexi," she said in a voice that smoldered like ashes. "What a reception."

"Don't make any sudden movements. I want your hands folded in front of you now," said the captain.

The witch complied, lacing her delicate fingers over her heart. I had heard it said that a witch's hands were her conduits of power. Bind them, and she would be rendered harmless. Break them, and she might never cast again. Of course, nobody ever got close enough to harm a witch before she unleashed unspeakable havoc, wind tunnels, raging conflagrations, and acid rain.

"Why are you here, witch?" asked Captain Dirk.

Her manicured brows furrowed. "Really, Lexi? Will you not call me by my name?"

"I seem to have forgotten it," he said, grinning sheepishly to the men on his left. His jest broke the tension across the deck as several in the crew chuckled.

"So this is your beloved Weasel I've heard so much about," said the witch.

"Wastrel," Dirk corrected. "She's a fine bird, finer than that pigeon of yours there."

"That pigeon, as you call it, is a globe copter. Its mechanized weaponry could decimate this rickety hulk in a matter of seconds."

"You wouldn't. You'd miss me too much."

She looked down her nose at him. "I would do worse, Lexi. Much worse. I have come to punish you for your crimes."

"Oh? And how will you punish me? Will it involve candlewax?"

Again, some of the crew laughed, but their mirth held a nervous cadence. The witch did not flinch or miss a beat. "I have learned you seek the emperor. And I know what you are bringing him. You truly have no conscience, no dignity, and no honor. Perhaps you lost those things in the bottom of your flask."

Her voice changed, and she pulled her hands apart. No sooner did she flick her wrists than both my hands ached under the pressure of a cramp. My cutlass clattered against the deck. I watched as every man dropped his weapon simultaneously.

When the witch spoke again, the air seemed to turn stagnant and make no sound at all. The clouds darkened, gathering in purple masses overhead. "May your most valuable prize be as worthless as your promises. May your ship fall to the earth in a rain of fire and ash. I curse you, sky captain. I curse you and the Wastrel and all these men you call your brothers."

Dirk only laughed at her, but the rest of us did not join in. We were eyeing the darkening clouds. Curses did not bode well for men who lived on airships.

"With luck, this curse might teach you some compassion," she said coolly. "Enough to see beyond your own selfishness, though I doubt it."

Dirk stepped toward her. "Maive—" He used a voice I did not recognize. It was softer than I had ever heard him speak. And that name—Maive—that was the name of the emperor's witch, the very same sorceress who served King Lucius before the revolution.

"I have no more words for you," Maive sneered.

She held her arms outstretched above her head and shouted a foreign word that was harsh and guttural in sound. A piercing hum split my ears, and a sunset-tinted aura glowed about her. Time shrank, and in a flash of blurred movement, she had returned to her ship and was soaring off into the horizon.

Maive had dominion over time itself. What havoc could such a woman wreak on simple creatures like ourselves? The back of my neck tingled. I looked around to see the many haunted expressions of my brothers.

Captain Dirk dropped his chin and glared off into the clouds. "Chasing her is pointless," he said. "Our prize is safe, gentlemen, and stands to make rich men of us all. We'll not let a woman frighten us off our course."

Generally, I trusted the captain. For all his faults, he had proved successful again and again in his undertakings. He wasn't young—the skies had aged him fast—but he had a fiery spirit that made him seem invincible. A captain like that could make any man feel intrepid.

A witch's curse was different however, for any man who underestimated the perils of real magic was a fool with an express ticket to the World After. I whispered a prayer to Ithicus for protection, but my heart was palpitating. The witch had left her mark upon us.

7

CERULEAN KNIGHT

Night fell, and the air grew choppy. It was my duty this evening to inspect the light bulbs throughout the ship. They burnt out constantly, but electric light was a luxury we could not do without. An open flame could kill us all. And so, each and every night, between the hours of four and five AM, the designated bulb mouse went through every passageway and common space, switching out the burnt bulbs, and turning off the lights so they would be ready for the next evening.

The ship lost altitude several times and sent my stomach lurching in my throat. I dropped my case of light bulbs and staggered up to the rail. I ate dinner too fast again. In the back of my mind, there was always an instinctive fear of starvation. Going hungry for days and weeks is a feeling the body never forgets, and I no longer believed any meal was guaranteed.

Some might say I became a pirate for the food, and they would be right. We ate well by our country's standards. Fresh fruit and vegetables filled the hold, along with sacks of grain, barley, and lentils. We had an array of meats packed with ice blocks from the Leffen Mountains. On this night, Cook had reheated frozen pigeon pies over our jerry-rigged electric stove. The first few times he tried this, he'd burnt the crusts, but tonight they had been perfectly crisped.

Now my pigeon pie took flight. I bent over the rail and hurled my guts out, lamenting the long and painful hours I would be yearning for breakfast.

I got that eerie feeling that was all too common out in the night sky. Perhaps it was our ship's dim electric lanterns glowing greenish in the fog, but it was more than just vertigo. In the abyss, I felt physically adverse to being in my own skin. The witch's curse had me nervous, and I could have sworn I heard a voice in the wind, something like the sad, sobbing sound of a child.

"They say spirits haunt the clouds up here, that there ain't no heaven. Only aimless mist," said Baker. He leaned his mop against the rail and tied back his dreadlocks as a gale rushed over the deck. He had a talent for finding me and hardly ever gave me a moment to myself.

"Shut up," I croaked. My vocal chords worked as well as my bow without rosin, and after a bout of retching, I could sound downright fiendish. "Ain't no ghosts up here."

"Are you scared, Clikk?"

"No." I closed my eyes, losing myself in my thoughts. "I'd rather like to see my dead. I'm an orphan, remember? Like every other bastard on this bird."

"Not every bastard. My mum's still alive."

"How nice for you."

An abashed grin crept across his lips, and he rolled his shoulders. "We're not on the best of terms."

"Why? You steal from her?"

"No. Nothing like that. I don't approve of the life she's made for herself."

"You mean whoring?"

He scoffed. "She ain't done that in years, not since she found herself a keeper."

"Is it the keeper you disapprove of?"

"Aye. He keeps her too often in bandages."

"I'm sorry."

"Don't be. At least I have a mother," he said. "Though that's not to say I didn't spend a fair share of my childhood in orphanages. Mum kept surrendering me. The orphanage was a bit like boarding school that way, with ever the possibility of going home with a new family." Baker often made light of the tragic events of his life. I always listened and chuckled along, but endured a buried, stabbing sympathy for the brute. He picked up his mop and dunked it in the bucket of water. "Anyway, I should get back to it."

"What are you doing? Since when are you a swabbie?"

"I got up to some games with Pierce and the cousins. We laid out the queens from a deck of cards and placed bets on which one Vincent would take as his wife."

"Vincent?"

"That spider we found. Sadly, though, Mr. Bentley walked right in on it. Squashed Vincent under his boot and gave each of us a list of menial duties."

"Bentley's a prig. I'm sorry about your spider."

"Thanks, mate. He's in a better place, I'm sure. Some kind of spider World After, full of them pretty lady spiders."

"Yeah. With all the crickets he could possibly eat. So, did you win anything? You still owe me two silver from our last game."

"Down to my last copper, I'm afraid."

"Course you are."

"It don't matter. We'll be swimming in coin soon enough. Have you decided yet how you will use your share?"

"Yeah. I'll buy weapons, loads of 'em, enough to form my own chapter of the resistance to see that damned usurper extinguished, a golden age of equality ushered in."

"Huh." Baker sighed. "Shame."

My heart pounded as it might have done on turbulent skies. "What do you mean by that?"

"Haven't enough people thrown their lives away for this same old lie of reform? It's a fairy story. The Blue Dusk was built on the foundations of it. What was it—a month—before Perceval declared himself emperor? The power merely shifted hands from the royalists to Perceval's cronies. Lands and titles were doled out to a new elite class. It don't matter how many times you overthrow your leaders. There just ain't enough pie for every brat on the street. And in the end, all you done is burn the world to trade one tyrant for another."

"You're a cynic!"

"Yeah, well, you're a damned monarchist!"

I scoffed. "It serves better than anarchy. And besides, a monarch is born to rule by his divine right."

"What does the opinion of the gods matter when a king murders his own people for sport?"

"No king of Elsace has ever done. A true monarch serves his people as he serves the gods."

"Except that ain't true. If Lucius had served his people, they would not have risen up against him. You forget, Clikk, it was *the people* what made Perceval emperor. It was *the people* enlisting in the Blue Dusk, *the people* marching on Locwyn palace and taking the heads of the royals. I was there, Clikk. They was killing each other like animals—royalists and Duskmen alike—blowing our city to pieces, filling our streets with dead."

"I understand the toll it took. Believe me."

He nodded, sighing as he let go of his tirade. "You was what? Thirteen?"

"Almost," I said.

"Whereabouts was you?"

"Shale." It was only a whisper, but the word hit hard.

Baker lowered his eyes. During the revolution, Shale had been razed, its people brutalized and disgraced. Blue Dusk entered the region and were met by a particularly zealous royalist resistance, which they crushed. After the trauma of that battle, they wreaked vengeance on the peasants.

"Is that how you got your scar?"

I touched the fibrous tissue at my throat.

"Such a mark must have quite the story," he said.

"A stupid story. A stupid story about stupid peasants. Not worth telling."

"All the best stories are about peasants," he insisted.

"Shouldn't you be working?"

Baker slumped his shoulders and snatched up his mop. "You're a grouse on rough air."

"It's a history I'd rather forget, is all."

"We all have histories we'd rather forget. I've shared all sorts of pain with you, but every time I ask about your scar, you look keen to rip my head off."

"I could do nothing but watch as the Blue Dusk killed my parents."

That silenced him. He leaned up against his mop like a walking stick.

"It was just after Locwyn fell. If you recall, the drought leading up to the revolution left our harvest meager. I was already weak with hunger when the Duskmen arrived at our door demanding we hand over our grain stores, our only goat, and the rest of our chickens. My father could not bear to see his only child starve, and thinking the Duskmen would not harm us, he begged their pity. He got down on his knees and asked they leave us just one of our hens."

A dark feeling gripped me as I recounted the tale. I could still smell the steel and the horses of those strange men. I could still see them in their blue military coats, standing over my cowed, stooping father.

"One of them, a Duskman called the Cerulean Knight, without a word, stepped forward and kicked my father down. He ran him through while his face was in the mud. Mother screamed and pulled me into the house. The Duskmen came inside, made themselves at home in our kitchen. The soldiers did nothing to stop the Cerulean Knight as he took my mother into the bedroom. He wanted her to behave, so he had his men bring me in. They made me watch as he ravished her. I begged him to stop, but every time I cried out, his men would strike me.

"The next morning, he finally slit her throat. And then he took me in his arms… and slit mine." I raised my chin so Baker could see my finger trace my scar. "I awoke on the bedroom floor, amazed the blood at my throat had clotted and I was still alive. For a long while, I lay next to my dead mother, holding her, too much in shock to weep. I knew I would not die there. The gods let me live for a single purpose, I was sure. I would find the Cerulean Knight and kill him. That idea gave me the strength to keep going. I got up, drank the last of the water in the kettle, and started walking."

Baker's eyes never left my face as I told him my story. "Blue Dusk," he said as though it were a dirty word. He spat over the rail. "If you ever see that knight again, I'll gladly help you gut him."

"I don't remember his face. The only thing I remember was his sword. It was curved steel with tear-shaped sapphires on the hilt. I'm certain I could recognize it if I ever saw it again."

"What if you found the blade but the man holding it was too young to be your parents' murderer?"

"No matter. I'll kill any man who holds that sword."

Fantasies of vengeance had carried me through my life on the streets. In times of famine and desperation, I pushed myself to survive for the sole purpose of finding and killing that evil man, even if deep down I knew it was unlikely. For now, any chance to damage the Blue Dusk gave me purpose, for it was their unchecked tyranny that orphaned children every day.

I watched the fields and forests pass below us. Elsace was an enormous country composed of forty-seven provinces. Southwest of the capital was my homeland, the valley of Shale. Farther south was the Wastes, a vast expanse of sand inhabited and controlled by anarchist gangs that had warred over the territory since before I was born. Five other countries touched our borders, and several of our crew came from those exotic lands, most commonly Leridia or Nazar.

Our air routes took us all over the different regions of Elsace. I had waded into the Poison Sea in Amaranthia, gathered sand of the Wastes into bottles, and nearly frozen to death in the harrowing mountain ranges of Leffen, but of all the experiences a human being might have in his short life, there was none so grand as seeing the world from an airship's carriage. At twilight, the clouds on the horizon could spread like ink on blue vellum. Or in the day, they could stack into pillars as tall as any canyon.

Soaring at this altitude, I saw Elsace as something so much cleaner. Lakes turned to puddles, cities into toys. The squalor of the slums went invisible, and everything smelled fresh like rain. It was one of the reasons I loved the Wastrel. I felt so far away from all that misery down below.

8

A Crying Shame

I was harnessed to the back of the gondola, frozen cold from the windchill of the dismal morning. A canopy of gray clouds loomed overhead, requiring me to shine a utility light from the front of my flight cap. I shuffled my spanner as I balled my hands in and out of fists. Fitz guided me through a routine engine inspection, a procedure I knew well.

The engines were about the only things on the ship maintained at a high standard. Our balloon had the face of a much-beloved rag doll, covered in gray stitched patches with sloppy weatherproofing painted across the envelope. Many steel cables between balloon and gondola were frayed and being reinforced by rappelling rope. Our engines held our pride. They were high-speed cloud-munching machines.

"All done! Everything is handy dandy," said Fitz, wiping the grease off his hands.

"Good," I said through chattering teeth.

"Wind making ice blocks of your bollocks?" Fitz brayed, juggling his spanner with one hand.

His flight specs, a steel plate with horizontal slits, gave him the appearance of a deranged cyclops. He was wiry like me and made a good mate for arm wrestling because he could make anybody look good. Nobody messed with him, however, for three reasons: the first, that he was also friends with Baker; the second, that he was our best mechanic; and the third, and most crucial, that he could muster the most horrid shriek. The bloke was off his rocker. I personally did my best not to excite him.

"Are we nearly done?" I stuttered, exhaling hot breath over my exposed fingertips. "I'm freezing."

"Invest in a pair of thermal trousers, boy. It's only summer yet." He smacked my posterior and used his pulley to scale the side of the ship. He was right, of course. Though we wintered closer to the equator above the hot sands of the Wastes, there were always difficult weeks in autumn and spring. The spring prior, I had worn a hole in my gloves and nearly lost a finger to frostbite.

Equipment was a regular expense. With the deck open to the elements, we had to acquire appropriate gear: goggles, flight caps, and gloves. My own cap was fashioned of cotton twill. It had rain guard flaps that fell over each side of my face. Flight shirts had to be both utilitarian and elegant. The cuffs were fitted to the forearm, but the sleeves hung loose for better mobility. Laces up the front of the tunic could be drawn tight to the throat or given slack down to the navel, as the weather warranted. We kept three shirts: a black one for labor, a white one for sleeping, and a red one for raiding. When it came to flight jackets, crewmen owned only one, made of wool-lined leather. Trousers varied, depending on whether a man preferred agility to insulation.

Upon returning to the deck, Fitz and I discovered our captain pacing, his brow clenched in frustration. With each shift in his walk, his hip scarf whipped about like a tail.

"Clikk!" he shouted, pointing at me. "There you are. I need to see you." I blinked in disbelief, glancing around deck to see if there was another man named Clikk. When there wasn't, I stepped forward and followed my captain into his chambers. He shut the door behind me, locked it, and then circled me in a slow, predatory fashion, sizing me up.

"Yes. It's just as I thought," he said, tilting back his flask and exhaling a groan.

"Captain?"

Dirk took a seat on a luggage trunk, resting his elbows on his knees. He sniffed, took another slurp of his liquor, and smirked at me. "Oh, Clikk. Poor, sweet Clikk. There is something that I've known about you from the start, but I put up with it because you can manage a sword and you fixed my puzzle wheel. It is time we addressed it."

This couldn't be happening.

"Addressed what?" I asked.

"Don't play daft! I know you're a woman."

His statement knocked the breath out of me. "Captain, I—"

"We have a few lads on board who are slight of figure and might even pass for a port in a storm, but if you take off that flight cap, we both know I'll see it plain as day! You're more than just a pretty lad with a rasp in his throat. You actually make a fine woman." He ripped off my cap, spilling my short blonde hair.

My face got hot with shame. "I'll leave the ship at the next port."

"You will not," he said and gripped me suddenly by the woolen lapel of my jacket. "I need your help." He lowered his voice, his eyes shifting to the door of his cabin and then back to me. "I am about to expose a dangerous secret to you, Clikk. I have reached the point where I have no other recourse than to ask you for help. I need to know I can trust you."

"Sure."

"Swear it, Clikk. Swear on your life."

"On my life," I stammered. "You can trust me, Captain. You have me at your mercy. The truth of my sex is my deepest shame, and I would sooner die than be exposed."

"You would sooner live, I assure you. You might be embarrassed, yes, but you would have the option of moving on. My situation offers no such luxury. I have exceedingly more at risk, for my secret affects the safety of every man on this ship. To compromise me, you would damn all your brothers. Do you understand me?"

"Yes, Captain."

His eyes flared with intensity as he brought his face close to mine. "Say it!"

"I understand."

"If you so much as make the slightest offhand remark to your friend Baker—"

"I would never—"

"—I will leave you copper-less at some rural port and post bulletins of your face in every tavern to see that you never work under the guise of a man again."

"Yes, Captain."

Dirk engaged me in a staring contest. "All right. Follow me."

He charged toward his sizeable four-post bed cloaked in heavy curtains. Pulling back the brocade, he switched a lever in the wall.

A hidden bolt crunched, and the wood panel flipped up on a hinge and spring, revealing a chamber beyond that barely had enough room for the luggage trunk and bedroll within. Inside sat a red-haired girl who looked to be about thirteen years old. She was like a doll in every aspect—plump, pale, and rosy-cheeked—but her eyes were puffy and wet with tears. When she saw us, her mouth trembled.

"Ugh! Are you still crying?" Dirk growled in a hushed tone.

The round-faced, freckled child clutched the skirt of her striped gown, bunching the black ruffled edge under her nails. "I'm sorry. I'm sorry," she whispered, sniffling.

"This is Molly," said Dirk.

Molly crawled out of the wall and onto the bed, swallowing her gut-wrenching sobs. "A friend at last," she said tearfully. "Oh, thank you, brother."

Rubbing his temples, Dirk closed his eyes. "Damn it, child. Have you no discretion?" The girl hid her face in her hands, weeping harder as he admonished her.

"This is your sister?" I asked, looking between the two. They had the same ruddiness to their complexions and the same greenish-blue tint to their eyes. Had Dirk not been so different from her in his style of dress and poor grooming, I might have surmised it myself that they were siblings.

"Our mother had her late in life. When she died, I became Molly's guardian. I spent a small fortune for her to go abroad to be raised up as a lady. Now she is old enough to marry. I want her future secured, and my investment returned. So I aimed as high as I could. I would make her concubine to the emperor himself, but because she is so young, his advisors considered her a better match for his son."

"The emperor's son?" I asked.

"Prince Torrent himself."

"The prince would wed a commoner?" I asked.

"She is a paragon of female perfection! Poised. Elegant. Cultured. And, as you can see for yourself, a rare beauty." Dirk faltered as he saw I was unconvinced. "I might have embellished the details of her pedigree. I got Prince Torrent on the hook, and then I pretended to kidnap her. As far as they know, we bear no relation. Hence the need for discretion."

"Naturally," I said. "So first you lied about her heritage, then you pretended to kidnap her, and now you are ransoming her to the fiancé?"

"They demanded a dowry! Can you believe it? I barely broke even. If Prince Torrent wants my Molly, he has to pay!"

I decided not to pry any further into Dirk's complicated scheme. With the girl crying so profusely, I could barely think.

"This tantrum came on only yesterday," said Dirk. "I need you to make her stop crying. You, being a woman, can surely understand the issues that plague the fairer sex."

I nodded in spite of being wholly perplexed and a little insulted. "I'll try."

"Good. Do it quickly. I'll give you some time to get acquainted; you can talk about your feelings, etcetera. Feel better, Molly, and good luck, Clikk." Without any further direction, he went out and shut the door, leaving me alone with the weeping child.

"Err," I started, sitting down beside her on the bed. "Hello there. I'm Clikk."

The girl said nothing but cried and cried as if her favorite mutt had just perished beneath a carriage wheel.

"What's wrong?" I asked.

"N-n-nothing!"

"If there's nothing wrong then why are you crying?"

"I don't know!"

I tried imagining what made girls cry. I hadn't wept since beggars cracked my lip with a pewter mug. There were a few tavern songs I'd seen bring a tear to a bar wench's eye and I tried to remember what they were about.

"Tell me true. Do you want to marry the emperor's son?" I asked.

"I should love to marry a prince." She sniffled. "It is to be a wedding in the clouds on his ship, the Crescendo. It's everything I've ever dreamed."

Tears dribbled down her cheeks. She smothered herself with the captain's pillow, bawling into it like a dying animal. Something had to be done or I'd be exposed.

"You have to stop that now. Little girl, stop it."

"I can't!" Her voice grew hoarse as she let out a mortified wail.

If I went back out there a failure, Captain Dirk would let everybody know Clikk was a woman. The men would never treat me the same again.

Baker would feel so betrayed. He'd pissed in front of me countless times and had even put faith in me to look at his little pirate whenever he had anything resembling a rash after whoring. Worse yet, I'd heard all his disgusting jokes about wankers and shite, and I'd actually laughed. I'd laughed because they were hilarious, but if he knew he was speaking to a woman like that, he'd never have the nerve to face me again.

I went and banged on the forecastle door. "Captain! Captain, I need you!"

Dirk opened it a crack, peeked in, and hissed, "What are you doing? She's still crying!"

"You can garnish my wages, Captain. I'll work for free. I can't help you on this account, but I swear to be the most loyal—"

"Every man on this ship is as loyal as they come. I could make them eat dog dirt and they would thank me for the honor of flying on the Wastrel. Have I asked you to eat dog dirt, Clikk?"

"I can work harder than anyone. I'll work doubles to the end of my—"

"Have I asked you to eat dog dirt?" he repeated.

"No," I said, "But what does that have to do with—"

"No, I have not," he said firmly. "If you cannot calm that girl down, you will be sent away."

"But I don't know what to do!"

"You're a woman! Figure it out!" He shut me in and turned the lock.

9

Siren Song

"**B**ugger!" I kicked the door, grumbling a string of filthy, hateful words.

It bewildered me to see a girl in such a fit without anything the matter. For a moment, I considered breaking out of the room, stealing a parachute, and trying my luck in the open sky.

I would lose everything I had built over the last year. I had survived the Fledgling phase and would earn my job assignment any day now. I had friends here, brothers who would risk their necks for me in battle. And if Dirk truly meant what he said and made sure no one ever hired me as a sky pirate again, I would become the most miserable wretch. I had come to love the skies, to crave the feeling of ascension and the thrills of bad weather. I had to make this work.

I returned to the girl, trying to think what helped me the night I was mugged. Beaten and robbed of my coin, I had curled up in the darkness, taking shelter beneath a broken cart as it began to rain. I had wept and pled with the gods to send me to my mother and father in heaven.

Then it struck me. Perhaps this girl was missing the maternal love her sod of a brother couldn't convey. Whenever I felt sad, my own mother would cradle me in her arms and sing to me. She sang a song passed down through the generations, a lullaby known only to our family.

I hummed the melody to Molly, surprised I remembered it. It was slow and a little melancholic, especially at the end. The girl rolled over, her teary eyes blinking themselves dry.

"What is that song?" she asked.

"I don't know the name," I said. "I'm sorry for my voice. I had an accident."

"I don't mind. Please, go on. It lifts my sorrows."

I continued to hum, hearing my mother's voice in my head as I did. The song conjured a feeling inside me that had been numbed for years. It was a yearning for something I knew I could never have again, and while the melody eased this child's pain, it nearly brought tears of my own. I heard the lock in the cabin door turn over. Captain Dirk re-entered.

"Ah, you made her see reason!" he cheered. "Oh, Molly. Whatever was the matter?"

"I swear it was nothing, brother. It was the strangest thing. The tears came upon me like a fever."

"Thank you, Clikk!" Dirk cried, kissing both my cheeks. "The wedding is the day after next, and you've saved us."

"Happy to help," I said. "I hope I might remain on the Wastrel and continue to serve."

"Yes, of course!" Dirk's celebration was a bit premature; once again, little Molly began to cry. "Oh no, no, no, no! What's wrong now?"

"I… can't… stop…" She had to force the words out as she choked on her sobs.

"Clikk! Do something!"

"Shhh," I hushed her and began to hum again. The tears vanished.

"Don't you see?" the girl said, exhausted. "The song helps me think clearly."

"Well then, by all means, keep humming it, Clikk!"

I did as my captain asked, but I couldn't very well do this for the rest of the girl's natural life, so I halted to present my theory on what was going on. "This has to be the witch's curse. If you recall, she said your most valuable prize would be made as worthless as your promises."

Molly began to weep yet again. Dirk bit his lip and scratched his head, pacing about the chamber.

"Damn. Damn. Damn," he kept saying. Molly sniveled helplessly. "Ugh! Clikk!" he snarled. "Would you please keep humming while I think?"

"Yes, sir!" I continued the song.

"Only stop humming to answer me. What is that song?"

"I don't know the name!" I spit the words out between notes.

"Do you know any of the words?"

"No!"

Molly tried humming it for herself, and I stopped to see if she could keep up the tune. She could not and collapsed back into her crying fit.

Dirk wrenched his eyes shut. "This is bad. This is really bad. Right. Clikk, I need you to be singing that song when we board the emperor's ship. And... throughout the wedding ceremony."

"Captain. My voice is rubbish, but I might play it on the fiddle instead so it would be more pleasing to the ear."

"Yes! Of course!" he exclaimed. "You must practice the song."

"Yes, Captain."

"Miss Clikk?" said Molly, sniffling. "Please. Keep singing. Just a little longer. I have not slept since this began."

Pitying the girl, I hummed the melody from the beginning.

Molly lay down on her side and closed her eyes. The cushion beneath her head was damp, so I turned it over and fluffed it for her. Then I pulled the fleece over her shoulder, withdrawing my hand suddenly. It was a strange role for me, as I had never taken care of anyone but myself. My only example of nurture came from memories of a mother as distant as the stars.

Dirk watched in silence, his eyes unfocused, his arms folded. As much as he pretended to have a callous heart, deep down lurked some familial compassion for the girl. Big brothers pretend not to care about their younger siblings, and pirates are the most adept men in the world at hiding their sentiments, but I could see the relief in his eyes as Molly drifted off to sleep.

10

THE THIRST

The crew liked to jest that an airship needed two kinds of fuel: fuel for the engines and fuel for the men. The pun came out of the fact that Skye was explicitly marketed to airmen for its qualities as a stimulant and mild anesthetic. Skye, the fermented concoction of gray bubbly, made a man feel like a supreme being, awake and full of spirit. It numbed all kinds of pains: toothaches, illness, hunger, homesickness, and the boredom that blanketed the hours and days between raids. At present, our Skye stores ran low due to economic collapse throughout Elsace. The thirst came upon us, and we had no means of quenching it in the near future.

The thirst was a mild sort of withdrawal that made men irritable and adverse to authority. During times of thirst, vandalism spiked. Arguments escalated quickly into fistfights. The men became sluggish and missed their shifts. They made mistakes that could put the entire crew in jeopardy. If we ran dry, Captain Dirk would have far more to worry about than a marriage deal with Emperor Perceval. Thus we moored in Briarton to refuel and conduct trade, regardless of our being pressed for time.

Not one of us was allowed to visit any brothel or watering hole. The crew had to fuel the ship and conduct maintenance inspections, while Captain Dirk and Mr. Bentley went to haggle at the general store.

It was a gloomy afternoon full of clouds and light rain. We sported our raingear: coats and caps of oiled leather that reeked of chemicals. I'd wrapped a woolen scarf over my nose to obstruct the fumes and strapped on a pair of kneepads I'd made of linen stuffed with chaff. After preparing myself accordingly, I lowered by rope ladder to the roughly paved ground below. Fitz was already down there, carting a fuel tank with the help of the tower personnel and some of our Hawks, Baker and Pierce amongst them.

There were distinct physical differences between our men and the people of Briarton. Aside from Fitz, ours had the bulk of muscle to fill the sleeves of their heavy dusters to capacity. The shirts and trousers of the tower personnel billowed in the wind around their bony appendages. Their faces were gaunt, their eyes weary.

Everyone wore weatherproof caps except Baker. His dreadlocks absorbed the rain and hung heavy down his back.

"Air pressure is fine," I called to them. "And we've plenty of reserve tanks. All we need is petrol."

"That's not *all* we need," said Fitz, a hint of desperation in his tone. "We need another kind of fuel."

"You won't get any here," said one of the fuel jockeys. "Spirits are all we have now to make these shortages bearable."

"I have four gold pieces," said Fitz.

The fuel jockey hooted deep in his throat. "Coin is worthless. We barter goods alone."

Fitz looked to Baker, who was working to unwind the fuel hose. "Should we fetch our rations for the day, you think? Split the drink? I know you're aching."

Baker shook his head. "Not worth it."

"Come on, Bakes!" whined Fitz. "Captain won't open that last keg until we've already found our Skye. You know that."

Baker just glared at him.

"What?" Fitz cried. "I'm aching, mate!"

"You ever worked a twelve-hour shift without food? You feel wretched! You make mistakes and let everybody down! We bear the thirst together. As a fucking crew."

"Fine. Gods above. You don't have to go ballistic," muttered Fitz.

Baker turned his back to him. As I wheeled a stepladder aft, I heard his deep voice carry over the squeaky wheels and the trickling rain. "Listen, mate. The captain might yet work out a deal. Chin up."

He followed me with the fuel hose and held my ladder steady as I went up. The engines were high on the back of the gondola. To reach them, I had to balance on the uppermost step.

I removed the fuel cap to the first engine, took the hose, and snapped it in place, waving to signal the boys at the tank that we were ready. The pipe made a soft hiss as it moved fuel. I sat down on the ladder stairs, slumping forward.

"How is the thirst treating you?" Baker asked.

I shrugged a shoulder. "I had aches for a day, but they've passed."

"You're young. Just wait."

"You're hardly old." I paused and gave him a discerning look. Baker could have been five and twenty for all I knew. He behaved like a child, but he was built like a man, and his jaded outlook suggested he had seen enough of life to grow weary of it. "How old are you?"

"How old you think?"

"One and twenty."

Baker laughed. "I'll be lucky to see one and twenty. I'm only two years older than you, ya prig."

I nodded slowly and stared off into space. I had too much on my mind to care what age he was.

I wondered if Baker—like Dirk—had always known the truth of my gender and went on pretending like he didn't. The other men rarely noticed me, and when they did, I tried not to say much.

Baker, however, noticed me plenty. We spent almost every waking minute together. He could not have known my secret. He was not the kind of man who let a woman's presence go unappreciated. In taverns, he liked to whistle at the pretty wenches and see if he could get them to smile for him. He even whistled at the ones who weren't so pretty, called them names like 'popsy' and 'lovey,' and shot them sly winks that left them in a tizzy. He might sometimes disappear with such a woman and return after a half hour with love bites running down his neck, for Baker just couldn't help himself. He tried at any woman who might have him.

We'd been blitzed and alone enough that surely if he knew, he would have made a pass. For to him, women were meant to be teased, scrogged, and forgotten.

"Everything all right?" Baker asked. "Fitz was saying the captain called you into his quarters yesterday. Are you in some sort of trouble?"

My chest got tight. I looked off over my shoulder, unsure how to answer. "No," I said quietly.

"Why didn't you mention it?"

"Because it's my business."

"If you're in trouble, it reflects badly on me, which makes it my business too."

"No trouble. It's a private matter. The captain needs my help, and I'm not to speak of it. I'll be going aboard with him during his trade with the emperor."

"Are you pulling my chain?" Baker grinned wide and gave me a friendly cuff on the arm. "He must see something in you!"

He did indeed.

The sound of petroleum flow went quiet. I unclasped the fuel hose and replaced the cap. "Let's do the next one," I said.

"Hold on tight, flyboy!" Baker shouted, wheeling the ladder down the pavement. I gasped and gripped the railings on either side as I dropped to my kneepads.

"Wanker!" I chuckled.

We came under the next engine tank and began the process again. That was when Captain Dirk and Mr. Bentley returned. By the looks on their faces, we knew there would be no new provisions.

"Shite," Baker grumbled.

"I'm sorry, mate."

The rain picked up. Baker hiked the collar of his coat up over his hair, groaning aloud. Those dreadlocks would be dripping for days.

11

THE CRUISER

We soared upon a flat plane of cloudsea that extended into the horizon. The watch sighted a shadow lurking just beyond a thick mist. A dirigible soared not far off our course. Determined to replenish our supplies, we hunted her.

The navigator, Mr. Weston, pinched a spyglass to his eye. The rest of us stood clenched at the ready as we waited for his call. Wind pummeled our flight shirts. "Cruiser," he said. "Should have plenty of Skye."

"Rich folk, I'd wager, which means good Skye," said Captain Dirk. There was a general murmur of approval. "She's a big girl, so we'll have to operate tactically and make her think we're bigger. Hawks! Suit up!"

In raids involving larger vessels, the Hawks infiltrated before we could be seen and assessed, offering the target's crew a chance to surrender peacefully. If they yielded their valuables, we would leave them unscathed. If they refused, the Hawks would signal for support, and a hundred grappling hooks would latch onto their ship. Sky pirates crazy with the thirst would flood in, spilling blood until we were wading ankle deep in it. It was an ugly bit of business, but we lived in an ugly world.

Baker stepped into his leathery wingsuit. I buckled the straps around his wrists, ankles, and throat. Inspecting his equipment was simple enough, but every time I dressed him before a raid, my heart pounded in my chest as if I were the one about to ride the wind.

"Pray for me, Clikk. Ask Ithicus for his grace."

"Always do."

"Pray for yourself too."

"I will. But not to Ithicus. I pray to Camilla for myself."

"Camilla? The trickster?"

"Chameleon. Hides in plain sight."

Baker turned to face me as he adjusted his crimson goggles. He stared a little too long at my face, and I put my head down. "I've never seen you hiding during a battle," he said with a shrug.

"Hiding in plain sight is different. No one pays any mind to a slighter fellow like myself, so when I strike, it's already too late. And right when they think they've got me, I drop my tail."

"Lizardman," he teased.

I secured the pocket just left of his heart with a stick of dynamite. Every Hawk wore dynamite on his person. If anything went wrong, it was protocol to threaten total annihilation. Blowing the ship up from within was a last resort if the Hawks could not signal for assistance. Although I had never seen any man use his boomstick, it still disturbed me to see Baker strapped with an explosive.

"What's wrong?" he asked.

"Just jealous," I said nonchalantly, examining all eight pistols on his chest. I inspected the grappling hook mechanism on his forearm and the dagger strapped in under his boot. "Have fun."

"Hey, now that you're all chummy with the captain, he'd probably let you ride the wind if you asked. Maybe he'll even make you his boatswain."

"Bugger off," I said, giving him a shove. Baker laughed, silver tooth winking in the sun. He backed up to the rail, spread his arms like a swan, said, "See you topside, Clikk," and tipped over backwards, plummeting headfirst. I ran to the railing to watch as he dived and spun and glided on the air. The other Hawks soared at his side. The Wastrel descended upon the cruiser and circled, settling just twenty yards above the aircraft. She was a beauty. Her elongated balloon had to house at least half a dozen gas cells. The gondola ran along the bottom of the envelope in two levels, having enough room for at least two hundred passengers, not including crew.

The Hawks grappled onto the base of the cruiser's envelope, zipping up to the rigid framework. They climbed down and kicked the round windows with their steel-tipped boots, swinging their bodies inside.

We waited for the white flag to appear. Ten minutes passed without any signal.

"What is happening in there?" I heard Mr. Weston whisper.

A blast rocked the body of our ship. Clouds of fire erupted from the cruiser, bursting from its gondola. Debris and carcasses spilt out of the hole, including one of our Hawks, unrecognizable beneath all the soot and blood that caked his scorched head. A man wearing a militant blue uniform fell out as well. There were Blue Dusk on board.

One of the cruiser's gas cells began to deflate in the middle of its balloon. Passengers jumped of their own volition, screaming as they met the sky. My lips and fingers went numb, and a screeching whistle filled my head. In the thickness of this physical terror, I heard Captain Dirk as he said, "Abort. They are lost."

"No!" I growled, my voice as raw and rough as stone.

Captain Dirk's eyes flashed with rage. He never had to explain his orders and would throw men to the clouds for insubordination. "Their chance to grapple back on board has passed."

"Captain, we can go under and catch them."

Dirk snagged me by my collar and yanked me in so close I could see the sun freckles under his eyes. "Did you not see that uniform?" he whispered. "Those are Duskmen. If we let a single man leave that ship alive, the emperor will never trade with us." He shoved me into the rail and turned to address the crew. "We cannot rescue our men without risking our going down with her! The Hawks have been compromised! Send that ship to oblivion, gunny!"

The mechanisms vibrated beneath my feet as our guns aimed at the cruiser. To Captain Dirk, the Hawks were expendable. He could train new men and have new wingsuits fashioned in the Wastes. But there was something he had clearly forgotten. If he wanted his deal with the emperor, he needed me.

I didn't think. I didn't give myself time to be afraid. I threw a rope ladder overboard.

"Clikk?" said Dirk behind me. And then, as I stepped up on the railing, and climbed over, he was screaming it. "Clikk!"

The Wastrel was in motion, and the ladder pulled more and more in the wind as I went farther down. The cruiser was moving too, tilting over as it lost altitude. It dawned on me that when I made my jump for it, I might miss and spend the next several minutes or however long it took, falling to certain death. I made sure to catch the cruiser's blimp with my eyes and visualize my descent. Then I let go of the ladder and gave myself up to the mercy of the sky.

12

FALLING

I've had nightmares of falling. Up and down mean nothing anymore. There is only vertigo permeating every bone and ligament in the body. The fall is synonymous with dread, for all falling ends either awakening in a pool of sweat or confronting the incorporeal mystery that awaits all men.

As my body yielded to the open sky, I rather felt like I was flying, like I had complete control. I belly flopped against the rigid framework of the cruiser's gasbags and clung hard. Pain throbbed in my ribs, but to my amazement, nothing felt broken. I climbed down the side of the balloon. The cruiser fell slow as if sinking in water. The shadow of the Wastrel lifted from off my back, and the hot sun beat down on me. It reflected off the balloon's metallic shell, and I had to squint as I dropped into the window of the cabin below.

I landed in the vessel's dining hall where chaos had taken hold. Tables were strewn about on their sides. The chandeliers leaned, their crystals clinking. As I moved through the cabin, I stepped over silverware and broken glass. A Duskman opened fire on me, and I jumped behind a long, overturned table.

Observing my surroundings, I saw Hawks and Duskmen slain by gunfire. This place was a battlefield. Civilians ran amuck, fighting over the last parachutes, all human decency abandoned. A mother and her young son clung to one another, while the so-called gentlemen resorted to communicating with their revolvers.

As soon as I saw his dreadlocks splayed out around his head, I knew I had found Baker. I crawled toward him and rolled him over, afraid he was dead. He was unconscious, his cheek swollen and cut. I dragged him behind an overturned table and smacked him awake.

"Clikk?" he mumbled dreamily. "What are you doing here?"

"There's no time to explain." I snatched a pistol from one of the holsters on his chest. A Duskman had us pinned down. I fired on him, missed, and ducked as he returned fire with an automatic rifle. When the barrage of bullets stopped, I used the second pistol from Baker's holsters and hit the Duskman's shoulder while he was reloading. My blood pounded in my veins and a rush of vigor gave me the strength to lift Baker to his feet.

We crouched and ran between the upturned tables. I reached into his holsters one by one, firing off the rest of his weapons as Duskmen popped out from behind their barricades.

We found another unconscious Hawk behind a pile of chair legs and other split wood. I nudged him with my boot, but this one would not wake.

Baker had begun to get his bearings. "The ship was full of Duskies," he whispered. "They would not yield to pirates. They killed Johnnie. Samson lost it and blew his dynamite."

"Can you travel?"

"Aye."

The hoarse screech of a hawk punctured the air. I looked and located four of our men behind the marble-countertop of the bar: Pierce, Henry and the cousins, Caleb and Nicolas. We darted toward them and crouched behind cover. The hard floor behind the counter was covered in shattered crystal and liquor that made my boots stick.

"What do we do?" Pierce asked Baker.

"Clikk?"

"The Wastrel will pass underneath us. We have to jump for it," I told them.

"You've no grappling hook," Baker noted.

I shook my head. "There was no time."

"Right. You'll hitch a ride with me then."

We came out from behind the bar. Most of the Duskmen were either dead or wounded, but a few stragglers tried firing revolvers at us. We slid behind a barricade of overturned tables. A Hawk came out of hiding behind a fainting couch, scrambling to join us as bullets whizzed past him.

"Brothers!" he shouted, crouching.

Baker was focused on the concussed man we had seen earlier. He was only a few feet away from our cover.

"Clikk," he said, handing me two of his pistols. "Give me some cover fire." Without any more warning than that, he bolted. I cursed under my breath and came up over the top of our barricade, searching, aiming, waiting. A Duskman popped up across the room. I fired, and he went back into hiding. Another tried. I fired once more and was spent, but by this time Baker had reached the concussed lad and was shaking him madly. The lad came around at last, waking to Baker's command. "Move! Move!"

The ship pitched sideways and, as furniture tumbled across the room, the Duskmen abandoned their last stand against us. We rushed the blast zone where the wind raged like a tempest. The ship continued to lean into it, and soon we were clinging to the floor so as not to fall through before we saw our rescue.

Dirk would not forsake me. He could not. But I had put him in an impossible position of choosing between his entire crew and me. He might just as well have cut his losses and fled. I kept anticipating the appearance of our ship through that opening, and every second that passed brought me closer to the bleak realization that Dirk likely abandoned his scheme. Time had run out; escape seemed hopeless.

Then a magnificent patchwork bubble appeared below. The Wastrel had come for us.

I jumped on Baker's back as gravity pulled us down. Together we fell into an open sky. This time, my fate was in another's hands, and I felt all the dread and vertigo I'd missed before. Baker aimed his arm at the Wastrel and released his grappling hook. It cast out and zipped like a fishing line. Its metal spokes punctured the railing of the Wastrel and gravity yanked us out from under the sinking cruiser. We swung like a pendulum and shot upwards, wind cutting our faces. A terrific feeling teemed inside of me as the Wastrel carried us with her upon ascension.

We vaulted ourselves on board. The other six remaining Hawks had made it back safely, but nobody was celebrating the rescue. They were all staring off behind us. Some of the men even bowed their heads out of respect. I turned to see what they were seeing and watched with them as the cruiser sank beneath the clouds. A feeling of grief for people I didn't know overwhelmed me. The Blue Dusk's refusal to surrender had cost all those passengers their lives.

A hand clutched me by the strap of my flight cap. Captain Dirk pointed his dagger at the center of my scar.

Baker started shouting, but his brother Hawks held him back from intervening.

"You disobeyed my direct order," said Captain Dirk. "You forced me to endanger all of our lives for the lives of a few. I'd cut your throat here and now if I didn't deem you to have the rustiest guts of any sky pirate I've ever met."

At first, I thought I'd misheard him, or that this was the beginning of a twisted joke that ended in me getting an ear sliced off, but Dirk lowered his blade and pulled me in under his arm. "Men! Clikk here just went overboard without hook or parachute and saved seven of our brothers."

A hush of awe and wonderment fell across the deck. In Dirk's eyes, I saw nothing of esteem or reverence. He was making this up as he went. This was all a pretty show to explain him not throwing me overboard. Dirk went on, "Clikk is a true sky pirate, a man with no fear of heights or gravity. From this day forth, he will be called Falcon!"

A great roar of approval exploded from the crew, a sound louder than all the engines and wind put together. They needed something to cling to in this moment of profound horror. We had hunted the cruiser for something as trivial as Skye, and as much as I wanted to believe the disaster was not our fault, I knew why the Hawks carried dynamite, and why Dirk did not allow transgressors to go free. We were criminals.

I'd seen death before. I'd seen Dirk and my brothers killing men on merchant vessels and supply ships, and I'd considered myself a mere bystander to their violence. But I was in fact complicit.

This had been the first cruiser. For the first time since joining their crew, I was no longer sure I could justify this way of life. Thinking of that young child and his mother made me sick. They knew what it was to fall. They felt the falling nightmare in their final moments of life, and for them, there would be no waking upon impact.

13

DYNASTY

We drank every cask of Skye that we had left. The men carried the last six barrels up from the hold as Captain Dirk encouraged us to indulge our thirst. After our exchange with the emperor, we would be so lousy with coin there would be no difficulty procuring spirits in a major city like Amaranthia.

The bitter drink went down like petroleum, but it charged me like an electric coil. I wanted to play my fiddle late into the night. I wanted to sing even if my voice burned in my throat. Fitz was climbing the cables, hanging off backwards, and tasting the mist. Meanwhile, Baker stirred up a game of Mercy, and the men took turns tensing their biceps and taking as many punches to the muscle as they could stand.

"Want to play?" Baker asked me.

I declined with a subtle shaking of my head, as I always did since those first few times when I'd attempted the game and had to tap out before anyone else.

I drank to forget the wasted raid, and leaned against the forecastle stairs, tuning my fiddle. I needed to get blitzed and lose my soul to song.

"What was the tune Johnnie liked?" asked William, the mandolin player.

I shrugged as I ran my bow hair over a chunk of rosin. I never really knew Johnnie, but I was sorry to have lost him and all the Hawks who perished.

"'Copper Monkey', I think it was," said William.

"That one's fast, Will."

"Yeah. You probably couldn't keep up."

I smirked and swept my bow over my strings to test the pull. "My pace would make your fingers bleed."

"That sounds like a challenge." William strummed the first chord. "Come on then, Falcon. For Johnnie." He played the first phrase and tapped his foot. I bounced my bow and quickened the tempo.

The speed duel began. I fiddled like a demon to keep up with William. The men stomped their feet to encourage our Skye-frenzied duel. I'd never been a spotlight musician before. Normally the men treated me like background noise, but on this night, they knew my name, which was now Falcon. At the end of our song, they applauded and brought us a round of drinks.

Everyone kept rehashing the story of the day. I secretly hoped they might all forget me by the next. I didn't want to be Falcon. Falcon was highly visible. How long would it be before one of them teased me for not having facial hair? I wanted to go back to being their taciturn minstrel who didn't like to be touched.

"Hey, Falcon! Play 'The Wench of Amaranthia'!" Even Baker was calling me Falcon now and grinning at me with a glow in his cheeks. I nodded and eased my bow into the first note of the evocative melody. Baker began to sing, and Fitz joined in, hanging upside down from the rigging as he took the tenor harmony.

She lived in a most mysterious port,
The pirate town Amaranthia,
She liked to sing songs of the lustiest sort

She drank like a man, and she laughed with a snort,
The Wench of Amaranthia!

Amaranthia! Amaranthia!
Ah-ha-ha-ma-ra-ra-ra-ranthia. Ha ha!

The other men joined in on the chorus, drinking at the end of each verse. By the fifth reiteration of Amaranthia's, they were spitting out random syllables.

When the song finally broke down into raucous laughter and shouts, Baker threw his arm over my shoulders and raised his tankard. "Falcon!" he roared. The crew roared with him and began a chant of "Falcon!"

"I need to talk to you!" I shouted in Baker's ear. He could barely hear me over the noise of the crew. Pierce grabbed me by the sleeve and yanked me into the center of a ring that had formed.

"Getting a big head now, are you?" he bellowed, putting on a show for the wall of men surrounding us. "Not a Fledgling anymore. It's time you proved your mettle." Pierce took off his shirt, beating his hairy tattooed chest at me as the men lost their wits to bloodlust.

Everyone was watching us. Someone shouted, "My money says Hawk beats Falcon!" Others revived the chant of "Falcon! Falcon!" with sporadic interjections such as "Take him out, Clikk!"

"I don't want to fight you," I said. Holding up my fiddle, I added, "I need my hands to play!"

"I won't hurt you. We'll just see who's stronger."

"You are!" I laughed, playing to the crowd. "And you've got about a hundred pounds on me."

Baker laughed. "Clikk just called you fat, Pierce!"

"What?" Pierce looked genuinely confused, as he had not an ounce of body fat amidst his chiseled figure.

"Little wanker called you fat!"

"I did not!" I cried in my defense. "You're a head taller than me, Pierce! That's all I meant."

"I'm going to make you cry uncle," said Pierce, his face turning sanguine.

I crouched, actually anticipating the possibility of fighting him now. Everyone was watching. If I backed down, it would raise questions.

"Come on, boy! Show us that pasty chest!" he goaded. "I'll bet you're as soft as a lump of dough."

"It's freezing up here!" I shouted back. I looked to Baker for assistance, but he misread my distress.

"Clikk's a beast!" Baker yelled. "He knocks out a hundred pull-ups each night before bed. I seen him."

I wished that were true. In fact, I could manage only fifty. And I never knew anyone had been watching me. It was a minimal effort to keep my shoulders broad enough to fill out my flight jacket.

Suddenly the captain's door flung open and everyone ceased their chatter. Captain Dirk cut through the crowd, brandishing a leather mug with a pewter spade on one side. He approached the open barrel of Skye and held his receptacle beneath the spigot.

"Give your captain a drink, old boy."

Ned filled it with bubbling libations. In one swift chug, Dirk polished it off. He almost never drank with the men. He looked over at the shirtless Pierce and the circle that had formed around us. "What are you idiots doing?" he asked.

"Bonding," said Pierce.

"Put your clothes back on."

"Yes, Captain."

"And, Fitz, get down from there!" Dirk smacked the banister beneath where Fitz was hanging. "Radar just picked up a storm sweeping through. Winds could send you flailing in the cloudsea before you know what hit you!"

Fitz pulled himself upright on the ropes and dropped to the deck. "Yes, Captain! Sorry, sir!"

The crew was no longer rowdy with laughter or reliving the story of the Falcon's daring leap. Lightning flashed like a spark of black powder and thunder bellowed in the distance. I could hear the wind reeling and my heartbeat did the same. Captain Dirk gestured for me to come with him.

He had saved me. But what terrors awaited me beyond the eyes of my brothers? I ducked my head and followed Dirk into his quarters.

14

A Shalean Vintage

Dirk led me through his cabin to an adjacent room where he'd built a small library. I appraised his collection out of habit, taking notice of the printing houses and the materials used to bind the folios. The sets of leather-bound encyclopedias and thick tomes were all in excellent condition.

Dirk plopped down on a pile of cushions and furs in the middle of the floor. He kicked off his boots, crunching and cracking his toes. I wasn't sure if I should join him. My conduct had to be different with him now that he knew my secret.

"Sit. Drink," Dirk said. He uncorked a bottle with his teeth and took a swig before passing it to me.

"Yes, Captain." I knelt on the edge of the furs.

"Wine from the valley of Shale. That's where you're from, isn't it?"

"Yes, Captain."

"Who better to share it with then? Drink with me." I took a sip of his wine to avoid insulting him and handed it back. "Quite an impressive stunt you pulled today. I guess we both know I can't give my sister away without you."

"What happens to me once you do give her away?" I asked.

"I don't know yet. I had to make the men love you to explain not killing you, which complicates things… Falcon," he said with a sneer, taking another gulp of wine. He knocked on his chest and belched.

I made an effort to veer the conversation in a new direction. "Why did the witch curse you, Captain?"

"Oof," he sighed. "Maive has been my paramour for many, many years, but recently we quarreled. Bah! It's amusing in retrospect. I was in Amaranthia when a couple of female bards offered me a night I couldn't refuse. The next day, I learned that it was my dearie sorceress in disguise."

"So Maive was one of them?"

"She was both of them!" he cried. "Of course, she called me a cheat, though I argued there was no foul as technically it had been her."

"Camilla's tail," I said, smiling in spite of myself.

"Camilla's tail, indeed. The woman is twisted," he scoffed. He tilted the bottle back my way, but I shook my head.

"Thank you, Captain, but I'm already—"

"Drink," he commanded.

I drank. I had a liver for wine from Shale, but I could already tell my captain did not. I took this chance to offer counsel. "You should swallow your pride and apologize to her. If you ask her forgiveness, she might undo Molly's curse."

"No. She won't. I have known Maive a long time. She is headstrong and proud." He reached for the wine again and I let him have it. He chugged it down to the last drop, the sod.

"You could still try. Your sister is suffering. Don't you care at all about her happiness?"

"Of course, I do! Haven't I said how tremendously expensive her housing and schooling have been? I've spared no expense for the girl, and because of it, I've not turned a profit in years. The Wastrel needs repairs, and I need a holiday, so the day Molly turned thirteen, I revealed to the emperor's advisors that I had her."

"Revealed to them?" I said. Dirk looked as if he wanted to suck those words back in, but it was too late. He was drunk on my countrymen's wine. "Why is the prince so keen on marrying your sister? Why would they purchase his bride from a notorious pirate? And why for such a high price? Unless she were—"

"Oh, Clikk," he groaned. "You ask so many questions. Now I truly will have to kill you."

I could not pull my gaze away from his eyes, those blue-green eyes renowned throughout Elsace as coming from the royal bloodline. Anyone with such a rare color could boast some noble lineage, and peasants did it all the time. But this was different. He was the right age. He had auburn hair. And his eyes weren't just a bluish tint of green. They glowed like pools of liquid jade. They revealed to me what should have been clear long ago, from that first moment I heard the pirate captain speaking with such refinement in that tavern hall. He was the dead prince of Elsace, and the little girl stashed away in his cabin was the lost princess.

There was a short time after my exodus from Shale when I thrived on the promise of royalist rebellion. The Luftburg royal family had been imprisoned in the black spire, and people spoke of a siege to liberate them and crush the Blue Dusk while they were still vulnerable. They gave me such hope back then. It never happened, and I was in Aixenport when they transported the prince to be executed. A local inventor had built the first guillotine, a device that could sever a head instantly without the precision or care of an axman. I was in attendance when Prince Derek von Luftburg put his neck through the frame. I saw the wide blade fall. I saw the executioner lift the disembodied head as the eyes twitched. He was dead. I saw it. And seeing him now resurrected was nothing short of a miracle.

"No, you're him," I whispered. "Anyone could see it. Captain Alexander Dirk. Prince Derek Alexander Xavier von Luftburg, rightful heir to the Elsatian throne."

"Careful. Those are dangerous words to put in that order."

"Was it the witch who helped you fake your own death?"

"Quite the imagination on you."

"You are him. I know it. Your people need you."

Dirk made a bitter laugh. "The people who, after the famine, murdered any person with a drop of blue blood in his veins?"

"You could restore your family's dynasty."

"What a perfectly mad thing to say! Prince Derek was publicly executed!" Dirk stood and wobbled over to take a fresh bottle of wine from a cabinet. He opened the cork with a knife, twisting, pulling, and guzzling it down like water.

"No," I said. "Perhaps you sent your double to the guillotine, a royalist willing to die for you. He knew as well as you that it is your destiny to retake the throne."

Dirk cracked his neck as he rolled his shoulders. He tumbled into the cushions, curling up like a cat around his new bottle. "Why is it my destiny? I never wanted it. I always looked to the sky."

Rain began to fall, pattering against our balloon in a noisy chorus.

"So you're just going to hand your kingdom over to the Blue Dusk? You really don't care what they stole from you? What they did to your family?"

"Ever notice that everyone you know is less than twenty? I am turning twenty-five next year. You know how I did it? I didn't start a war. I didn't hold a grudge for what could not be undone. It's a nasty world out there. We need coin. And our girl Molly—everything she touches is made pure. She will heal the leadership from within."

"Unless they kill her. How will she fare when they realize she's enchanted? Or what happens once the prince has his heir?"

"They're not barbarians, Clikk. She will have a better life as Prince Torrent's wife than she will in exile, ever at risk of being discovered and assassinated. I am doing the best thing possible for her."

"For her? Or for you?"

Captain Dirk reclined his head all the way back and closed his eyes. "How old are you, Clikk? Fourteen?"

"I'm seventeen. I know I ain't as learned as you, but you must listen. Only you can heal our country. The Blue Dusk will never change. They've held our people hostage since the revolution. They force us to either steal or starve. If you made a claim, it would unite every rebel group across the provinces. Thousands would rally behind you. Because you're different. You're the first man with a claim who knows what it's like to be one of us. You understand suffering, and it makes you a fine captain, and it would make you the finest king who ever ruled."

"Lishen," Dirk slurred. "The old bird's full of mold. It's not even safe to breathe the air in here. This operation ain't going to last, and what do you think happens to my sister when I can no longer provide for her? For all we know, the prince could break her curse. That's what princes do. True love's kiss and whatnot." The wine bottle fell from his fingertips and rolled, spilling a streak. I chased it across the floor and plugged the neck with my handkerchief. "Throm, have mercy. What was in that wine?" he asked.

"The berries in Shale carry a toxin that knocks foreigners off their feet."

"How about that?" he said, his laughter skidding. "A woman drank me under."

"No shame in it," I told him. "I've been drinking this piss since I was thirteen."

"My kind of girl." He winked, which I found more repulsive than if he had blown chunks across the furs.

"Will you think about what I've said?"

"What do you think I've been doing these past five years? I've thought and thought and thought. Holding a grudge is like squeezing a blade in the palm of your hand. Better to let go than bleed to death." He lurched forward, covering his mouth and then relaxing when only a burp came up. "Go to bed, Clikk. Do your job. It's the best you can do in this life."

The Shalean wine and Skye fueled the rage swelling in my heart. The great prince I had mourned for all these years was nothing more than this useless, drunken reprobate. I slammed the doors on my way out.

The men outside cheered, "Falcon!" when they saw me again, but I passed them without a hint of notice. Craving some time alone, I went to the sleeping quarters to lie down.

15

THE PACT

Silver light crackled in the storm that seethed outside. With every maneuver of the ship, my hammock swayed, threatening to dump me out onto the floor or the hammock beneath. The sleeping quarters were deep in the hull. It was a wide-open room with little round windows all around and hammocks suspended from a low-hanging ceiling. All the men slept here in a cabin that creaked and moaned under the pressure of the air currents. I liked it here. It was quiet. Nobody talked to me except Baker, who always needed something.

"Can you fix this?" Baker came up to me and tossed me a gold pocket watch. I caught it mid-air, turning it over in the meager light of dimmed bulbs. It had the initials T.M.B. engraved on the back. "Pierce nabbed it off a waistcoat on the cruiser. Said he couldn't leave empty-handed from such a calamity."

"For shame, Bakes. Withholding a prize."

"Tch," Baker scoffed. "Like you never broke the rules."

"It's a nice trinket is all, nice enough to get the both of you wind-hauled."

"It has my initials, so Pierce let me have it for only twenty copper."

"TMB? But I thought your name was Thomas Quinn Baker."

"It's close enough."

I motioned for my kit and Baker brought it over. "Watches are easy," I said, popping it open with a lockpick. I'd have asked for payment from any other man, but I never minded helping Baker. Besides, I preferred to work over dwelling on the issue of my captain prince and his sister's curse.

Rain and wind pounded the ship, rocking the gondola and rattling the hooks and chains that dangled upon the wall. The electric bulbs kept flickering, thwarting my attempts to see into the watch.

"Damn," I whispered, squinting. "Wouldn't you rather melt it down?"

"I always wanted myself a proper watch," he said.

"Something to measure your short life?" As I laughed, my ribs ached and I winced.

Baker sobered at the sight of my discomfort. "Clikk… maybe you should let Cook take a look at you."

"I'm fine. Just a bit bruised." I used my pick to wobble the balance wheel for him. "There it is. Broken balance staff. I can fix it when we get to port." I closed the watch up and returned it to his hand.

He put it away in his knapsack and returned with a head of cabbage. "Here," he said, peeling away the leaves and tucking them under my shirt. "My mum taught me that cabbage heals a bruise up quick."

I stayed his hand, taking the leaves and setting them myself. "Thanks, mate. I s'pose she'd know."

"I'm grateful for what you did for me back there. There's something I want you to have." He removed a steel ring from his finger and handed it to me. Upon closer inspection, I realized it was a twisted nail. "It's good luck."

It was a strong piece of jewelry, a ring for a man. I didn't dare put it on. It would draw attention to the fact my fingers were so much narrower than his. I stashed it in a pocket that zipped. "That's kind of you. I've never been lucky." I closed my eyes and let the cool oils of the cabbage seep into my skin. "You still owe me two silver."

"I know, I know."

"That new watch of yours is eighteen karat gold. You could fence it for much more than twenty C, even broken."

"You know that just by looking at it?"

"Gold appraisal was the first thing Mr. Greyson ever taught me."

"From pawning to piracy, legend of the Falcon," he said as if it were an epic to be recited.

"I'll thank you not to call me Falcon."

"You need a woman to call you such; that will change your tune." Baker reclined into his hammock beneath mine, and I heard his boots hit the floor. "Are you a virgin, Clikk?"

"No, you glock."

"I've noticed you never visit the brothels when we go to port…"

"I have standards. Women are like locks. If they give too easy, they aren't worth the trouble. The ones that require precision, effort, and clever maneuvering are those that hold the greatest treasures."

"True, true," he said. "And women are also like light. Go long enough without them, and you start going mad, to the point you contrive disturbed ideas about women and locks."

"I had someone long ago, Baker, an angel so pure she'd make your cock fall off for longing."

"What was she like?"

"She was a village girl."

"You dog." Baker kicked my backside from below. "Tell me about her. I like a story in a storm."

"I'm not your bard."

"Did she have good tits?"

"They were all right. She was poor. Very skinny. But she had hair that shone like wheat in the sun. And she did all these nice things that village girls do, like picking larkspur on the cusp of May."

Baker yawned, already weary of my tale. "What was her name?"

"Ramona... You think I'm a pansy, don't you?"

"You are a pansy," he said, snickering. After he'd had a good laugh at my expense, he added, "Still, I do hope you get back to your Ramona someday."

Pirates were interesting fellows. Baker could say things about women that made me want to break his nose, but then he would out of nowhere show a glimmer of sentiment for them. I leaned over the edge of my hammock. "Baker? If someone were to unite the rebel factions and organize them to take back the kingdom, would you ever consider joining the rebellion?"

"No," he said and snorted a gob of spit into a bucket.

"But what would you say if I told you the Luftburg princess was still alive?"

"I'd say you'd been putting Skye up your arse."

"Well, let's just say she is alive, and let's also say, she's been taken hostage by our captain and resides on this very ship."

There was a pause and a sudden commotion as Baker jumped out of his hammock. He stood and looked me dead in the eye as he said, "Are you telling me there's a woman on board?"

"Lower your voice!" I hissed.

"Why would the captain trust you with this?"

I glanced about. The sleeping quarters were empty. The men were still getting blitzed above us, singing rowdy songs to drown out the storm. I lowered my voice all the same. "The girl is cursed. She can't stop crying except when I play my fiddle. The captain made me promise not to tell—"

"Throm have mercy." Baker rushed the porthole. Just outside the smudgy glass, a bolt of lightning veined across the sky. Thunder boomed and shook the very framework of the Wastrel. Baker spun around, his eyes full of terror. "We need to get off this bird."

I couldn't believe that was his first concern. "Don't be absurd. Those old wives' tales are nonsense, you know."

"Where is he keeping her?"

"Baker, shh!" I hopped down from my hammock, surveying the room again to make sure nobody was around.

"If we find her, we can toss her off the ship."

"You wouldn't!"

"Everything the witch said is coming to pass. May your most valuable prize be as worthless as your promises. May your ship fall to the earth in a rain of fire and ash. We have to find the girl and toss her before this storm engulfs us."

"She's a child."

Baker inhaled sharply, holding his head as he paced. "All right," he said. "I'll do it."

"Baker!"

"I'll give her a parachute!"

"Then you'd better give me one as well because she's not going anywhere without me."

He blinked, gasping a little. "You've fallen in love with her."

I wanted to punch him.

"Yes! It all makes sense now," he said. "So much for your Ramona then."

"I'm not in love with her. She's a little girl."

"How old is she?"

"It don't matter how old she is!" I snapped. "This ain't a romance novel! It's a revolution!" Revolution. The word hung in the air between us. "Baker, I saved your life today."

"You did."

"And now I need a favor."

"Already?"

"You will help me rescue the princess and restore her to the throne. We'll take our parachutes and make the jump together."

"You've never made a jump like that, Fledgling."

"I have to do this. Dirk is planning to just hand her to the usurper and that will only cement their regime. If we rescue her and show people that she's still alive, I am certain they would fight for her. She would unite royalists and rebels alike all across Elsace."

"Rescue her?" Baker scoffed. "Unite royalist nobles and insurgents? Do you hear yourself, mate?" Baker leaned in until he was only an inch from my face. "You're talking about mutiny," he whispered. "And against the most dangerous sky pirate in all of Elsace."

"This is important."

"Dirk will hunt us, and he will kill us."

"Our queen would protect us. We would be the men who put her into power."

Baker was torn. He chewed his lip and scratched his matted head. "One hell of a favor, Clikk …"

"You promised to help me find the maggot who killed my parents, to help me avenge their deaths. Well, trust me when I say that this is more important to me. This is our chance to change the world." His hesitation was beginning to aggravate me. "You would be dead right now if I hadn't helped you! Dirk wanted to leave you all on that cruiser. Had I not jumped, had he not needed me for his deal with the emperor, you and the other Hawks would all be dead. To Dirk, our lives are expendable. I don't want to see you dead, Baker. I want to see you exalted."

"Exalted how?"

"We would be the nation's saviors. We could retire, own our own land, and eat all the cricket fudge you could ever want."

"Would our queen see us compensated for our services?" Baker asked.

"Are you kidding? We'll be showered in riches, celebrated in epic poems. You'll have more women than the sultan of Nazar."

"I don't know," he said. Behind his posturing, I could tell he was mulling it over. "All right, all right, fine! I'll help you, Clikk. I owe you a debt. But when we're done, we are getting blitzed, and you're buying the Skye."

I could not believe it at first that he had agreed. After getting to know Baker over the course of a year, I had come to realize he was a better man than most. It made me proud to call him friend, prouder still to call him brother. Now that Captain Dirk had revealed his determination to sell our princess to the Emperor, I had to oppose him. I could never—not for any promise of wealth or peace—allow Dirk to sell our last chance of removing the Blue Dusk from power. It would be treason against my very soul.

Had Dirk grown up on the streets like myself, he would have known not to build an alliance on blackmail. He would have known not to underestimate an urchin's guile. We build networks wherever we go.

Try and see how a little bloke does a card trick; you should be looking for his friend behind you.

16

SUBTERFUGE

The last barrels of Skye were empty now. Our boisterous crewmen had finally gone to bed, and the decks were mostly clear, guarded only by a pair of scouts, one on each flank. Dressed in their trench coats and wide-brim waterproof hats, they watched the rain spilling off the side of our balloon. Baker and I slinked past them, keeping to the shadowy edge of the main deck.

Suddenly he grabbed my shoulder and pulled me back. "Wait," he said.

Palpitations thrummed in my chest as I watched a few mechanics come up through the scuttle.

"Can you believe it's busted again?" one of them whined. "Sometimes I wonder how this wreck stays afloat." After they'd closed the hatch and moved on, Baker gave me a nod to signal we should keep moving. We crossed the main deck, heading aft until we reached the captain's door.

I crouched, my thieves' kit slung across my chest in a satchel. As Baker kept watch, I used my most reliable betties to pick the lock.

Baker's whispering—"Come on, come on, come on"—distracted me.

"Stop it," I told him. "Let me focus."

"What are we doing? Dirk'll toss us in the cloudsea for this."

"He won't. I promise you he is dead drunk tonight. Have you ever had the wine in Shale?"

"Course I've had it. Remember my story about Mathilde?"

Baker had a story about Mathilde for every occasion. As I recalled, one such episode had taken place in a Shalean vineyard and involved an old woman going blind.

"My elbows and knees were purple for a fortnight. And you should have seen Mathilde's backside."

"Be quiet before someone hears you. I'm ready for that oil."

I tripped the pins in the lock, nodding to Baker as I twisted the handle. He poured oil into the hinges in perfect synchrony with my opening the door. Beautiful silence ensued.

We crept in, closing the door behind us. Lightning illuminated the captain's dark chambers. Dirk wasn't in his bed. He'd likely gone unconscious right where I left him on the floor of his library.

Once we were inside, I could hear the muffled sound of Molly weeping behind the wall. Baker closed the door behind us. When he could hear the girl for himself, his demeanor changed. He no longer looked so nervous or begrudging of our quest. A touch of genuine sympathy appeared in his eyes.

"Poor little lamb," he said.

"Shh."

I led him toward the bed where I pulled back the brocade curtain and tried the hidden lever. Nothing happened. I jiggled it up and down. Still nothing.

Baker and I looked at each other. "This was how he did it," I said. I pulled on the trapdoor's outline. It would not come away.

"That's not good," said Baker.

I slid my thieves' kit up toward my chin and fished out a paint can opener. As I was putting it in the wedge, we heard Dirk expectorating in the adjacent room. My blood turned to ice. I tried prying the little door open. It wouldn't budge.

"Who's there?" asked Molly.

"Let me," said Baker. I stepped aside. He tried to force it, succeeding only in bending my tool.

"By gods, man! This is a delicate mechanism!"

The floorboards creaked in Dirk's library.

"Shite!" I hissed. "Abort! Now!" I smacked Baker's upper arm and made a dash for the exit, hoping to Throm that he was right at my heels. I locked the captain's door from the inside and closed it behind us as we came through.

The main deck appeared empty. Breathless and paranoid, we put our backs to the wall. "What now?" whispered Baker.

"We'll have to board the Crescendo tomorrow, retrieve the princess there."

I looked up and saw we were not alone. Nicolas Fitz dropped from the underbelly of the ship's balloon. He holstered a caulk gun in his utility belt and folded his arms. "Hello, friends," he greeted.

"Oh, Fitz. Hello. Banging out a few late night repairs, are you?" I laughed nonchalantly.

"Can't sleep thinking about them cracks in the envelope. Had to caulk 'em up," said Fitz. "I thought you boys turned in early. What were you doing in the captain's cabin?"

I grabbed him by the collar. "Listen to me, you caulk-sucking scum."

"Agh!" he cried.

"You can't tell anyone what you seen here. I'll take your eyes out—"

"The captain has a woman on board," said Baker.

I glared over my shoulder at him. "The hell is wrong with you?"

"I think it's vital we bring Fitz in on this. If we take her from the Crescendo tomorrow, we'll need a ship if we want to escape the Blue Dusk. You're sneaky, and I'm tough, but neither of us is an engineer."

Fitz giggled, genuinely amused. "Are you boys trying to steal the captain's woman?"

"We are! She's the true princess of Elsace," he explained. "And tomorrow the captain is going to surrender her to the usurper."

I wanted to kill Baker. I wanted to walk his arse back to the stern and push him down into the ship's propellers, waving gleefully as his dismembered body parts twirled on the wind.

But it was too late now. Fitz was on board.

17

A NEW PLAN

L ate into the night, we discussed how we would liberate the princess. A consensus was reached that we had no choice but to act after the exchange with the emperor. As morning broke, I lay in my hammock, practicing the mysterious lullaby until the music came away from my fingers without the slightest concentration. I would have to go through with the exchange, after all, but I made myself a solemn vow that I would not leave that ship without the girl.

The gentle light of the cresting sun peeked through the portholes and made visible the rest of the sleeping quarters. The many white canvas hammocks swayed, matching the pace of my bow as I made long strokes across my strings. The song sounded far more agreeable on fiddle than in my strained vocal intonations. The men who had done the graveyard shifts the night before did not mind my music enough to throw anything at me or ask me to stop. The melody seemed to put their souls at ease, much in the way it had done for young Molly.

Baker came in from the mess hall, juggling an orange. "Is that your mum's magic song?" He dipped his elbow into my hammock as he leaned against it.

"Aye, sir."

He scowled at me. "What have I said about calling me *sir*?" He dug his nails into the peel of his orange, to no avail. Then he tried using his teeth. This poor creature who could barely feed himself was my primary ally in rescuing a princess from the Imperial Guard.

"How was breakfast?" I asked.

Baker pierced the orange peel with his silver tooth. The aroma of citrus imbued the air as the skin came away at last. "You missed out. Cook made blood pudding."

"I can't eat right now. Got too much on my mind."

"At least have this orange I brung you."

"Nah, I don't want sticky fingers. Besides, I have to practice."

"Open your pie hole. I ain't asking. I won't have you getting scurvy on account of your shoddy diet." He broke off a wedge and shoved it in my mouth. "Eat, boy."

I suppressed a cough, swallowed hard and said, "Camilla's tail, man! You're bound to choke me!"

Laughing throatily, he shoved another equally large bit of orange in my mouth. "Don't take the goddess' name in vain. I'll not put up with your impudence today."

"I'm not a bloody snake!"

Boots thundered across the planks over our heads. A voice came through the ceiling. "Ship! Imperial!" More boot falls followed the call. I strapped my fiddle over my shoulder and hopped down from the hammock.

Baker and I rushed to observe through a porthole as the Emperor's ship, the Crescendo, came floating in next to ours. The magnificent vessel was rival to the sun itself. Her enormous gold-rimmed propellers dwarfed those of the Wastrel. The engines knit the clouds. They bore the emperor's crest, a crescent moon descending on a crown.

I had never seen such a vessel. The ship was hardly aerodynamic, its deck resembling a horseshoe-shaped tower. For lift, she used a multitude of balloons tethered all around her circumference. Their spherical frames had been sealed with gold silk, an effective, albeit expensive, material.

"This is the day we've dreamed of all our lives," I whispered. "We'll steal a rescue bird and be off before anyone has time to react. We will be the saviors of Elsace."

"I don't see any rescue birds," said Baker.

"An airship such as that has to have escape vessels."

"Couple of lunatics you are," said Fitz. I looked over my shoulder to see the grease-smudged lad grinning behind us. Nicolas Fitz was the last man I would have asked for help. His metal eye plate with the slits was pushed up on his forehead and crowned in spikes of messy hair. The plate had acted like a stencil, leaving soot lines over his eyes and forehead. He crossed his arms over his pigeon chest and brayed. "We might as well kill everyone and take the big boat. Quite a prize that."

Baker and I just stared at him. The notion of hijacking the Crescendo was preposterous. She was rumored to carry enough guns to ward off two ships on each flank.

I shook my head. "Baker, I need to talk to you."

We walked several strides away, far enough that Fitz most likely couldn't hear us. "How do we know he can be trusted?"

"It's Fitz," said Baker plainly. "Of course we can trust him."

"He's half-mad. And extremely annoying."

"You just haven't got to know him. He was my Fledgling before you."

"If he tells anyone else, we could be walking into a trap. The captain could have us arrested the moment we set foot on that ship."

"That's the risk you must run for progress. Think about it. The captain himself is taking a risk. He is selling them a princess with nothing but the emperor's word that he won't be arrested. They could capture him right there and take him to Locwyn to face trial."

"I'm sure Dirk has an escape plan in the event of such betrayal."

"Yeah. What if his escape plan gets in the way of our kidnapping plan?"

"Don't call it that. It's not kidnapping. It's rescuing."

"Right. Whatever."

"Just don't tell people our business anymore!"

"Fine. I won't tell no one nothing from now on. Ah. But I already told Pierce you could play magic songs."

I took a breath. I made an honest attempt to contain my temper. Then I shouted, "Did your mum drop you on your head?"

"I didn't mention the princess."

"Just. Shut it. Now." Shaking my head, I returned to Fitz by the porthole. "Fitz," I said. "Why on earth have you agreed to help us?"

"I told you. I want the big boat. We could be captains, hire our own crew out of Amaranthia, make our fortunes on the high skies."

"Three captains?" said Baker dubiously. "I'll be Captain. Clikk will be Quartermaster. And you can be Swabbie." He laughed, grabbing Fitz in a headlock. Fitz slipped it as easily as if he'd been greased with oil. In all fairness, he practically was.

"It's my idea!" he cried. "I get to be captain!"

"Nobody is taking the Crescendo," I told them. "We have a straightforward mission. You two will sneak aboard the ship and assume the identities of Duskmen. The wedding is tomorrow morning, so before it begins, we will spirit the girl away on a rescue bird."

"In what universe is that straightforward?" asked Baker.

"You never know! We might bring it off without a hitch!"

As the Crescendo swerved on the wind, we got a look at the ship's stern. Just as I had expected, smaller sky vessels were docked on perches, and amongst them, was the witch's bird-faced globe copter.

"Look!" I squawked. "That's the witch's ship."

"What's she doing there?" asked Baker.

"Didn't you hear when Dirk called her Maive?" I asked. "She is the emperor's sorceress."

Fitz salivated over the globe copter's mounted machine guns. "Phenomenal firepower," he whispered. "Just look at those guns. Oh, gods." He made an automatic weapon noise, spraying us with flecks of spit while pantomiming the act of self-manipulation. "Pop, pop, pop, pop, pop! Ahhh, spent!"

I glared at Baker, letting him know I held him fully responsible for Fitz being part of this. There was nothing I could do about it now. Unless I wanted to spur a full-blown mutiny, unless I wanted my captain's blood on my hands, these two dunderheads were all I had.

"Let's do this, boys!" squealed Fitz, patting our shoulders.

I shrugged him off. "Don't touch me."

"Or at least wash your hands first," said Baker.

Our plan was simple. That evening, Baker and Fitz would find a way to hijack the witch's ship while everyone was asleep. Meanwhile, I would open whatever locks confined the princess, and at the sight of a flare or other such explosive fired from the globe copter, I would walk her to the edge of the ship's starboard flank. Easy as pie, right? Baker sounded confident he could pilot the globe copter, and Fitz vouched for him.

"What of our captain?" asked Fitz.

"What do you mean?"

"Won't he be blamed when a gang of his men fly off with the blushing bride?" He made a point I had not thought about.

"He'll hunt us himself," I explained.

"Unless he's jailed," said Baker. "Fitz is right. We can't leave Captain Dirk to pay for our sins. We'll have to warn him, give him a chance to bolt before the Duskmen put him in irons."

"I'll do it," I said. "You have my word."

Our foolhardy plan could go wrong at any time, and we would all be killed if we were caught. No matter. I had my lucky nail around my thumb, and I wasn't about to give up our trueborn princess without a fight.

18

MY PRETTY MINSTREL

The fence of cables tethered to massive golden orbs allowed sunlight to fall over the Crescendo's deck. Duskmen stood in rows along the fringes. In their double-breasted uniforms with rows of shimmering buttons, they embodied the pristine, militant aesthetic of the new empire. Not one of them was smiling. Seeing them reminded me of our many differences. While they had their coiffed mustachios and elegant customs, we had reverted back to a darker age when a comb and cologne would satisfy the grooming standard.

They allowed only a few escorts to board with Dirk. We rode a blimp between our mighty sky vessels, taking the quartermaster, two Hawks and our cloaked princess. Nobody understood my purpose there, but Captain Dirk being the eccentric man that he was often had a flair for the dramatic, and having a minstrel accompany him to a hostage exchange was not entirely unanticipated.

"That wine did not sit well with me last night," he said as I hopped down from the gangplank and joined him on the Crescendo. We had made it this far without a confrontation about my breaking in. He could not have noticed anything amiss.

"It's hard on people who don't drink it all the time," I said.

"Yes. I've read about the neurotoxin in the berries. But every source claims it's harmless."

"Harmless, true, but it ain't good for you neither."

He chuckled, then leaning in, asked, "Did you try to get into Molly's room last night?"

My knees buckled. I stopped in my tracks. Dirk smiled to put me at ease.

"Don't worry. I'm not angry. I know you're fond of the girl. I'm going to assume you only wanted to help her get to sleep again."

"Yes." I seized the excuse.

"The bolt only moves when the curtains are fully drawn."

"Ah, I see."

"You could have asked me."

"Yes. Of course."

I spied the emperor and his son Prince Torrent. They wore similar robes of green silk embroidered with gold and silver thread. Somehow the lean, ghoulish Perceval had sired a chubby dumpling boy with the pouty mouth of a flat-faced cat. Maive stood beside them, arms folded. Her skin glowed pearlescent with the faintest hint of lavender in her lips and her eyes. She wore a structured dress of silver cogs and clockwork. The collar came up behind her head like steel lace, and a system of gears turned along her corset's metal boning, compelling her brooch to keep time.

Anxiety coursed through my chest in her presence. How easy would it be for her to hex me? To set all our men ablaze? How would she feel if she knew I was the reason for Molly being so composed?

The emperor came forward, looking down on us with a haughty, stately air. He spoke at last. "Welcome to the Crescendo, pirate captain. Have you brought me my tribute?"

I drew my fiddle and played my mother's lilting melody. Dirk removed Molly's dull, brown cloak. The girl beneath was radiant to behold in direct sunlight. Her heaps of blood-red curls, her eyes that were as vivid and lambent as a lagoon on the western shores, and her creamy, sun-kissed complexion all came together in the amalgamation of what one would expect in a true princess.

Our Hawks gasped. Mr. Bentley only smirked, having already known about the young lady stowed in the Captain's Quarters. She stood before Torrent in her fine pink satin gown, her eyes glowing with adoration. She was composed upon hearing my mother's song, perfectly regal in her natural state. To see her traded like chattel sickened me. As much as I wanted to throw down my instrument and strangle the emperor with my bow, I could not compromise the plan. I was to wait for Baker's signal so we could actually escape.

Molly curtsied and presented her hand to the prince. He kissed it and smiled up at her with cheeks like apples.

"Miss Luftburg," he said.

"My prince."

"You are truly she?"

"I am," she said with a modest smile.

Maive scowled. She spoke in a loud, clear voice as she said, "How can we be certain, Magnificence?"

"I remember her mother. This girl is the mirror image of her," said a woman, stepping forward from a cluster of ladies in gentry' robes. I recognized the empress from a painting I'd seen hung in a tavern in Aixenport. She had been the princess of Edwin, a nation eager to see unrest in its southern neighbor. It came as no surprise when the emperor announced her as his intended. No doubt her parents had supported his efforts to unseat King Lucius. It was strange to see such figures in the flesh, for I had always imagined them in some demonic perversion of their portraits. She was just a woman, a petite blonde encased in purple silks and shimmering stones. No claws. No blood dripping from the corners of her mouth.

Prince Torrent smiled and patted Molly's hand. "The ceremony shall commence at three o'clock, followed by a reception. As a member of the former dynasty joins our great house, a civil war is prevented!" The company of Duskmen applauded.

I hoped the wedding would be a short ceremony; I was having the most vivid homicidal fantasies about the emperor's family, and Molly looked like she was going barmy from hearing the same musical phrase repeated over and over on the fiddle. The emperor and his son were also staring at me with baffled expressions.

"Who is this?" asked the prince, gesturing.

"This is my minstrel," said Molly. "She plays beautifully, doesn't she?"

"She?"

The blood went cold in my face. I heard some confused whispering from our Hawks Pierce and Caleb. Mr. Bentley shushed them.

"Oh yes! She dresses like the men, but she is a lovely young woman," prattled Molly, fidgeting with the lace ruffles at her wrists.

Caleb laughed and Pierce elbowed him in the ribs.

The prince came toward me and stared intensely at my face. To my amazement, he smiled wide, his little teeth glistening. "Indeed she is," he said. "She will be the handmaiden."

Captain Dirk stepped forward, murmuring, "My prince, this woman is but a lowly peasant, a minstrel no less."

"No matter," said the prince. "Any woman whom both bride and groom fancy may fill the role." He turned to address me. "You, girl, put down that fiddle and go with the servants. They shall make you presentable."

I didn't know what this assignment entailed, but if it involved being made presentable, I did not want to comply. I kept playing until a servant girl snatched my instrument away.

Molly shook her head, tears welling in her eyes. "My sweet, sweet prince!" she cried. "I am overcome with joy." She could barely stand. I caught her by the arms and supported her weight.

"Not so fast! We need to be paid," demanded Captain Dirk. "I've brought you the girl."

"Aren't we eager?" said Emperor Perceval with a malicious grin. "You wouldn't want to miss the festivities, would you?"

I felt the ship rise. More of those golden orbs inflated and surrounded the deck like a bubbly fence. Visibility from the Wastrel was blocked.

"Besides," he added. "I know how you pirates can get on your long and lonely voyages. Tomorrow my son will confirm that Miss Luftburg is still a virgin. Then you will be returned to your ship."

Dirk squinted, matching the emperor's manner. "No, I think not. I think you will pay for what you have bought and return me to my ship this instant. If my men do not have me returned within the hour, you can expect a battle."

Emperor Perceval laughed, and it sounded so genuine that, at first, I thought he was about to comply.

Then the guards seized my captain and twisted his arms behind his back. Emperor Perceval backhanded him with a force that cracked his jaw like a whip.

"Stop!" Molly cried, exploding into a wild tantrum. I held her back from running to him. If she gave him away as her brother, he was dead.

Dirk spit a gob of blood. "Be strong, little girl! Don't weep for pirate scum."

"Come, child," said the empress, snapping her long, white fingers. "We have a wedding to prepare for." A group of maids ripped her from my arms. There were four of them, all in white gowns, white aprons, and lace headdresses. Their faces were monotone and severe, hard and sharp like broken glass. I froze where I stood.

Mr. Bentley drew his pistol but could not bring it up before the Duskmen brought knives to his, Pierce's, and Caleb's throats.

The emperor addressed Pierce. "You there. You will return to the Wastrel and tell the men that your captain wishes to remain for the ceremony. Any sign of retaliation from your decrepit vessel and we will execute your friends and destroy your ship. Understood?"

Pierce nodded. Blue Dusk escorted him to the blimp that had carried us over. Once he was gone, the emperor signaled to the men holding Mr. Bentley and Caleb.

They cut their throats open in one vicious motion. Blood cascaded down their fronts and they fell to their knees.

"No!" screamed Molly. She had escaped the maid's clutches briefly enough to run back on deck. "You villain! How could you?"

"Somebody tend to this girl's hysterics," said the emperor.

Dirk stared in wide-eyed horror at the bodies of our friends. "We had an agreement," he growled. "You swore on your honor that none of my men would be harmed."

Emperor Perceval clutched him by the jaw. "And so did you, Captain Dirk. You think I don't know who sank my cruiser? That ship had wedding guests on board, friends of the Order. Your kind will no longer be tolerated in the skies. Once the insurgency is crushed, our military will focus on eradicating piracy from our airspace. Now over the next few days, I will determine whether we kill you quickly or draw it out. As I said, all of that depends on the condition of Miss Luftburg." He delivered a swift kick into Dirk's ribs.

"Miss Luftburg," Dirk coughed. "You offend the gods themselves calling her that. She is of royal blood."

I did not see the rest. The maidservants' nails dug into my wrists as they pulled me down below deck. In the passageway, they paused as a crone in white lace dictated orders.

"A bath of milk and roses for the girl," she said. She was a wiry old thing with a weak jaw that hung wrinkled about her throat. "The empress left a gown for her in the blue room. When she is washed and has had her hair and makeup fixed, take her there."

"What of the peasant?" asked the maid who wrung my arm.

"Just what I need. Another project," the old woman groaned. "You'll have to sort her out downstairs. Take her to the kitchens and have her scrubbed. Then send her to the red room."

Molly screamed, reaching back for me. "Clikk!"

"Be brave, girl!"

The maidservants dragged Molly one way and I another.

19

A Girl with Yellow Hair

The staff forced me down into the belly of the ship where the sweltering heat of the kitchens raged. The rooms were noisy with the clink of crockery and the hiss of boil and steam. The staff here dressed in beige stripes bearing the stains of animal blood and sweat. Judging by their haggard and starved appearances, I could tell they were a mistreated bunch.

The heat was oppressive. Both of the maids pulling on me had nervous round eyes. All the stress and strain of preparing a wedding at sky had driven them mad.

"Out of the way!" one of them snapped at a kitchen boy, shoving him by the head. Another kicked the basin being scrubbed by a scullery wench and told her to fill it with water and bring it to the pantry.

We arrived in a small hold filled with grain and flour and other bulk goods. A single light bulb illuminated the space. It flickered out as we came in. My captors shouted for someone to bring another and a young man came running. When we had light, the maids stripped me of my clothes, starting with my flight cap.

Though they debased me no different from a swine up for slaughter, I did not bother fighting. I shut off my mind. My armor had already been stripped away when they knew my sex. Whoever they saw standing before them in all her nakedness and shame was not a full picture of my soul. I had to remember that. There were things inside my heart they could not touch. They could not have the part that was my father's kindness, nor Mr. Greyson's wisdom, nor Mikhail's ruthless grit.

The women pulled my grease-ridden shirt away and gasped when they saw the bruising over my ribs and the scars on my neck, shoulders, and back. As they peeled away the bindings around my chest and removed the rest of my clothing, they saw more scars and recoiled in disgust.

"Who would do this to a woman?" one whispered to the other. I ignored her. She knew nothing of the life I'd lived, and my scars could speak for themselves. I'd been shot in the shoulder, and the mark there was from the barber who cut out the bullet. I'd earned the lashes on my back mouthing off to a knight. On my ribcage, I had three brands from a hot poker. That was a test of toughness I passed to join the Kindred. And maybe they could see it, and maybe they couldn't, but I also had a faint white mark under my lip from when I was robbed. I had many scars, and I was proud of every last one.

The women guided me into a basin of water and lathered me in soap that smelled of cloves. With a pitcher, they repeatedly doused me in freezing cold water.

The crone came down after my bath. They wrapped me in a robe of porous linen and had me stand before her with my eyes forward. She pulled at my hair, inspecting it as if I were a horse. I had neglected to cut it over the course of the year. It came down past my chin, and the back was rather shaggy. "Hmm. It's a good color. I'd hate to hide it with a wig. Fiona has a similar color, hasn't she?"

"She does," said one of the maids.

"Call her down here."

They did so, and a girl about Molly's age came down. Her thick blonde locks fell all the way down to her hips. They had us sit down, side by side, and combed my tresses dry. With a pair of shears, they cut the girl's hair and clamped the locks in hot wax. Then they wove them into braided rows against my scalp. When they were done, I felt a heavy mass on the back of my head. I had long yellow hair and the girl called Fiona was in tears.

"There, there," said one of the maids. "It will grow back."

"Why did she have to be blonde?" the girl wept, touching her bare nape.

The two maids led me upstairs. They took me into the so-called red room, with its curtains and bedspread of rose-patterned brocade. There they pulled a floor-length kirtle over my head. An emerald green dress lay spread open across the bed. It had such shape to it, the kind that groped and squeezed a body, accentuating and exposing every womanly effect.

"Drat! They forgot the corset."

"I'll let her borrow one of mine. I don't want to be a bother. Everyone is so busy as it is."

"Yes. You're quite right."

"Stay here with her."

"With her?" The young lady looked ill at the idea. "Do not forget this woman came with the pirates. I'll go with you, thank you."

"Perhaps she was their captive. Were you their captive, Miss…?"

"I hold the second highest confirmed kill count amongst our crew," I lied. "The men of the Wastrel would be fools to try and hold me captive."

"Let's lock her in," said one maid to the other. "Let's do. I'm not staying here alone with her."

I fought the urge to laugh as they shut the door and turned the key in the lock. I donned a robe with a high lace collar on top of my kirtle and fastened it with a sash from the green dress. In the armoire, I found some wire hangers. With these, I fashioned a set of shoddy thieves' tools. Fortunately, the lock on my door was a simple deadbolt. It tripped easily.

I ducked my head and walked briskly down the passageway. I had to improvise from here. Dirk was in trouble, and I had no idea where they'd taken him, or Molly, for that matter. I pulled on the long yellow hair sewn against my scalp. Nothing would get that off short of sawing it with a blade, and I might need it to blend in until I had the princess in my keeping.

Down the passageway, deep voices echoed dimly. I slipped into a nook before a laundry chute and waited for the men to pass. But they stalled at the window, suddenly lowering their voices. As I peeked out from around the edge of the wall, I noticed the emperor was speaking to one of his officers, a man wearing more ornamentation on his uniform than any other Duskmen I had seen thus far. Rows of silver badges hung from stripes and he wore epaulettes corded thrice on one side. The man was tall and ivory-skinned, his eyes as blue as twilight. He had a long and severe brow, a natural sneer, and a square, clean-shaven jawline.

He spoke, his voice eerily familiar. "The rebels of Locwyn have been inciting riots since you've been away, Eminence."

"How is that? We left enough forces there to sack a small nation!" hissed Perceval.

"Some fools are defecting. My absence has lowered morale."

"Go on, then. Go and crush it."

The officer nodded, and as he turned, I could see the sword tied to his left hip. Its tear-shaped blue stones caught the sun. Sapphires.

He glanced away from the emperor for just a second to look at me, to raise one brow, and take me in. I slipped back behind the wall and suppressed a shudder.

"I regret I will miss the reception tomorrow. I wish your son all the happiness in the world. Goodnight, Your Eminence." His words came off heavy and muffled in my ears, which were ring-ing. I fixated on the sword as he stepped into view. Its sapphires gleamed like the eyes of snakes.

That was him. He was there, right in front of me, and now he was speaking to me directly. "Why, hello there." I could not meet his eyes. I had sworn to kill the man who carried that sword, but now, as I beheld him, I found my body turned to stone. "I must know your name."

My glare shot up at him. I whispered my mother's name, "Sera."

"Beautiful," he said, oblivious. Part of me hoped he would rec-ognize me, but it was better he did not. "You don't know who I am, do you?" he said with a laugh.

"You are the Cerulean Knight." It took every ounce of self-con-trol not to reveal my true hatred for him.

He laughed again, but his laughter was like venom dripping from a serpent's fangs. "You may call me Rex, pretty flower. Gen-eral Rex in polite company. May I ask your affiliation with the Imperial family?"

I cast my eyes downward. "I'm only a servant. Forgive me, General." I bobbed and hurried away down the hall.

"A pleasure to meet you, Sera!" he called after me. For all my talk of vengeance, for all my vows made to my dead, I had been meek as a mouse in that murderer's presence. I hated my cow-ard guts. I wondered, was it this womanly transformation that had made me so pitiful?

Before I could loathe myself too thoroughly, I saw Duskmen approaching in a single file. Their faces stared straight ahead as they passed, except for the last one, a dark-skinned soldier with dread-locks. Throm's grace, it was Baker. And rather than recognize me, he took notice of everything below my neck. Typical Baker. And thank the stars for that for he passed without once making eye contact. I realized it had been Fitz walking in front of him. Hopefully, he had also failed to recognize me.

I had to find Molly. But I also had a duty to my mother and father to end that wicked Knight. How many lives had he destroyed? How many would he continue to destroy if no one stopped him? I made a vow the day I awoke in a pool of my own blood. The gods brought me back for one thing and one thing only. It was vengeance that had compelled my heart to go on beating as I pulled myself up from my kitchen floor, vengeance that kept me conscious and on my feet long enough to reach the neighboring farmhouse, vengeance that filled my belly at night when I had not eaten in days. I would make Rex look into my eyes and remind him what he stole from me right before I sank a dagger in his heart.

20

THE GENERAL

Had I been a different sort of girl, I might have seduced Rex and killed him in his sleep. He had been drawn to me and apparently had a type. I did consider how easy it would be to knock on his door and offer myself to warm his bed, easy only until I felt his cruel hands upon my skin. The mere thought of it made my eyes water.

The prospect of prostitution had always horrified me. I decided as a young girl that I would die before selling my body to a man. The feel of it would be insufferable—the smell, the risk, the shame. There are some memories one never escapes. They bubble up in the night when you think you are safe in your bed. You feel the shadow fall over you, the weight of a man's hands crushing your throat. I rather admired ladies of the night for their ability to suffer vile men in their beds, to go on smiling like dolls after taking such rot into their hearts.

I had followed Rex to his room in first class. His attendant greeted him in the hall, taking him inside and closing the door. I could have forced my way in and cut him down, but I would inevitably be discovered and would miss my chance to rescue Molly.

The only way was to spend the night with Rex and wait until his servant had retired and he had let down his guard. I could not bear to do it. Neither could I bear to lose the princess to the Blue

Dusk. And so I was frozen, trapped in the limbo of indecision, watching Rex's door from the stairwell.

How could there be gods, I wondered, if such a man as he can live so well and earn so many honors after committing such atrocities? The scar over my throat began to itch beneath my lace collar. A wound like that never fully heals.

"The prince wants you to be present for the consummation," snarled a voice from below. I went higher upstairs without making a noise, concealing myself as some Duskmen ascended with Captain Dirk in chains.

"Quite the exhibitionist, isn't he?" said Dirk.

"If it turns out the girl is no virgin, you can expect our prince to spend the rest of the evening torturing you."

Dirk laughed, though I knew he cared more than he let on. "It will be torture enough watching a pair of virgins navigate the mysteries of each other's bodies," he said. Their voices faded away as they entered what must have been the prince's chambers at the end of the hall.

The scene put my mission into perspective. I would rescue my captain, granted that he agreed to my conditions. He would have to help me save Molly as well. I could see the plan so clearly in my mind when suddenly a hand fell on my shoulder.

"Look what I found!" a woman exclaimed. My eyes were drawn to the diamonds glittering up her sleeves. "It's the Lady Molly's young minstrel!" Her breath reeked of sherry. Four other women of her class squealed with delight.

"Come to our room, little dove! Play us a song!" They snared my waist and pulled me upstairs with them. If I protested, they might ask what I was doing on my own out there. They were drunk enough, however, that if I appeased them with a few songs they could very well let me waltz right out of their chambers.

Their luxuriant suite was papered with a rose lattice pattern. Small, wood furniture upholstered in striped satin stood around a mirrored coffee table strewn with open snuff boxes and empty bottles of sherry. The ladies sat me down on a hard, little chair and handed me a lute.

"I mostly know sky shanties," I said. "Hope that's all right."

"Oh, yes!" cried a brunette with tiny pearls on the tips of her eyelashes. "She is part of that pirate's crew! Do teach us a shanty!"

As I toyed with the strings and figured out some chords, the ladies poured a round of sherry into sparkling chalices.

"I should love to sing a lewd shanty! Make it the lewdest!" the brunette cried, cackling with delight. I played them some of the filthy songs Baker and I had written together. These upper-crust ladies choked on their laughter as if they had never heard a joke in their entire lives. They didn't mind my raspy voice or my contrived lyrics. They were the best audience I'd ever had.

After the third shanty, I bowed my head and said, "Thank you, ladies. You've been lovely. I must retire now for we have the wedding at sunrise, and we all need our precious sleep."

I laid the lute on my seat and tried to go, but they blocked the door and protested at length. "You must stay for another song!"

"Please!"

"I cannot. Surely you understand."

They did not, and as much as I fought them to get through the door, these ladies were unreasonably strong, fortified by the sherry in their blood. For all my might, I could not get away.

"Another song then," I conceded, catching my breath and returning to my seat. They cheered and toasted with another round of drinks. I played "Wench of Amaranthia" and taught them the ridiculous chorus. I'd never seen such a raucous bunch of ladies. They were wilder than pirates, hiking their skirts up over their bloomers and stomping about the room in a crazed, militant dance. The ringleader with the diamond sleeves rang a little bell attached to a string on the wall.

Not long after, there came a knock.

"Shh!" cried the ringleader and the laughter tapered off into low giggling. She opened the door and a maid came through. Seeing me, her eyes went wide.

"Lydia," said the fancy lady to her maid. "We need some more sherry. One last bottle, I think. And then we will retire."

"Lady Margaret, you must forgive me, but the wedding is in only a few hours. This girl needs to be made ready."

"A few hours!" cried the ringleader. "Heavens! What time is it?"

"Five o' clock in the morning, ladyship."

"We must go to bed! Oh, my girls! We will look wretched tomorrow if we do not sleep."

As the ladies became anxious and distressed over the hour, the maid snared my wrist and hauled me away without their noticing. "You could have cost me my job!" she snapped, dragging me like a child. "Wretched little weed, vying for the favor of ladies far above your rank. Because of your ambition, we've hardly any time to make you presentable!"

Beyond the clock window in the stairwell, the sky had the early tints of daybreak.

"We still need to paint your face, set your hair, dress you—do you have any idea how long dressing you will take?"

"A quarter of an hour?" I queried.

The maid suppressed a shriek. "Idiot peasant."

We came into the red room where that garish dress still lay. Beside it, a whalebone corset hung halfway off the edge of the bed. There was hardly any fabric to it. Skinny as I was, I could not possibly stretch that fabric around my waist's circumference. I fought to get away, twisting the skin on the maid's forearm and pulling with all my strength.

"I cannot wear that!"

Her accomplice came in behind me. "You found her! Thank the gods!" she exclaimed, pushing me forward against the bedpost and yanking down my robe. The air was cold, and my kirtle did nothing to keep it from puckering my flesh. I held both sides of the bedpost as they brought the unlaced corset around my waist. At first, the laces merely held it on. I thought, *oh, this isn't so bad, after all.* Then the tightening began.

21

THE GIRL RAMONA

Mother taught me my scales before she died. One of the maids hummed as she laced me in the bone-crunching corset; I used her lilting melody to escape to a memory of those mornings with my mother when we used to hum while washing our clothing with lye. Mother taught me how to harmonize, how to keep a steady rhythm, how to improvise with notes. Strangely, almost every good memory I had of her involved music somehow, making me wonder, did we ever speak of anything meaningful? She gave me tidbits of knowledge over the years, most of which I would never use as I would never have a proper household to keep. She made promises to me about my future before the world tore it all away. She said I would marry, I would have a daughter of my own, and I would teach her the songs.

There had been other songs. I could only remember the lullaby.

I asked her once how she met my father. A demure smile curled her lips. "We met as children very far away from here. He stole me from a tower. I will tell you when you are older."

"Tell me now!" I had pleaded, longing to fancy that my mother had been a princess from some distant land, liberated by her true love. "Were you enchanted? Did Father have to fight a dragon?"

"It is no fairy tale as I have made it sound. We were both servants who ran away together. It is best I leave it there."

I never learned from whence they had come, but my mother spoke with proper grammar and knew how to read and sing and play the flute. I used to imagine she had been a lady's maid. Now that I was older, I suspected she might have even been a courtesan or a concubine. With both my parents dead, I would never know. Our last name sounded vague enough to have come from any of the northwestern continental countries.

The lacing of my corset now made it impossible to concentrate on anything but the pain. The garment went on like a piece of armor, hard and heavy. I was used to discomfort, but the tightening of that garment exposed me to a new level of torture. My bruised ribs screamed in agony as the women cinched my waist to an inhuman measurement.

"There we are!" cried the maid, catching her breath as she knotted the laces. She and the other woman fitted me with a hoop skirt weighing at least ten pounds; they added another twenty with the gown.

"Stand tall!" said the meaner one as she grabbed my shoulders and forced them back.

The first maid said, "Go easy. Girls like her don't know how to wear a dress like this."

"At the very least, try and keep your chin up and your eyes open."

They worked together to secure over a hundred buttons in the back and along the cuffs that came up to my elbow. The off-shoulder puff sleeves offset the width of my shoulders. The low neckline clung tight around my arms, securing me in a prison of stiffened silk.

They did not have any shoes that fit me, so I was permitted to wear my boots as long as I walked slowly so they did not peek out from below my hemline. I was glad for it; it gave me a place to hide my lucky ring when they weren't looking. I fastened it against the laces.

They added a choker to hide my scar, and when my look was complete, showed me my reflection in a gilded hand mirror. "There's a whole new person in there," said the kinder woman.

They both smiled and looked as if they expected me to do the same. I'd never seen my own cleavage before or even known I had any. The sight of myself made me want to retch. It was like seeing my body flayed: exposed, filthy, and yearning for death.

The crone from the day before came in to inspect me. She paced about me, her heeled boots ticking like the pendulum of a grandfather clock. "Yes. This will do. Well done, ladies."

"Where is Molly?" I asked her.

The crone folded her hands at her waist. "Your whiny mistress is still getting ready. It is taking an eternity to do her makeup because she will not stop crying. Nothing in the world can console her."

"If I could just see her."

"No. You must go above deck to scatter rose petals down the aisle."

"I need my fiddle. My lady requested I play it."

"It's not necessary. We have a quartet from Leffen."

My patience dissipated. "Where is my bloody fiddle, woman?"

The crone's face grew severe as she lost her patience as well. "Stay that vile little tongue of yours."

"Or what?" I spat. "You'll put bows in my hair?"

She huffed. "The prince will have fun breaking you in."

I stumbled over my words when I begged her pardon.

"Don't you know what is expected of a royal lady's handmaiden? You're to be your mistress's servant and quite likely the prince's lover," she explained.

My heart sank like a dagger into a boiling sea. "That swine won't touch me."

The crone shoved a cast-iron cauldron of flower petals into my arms. "Do as you're told, peasant."

I had heard that phrase before on that awful day when the Blue Dusk came to Shale.

"It should be quite an exciting night," she went on to say. "A wedding feast followed by the destruction of that ratty old pirate ship below. They say its balloon will combust if it's punctured."

"The Wastrel will blow the Crescendo out of the sky," I hissed. I saw my own temper reflected back at me.

The crone slapped me across the face. It stung, but not as much as her words. "Quiet, slattern. You may be dressed as a lady, but do not forget that you were born sullied."

This poor woman. She didn't know any better. She only saw Mona, peasant girl of Shale. She didn't know Mona died long ago when the Cerulean Knight cut her throat. I was Clikk, a picklock, a thief, a sky pirate. That thought of pity for the old woman fluttered in my mind like a lone feather on the wind, and then Clikk took over.

I smacked my cauldron into a maid's head, stole the hair pick right out of her bun and stabbed the crone in the shoulder. She screeched and I slammed her head into the bedpost to silence her. The remaining maid tried to flee, but I caught her by the apron sash and pulled her in like a prize of war.

"Shhhh," I whispered in her ear, stealing her hairpins one by one and tucking them down the front of my corset. "You have the long, white neck of a swan, easy to break. So keep quiet and help me tie up these ladies."

22

CLİKK

And now I was improvising again. The original plan had been dodgy from the start, and I could not in good conscience abandon my captain to the mercy of the Blue Dusk.

The sumptuous halls of the Crescendo were well serviced. The fruit bowls overflowed with bright tangerines, apricots, and berries. Floral arrangements towered over me on all sides, roses and crabapples tinged with a hue like a mingling of cream and blood. I popped in and out of rooms, bobbing and apologizing.

"Sorry." Again, "Sorry." I did not find my fiddle and accepted it was lost to me. My professions of "Sorry" began to lose their meaning, though everyone I crossed would bob in return, say, "That's quite all right, Miss," and be on their way. Everyone's politeness was refreshing. I had never known polite society to live up to its name. Only one of the well-dressed lords was discourteous. As I came through a narrow spiral staircase, he moved aside and said, "You're welcome," without my saying anything at all to him. I ignored the toff.

Finding Dirk was my first goal. I kept my head held high with an air of belonging, as I had done when I first hit the city streets of Aixenport in search of work. I smiled courteously to each person I passed, conjuring Molly's innocence and propriety. Nobody bothered me or asked what I was doing. Not a single guard had any suspicion about the yellow-haired noblewoman holding a cauldron full of rose petals.

The staff was overwhelmed, screaming orders at their inferiors and running about in a craze. The only person who spoke to me was a maid, and it was to apologize for losing her temper at another maid in my presence.

There was a shift in the Duskmen's attitudes toward me as I neared a more secure area of the Crescendo. One of them halted me and asked, "Are you lost, Miss?"

"Yes," I replied in my best impersonation of a noble. I raised my chin, enunciated every consonant and tried to remember how grammar worked. "Forgive me. Where am I?"

He smirked upon hearing the rough quality of my voice, but didn't seem to assume anything other than I might be ill. "You were about to wander into the prince's chamber, Miss. You wouldn't want to go there."

"I am the bride's handmaiden," I said. "I thought I might prepare the chamber for the wedding night. I have these rose petals. See?" The sugarplum damsel act was actually quite amusing. I lifted my cauldron for him. He peeked inside.

"The prince has the key, so I couldn't let you in even if I—" Before this hapless guard could finish his sentence, I swung my cast-iron pot into the side of his head, dropping him to the floor with a spray of petals.

I wound my bent hairpins into the keyhole. This lock had a number of tricky pins and without my tools, its securities proved a decent challenge. I twisted, scraped, and timed my picks, and finally, the lock gave.

On the other side of the door, Captain Dirk was chained to a steam radiator. For a second, I thought I had broken into a torture chamber, but then I saw the luxurious bed. Torrent's bedchamber was the stuff of nightmares. Frightening projects covered every surface and shelf, baby dolls with taxidermy bird heads, stitch-work chimeras combining cat's tails with rodent's bodies and monkey's feet, masked with the scratched faces of porcelain dolls. I didn't let this distract me. My primary task was removing Dirk's gag, which I regretted upon completion.

"You look beautiful, Clikk."

"Shut up," I said, concentrating on the padlocks confining him. These were much simpler than the lock on the door, and I could easily pick them with hairpins.

"I am going to kill that imperial snot. He's a twisted pup," said Dirk.

"I saw the dolls." I moved onto the next padlock, stabbing fiendishly as I hurried to get him free and get us out of there. If anyone discovered us, all was lost. I envisioned myself fighting tooth and nail for freedom, only to be subdued when they sounded the alarm and a dozen guards swarmed me.

"I mean, to think of him putting his grubby mitts on Molly." Dirk shuddered. "Ugh."

"What did you think would happen after the wedding?"

"The boy looks like an eight-year-old! I only just learned he's sixteen. And I never imagined he would be so..." His eyes wandered back to the doll creatures and he cringed. "...depraved."

"He is Perceval's son! The man who killed everyone in your family, including the children! Have you forgotten them already?"

"I have not forgotten them."

"And you would just trust your sister to be happy marrying into their family?" I opened the last of the padlocks. Click. Click. Click. As the chains fell away, Dirk took hold of my arm.

"What choice did I have?" he cried. "I want to keep her safe, don't you see? But whether we live as peasants, or thieves, or whatever, she will always be in danger for her resemblance to our mother. And if I made a claim for the throne, I would be risking both our lives. I thought if I gave her to them, assimilated her with their family, she would be safe. There could be peace." Dirk hid his eyes in the palm of his hand. "I've only tried to protect her, but as it turns out, I'm rubbish at it."

"Yeah, you really are. Maybe if you spent less time drinking, you'd have a clearer head."

"I haven't had a clear head in years," he whispered, tensing his jaw in an effort not to show his emotions. "Whenever the drink wears off, I remember everything the royalists did to help me escape my execution. I remember my family. The last time I saw them alive was the day I escaped. The royalists had made arrangements to save only one of us, the one who would lead the revolution. I switched places with a young man who came disguised as the physician. My mother, ill, her color fading, asked one last thing of me. She begged me to take Molly under my cloak and see that she never fell into the hands of the Blue Dusk again. I promised her—promised on my life—that I would protect her at any cost. That young man who took my place in the spire died so I might live. See how I've failed him. I've failed all of them. My mother and three of my siblings never left that cell. My younger brother was killed alongside my double. I wasn't even there to see him through to the World After. Then, in the weeks that followed, one of my little sisters died from a fever. When they executed my mother, my other sister took her own life. And all that remained of them, that innocent child, has been sold to the very people who murdered her family. Oh, Molly. What have I done?"

I unraveled the heavy chains from around him and offered a hand up. "We can make it right, Captain. I have a plan to get her off the Crescendo. You must run to the place where the witch's globe copter is located and join Baker and Fitz there. I will go above to the wedding, and when you boys signal me, I will grab Molly and run to the starboard flank."

"How do Baker and Fitz figure into this?"

"We planned to save Molly all along, against your orders. I'm sorry, Captain, but I couldn't let you give her to the usurper."

Dirk grimaced at first, but his anger allayed, and he said, "You came back for me when you didn't have to. I just wish I understood why."

"Because even though you're a drunkard and a terrible brother, you don't deserve to be tortured and killed by the Blue Dusk. And you gave me a chance on your crew even though you knew I was a girl."

"Well, thank you for that, at least. Still, someday you will have to learn how to follow orders, especially if we are to start a revolution."

My heart felt light and sunny upon hearing this. "Will you fight to overturn them?"

"No man humiliates Alexander Dirk and lives to tell the tale. Seeing as how you seem to already have a plan in motion, I shall follow your lead." He looked at my hand. "I would shake on it, but I never shook a woman's hand before."

I gripped his forearm, and we sealed the alliance with a mighty jolt. "I'm proud to be your first."

"Said no woman ever," Dirk quipped.

"Have you got any weapons, Captain?"

"They took everything."

I slipped out into the nook where the unconscious guard still lay. We dragged the Duskman in, undressed him, chained him to the radiator, secured the locks, and gagged him for good measure. Dirk slid into the Duskman's uniform, which was a bit tight in the arms. With pocket automatic in hand and a short sword and dagger on his belt, he fled down the hall to make his way to the copter. The tuning of stringed instruments sounded above my head. It was time. I knelt to gather my rose petals back into the cauldron and ran to join the wedding party.

23

THE BRIDE

Above deck amidst the array of opulence and frivolity, I smiled and bowed my head to each guest I passed and prayed none of my carnage had been discovered. The people were finding their seats along benches that were arranged before the helm. The ship's wheel had been decorated with rose garlands. Two thick, white candles burned on either side. Whether or not this was a helium ship, it seemed highly dangerous, not that it mattered to me. If I had my way, this whole ship would be torched once we got Molly to safety. A tiny woman jumped out from behind a pair of rotund nobles.

"There you are! Where is Clarice?" she squeaked as she shoved her face in mine. "Miss Molly was in the bath until she was as pruned as her! We had to dress her ourselves!"

"There was an emergency. Clarice said to move forward without her."

"Ugh!" groaned the maid. "Just toss your petals already."

The string quartet began to play a Leffenese ballad. I followed the velvet runner to the altar, walking as gracefully as any person could with her heart drumming out of control. It was a short walk, fortunately. I dropped a handful of white rose petals every few paces.

The glittering aristocratic guests were less than twenty in number. I recognized the ladies from the night before. They had dark circles under their eyes. The ringleader leaned forward to yawn into her fan, nearly losing consciousness before she jerked awake. The empress had some friends around her, nobles whose badges suggested they belonged to the imperial cabinet. Maive was present as well and seemed none the wiser that her ship might have been hijacked.

As I reached the altar, I saw General Rex boarding a small blimp with several Duskmen. I had missed my chance, and I might never have another. I wondered whose innocent lives would be ruined as a result of my failure.

"I could tell you were a pretty one. Even under all that crud, I saw it." The prince spoke to me, but his voice came off heavy and muffled in my ears, which were ringing. I fixated on the blimp as it floated away from us. Its fuel burned blue, blue as sapphires.

He had been here, right here on this ship, and now he was getting away. I could not chase after him, not without Molly.

A Duskman jabbed me with the butt of his rifle. "Your prince addresses you. Thank him for his generous compliment."

I met the gaze of the pudgy youth in his stolen crown. "Thank you," I said. Prince Torrent had nothing else for me.

The band played the bridal march as a trio of maids sang harmony. Molly appeared from below deck. Her thick, many-layered veil danced in the wind as she surfaced. I couldn't see her face, but I saw the V-shaped cuffs of her sleeves where she held a bouquet of white roses with dark leaves weeping down. The child's hands were trembling; she still suffered the curse. She walked so stiffly, so hurried, and was only a few feet away from the altar when a maid came running out behind her.

"Wait!" the servant screamed. "Stop the ceremony!"

Gold fire split the sky in a vertical streak. It whistled, and then with a thundering boom, showered a sparkling spray of tendrils across the deck. Everyone gawked, and there was scattered applause amongst the nobility.

The witch's avian globe copter wheeled through the sky, wobbling on the air like a drunken crow. It tumbled and tripped between clouds, and I could see Baker through the windshield fighting the controls.

Molly, meanwhile, swept her veil back over her head and wasn't Molly at all, but Fitz dressed head to toe in white chiffon. He drew two mechanized pocket automatics from his shoulder holsters, gritted his teeth, and fired into the crowd. The weapons popped like kernels over a flame, propelling waves of tin debris. I dropped down flat on my face. A cacophony of screams lifted off the wedding party, blood spraying the deck.

When the shrieking of the weapons halted, I peered up, squinting through the smoke. I made out what I could through the mist and the gunpowder clouds. Fitz in all his bridal attire was drenched in the blood. Torrent's face had become a shell of gore and over half of the Duskmen lay dead. Emperor Perceval had taken bullets in his arm and shoulder. His guards surrounded him, shouting, "Down, down, down!"

Nobles rushed the Duskmen, trying to get them between themselves and Fitz. The Duskmen were unable to open fire until everyone hit the deck. Laughing like a lunatic, Fitz bolted for the open sky.

The globe copter swept in and hovered at the railing, its glass doors hanging open on both sides. In my head, I kept thinking, *please gods, let him make it.* He ran hard, chest puffed out, legs pumping like piston rods. The copter's propeller blew everything about and launched Fitz's veil right off his head.

Shells sprinkled the ground around me as Duskmen fired on Fitz with their many pocket automatics. I could barely see through the wisps of gun smoke curling up on the wind. The wood balustrade shattered, disintegrating into dust carried on the wind. If Fitz made it out alive, this would be the greatest assassination stunt in history. Just as I thought he could make the jump, the Duskmen's bullets shredded through his right calf. Fitz reached for the copter as he stumbled. Wood splintered off the gunwale. With the last of his strength, he sprung over the ship's edge and took a leap of faith into the dust.

24

THE CRESCENDO

Fitz nearly met his end with a long and harrowing descent, but as the dust cleared, I could see Baker leaning out of the copter, clasping the imposter bride by his forearm. He yanked him up and slung him into the vessel. This was the moment we'd planned.

I needed to join them, but the Duskmen were laying down too much heavy fire. Baker and Fitz had no choice but to flee. The doors closed, deflecting bullets off their coppery armor. As my compatriots flew away, I caught a glimpse of Molly through the side window. She had been saved.

It did not matter if I lived or died.

Reinforcements came up from below. Two of the Duskmen had captured Dirk, and they held him with his arms twisted behind his back. They shoved him to his knees, and one of them gripped the top of his head. Blood streaked the side of his face, running down from his eyebrow. My ability to go unnoticed as a guest gave me an advantage. I blended with the other nobles, watching from the outskirts of the crowd and maneuvering my way closer to him.

Maive knelt beside the emperor, running her hands over his wounded arm and whispering strange words. His blood got thick like honey, and while his sleeve remained torn, his arm materialized as unscathed flesh. Perceval stood as if nothing had happened, but upon seeing his only heir in a pool of blood and brains, was too much in shock to speak.

"Your Grace," said a Duskman, holding my captain. "The pirate captain escaped and killed three of our own before we could apprehend him."

Emperor Perceval glared down at Dirk with a hatred I knew all too well. Everything that had happened, the loss of the princess, the massacre of his friends, and the death of his son, would be blamed on the pirate captain. "Shoot his ship out of the sky."

"No!" cried Dirk.

The men lifted a tarp and rolled a ballista toward the bulwarks, aiming its spear down at the Wastrel's gasbags. They cranked a lever that pulled back on the slack. I shut my eyes, unable to watch. My brothers.

"Stop this at once!" Dirk yelled in a most imperious voice. "I'll give you the prince! For the true prince of Elsace is still alive! In exchange for my men, he's yours."

"You're lying," said Perceval.

"I'm not! I swear it! Act now, sir, or the true prince of Elsace will take back what you stole!" Dirk shouted. Sweat poured down his neck and his eyes showed the fear captains hide at all costs. A hush fell. Even Maive's shell of smug composure was cracking. She almost looked sorry for him.

The emperor shook his head. "Lies of a desperate man."

Dirk lifted his chin high. "Do you not see the truth in my face? Why don't you look at me again?"

The emperor gazed upon my captain's face, crinkling his eyes. The crimson of his cheek turned white as a sheet.

"My father," said Dirk, "was Lucius von Luftburg. I am the true heir to the Elsatian throne, Prince Derek Alexander Xavier, the last son of the Luftburg dynasty!"

"I saw your head come off your shoulders. The princess was never found, but the prince we executed." The emperor's face colored.

"Yet here I stand, usurper," said Dirk calmly. All were in awe of him, clinging to his every word. "I was a young man when you took Locwyn palace. I was not ready to oppose you. I admit I was afraid. But you have held our nation captive, and I shall no longer allow you to brutalize and starve my people. I denounce you as sovereign! I declare war on your regime!"

Perceval waved his hand dismissively. "Fire the ballista."

"If you fire, it is treason against your true king!" Dirk roared.

The Duskmen were bringing down the hammer on the ballista's release, when suddenly the entire mechanism went rolling backwards. They jumped out of the way as the ship tilted and sent the contraption flying, breaking the railing right off its pegs. The witch Maive held her arm outstretched, all five fingers spiked like a cactus flower.

"Maive," said Dirk, grinning with as much joy as a bloodied, beaten man could muster.

"What are you doing?" demanded Perceval.

Maive did not answer the usurper but addressed Dirk instead. "I would have never let them kill you, you know."

"I did not know," said Dirk, being as much shocked as the rest of us by the witch's actions.

"I hoped you would withdraw from this foolish exchange."

"You underestimate my foolishness."

"Never."

Perceval's eyes channeled all the rage of an inferno. "Traitorous witch," he growled. "Have you aided him with some enchantment to make him and that girl look like the dead Luftburg heirs?"

Maive raised her eyebrows and blinked. "I don't even know a spell like that."

"Maive," Dirk said urgently. "I beg you. You must lift Molly's curse. She has nothing to do with our quarrel."

"Throw her to the clouds!" commanded Perceval. Two Dusk-men grabbed Maive from behind. She shrieked and writhed, kick-ing her legs as they dragged her and held her over the railing. They gripped her hands tightly so she couldn't cast. The wind whipped her black hair in front of her face.

Dirk struggled against his captors. "No!"

Maive called out to Dirk, "You are the only one who can break the child's curse!"

"What?" cried Dirk. "How?"

"Who is this man to you?" demanded Perceval.

"He is my king!" cried Maive. The Duskmen thrust her from the ship.

"Maive!" shrieked Dirk, twisting and fighting to get away. "You will die this very day, Perceval! I swear it! The Wastrel won't go down without a fight! We will take your Crescendo with us!"

Like a mountain rising from the earth through a sea of mist, the Wastrel became level with the Crescendo. Our men lined the flanks, beating the rail with their grappling hooks and shrieking like animals. Their display of terror was followed by the purr of a stealthy aircraft.

The globe copter rose with Maive clinging to a red fin, one hand signing over her head. She moved with lightning speed as she leapt on board and tackled Dirk away from his captors. A field of energy knocked the Duskmen back and formed a shimmering dome around the lovers.

Through the globe copter's side door, I saw Fitz revving a sta-tionary minigun covered in pressure gauges. He had a wild look about him. I dived behind a bench, covering my head with my arms. The chamber whirred as it gained rotating speed, and then it dealt death across the deck. My ears ached and hummed. I screamed noiselessly against the roar of artillery.

When the minigun finally ceased, zip lines planted into the Crescendo and mobs of pirates rode in, parachute packs already prepped on their backs. They discharged pistol after pistol from holsters running across their chests. The Wastrel's cannons unleashed a full assault on the Crescendo's hull. Through the swells of gunfire, I saw the emperor ripped apart by bullets. My barricade burst into splinters, and I sank deeper into a prone position. The pattering of gun panels flipping open sounded along the side of the Crescendo.

By the end of this battle, both great ships would surely be irrevocably destroyed, which meant there was no way out but down.

25

ABANDON SHIP

In the chaos of battle, the globe copter was able to set down on the central deck of the Crescendo. Baker jumped out, beckoning for Dirk and Maive to board the vessel. He stormed across the bridge, shouting my name over the whir of the copter blade and the noise of firearms discharging.

I ran toward Baker, waving my arms to alert him to my position. He looked at my clothes and then at my face and then down at my clothes again. I blenched to see the change in his eyes. For the first time, he saw Mona.

"Clikk?" he mouthed. He averted his gaze as I got closer, for he could see it plain as day that, unlike Fitz in his bridal attire, I looked far too convincing as a girl to be anything else. "Earth and sky," he said. The Crescendo quaked as the cannons blew, jarring Baker from his stupor. He grasped my arm and flung me into the back of the copter, squeezing in behind me.

Crammed between Baker and Fitz, my hoops bridged up and covered our laps. Fitz had torn the skirt of his bridal gown and was wrapping his leg.

"Hold fast," Maive told him, reaching back from her place in the pilot's seat. She ran her hand over his calf. The bullets dropped out of his flesh, clinking against the copperplate floor. Fitz sighed in relief, but his calm was short-lived, for as he recognized me, his jaw fell open.

"Ithicus' grace, I don't believe it!" he shouted. "Is that you, Clikk?"

"Where's Molly?" asked Dirk.

It was Baker who answered him. "She's on the Wastrel."

"What!"

"We heard they was going to kill you, Captain. We had to come back for you. We had to come back for Clikk. We told the men on the Wastrel to flee with the girl, but they saw fit to attack."

With the doors still open, we heaved upwards and down in a perfect arc toward our beloved Wastrel. The men were abandoning her, strapping on parachutes and diving into the clouds. Cannonballs shredded the gondola, splintering wood and snapping cables. I clenched my whole body, dreading that those iron hulks might stave our tiny vessel.

Dirk took Maive's hand in a firm hold. "We are south of Nelise. Go there and find Dorian Belle. He is the man who helped us escape our executions."

"You're not coming with me?" she asked.

"I have to save Molly."

"You haven't a parachute, and you likely won't find one on a sinking ship."

"I'll find one. I made a promise to protect her and I intend to keep it."

"Very well," she said, staring through him and nearly smiling. "Be careful, Lexi."

"You can't!" I shouted, reaching for Dirk as he leaned out the side of the globe copter. "Without you, we have no claim to power!"

Wind ruffled his hair and his clothes. He said, "You're not the only one mad enough to jump into the sky for someone. Until we meet again, Falcon." With those words, he leapt down to the crumbling deck. As he fell, an explosion of dust obscured him and rattled the copter.

"We can't stay," said Maive, sealing the copter airtight. The ship did a backward roll as we took to the wind. She swept around the side of the Crescendo and fired a rocket at one of its golden orbs. A cluster of them exploded, and the ship leaned. My stomach flipped, and I looked at Baker, terrified because I couldn't read him.

"Are you pissed?" I asked.

"It's odd is all," he said. Fitz chuckled, but something about Baker's tone suggested he had not meant to poke fun or belittle me.

"I understand now why you two got so close," said Fitz. "You knew, didn't you, Bakes?"

"Don't be daft!" I smacked the back of Fitz's head.

"Enough!" Maive reproached. "Fighting amongst yourselves is the last thing we need."

Baker didn't intervene. He just shook his head. "I must be a blinking imbecile," he said.

My eyes stung. I'd never in all our time together seen him so flummoxed.

A fire erupted in the Wastrel's balloon, eating its way across the envelope and exposing the coppery skeleton beneath. The ship spewed a tail of black smoke as it circled the Crescendo. It continued to return fire even as it began its inevitable descent.

"May your greatest prize be as worthless as your promises. May your ship fall to the earth in a rain of fire and ash," Baker murmured the words in a tone of resentment. He leaned to whisper to Fitz, "All of this is the witch's fault. Why does she help us now?"

"I can hear you, pirate," said Maive.

"Then explain yourself, witch."

"I cursed the girl for her own protection, as well as that of your captain."

"That's not the entire story," I said. "The witch was the captain's lover. She caught him being unfaithful—in a sense—and set the curse as revenge."

"Is that what he told you?" Maive shook her head. As though to unleash her vexation with Dirk, she opened fire on the Crescendo, taking out a row of mounted machine guns poking through the hull. The globe copter's blades hummed as we accelerated. We soared away from the Crescendo before they could return fire. "Granted, I was peeved at him over that affair, but our quarrel had everything to do with his plans for his sister."

"So you knew he was the lost prince?"

Baker and Fitz both looked at me suddenly. I forgot I had not mentioned that little detail when I enlisted their help.

"Of course I knew," she said with a huff, steering the copter into the safe haven of a cloud. We hovered there. "I have been your captain's lover since he first went into exile. I remember when he first sent the princess away, claiming it was because of a promise he made his mother. The girl must be protected from the Blue Dusk at any cost. Any cost. Which is why it enraged me when he told me that he planned to give her in marriage to Prince Torrent. I cursed him, thinking he would have the sense to withdraw from the agreement."

We descended from the cloud, and as the skies became clearer, we saw we loomed over the floating wreckage of the Wastrel. Our glorious ship broke apart in the sky. This refuge for aimless wanderers had been my home for almost a year. Throngs of men leapt off, opening their parachutes. They were well trained, and I took solace knowing many of them would survive.

"She's gone," Baker said, placing his hand against the glass door. I did not know what to say to comfort him. I did not feel like his friend anymore, but more like a woman he had just met. Even if he wasn't angry now, I knew once the shock wore off, he would be.

Maive swore under her breath. "Will you look at that." My heart raced as a million terrible thoughts polluted my head.

Then I saw what she saw: a man and a little girl falling out of the sky. Dirk clutched Molly to his chest. The child's hair shot up like a pillar of fire. We circled their descent from afar, holding our breaths right up to the moment their parachute sprang upwards and inflated.

"This shall have done it," said Maive. "He has broken the curse. He has kept his promise and made his own redemption."

I felt something odd stirring in my breast, a vague little flutter of a feeling I had not felt in many years. Was it hope? Did Elsace have a future worth fighting for? To trounce the Blue Dusk whose military had radically superior technology, we needed to best them in numbers. We needed the people. And the only way to rally that kind of force was to restore the people's faith.

Seeing Dirk and little Molly united, I realized he was the beacon of hope I had been searching for, the very spearhead that would usher in an age of peace.

26

The Forest

Maive steered her ship toward the thicket of trees where Dirk and Molly had fallen. She flew with daring audacity, plummeting suddenly, swooping around and skimming over the treetops. A flock of blackbirds exploded from the canopy as our vessel's winds rustled the dark leaves. This vast and impenetrable forest stretched as far as the eye could see.

We had abandoned ship in the Valley of Shale, land of lavender and wine. I knew this woodland from my father's stories. It was the origin of several prominent Shalean fairy tales, a sprawling forest of pine, yew, and juniper. Once upon a time, a witch lived there and lured children to her home full of wind-up toys, and every child who went inside became one hence. I always liked that story. The witch turned a little boy into a monkey that slammed a pair of cymbals together. She turned his sister into a mouse that wheeled in circles across the floor. The two siblings worked together, the sister moving the brother into a hidden place behind the wall, where he rang his cymbals night and day. The witch could not find him, and as time wore on, the chiming of his cymbals began to drive her mad. Finally, she became so irritated by the noise, she took an axe and chopped through the wall.

Unfortunately for her, by the time she made a hole, the sister had moved her brother to a new hidden place. Again, the witch hacked away at the wall. And again, the sister moved her brother. She kept moving him until the witch destroyed enough of her house that it toppled and crushed her. All the wind-up prisoners escaped, and once they found their way out of the rubble, they returned to their human forms.

Father also said wolves inhabited these woods. They wove between the trees at night. I must never go into the forest, he told me. It was a place for madmen, criminals, witches, and other such malevolent characters. But Father had not been there to protect me from the world's evils, and now I was a criminal living amongst other criminals, and we had enlisted the aid of a witch. I belonged in the forest more than ever.

We hovered and discussed our course of action. With no place to land, Maive suggested one of us take a flare gun, climb down by ladder, and gather as many survivors as possible until rescue arrived. Baker volunteered.

"I'll go with him," I said.

"Absolutely not," said Baker.

"Why not?"

"Your dress alone will slow us down."

"Not as much as your shoddy sense of direction!"

"Both of you, get out," said Maive.

I stuck out my tongue and made a nasty pig face. What would have normally made Baker laugh and punch me in the shoulder only made him roll his eyes.

"If you wish to climb out of a copter in a ball gown, go right ahead," he said.

Fitz cleared his throat. "I should accompany Maive in her search for this Belle fellow. Women should never travel alone," he said. "I wish you luck, brothers." He blinked and looked me over, but didn't bother correcting himself.

A vaulted trapdoor lay at our feet. Baker twisted the release and swung it open. "Ladies first," he said, kicking out the rope ladder.

Descending a ladder in a ball gown was more difficult than I expected, and I had expected it to be difficult. The wind blew my skirt about like a bell, and the weight of it threatened to fling me into the sky. I compressed the hoop structure and pinned it to my abdomen, but as I lowered from the aircraft, it fell and tripped me. I grasped the rungs and calmed my body, regaining good form. At the bottom I dropped onto a twisted branch and traversed a twiggy maze of tree limbs and leaves, my dress catching on every little snare.

Baker waited behind me and said nothing as we climbed down, even when I stopped to rip my hem free. Coming out of the leafy canopy, I saw Dirk and Molly hanging from a tree, harnessed together with layers of leather belts. Their parachute was tangled in the branches above; they were too high up to cut the lines, and too precariously situated to swing from side to side.

"Captain!" I called out. Dirk searched the ground below, but he couldn't see me.

"Clikk? Is that you?" he called back.

"We're coming to help you. Don't move!"

"Someone there?" One of the men moved between the trees below us. It was our cook, Jasper. He dragged his deployed parachute behind him. Baker and I dropped from the tree and landed nearby.

"Left my dagger on the Wastrel," Jasper said. "Buckles jammed."

"I'll cut you loose." Baker used the dagger from his boot. "Bring your canvas with you. We'll need it to get the captain down."

"Who's yer friend, Baker?" asked Jasper, licking his teeth as he undressed me with his eyes.

"Don't ask," said Baker. "It's Clikk. He's a…"

Jasper frowned. "Falcon's a girl? Camilla's tail. I'll be damned." We left it at that and pushed on. The cook gathered his knotted parachute into a ball and carried it over his shoulder.

At the small clearing beneath Dirk and Molly, Baker took on the role of delegation. "Tie the strings to the stronger branches, and we'll move around to make a sort of trampoline." We started at three different points and moved clockwise, attaching the cords to various trees.

We had to keep the bottom of the tarp high enough off the ground so when Dirk and Molly came bounding down, they wouldn't smash into the earth. Baker and Jasper were able to shimmy up the trees to tie their knots, but I was stuck on the ground in my ludicrous dress.

It was difficult work. Though we had shade enough, the breeze hardly made its way down through the trees. The air was thick with moisture, and I could feel the earth's heat radiating from the soil.

"Baker, lend me your dagger," I called, wiping my brow with the back of my silk sleeve.

He was three meters over my head, but he dropped down, and handed it to me by the hilt. "Be quick about it."

"This will only take a moment." I slashed out the elbows in my sleeves and cut my dress a few inches below the waist, detaching skirt, hoopskirt and petticoat in one rigorous go of sawing and stabbing.

"Careful, turtledove," Baker said. "You'll clip a wing."

"Don't be a cad." In my bloomers, I would actually be able to move about and climb. Once I had a moment to myself, I could remove the corset for even more range of motion.

Baker retrieved his dagger but was too distracted to sheath it. He raised his eyebrows as he observed me.

"What?" I said. "Now I won't slow you down."

"No, popsy, but now Jaz will try and have a peek at your money."

I grabbed him by his collar and pulled him in as I whispered, "Call me popsy, or turtledove, or any other name that ain't my own, and I will cut out that rude tongue of yours."

Baker didn't back off but instead tapped my chin with the hilt of his dagger. "With what now… sweetheart?" He winked at me.

I nodded and feigned a little laugh. Then I sucker punched him in the gut. Baker pushed me and staggered back.

"Knock it off!" ordered Captain Dirk. "Get us down from here!"

Baker spit in the dirt like the hit was nothing and went back to climbing trees. I was able to knot my parachute cords as high as the rest of them, and we soon had a stable trampoline.

Dirk helped Molly slip the belts. She screamed as she fell and bounced on the tarp below, layers of pink satin fluttering. I helped her down.

"Oh, Clikk, thank the stars!" she exclaimed, leaping into my arms. "The pirate man said to trust him, and so I gave him my dress and went with the other pirate in his ship!"

"Oh, good," I said. "But next time a pirate tells you to trust him, you mustn't. Understand?"

Molly frowned and nodded.

"Good girl. Help is on the way."

Next came Dirk. He cut himself free and came down thrashing his legs. The parachute canvas broke his fall, and we helped him to his feet as well.

"Good work, boys," he said. "Where is Maive?"

"Off to find your contact," answered Baker. "Gave us this flare and told us to gather survivors."

"Right. Let's find the rest. We'll need everyone we can get. We just murdered a bloody emperor."

"Captain," said Baker, motioning toward me all of a sudden. "Clikk… um…"

Dirk nodded. "Yes, I know."

Baker folded his arms and scowled. "How long have you known?"

"Pretty much from the day she asked to join our crew," said Dirk.

"You told us it was bad luck having a woman on the ship."

"I also told you your cock would fall off if you pissed over the rail."

Molly spewed giggles.

Dirk grinned and said, "Superstitions are made up with practical reasons behind them, brother. A woman on a ship is only bad luck if the men know she's there, for it is the men who are the unlucky bit of the equation. I can explain it all—"

Something scurried through the brush. Innate panic paralyzed me where I stood. I watched the shrubs that pulsed in the creature's wake.

"What was that?" Jasper whispered.

Dirk shushed him as a low growl rumbled beyond the leaves. "Let's not tarry here any longer."

27

THE APPLE TREE

We began our forest hike as we searched for more of our brothers. The thick brush took a toll on our clothes and bodies, decorating us with twigs and scratches. Molly's pink satin shoes became shredded along the soles. I was more grateful than ever for my boots, but I could not idle while the girl got herself all torn up. I took her aside and used some vines to reinforce her shoes' structure.

As we walked, Captain Dirk fed Baker some morality tale about two neighbors who quarreled over a tree planted on the border of both their lands. When the tree yielded naught but shade, the men became friends and would go there to rest and dialogue together.

But one day, while climbing, one of these men—he was called Jon—discovered the tree grew an occasional apple. His neighbor, Adam, saw him eating it and asked where he had got it. Jon told him about the tree between their lands. They decided it would only be fair to divvy up the apples. But the next month there was an uneven yield, and sometimes they would argue over which of the apples were bigger or brighter than others.

At this point in the story, we had discovered four more survivors, including the mandolin player William and good old No-Nose Ned. He'd lost the tin patch that covered his missing nose, forcing us to witness the unsightly effects of syphilis.

Each time we found some more of our men, they asked who I was, went through the same amazement as everyone else, and then asked Dirk how he could allow such a thing. Dirk would summarize the beginning of his bizarre parable and continue in his explanation.

He went on to say the two neighbors decided they should divide the months. Jon would take fruit one month, and Adam would be able to harvest the next. This worked well until the season for apples ended, and Adam had to go longer without them than Jon. When the apple season returned, it was yet again Jon's turn to harvest. So the unlucky Adam was angry and consumed with hate for his neighbor. One day, he waited beneath the tree with a knife in his hand. When Jon arrived to take his first harvest of the season, Adam stabbed him in the throat, killing him forever.

"As opposed to killing him temporarily," giggled Molly.

"What is the point of this story?" asked the twentieth crewman we had found.

"Well," said Dirk, cutting down a spider web, "I don't remember the ending exactly, but this is why men have Adam's apples."

"You messed it up from the start," Molly said. "The tree is a woman, and she gives her fruit to the men because women are nurturers by our very nature, and she wants them to be happy. So when Adam kills his friend, the tree is unimpressed with mankind. She puts the core into the apple as punishment, because women can be vengeful too. The next time Adam goes to eat one, he chokes. And men have had Adam's apples ever since so that women will remember they are greedy and should not be trusted."

"What does that have to do with bad luck on an airship?" asked Baker.

Dirk stared blankly.

I groaned in frustration and raised my voice to a shout, "If the two neighbors had never known the tree had apples, they would have remained friends! Just as if there is a woman on the ship, and nobody knows, her being there won't cause any fights or fires!"

"Perhaps not fights, but what about the fires?" asked Jasper.

"We have only another hour of light," interrupted Dirk. "We should make camp."

He was right. Already the sky was changing to a dull shade of orange. We needed a fire to keep predators away, and we had to get off the ground if we didn't want to be eaten alive by insects. We used the canvas from the parachutes to sling hammocks. I chose branches high up and situated amongst smaller branches that would make noise if anyone tried to climb my way.

Suspended above prying eyes, I adjusted my clothing. The bodice was too tight for me to loosen the corset underneath, and I had reached my breaking point. I ripped it down the middle and pulled at the laces of the infernal undergarment. When it came loose by several inches, I reclined in the hammock and caught my breath. The ability to draw long, deep breaths was a liberty I had taken for granted. Even though they ached against my sore ribs, I savored the relief.

"Nobody is to bother Clikk or Molly tonight!" ordered Dirk. "Save it for the brothels in Nelise."

His warning didn't make me feel any safer, but as I settled into my hammock that night, I no longer cared what happened to me. I swayed in the strong arms of an ancient oak tree, watching the leaves caress the star-ridden sky overhead. The prince and princess were alive, and their cause gained strength with every brother we found.

The sounds of the forest after dark were louder than I expected. At times, the crickets' volume swelled to such a height I could barely hear my own thoughts, and in the distance, a pack of wolves was howling at the moon. An occasional laugh shared amongst the men below stirred me out of my sleep state. I rolled onto my side and peered down at them.

Baker was still up, regaling a few sleepless mates with the story of how he and Fitz stole the witch's globe copter. I couldn't help but listen. In fact, I longed to join them, longed to tell Baker that I had seen the sword that killed my parents. I had found the Cerulean Knight. A dark thought pulled at my heart. Would he even care anymore?

I no longer belonged sitting at a campfire with their lot. They would only laugh at how funny it was to finally know why Clikk was such a loner, never pissed in front of others, or took his shirt off to sunbathe at dawn. Maybe I could sleep instead. Something about the crackling of the fire and their soft voices put my nerves at ease. Even if I were no longer their brother, I still had their protection.

As Baker told his story, I listened in, eager to hear his version of events.

28

FIRE STORIES

The flames danced across their faces. I leaned out of my hammock to secretly drink in Baker's storytelling, which I had enjoyed ever since those first nights he stayed up with me on the Wastrel. Of course, this tale would not involve Mathilde. But I had to hear him finish so I could know what kind of role I played in it.

"So to board her," I heard Baker say, "Fitz and I climb down the hull of the Wastrel and grapple onto that of the Crescendo. The ship starts rising right as we're reeling in our lines. Not a pleasant feeling. Fitz almost loses his breakfast. I'm telling him to pretend he's taking a lift in Aixenport but that ain't helping him. We reach the ship's underbelly, stuck on like a pair of cockroaches, and—poor Fitz—he's turning green. I say, 'Think about placing your bare feet on the earth! Think about rich, dark soil!' It's no use. He scarfs up big gobs of the blood pudding we had for breakfast, which nearly makes me ill for watching him. The ship, thank the gods, stabilizes. So we move on, climbing up the gondola's side with our hooks and our ropes. Like a couple of deviants, we go peeking into windows. Accidentally saw a room full of servants bathing. I wish I could say they was attractive. I won't go into details here. We find a room with only a single guard posted. I pry the window with my dagger, Fitz leaps through, and he chokes the Duskie out from behind, drops him like nothing. But as soon as I hop in, another Duskie shows up. He sees his friend, looks at me, screams, and charges me like a wild animal. Bloody oaf lands himself right on my dagger!"

The men laughed and Baker shushed them down to a chuckle.

"I never thought that could actually happen! Anyway, so much for Stanton and Pratt. These were the names on their badges. We toss the pair of them out the window, but not before taking their uniforms and guns. In our new disguises, Fitz and I move about the ship, learning the map. An officer approaches us and tells us there's an assembly in the mess hall. Once we attend that, we're in. Nobody seems to miss old Stanton and Pratt. My guess is they were part of a battalion that flew in for the wedding. Some officer writes me up for my dreadlocks. I got off with a warning 'cause I tell him I'm new."

"It's true though, ain't it?" said a gunner.

"Aye, it is. So in the assembly, they explain to us the situation with the pirates. Very grim, mind you. We are to be on high alert and to guard every orifice of the ship."

A few of the men began to chuckle.

"I know, I know. It was so hard not to laugh. And his exact words were, 'We need to protect her every orifice.'"

As they chuckled harder, Baker raised his voice. "Well, once we're told to turn in for the night, Fitz and I creep off on our own and start disabling alarms. We locate the globe copter, watch the officers posted to guard the vessel, and wait for them to take a break or shift out. We wait the whole bleedin' night and then an officer approaches us and asks what we're doing, reprimands us for being lazy sods, and tells us to investigate some noise heard by one of the maids. So's we head into this room with a red door, and inside is three women all tied up and gagged, one of whom has had all of her hairpins pilfered. We can guess this is Clikk's handiwork.

"We return to our superior officer, and Fitz contrives some story about the bride having wedding jitters. The officer informs us that the bride is supposed to be in the blue room and that we must escort her from the red room at once. So off to the blue room we go. There, waiting patiently is the little princess in her wedding gown. That's when Fitz gets his great idea. He actually fits into the dress."

The men burst into laughter and then quieted themselves as some of the restless sleepers cursed down at them. "Shut up, you wankers! Go to bed!"

"Is Fitz a woman too?" whispered Jasper.

"No," laughed Baker. "At least I don't think he is. Anyway, while Fitz and Molly change their clothing, I go to where the witch's ship is being held. I rewire it and fly it around to the window of the blue room. The princess hops in while Fitz goes up to get married. Then greets his blushing groom with a pair of pocket automatics."

"Had you alerted the guards at this point?" asked one of the listeners.

"Yeah, and they went running up on deck to warn everyone, but it was too late."

Baker lowered his voice for what he said next, but I could still hear him. "Now, Fitz and I had lost track of Clikk. See, Fitz couldn't find the kid anywhere, but it's because he was looking for our little street urchin, not some popsy in a silk dress."

My body was exhausted and hungry for sleep, but now Baker had reached the part of the story about me. I had to listen in case he told lies about us for the sake of bragging.

"I think we passed her in the hall and did not recognize her," he said. "I remember seeing a pretty girl and thinking to myself, who is *that*? And what is she doing out here in her shift? Forgive me, gentlemen, but I was so preoccupied with her gauzy dress, I barely took in her face at all."

"You saw her naked?" It was only a whisper from one of them, but I heard it pierce the air like a javelin.

"No, no," he said.

Tread carefully, Baker, I thought to myself, *lest this fantasy take on a life of its own.* I took a deep breath to calm my nerves.

"I mean, sort of."

Bastard needed to shut it. The whispers bubbled up as all of them began speaking at once.

"But who's to say it was really her? Might have been someone's mistress stepping out to use the privy."

"Wait now, Baker. I don't believe for a second you weren't shagging your Fledgling," said a gunner who had just made my hit list.

"Yeah," said another. "You knew, didn't you? Like the captain."

"Now that's a secret worth protecting," said another.

"No," said Baker. "It was never like that."

"You think she was shagging the captain?"

"No."

"Oh, come on," insisted that same churlish gunner. "You must have been shagging. You knew her better than anyone."

"It was never like that," Baker repeated firmly. "Clikk was my friend, yes… slept above me for almost a year. I never suspected. We drank Skye, wrote dirty limericks, talked about wenches. Yesterday, I thought I knew everything about the urchin… when really I didn't know the first thing about her." Baker went quiet, and so did the men.

"So what happened next?" asked the gunner. "You got the princess. She traded places with Fitz. What happened after that?"

"The rest you know from when we returned to the Wastrel."

"Aw," whined the gunner. "You skipped over all the best parts."

"It's late."

The blunt finale to his rollicking tale inspired a long stretch of silence. Finally, one of the engineers spoke. "We'd best get some sleep if we're to survive the morrow." With that, the night owls dispersed and climbed into their hammocks.

The music of crickets and cicadas droned on in a hypnotic rhythm, punctuated by the occasional croon of the nightingale. I thought of lullabies and how as a child they would placate my disappointment that another day had ended. I was used to sleeping in strange places and would always focus on sound to relax.

In the pawnbrokers' shop, it was the ticking of grandfather clocks or the tuning of antique instruments. In the Thieves' Den, it was the striking of a match, the bubbling of a water pipe, and the gentle murmur floating in off the streets. On the Wastrel, it was the wind or the creaking wood. It was important to me to find lullabies where I could. If death came with a lullaby, perhaps fewer men would fear it.

There came a low rumble in the distance, something like motors. The noise swelled and jostled the leaves as an aircraft flew over. I recognized Maive's globe copter. The men fell out of their hammocks and fumbled for the flare gun. Someone discharged it, and it soared overhead and burst above the tree cover. The wind channels coming off the sky vessel rocked the branches upon its return.

A wooden box floated down by parachute and landed on the forest floor. One of our gunners pried it open with his short sword. Inside were provisions of water, bread, and preserves. There was an attached note that told us to head north at sunrise to a rendezvous point on the edge of the forest.

29

OUR HOSTS

I awoke to the agonized murmur of men suffering from the thirst. Cylinders of bright sun slid between the leaves overhead and my torn, sweat-drenched garments clung to my skin. I despised the heat of late summer. I peered over the edge of my hammock and saw our company below. They had wrapped their shirts around their heads like turbans and were taking rations from the supply crate.

"Ahhh!" Dirk sighed after his first sip. "It's better than Skye, my brothers!"

The men reveled in the simple joy of hydration. Water couldn't possibly ease their withdrawal, but they all played along with the idea that it did. Molly's complaints of still being thirsty after finishing her water ration went unnoticed or, at least, unheeded. Being this hot was never a problem a thousand meters from earth. I knotted my damp hair into a bun. The extensions fell out in wisps as some of the braids came loose. I wanted to rip them all out, but they were sewn in tight, and some of the wax had melted against my scalp.

I joined the men for breakfast. We ate half a roll each with a spoonful of jam. The meal was enough to ease the churning pain in my gut, but my hunger remained bottomless. We headed north. I found a sturdy walking stick nestled in the brush and used it to keep myself going at an even pace. I needed to stay near the front of our party with people I trusted.

We wound through the forest, climbing over felled trees, and cutting away plant debris. The heat rose to abominable temperatures. Even beneath the tree cover, our faces dripped with sweat. I noticed Molly stumble against a tree.

"I can't see," she cried, gasping.

"She's fainting!" I yelled, running toward her as her legs gave out. I caught her before she collapsed. Dirk came dashing over and lifted Molly onto his back. She mumbled an apology, which her brother hushed.

"Thank you, Clikk," he said.

The remainder of our slog through the woods took several hours, but eventually we reached a meadow, vast and radiant with tall, yellow-tipped grass. Molly slid off Dirk's back and went running to greet our rescuers.

Maive stood in front of a large hay wagon pulled by two white horses. The cart had ample space, but not enough for all in our company. A pair of well-to-do country folk accompanied her, a rotund old man and a young blue-eyed woman. Both wore gray linen clothing; the structured silhouettes of their tailored garbs gave them away as being upper class. While the wealthy wore the fashions that emphasized the male and female silhouettes, the lower class still wore styles of an earlier century design, simple ensembles such as tunic and skirt or trousers tied together with a bodice or vest.

Dirk went running. "Dorian!"

"Derek, my boy!" The rotund aristocrat waved. Dirk opened his arms and gathered Dorian Belle into an embrace. The affection made the man blush, but he took it with a smile, patted Dirk on the shoulder, and slipped something into his hand, whispering, "I held onto it for you. Just in case this day ever came."

I could not see what he had placed in his hand, but whatever it was, it made my captain's eyes lose their sharp edge. He slumped his shoulders and hugged the man once more, this time holding him for much longer. Molly and the young noblewoman bobbed politely to each other, displaying more conventional social graces.

"Who is this angel?" Dirk asked.

Dorian moved apart from Dirk so he could introduce the lady. "My daughter Lily. You remember her, don't you?"

"Lily! You were just a child the last time I saw you. How are you, my dear?" Dirk kissed her hand.

"Better now that you're back. We've missed you, Derek."

After the pleasantries, Dorian and his daughter Lily proceeded to load a little less than half of our party into their wagon and took their seats at the front. We would lodge at the nobleman's estate as we regrouped and recovered from the crash. Dirk kissed Maive farewell and remained with the men who would be traveling on foot.

"Yah!" cried Dorian, cracking the reins. The horses began a brisk trot and we bounced along the uneven ground. The daughter glanced back at us and seemed to marvel at our appearances, especially mine. When she saw me take notice of her staring, she quickly turned her head to face forward.

I rode next to Molly and Maive. While taking in the vista of lavender country, we shared some conversation along the way.

"Beautiful," sighed Maive, tilting her head and inhaling the perfume on the breeze. "Absolutely breathtaking crop fields."

"Beautiful, yes. And inedible," I said. "I remember walking through such fields, surrounded by so many pretty flowers, and starving."

"How awful," said Maive. "Queen Anna von Luftburg washed only with lavender soap and kept fresh bundles in all her garment chests. Ladies of refinement followed her example, and Shale has been lavender country ever since." She touched my shoulder and I jumped a little. "So tell me, how is it a peasant girl from Shale knew the only song that could muddle my curse?"

"My mother used to sing it, is all," I confessed.

"Was your mother a witch?" She tucked my hair behind my ear so she could see my face.

I shrugged off a shiver as the woman's nails ran against my scalp. "She and my father were farmers."

"That song is ancient. Legend says it was stolen from the sirens, and only a very special kind of witch can wield its power."

"Are you saying I'm part witch?" I asked.

"There's no such thing as being part witch," Maive said. "You either have the gift or you don't." She leaned in like she was telling me a secret. "You have it."

"What does that mean then? Do I start dressing like a black-bird and setting hexes on little girls?"

Maive rolled her eyes. "By the letter of the law, it means you must present yourself at the Moonstone Library in Leridia to begin your training. Until you are deemed to be in control of your powers and in a stable state of mind, you are not permitted to leave the society of your peers."

"Is that right?" I asked. "How did you get out then?"

"You would make a fine witch, Clikk. You should go to Leridia. When this is all over, I would offer you my services in honing your craft."

"I've been a lot of things in my life. Not sure I want to be a witch."

"Hold still." Maive dabbed my cheek with her fingertip and showed me one of my eyelashes that had fallen off.

I smirked. "Should I make a wish?"

"Actually, I was hoping I might keep it."

"Um... go ahead." Molly's eyes and mine met briefly as we both stifled a chuckle.

Maive tucked my eyelash into a velvet pouch. She had an odd social character that might have been considered inept in most settings. Perhaps that was how witches conducted themselves. Having so much power, they had no reason to accord with ordinary folk.

"How did you come to be Dirk's lover?" I asked.

Molly perked up at this, watching Maive from the corner of her eye as she pretended to stare out over the lavender fields. A fond smile worked its way across Maive's lips, but only briefly before she cloaked it with indifference. "I was the court-appointed witch to King Lucius, Dirk's father. Dirk requested that I tell his fortune one night. There was an immediate kindling between our spirits that ignited and flared. We've been lovers ever since, convening in secret off and on for the past decade."

"Why in secret?"

"Because of who he is. That, and our temperaments are too caustic for anything else. We must walk different paths and keep our distance until the longing returns and draws us back into love. It is our way. Like majestic oaks, we need room to thrive."

Their way sounded strange to me, but it was moving how two independent people with fiery passions found something functional.

My own parents had cherished a much simpler existence. Mother and I cared for the house and the animals, while Father worked the fields. At day's end, Mother would sing me to sleep and Father would stand in the threshold. I still remembered his outline as he leaned there, arms folded against his chest. He and she would go into the kitchen to talk, or if the weather were fine, they would go outside. I never understood how they slept so little. They shared these moments while they had the chance, as if they could see the Blue Dusk on the horizon and understood their time was limited.

I wondered when Dirk would address the questions festering in everyone's minds. Without knowing what came next, I couldn't imagine the men remaining after a night or two recuperating in

Nelise. As conservative agricultural towns go, it somewhat lacked in entertainment.

As we rolled down a tree-lined avenue, I wondered if we could trust these aristocrats. If they still had land and money, it meant they had pledged fealty to the usurper. What would they get, I wondered, for turning our prince over to the Blue Dusk?

30

THE MANOR

Dorian Belle lived in a stately manor with his daughter and a host of servants. The home had a character both pastoral and elegant, its high-ceilinged rooms painted white with accents of gray and charcoal blue. There was no electric. The tall windows allowed natural light into every room and there were a great many candelabras and wall sconces. The Belles might have appeared modest for members of the gentry class if not for the majestic splendor of their ballroom. The grand space had a ceiling painted with clouds and cherubs, stretching up into an oval dome. Its gold-plated walls bore portraiture of old-world Elsatian aristocrats, stuffy old men in tight frilly collars and powdered wigs. Across the parquet floor, dozens of sleeping mats lay in rows for our men.

Dirk went for the phonograph on a buffet table. He looked through the wax cylinders scattered about, eventually settling on one. As a lively polka started up, he pulled Maive in by the waist and began to spin and lift her. Such girlish laughter burst forth from her; I almost forgot she was a witch. She seemed so like a child, twirling and grinning.

I was always curious about lovers. I often watched them in candlelit corners of taverns, or on benches in city parks, and wondered what miracle had brought them hence.

I never knew love like that. I made the mistake of thinking I did with Mikhail, but he was too good a liar, and in the end decided I had nothing to offer that he couldn't have with the flower girl on Bartleby row.

After everything we had been through together, I made the assumption Dirk and I were on renegotiated terms. I might have even dared to call him my friend. It only made sense I should sit in on his council, but as I tried to follow our host into the billiard room along with the boatswain and navigator, Dirk closed the door on me, whispering, "Clikk, love, I need you to look after Molly. You're the person I trust the most."

A scowl cut across my face, but I nodded and accepted my role as Molly's keeper; I had no experience to suggest I should be any good at it. If the girl needed a governess, our navigator Mr. Weston would have been the better candidate, as he knew far more about grammar and geography. My only qualification was being female.

I ticked my head to signal for the girl to follow me into the ballroom where we idled while I partly listened to the men's conversations. They were mostly complaints. As one began to whine about the thirst and his aching legs, I lost interest. I sat down on a loveseat with little Molly at my feet. She got my attention when she nudged me in the knee.

"What you want?" I said under my breath.

"Why don't pirates have any buttons on their shirts?" she asked.

"Because laces don't pop off in the wind."

The girl and her questions were a nuisance, but they did serve to distract me from the attention my corset and bloomers had enticed. I'd abandoned the handmaiden gown and chose to go about in my undergarments, which were now transformed from their pristine white state into rags the color of sand.

Our host's daughter Lily came into the ballroom, having changed her garment to one with a plunging neckline and an ornately trimmed bustle. She had a magnetic presence, though her beauty was not without flaw. Her eyes had thick lids, and her teeth came a little too far forward in her mouth. Yet these features suited her. Her full lips and demure glances redeemed her. Everything seemed pulled together by her luscious mane of raven curls, which she wore in a loose low bun. It could only be said that she was ugly in the most beautiful way.

Lily stuck her fingers in her mouth and whistled, hitting a frequency that pierced my brain like a spear. Everyone turned and then was taken aback to see the skirt.

"So, they tell me you're a bunch of fugitives!" she declared, projecting across the ballroom with that proud confidence wielded only by people of noble birth. "Every last one of you. You might have survived falling out of the sky, but you'll hang for treason if the Blue Dusk find you. Now your captain has your best interests at heart and has brought you to our doors pleading for your sorry souls. We're only helping him because he is a very old friend of ours.

"You're all welcome to stay here while your captain gets your affairs in order, but there are some house rules—" The men began to grumble over her and she had to shout to be heard. "As there were rules on your ship! No stealing or harming anyone in our company. Treat our home with respect and use the outhouse to do your business. Dirk assures me that he will still enforce the same disciplinary consequences observed on the Wastrel."

Molly had asked for my handkerchief and I now noticed she had been stitching a bouquet of pink roses on the corner of it.

"Where did you get that?" I asked.

"I found the needle on the floor, and I used some of the loose threads from my skirt for the flowers."

"How resourceful."

"Do you enjoy needlepoint?"

"No."

The fifty-some remaining men laid down on their bedrolls and organized what few things they had left to their names. They never owned much to begin with, but the loss was evident on their faces. Any small mementos like photographs, family weapons, or lucky flasks had likely gone down with the Wastrel. Even if they had not, all of us still mourned our ship's destruction.

"Do you have a beau?" Molly asked.

"No."

"Probably because you don't know needlepoint. Men like a lady to know these things if she's to manage a household."

"I never said I didn't know needlepoint. I said I didn't enjoy it."

"Oh," said Molly. "I could mend your bodice if you still have it. I could shorten the sleeves."

"There's no point. It doesn't fit unless the corset's drawn as tight as a finger trap, and I've got to breathe, haven't I?"

Molly nodded and was quiet. It was then I spotted Baker near one of the two fireplaces. He leaned against the mantle beneath three sculptures of ladies in alabaster. Beside him was Lily, speaking that alien language of femininity that made men powerless. I recognized that look of intrigue in Baker's eye.

Just then I felt a hand clap me on the shoulder. "'Ello there, Clikk," squeaked Fitz, sitting down on the armrest.

I shrugged him off. "What have I told you about touching me?"

"Yes, yes, I know, but I haven't seen you since—"

"Yesterday, Fitz. You saw me yesterday."

"And here I was worried you'd been eaten by wolves. I'm happy you made it in one piece… if only slightly disrobed."

I hardly listened to him. Baker had just leaned close to whisper in Lily's ear. The young lady held the back of her neck to suppress a shiver. She tilted her chin up to whisper something to him. A couple of men walked past and Baker's hand touched Lily's waist as he moved her gently out of the way.

"Do you think she's pretty?" I asked Molly.

Molly nodded. "She's beautiful."

"Does he think so?" My throat became suddenly so dry I found it difficult to speak.

Fitz chuckled. "You never know with him. He'll tackle anything that moves."

New emotions were swelling inside of me like dark clouds. If Baker made advances on a lady of aristocratic stock, it meant certain peril for both of them.

Molly focused on her needlework, but eventually said, "You should go over and ask him yourself."

I did not dare approach. "No, Molly. Sabotaging a man's conquest is the worst thing a friend can do to him."

Just as I was saying that, Fitz went speeding across the ballroom like a bullet. He leapt on Baker's back, screaming, "Shite! Shite! This Hawk got dynamite!" The two of them laughed, and Baker spun until Fitz tumbled down.

Lily caught me staring. I shot my gaze to the floor and tried to find something to occupy myself with, but all I had at my disposal was Molly's damned needlepoint project. Lily's shoes plunked against the waxed floors as she neared. I readied myself for what would undoubtedly be the most awkward conversation I had ever been forced to endure.

31

LADY BELLE

"Princess Molly!" called Lily as she joined us near the posh little loveseat. "Please, forgive me. I have neglected to show you to your room. Come, come. You may wash and ready for bed."

Molly bowed her head. "Thank you, Lady Belle."

"Lady Belle?" Lily laughed prettily. "You don't remember me, do you? You must call me Lily. You and your brother lived with us before you were old enough for school. You and I used to have mock tea parties in the attic."

"I'm sorry to not remember," Molly said. "Everything from that time is something of a blur."

Lily's dark blue eyes moved over me from head to toe, observing my state of dress. "Who is your... friend?"

"Oh! This is Clikk. She's a pirate."

"A pleasure to meet you, Clikk," said Lily, extending her hand. I looked at it. So soft and white, her hand must have never seen the light of day, much less a scouring pad. I took it in a firm handshake and she surprised me by matching my grip. She smiled at me in a way nobody ever had. It was a uniquely female expression, the kind of look that said, "Let's be friends." I found it immediately suspicious.

"The pleasure is mine, lady." The rasp of my voice startled her. She went as still as a doe with an arrow aimed at its heart. "I suppose you'll take the child from here then."

"What?" cried Molly. "No!"

"Yes, child. I have important work to do. Important inner circle work."

"What is it you have to do?" she whined.

"Nothing that concerns you. Go with the nice lady."

"I won't! You are my chaperone!"

"Go on, girl. I am hardly a proper chaperone. Not like this fine lady here."

Lily tittered against the back of her hand. "Looks can be deceiving, dear Clikk. Molly and I could get into all sorts of trouble together."

"Oh?" Molly's eyes lit up at that.

"Well, alas," I said, "for I must go." With an impertinent little bow, I left them, striding across the ballroom back to the hall.

I had to find a way to listen in on the meeting. Information was power, and if I knew some of what Dirk was planning, I could try and coax him into accepting my counsel. The main hall was empty. I glanced over my shoulder several times, making sure the room was clear before I went to the door of the billiard room and pressed my ear to it. I heard low murmuring, but the wood was too thick for me to make out any words.

"Is this your important work?" asked Molly.

I jumped, turning to find her and Lily standing behind me. "How did you—" I scoffed. "—Not many can sneak up on me." I noticed Lily holding her shoes. "Clever."

"You should have said you wanted to eavesdrop," said Lily. "It is remarkably easy to eavesdrop in this house. This way." She beckoned me to a door beneath the stairwell.

I looked at Molly. "Not a word of this to your brother or anyone."

"Do you consider me an idiot?"

I tried—poorly—to imitate her voice. "Oh, yes, this is my minstrel. *She* plays beautifully, doesn't *she*? Did I mention *she* is a girl?"

Molly scowled. "I won't let anything slip. I promise."

We followed Lily through the door under the stairs. The air stank of dust and mildew. I held in a sneeze by cramming my nose into the crux of my arm. Lily took my other arm and guided me through the dark. She slid a ruined painting aside, and we entered a narrow passageway behind the wall.

This girl was not at all what I expected from a lord's daughter. Hanging about in crawl spaces and listening in on men in the billiard room was hardly the behavior expected of a lady. A speck of bright light glowed where it came in through a peephole.

Lily brought her face to it, the fleck of light dancing on her pale cheek. She stepped aside and waved me forward. "Go ahead," she whispered.

On the other side of the wall, I saw two low-hanging chandeliers above a billiard table of dark green felt. Dirk leaned against a mural, puffing on a black cigar, his billiard stick resting against the wall beside him. Lord Belle was speaking from somewhere else in the room.

"Jon Arnault could easily be persuaded to our cause. I know him to be a royalist, though in the eyes of the Blue Dusk, he is nothing if not loyal."

"Would he supply us with weapons from his factory?" asked Dirk.

"The Blue Dusk keeps a close watch over his inventory, but he has supplied rebels before. It might take him a great deal of time to produce them. There is also Lord Terrence. He's still in Locwyn. Many thought him a turncoat when he began managing the emperor's finances, but in fact, his loyalties have always resided with whoever stands the best chance at winning. I will write to him. It would be useful to have someone so entrenched in the enemy's inner circle."

"And what of the people here? Would they join our fight?"

I saw Lord Belle's arm as he leaned over the billiard table and took a shot at the eight ball. "While I am aware of royalists amongst the gentry, I cannot speak to the attitude of Shale's commoners. There have been some uprisings, rather small, disorganized ones. Perhaps Jon would know more, seeing as he's the one whose guns they're all using. I'll invite him to come here."

"The strongest rebel groups are in the North," said our boatswain, Mr. Pugg.

"This is true," said Lord Belle, "but remember, Shale is the breadbasket to all of Elsace. If you could sway the people of this region to your cause, you could essentially cut off the Blue Dusk's supply line, starve them out—"

"And starve the citizens of Locwyn? Of Vane? Skalway?" Dirk shook his head, biting his cigar as he went to take his turn at the eight ball. "I will not do that. These cities are massive, and their people have suffered enough already under the Blue Dusk. People would die in the thousands. Men, women, and children."

"War is no time for sentiment, my boy. You can afford your moral high ground *after* you have crushed your enemies."

It sickened me that neither Mr. Pugg nor Mr. Weston would speak up for the common folk. We were common. Some of us— like Baker—still had family in the northern cities.

"You may stay here as long as you like while you formulate your next move. Our village is remote and very distrustful of the Blue Dusk ever since it was razed in the revolution. We will protect you and your company as you gather allies."

"I am grateful, but I would not want to put your family in danger. If you were caught harboring us... There is Lily to consider."

"My daughter is a capable woman." As Dorian came around the side of the billiard table, he looked directly at the peephole. He made eye contact with me and I jumped back.

"Go. Go," I whispered breathlessly, shooing Lily and Molly with my hands. We slipped out of the crawl space and scurried into the hall.

Lily closed the door under the stairs, letting out a relieved sigh of laughter. "Well," she said. "Now that I have helped you, you must oblige me. I am going to have my lady's maid dress you. It does nobody any good for you to go about in your undergarments."

"Your father saw me," I blurted.

"He—what?" stammered Lily.

"He looked right at me."

"You must have imagined it. Father has terrible eyesight. His eyes seem to be looking everywhere at once."

"No. He definitely saw me—"

The door to the billiard room swung open, and the men came out laughing and holding diamond-patterned glasses of port. Lily stepped out in front of Molly and me, bowing her head to her father.

"Lily." Dorian greeted her with a knowing smirk.

Lily bobbed. "Hello, Papa." They passed us as they headed into the ballroom. Lily faced me, a disconsolate look wrinkling her pretty face. "He knows."

32

LOYALTY

A guest room with a day bed and trundle was arranged for Molly and me. The room was tucked away in the quiet part of the house, where the windows were narrow and the ceiling slanted in. The housekeeper pulled out the bed's white iron frame and dressed the mattress with fresh linens, pillow, and blanket. The goose feather bed was more comfortable than anything I had ever rested upon, but I wondered how I would fare without any rocking or sudden loss in altitude.

Lily's maid helped Molly undress. I told her if she touched me, I would break her pinky, which was enough to keep her at arm's length for the rest of the time she was present. Molly and I changed into clean shifts and used the steel basin to wash our faces. The lady's maid took our clothing to be laundered, looking at mine as though I had handed her a carcass and asked for some taxidermy.

Lily came in and ran her hands over the two housedresses her maid had brought us to wear the next day. They had been draped over the chair where Molly sat combing out her curls.

"I hope you like them," said Lily. "For you, Molly, I chose one of my favorites from when I was a girl. Clikk, I thought you might like something more austere, hence the brown."

"I won't wear a dress," I said.

"It's only for a little while," said Molly.

A burning sorrow swelled inside my chest as I thought of those maids aboard the Crescendo tearing my clothes away. I wanted my things back. I wanted myself back.

"Perhaps the servants might have something," suggested Lily.

"I need a pair of cutting shears as well."

"All right," said Lily warily. "Just please don't do anything to alter the clothing."

"It isn't for the clothing."

Lily reached into the vanity's center drawer and handed me a pair of shears. She bid us goodnight and was gone, closing the door behind her.

Molly glared at me.

"What?" I asked.

"She's trying her best. You don't need to be cross with her just because you're jealous."

"I'm cross with everyone." I scratched the rash on the back of my head. "And I'm not jealous. I'm vexed. My scalp's flaked down the back of my neck, I'm dressed like a pansy cherub, and everybody hates me."

"I like you." Molly took the scissors from me and set them on the vanity. "Take a seat and I will sort you out."

I did, resisting the urge to spew profanity at the first pull of the comb. Molly snipped the tangled nests where necessary, cropping my hair close to my scalp in the back. "We need a straight razor to scrape some of this away. I could ask my brother."

All evening I'd been hearing a rhythmic smacking sound coming from the bedroom where Dirk and Maive stayed. "Use the edge of the shears. I'll show you how."

Molly shaved parts of my head around my ears, artfully covering it with what she hair could salvage. When she was done, my head felt five pounds lighter.

"We should use this to make hair work," Molly said, already winding the discarded strands into taut coils. "One of my tutors taught me. She had woven the hair of all the women in her family into the image of a bouquet and framed it in glass."

"Perhaps tomorrow. Now it's time for sleep."

Molly had no qualms with that idea. We crawled under the blankets of our respective beds and blew out our candles, settling into the calm darkness.

"Clikk?" squeaked Molly.

"Hm?"

"I'm glad we're friends."

"Me too." I closed my eyes and let all the tension release in my neck and shoulders, allowing my body to sink into the mattress.

Hardly a minute had gone by before Molly nudged me. "Clikk?"

"What?"

"What is it like to have parents?"

"I'm not the best person to ask."

"Dirk won't speak of ours. And I hardly remember them. Most of my childhood is lost to me. I have vague memories of being surrounded by nurses and tutors, of looking out a tower window and seeing birds. Sometimes, I dream about a woman who looks something like myself only more grown up. I think she is my mother, but there is nothing to suggest she isn't simply the mother I imagined for myself."

"Most orphans find it helps to find a new family."

"A new family?"

"Yeah. People you trust. My family's the crew. Or it was, at least. Yours could be this family here. They seem like decent folk."

"Before my brother came to collect me, I had that kind of family at boarding school. Do you think I will see them again someday?"

"Likely not. Families tend not to last. I've had enough of them to know. The man who gave me my first job was like a father to me. He took me in as an apprentice at his pawnbrokers' shop, dressed me like a boy, and named me Clikk when I popped my first lock."

"What was his name?"

"Mr. Greyson. He showed great pity taking in a child with no voice. Most employers want youngsters who can raise a ruckus in the square, announce the business name and practices. Mr. Greyson gave me such charity. If it weren't for him, I'd have never learned to fiddle. He let me have one of the old fiddles from the shop, said it could supply me a voice, and gods bless him, it did. I swear, he taught me how to be a man before I'd even learned what it was to be a woman."

"Where is he now?"

"He's passed. I will never see him again, but he'll always be part of who I am, just as your schoolmates will be a part of you. Having people to keep in your heart, people who make you who you are, I think that's what it's like to have parents."

"Yes. I think so too," said Molly. "How did he die?"

I took a breath, remembering the old man's blood spreading across the floorboards. "He got sick," I said. "He willed his shop to me, his boy Clikk, but then his estranged son came along and made his own claim, took everything."

"How could that happen?"

"Well, you know, girls can't inherit property. I would have had to lie about my age too. I didn't know how business was done. I thought that if it came to a dispute, they might make me prove my gender to a physician. So I ran away. Found myself a new family. You have to in this world."

"Who was your new family?"

I felt a twinge of pain in my heart as I thought of the Kindred. "It don't matter. They're gone now too."

That pain struck deeper as I remembered Mikhail. I could not help but think of him, being in such close proximity to Aixenport. I could walk there in a day. I knew all his old haunts. I might find him having coffee at the Foxglove or busking outside Camilla's temple during the weekly summer street fair. Yet even if I found him, he would not know me as I was today.

"I'm so sorry," said Molly.

"Don't be. I don't deserve your pity. I've done too many wicked things in my life. I've robbed and hurt people, good people. And I'm too weary to feel sorry for it anymore. This world makes ugly work for us."

Some silence passed between us and at last she said, "Goodnight, Clikk."

"Goodnight."

Drained from the strenuous day, I stared at the blurry shadows on the ceiling. My mind refused to be still. A pervading emptiness consumed me. An hour passed and I was still awake, remembering all the faces from all the families I had found since I was orphaned.

I crept out of bed and went downstairs, treading on tiptoe. Even though it made no difference in the creaking of each stair, I held my breath on my way down. A muffled laugh sounded in a room above me. It was only Maive, but it startled me enough that I bumped against a picture frame. It rocked on its nail but did not fall. I paused and collected my senses.

In the ballroom, I steered my path through the bedrolls, stepping over the arms and legs of dozing men. Baker lay asleep on his face like a fool. He might have suffocated himself like that, so I rolled him over and shook him until he stirred. He started for his dagger but subdued upon recognizing me.

"Oh, gods. I thought you were a bloody spirit," he said.

"I can't sleep."

"Did you not hear the house articles? You shouldn't be out here."

"I should though. I might steal things. These nobles have no idea putting me in a room with all that finery."

"What you want, girl?"

"Don't call me girl like that. I'm still Clikk. I'm still the friend you knew, who fixed your busted trinkets, and had your back when you needed me."

"I never said you weren't."

"No, but you treat me different, teasing me like you did in the forest."

"I never teased you before?"

"You did, but it were different."

"It were, but that ain't my fault. I can't well tease you for having no cock. It's a blooming fact. Ain't funny no more. You should go to bed before you get us in trouble. You can't just run about the house in your ghost garb, waking people up."

"Are you even my friend anymore?"

Baker rubbed his eyes with the heels of his hands. "Truth is, *Clikk*, I feel like we only just met. I don't even know your real name."

"Clikk *is* my real name. Why can't things be like they were?"

"Because you're not who you said!" he snapped. "You're not my brother."

A sting like clenching broken glass burned in my chest. I couldn't speak. I could barely breathe.

I went running back upstairs to the guest room. There I threw myself down on the trundle and pulled the blanket over my head. Even after my face got hot, I remained entombed beneath the quilt. I felt like a freak one should not suffer to live, a creature worse than something in between.

Invalid; abnormal; queer.

A hateful voice threw these words at me until I wished I had never been born.

I tried listening for some ambient lullaby to drown it all out, but the room grew eerily quiet. Molly slept as silent as the dead, and suddenly all I could hear were Baker's words repeating over and over.

You're not who you said. You're not my brother.

33

REMEMBRANCE

A loathsome feeling consumed me as I remembered the countless times I had been there for Thomas Baker.

I was with him in Amaranthia at the Hemlock Tavern on the night he was attacked and chipped his tooth. Baker and I had taken seats at the bar, and one of them belonged to a bloke who had gone outside for a piss. When he returned, he didn't even ask Baker to move, just ripped the stool out from under him and broke it over his back. Baker came up swinging a leg of that broken timber and clocked the fellow over the head. The man's friends joined in on the brawl, making it four-on-one.

I couldn't have that, so even though I was smaller than every man in the fight, and even though we were still outnumbered two-to-one, I clapped the first pisshead on the ears and stomped the back of his knee. As he came after me, I hopped up on the bar, leaned back, and kicked him in the throat. The bouncers came running but got there just as two of the men were slamming Baker's face into the bar. And that was how he chipped that incisor of his and ended up with that ridiculous silver fang.

We left out the back. Baker held his mouth with his hand, cursing the unfairness of it. I handed him a handkerchief, which he used to soak up the blood pouring down his chin.

"You're good in a fight," he'd said. "Better than I expected."

"Kindred. Remember?"

"True, but I always thought you only picked locks for them."

I rolled my eyes, scoffing lightly. "No."

"Well, thank you. You didn't have to get involved."

"You'd have done the same for me."

"I would," he said. "Because I'm loyal to a fault when it comes to my brothers. I never surmised that of you until tonight."

It was a turning point in our friendship, the first night he saw me as anything other than just another Fledgling. I thought nothing would come between us after that. He made me forget I was a girl hiding in men's clothing because in his eyes, I was so much more.

I came out from beneath my quilt and took a breath of cold air. My body had overheated. Those words of his repeated in my head again. *You're not who you said. You're not my brother.*

That night in Amaranthia meant nothing to either of us in the end. I wrapped my blanket around my shoulders and fled the little room, bounding down the stairs to the world outside where the crickets shrieked and the moon cast its silvery light across the estate grounds. I fell against a post on one side of the veranda stairs and pressed my forehead into the wood.

For the first time in many years, I cried. It came upon me like a spell, in the way that spells seem to catch one by surprise. Tears drenched my face, and my sobs were ugly and stabbing.

Damned brute. How had I ever called such a man my friend?

I'd thought I knew him. I thought that out of everyone, he was the person I could trust the most.

Someone cleared his throat behind me. My first instinct was to run, but I turned sharply, half expecting Baker to have come through for me, a ridiculous fancy.

There stood Fitz, arms folded as he slouched to one side. I stared at the green boards beneath me and closed my blanket around my shoulders.

Fitz's breath showed in the cold night air as he spoke. "I heard that unfortunate exchange." He came toward me, reaching for me.

Wiping my eyes on my blanket, I edged away from him. "Don't touch me. I swear I'll bloody scream!" I snarled.

His hand drew back and I saw he was only offering me a handkerchief. He sat down on the veranda stairs, pulling out a pouch of tobacco. As he began rolling a fag, he said, "You're wound pretty tight. Care to smoke?"

"I don't smoke."

"Suit yourself." He sealed his rolling paper with a lick, pinched it between two fingers, and struck a match. His first inhale was a hard pull. He sighed, releasing a dense mist.

"I'll take a drag," I said, taking it from him. The smoke burned my throat, but I didn't care. I wanted to hurt whatever part of me was still that powerless girl child from Shale.

Fitz looked at my face as if he were trying to discern something. I sneered at him. "What?"

"He really gets to you, doesn't he?"

"He's a piece of shite. Always had been. Treats women like dirt, he does. Disgusting."

Fitz nodded, taking the cigarette and tapping out the ash. "You know about his mum, right?"

"I know all about his whore mum. She don't excuse his treating me like this."

"So you know he tried to save her? Even when he was just a little kid, he tried to make money so she wouldn't be selling herself."

"You think anyone on this earth knows Baker better than me?" I stole the cigarette again and pulled on it. The ember burned so fast it started to singe my fingers and I handed it back. "I know he took his first whore when he was fifteen. I know he hates himself for being a johnnie, and every time he lies with a girl he's paid, he's more messed up than before. But he keeps going back because it's the only sort of love he understands." Tears burned in my eyes. I wanted to think it was only the smoke, but it wasn't.

Fitz listened, finished his cigarette, and flicked the end into the damp grass. "I know. I was his Fledgling before you. Believe me when I say that he respected you more than any man in the crew."

I scowled, digging my nails into my blanket as I squeezed it tighter around myself. "So much for that. He's never respected a woman in his life."

Fitz looked at me. Standing, he said, "Exactly. And now his whole world has gone upside down. He was just coming to terms with what he felt for you."

"What are you saying?"

"What a man like him would never admit."

I might have burst out laughing if I weren't brimming with anger. Fitz had caused me such offense I wanted to crack his skull against a post. "He loved Clikk as his brother," I said.

"Why does that scare you?" asked Fitz. "Are you so convinced you're a man you're afraid you might be an invert?"

I did not answer. I looked out toward the dark forest. Some fireflies flickered and a breeze rustled the blue-black leaves above them. Dark clouds rolled in and stifled the moonlight. I thought about the night Baker tended to my bruises, gave me his lucky ring, and asked me why I never visited the brothels.

"Tell me, Clikk. How long has it been since someone loved you? The real you."

With that last remark, he was gone. I took some time to myself, watching the trees and twisting the iron nail on my thumb. It started to rain. The sound of it pelting the roof of the veranda reminded me of the hush that fell over the city on the night I met Mikhail.

34

THE THIEF BOY

As it turned out, being a boy came with its own set of difficulties. Beaten bloody by a gang of Aixenport thugs, I curled up beneath the broken shell of an old hay wagon. Waters droplets drummed against the wood over my head. Every hard surface—the cellar doors, the cobblestones, and the cracks between—deflected the rain. The mid-morning sun was swathed in gray veils, but some light shone through the vacant alley.

I jolted upright when the wagon wood creaked. A youth lifted the cart and shouted, "Move over!" He squinted through the streams of water pouring down his face. "I am getting soaked out here!"

"This spot's taken! Find another!" I rasped.

His hair was dark with all the rain it held, and he ducked in against my wishes.

"Get lost, I told you!"

Still, the lad ignored me and sat down. Even at my best, I couldn't have physically forced him out, and here, at my worst, I was rather at his mercy.

"There is room for three or four under here! When storm is passed, I will go," he said, setting his short sword on his left, away from me. I did not recognize his accent, but that was common in Aixenport. It was major hub in international sky transport, drawing people from all over the world. I could tell immediately he was not a native speaker by the way he would omit his articles or stall in the middle of a preposition.

I examined his clothes in an attempt to guess his trade. His boots were crafted of leather, scuffed and worn around the heels. His pants were lightweight and tailored close to his slender limbs. Over his shirt, he wore a vest of many different colored threads, all in earth tones. Its patchwork was festooned with pockets and loops that held keys, nail files, wire-cutters, and loops of elastic cord. I guessed he was some sort of scrapper.

He stared at the way I held my abdomen and gestured to the dried blood on my chin. "Who did this?"

I stared off away from him, hoping he would lose interest.

"Do you have name?"

"No."

We sat in silence a long while, just listening to the rain. The youth started humming a ditty to himself, something kind of pretty. I didn't mind it, but I tried to ignore him all the same. The rain picked up, developing into a deluge. It became increasingly clear that we would be stranded here for a while.

"I am Mikhail," he offered.

I sniffed, leaning forward against my knees. A ragged breath slipped out as my body clenched in pain.

"Do you have place to stay tonight?" he asked.

I nodded, even though I didn't. I'd been sleeping in an alcove of Camilla's temple. I believed she kept me safe as I slept.

"Is there someone who takes care of you?"

I didn't answer. He nudged me.

"Don't touch me!" As I tried for his short sword, he caught me by the hand, but not before I'd drawn it out by a half a foot.

"You need to calm down, boy."

"Don't call me boy. You're a boy yourself."

"I am fifteen. A man."

"Well, so am I."

"If I knew your name, I would not call you boy."

I let go of his sword in exchange for my hand. Sheathing and buckling it down, he said, "Your lip needs stitches. Tell me your name. I will leave you alone if you do."

As much as I doubted his promise, I told him. "It's Clikk."

"What kind of name is—"

"You promised to leave me alone."

Mikhail let out a vexed laugh. Not ten seconds later, he asked, "Is Clikk short for something? Clikolas? Clikolai?"

"No. Just Clikk. I pop locks. They click. So that's my name."

"You pop locks?"

A leak sprung between two planks of wood over my head. I gasped as freezing cold water slid down my back.

Mikhail edged farther to the edge and beckoned for me to come nearer. Reluctantly, I went and sat near to him.

"Where you learn to pop locks?" he asked. He seemed not to be getting it through his thick skull that I had no intention of conversing with him. As he went into his own monologue, I came to believe that he must be lonely and desperate for friends. "I came here from Dassan with my father. He is dead now. He died in factory accident when I was twelve. So I make my own way. You make your own way too, no?"

"Sure," I said.

"Like you, I was homeless and suffered my own share of beatings. And then I met Ordrick."

He spoke of a man who was kind to orphans. He adopted them as his own children, took them in by the dozens. And his only condition was that they respected him and their fellow Kindred. This was the first I'd ever heard of the Kindred. By the time Mikhail finished his story, the percussion of rain had softened to a drizzle.

Noticing this, I said, "Best you were on your way, Mikhail."

Mikhail hoisted the cart up and stepped out. He paused. "Listen... Ordrick would let me take you in for the night. We could stitch your face and feed you supper."

I could not afford the pride to refuse. "What do you want in return?"

"You teach me about locks."

Mr. Greyson had always stressed the importance of guarding locksmiths' secrets. I hesitated on his terms.

"Or don't," said Mikhail. "I will still help you."

"All right," I said.

I walked with him along the slick cobbled streets of the Aixenport slums. Whenever it rained, this part of town smelled faintly of sewage. Rats, chased from their dwellings, scurried along the edge of the brownstones.

My vision grew poor, and the sounds of the city melted into a tonal hum.

Not far into our journey, I crumbled against the wall of an alley. Mikhail asked if I was all right, felt my forehead, and said, "You are burning up. Take my arm."

Everything around me began to go dark, absorbed into a blur of heat and ache. He offered his hand, which I accepted in my desperation.

I did not quite pass out, but I could barely remember how we arrived at our destination. I recalled flashes here and there of walking under his arm, stumbling through crowds, slipping into alleys, eventually going up a side street and entering a dark cellar that smelled of cloves and citrus oil. I collapsed into a pile of tweed cushions and ratty quilts. I could see the wall had chipped blue paint and a streak where water had leaked down from the ceiling. Mikhail's voice sounded heavy in my head.

"We need water. Now."

Another answered him. "Look what the cat dragged in. A bloody sewer rat."

"The rat pick locks. So shut up and help me."

They brandished lanterns near my face. The warm glow blinded me, and I had to close my eyes. Someone wiped away my sweat with a bandana. Then Mikhail's warm hands unwrapped the weathered garment around my throat.

After a spell of darkness, I awoke on my back in that same pile of blankets. The room had no hearth, but in the corners, glass lanterns glowed with flame. Through a row of windows high up on the dilapidated wall, I saw the sky was dark.

A piece of coal burned atop the bowl of a hookah and a man with dark skin and a shaved head was pulling smoke through the hose. He flicked his cheek, his lips forming a perfect O as he blew smoke rings. The edges of his eyes were stained black, and he had ornate lines inked along his temples, behind his ears, and down his neck.

Behind him, a man and a woman kissed passionately in the shadows. All I could see of them was a hand fumbling with a garter.

An arm's length away, Mikhail dipped rags in a steel basin and rung them out. My midsection was wet. I saw that my chest was covered in cold compresses. My bindings had been cut open. I sat up, closing my shirt and tying it in the middle. Pain shot through my core, pain so intense that I fell back on my elbows.

"Careful," whispered Mikhail.

"Get away from me!" I cried, my throat aching as I held back a sob.

"Calm down. I did not bring you here to sell your teeth." He and the man at the pipe shared a chuckle, which only made me more nervous. "Can you believe this, Remi?"

"I wouldn't trust you either," said the man called Remi. He too had an accent I did not recognize, but it was different from Mikhail's, more proper in its grammar.

"What happened to you?" asked Remi.

I tried sitting up, only to buckle against the pain. "I was robbed," I answered.

Remi raised a glass of dark green liquor. "Hope it wasn't one of ours." His white teeth glistened prominently against his black goatee as he smirked and smothered his drink. "Welcome to the Thieves' Den."

"You're thieves?"

"We are the Kindred," said Mikhail. "You are safe here. I give you sanctuary."

The Kindred were, as Mikhail had said, a family of sorts. They ate together every night in a long dining hall. Their company spanned across generations with white-haired old men and children as young as seven. Some small part of me was still innocent enough to believe their patriarch Ordrick had created something beautiful.

Mikhail took care of me until I got my strength back, and never once did he take advantage of me. I repaid his kindness by teaching him everything I knew about locks. Poor old Mr. Greyson likely tossed in his grave.

I never intended to join the Kindred permanently, but spending time with Mikhail was a bit like running downhill. Once I built enough momentum, I couldn't stop my falling head over heels for him. After helping him with locks, I suggested we continue an exchange of our knowledge. I taught him fiddle and he taught me swordsmanship. He taught me how to hold a blade properly, how to position my knuckle against the cross guard to keep a firm grip. He showed me the clockface of blade work, how to intercept an attack and knock a man off kilter.

I began to visualize my vengeance against the Cerulean Knight. My sword became part of my soul, an extension of my power. As I came to know the tempo of Mikhail's body, his strength, and his confidence, I found myself wishing I could mirror him in every aspect.

We became inseparable. I shared his bed, his clothes, and spent every waking minute at his side. Eventually, I went under the hot iron for him and joined the ranks of the Kindred.

Our romance lasted only a year. I could still remember the wretched day I learned what it was to be betrayed. I found him at the end of the alley rutting like a hound with the local flower girl. I watched them for a time, long enough to be sure I would never forgive him. He did not see me and, rather than confront him, I vanished overnight.

Despite all my best efforts, I could not forget Mikhail. Like the brands tracing my ribs, he had seared himself into my skin. I continued to dress like him. I kept and wore clothing that had belonged to him. I used his mannerisms and mimicked his deportment.

As I stood on the veranda watching the rain fall outside the Belle Manor, I had to ask myself, why did I care so much about having lost Baker as my friend? Perhaps I yearned for something of him to be present in myself. Perhaps I craved his acceptance as validation of my masculinity. Or perhaps—and I could hardly admit it to myself—I had harbored a quiet desire to be more than his friend.

35

Brother Starling

T he sun shone so brightly the following morning; I noticed a skylight tucked high in the slanted ceiling. Molly was still fast asleep when I awoke, so I did a bit of light snooping in the room. I could not help my curiosity. What kinds of luxuriant items had these nobles trusted in the room of a known thief? When Lily came in, she caught me flicking the strings of a violin I had found under the bed.

"Forgive me," I said, instantly laying it back into its velvet-lined case. "I was only tuning it." I had considered stealing it. The instrument had the stamp of Cecil Lariat, a world-famous luthier, and it was practically untouched in its dusty, forgotten case. Nobody would have missed it.

Lily set a pile of folded clothing on the vanity surface. "Please, go ahead. I've brought you some clothing. One of the footmen had an old uniform that didn't fit anymore."

"That's kind of you," I said.

"My!" exclaimed Lily, looking more closely at the violin. "You've fixed the crooked neck."

"Minor adjustment."

"Would you like to keep it? You should have it. You will care for it better than I ever did. I never have time to play anymore."

"Are you sure? This is a Lariat."

"Quite sure!"

I thanked her. Not only had she gifted me a violin I could have never afforded on my own, she had also spared me the guilt I would have felt after inevitably stealing it.

I asked that she and Molly turn their backs as I changed into the uniform. I wore it with three buttons undone, the vest open and the trousers rolled up. In all the chaos that had taken place on the Crescendo, I delighted that my lucky ring and boots remained with me. Lily helped Molly into a dress with a floral pinafore. She tugged hard on the sash in the back.

"Your dress is a bit tight on me," Molly sulked. "I wish I weren't so chubby."

"No, Molly. You're a lovely, healthy girl," said Lily in her melodic way. "I was a rail when I used to wear this, like Clikk."

I eyed her dubiously. "Were you?"

"I didn't get my figure until I was about fifteen."

"I'm still waiting for mine," I said. It was a lark made in good fun, but Lily and Molly both frowned and looked away.

"Does Derek feed you enough on his ship?" Lily asked.

"'Course he does," I said. "Still, it's hard work on a pirate ship. No matter how much you eat, you're always hungry. But I'm strong as steel, stronger than some of the men." I was only stronger than Fitz, but I rolled up my sleeve to show them my lean muscle. The ladies oohed in approval.

"Speaking of which, the crew needs to be fed. I should go down," said Lily.

"Do you need help?" I asked.

"No. It's fine. I have staff for that."

"The men are a rowdy bunch. I know how to keep them in line. Should they show any disrespect, it would be my pleasure to put them right."

"Very well then," Lily said. "I would enjoy the company."

We went down together to dole out the men's rations. Back in the stuffy, hot servants' quarters, her cook and ours had collaborated on porridge. The concoction was a runny mush, but I doubted the men would mind. Lily and I heaved the ceramic pot into the ballroom and set it on a long buffet table next to stacks upon stacks of bread bowls.

Captain Dirk leaned against the wall in the far corner, reading a note, but not so much reading it as burning a hole in it with his rueful gaze.

"What's eating him?" I asked.

"Maive left this morning," Lily whispered. "Derek won't speak to anyone, just stares at that letter."

In addition to Maive's disappearance, about twenty of our men had deserted. I was surprised to see Baker remained. I assumed he still expected a reward and a pardon at the end of all this.

"Clikk!" Captain Dirk waved me down. I crossed the ballroom and reported to him directly, even though his tone suggested I was about to get a lashing.

"Captain?" I said.

"I told you she was twisted," he muttered.

"Why would she leave now?"

"She thinks she's helping me. Here. Just read it." He shoved the parchment into my hand.

Dearest Lexi,

Fitz and I are leaving for the capital to infiltrate the cabinet of the Blue Dusk. I will tell them my ship was commandeered and I was held captive until a compatriot helped me to escape. One of your crew is a witch, but her powers are dormant. Still, I can use her as a conduit and convey information that I gather from within. I've taken her eyelash to create a bond between us. She and I will communicate through her dreams, but she must take care to be asleep at the hour of three in the morning. I will give you significant advantage in doing this.

I am sorry to leave you without a proper goodbye, but I knew you would never let me undertake such a dangerous errand. Please trust I will return to you. Burn this letter, lest it should fall into the wrong hands. When you liberate Locwyn, we shall be reunited once more.

With love,

Maive

He grabbed the letter. "If any survivors from the Crescendo saw her helping us, they'll kill her. And for future reference, don't ever let a witch get her hands on your hair, jewelry, clothing, any of it! Have you never heard a fairy tale in your life?"

My face burned crimson. "It was an oversight and I apologize, Captain."

"You could have mentioned you were a bloody witch!" he whispered.

"I would have told you in the meeting yesterday, but you had me tend to Molly instead."

"You could have told me at any time."

"You knew as much as I did about my abilities. And Captain, I would prefer not to be called a witch on top of everything else."

"On top of what?"

"My standing with the men was compromised when they learned my secret. Even you bar me from your meetings, preferring the counsel of gutless yes-men and a lord who would have you starve out thousands of your own people."

"Were you listening in? When I gave you a direct order to watch Molly?"

"All due respect, this revolution would not be happening if not for me. I did not start this to starve out civilians. I actually know what it is to starve, unlike your Lord Pomp in there."

"This is not *your* revolution. You may have saved my arse on the Crescendo, but I do not take orders from you. I am your captain and commander. The hard choices are mine to make. If I want your opinion, I will ask for it. And if I need you to watch my sister, I expect you to do so without question. If you are to remain in my service, I need to know that you will follow orders without hesitation. I say, 'Fire,' you fucking fire. I say, 'Retreat,' you run, even if it means leaving friends behind. If that doesn't work for you, say so now and you may go your own way. Go make bombs with the Aix Resistance, for all I care."

"I am with you, sir. I will follow orders. But I will also speak my mind to you even at the risk of exciting your wrath."

"Fine," he said. "You'll tell me the first dream you have."

"Yes, Captain."

"You are dismissed."

I returned to Lily to help her set up. She had a big wooden bowl full of figs, and as the men formed a queue at our table, she went to pass them out. I spooned porridge into bread bowls, watching her move from brother to brother. I couldn't help but take interest as she reached Baker, watch what she did, watch what he did. Their eyes locked and he shot her a daring smirk, which made that milky complexion of hers turn rosy. She handed him a fig, and he took her wrist in his hand and said something that roused her smile. One of the men snapped his fingers at me. I'd neglected my duties as porridge scooper.

"Sorry," I muttered, giving him his meal.

Lily returned to me, flushed and giddy. "Oh heavens," she tittered. "That one is so droll."

"Who? Baker?" I asked. "He's a character, isn't he?"

"I never heard a man say such a thing."

"What did he say?"

"He said I had to stop making eyes at him, or we would both be ruined," she said, gasping up a little swoon as she looked his way. "That charmer started it yesterday. Oh, I love that silver tooth of his."

"I might have noticed you two together. What happened?"

"He asked about Shale, about its people and culture. I was more than happy to tell him. He said that if he ever settled down, this was the place for it."

"Ha. Baker settling down," I muttered, spooning out porridge like a factory machine.

"Is he a rover?" Lily asked. "He seems the sort."

"Calling him a rover is putting it nicely. Baker is a dog when it comes to women, a real libertine type. There ain't a brothel in Elsace that hasn't seen his face. You know they named the Wastrel after him? Started out as a joke after he got his first shanker, but now that he's pissing needles, it's not as funny as it used to be."

I saw a shadow darken Lily's face.

"Morning, Clikk, you old joker, you," said Baker, having arrived at the front of the queue. "You know, on my way up here, I was thinking I should apologize for what I said last night," he said matter-of-factly.

"Is that right?"

"Yeah. Truth is, your gender don't bother me one bit, nor the fact that you lied to me about it. You'll always be my brother, even when your conquests get in the way of your loyalty."

"My conquests?" I laughed outright, glancing at Lily. "Her? No thank you, Baker. I've no interest in being your brother starling."

Lily's face went from rosy to sanguine. She excused herself, stammering some nonsense of seeing to Molly's needs. She knew more about starlings than I anticipated or at least understood the polyandrous mating practices of birds. I saw no reason for her to get upset, as my sharing her with Baker was an absurd idea that hardly warranted any credence.

When she was gone, Baker shot me a derisive stare. He leaned in close and whispered, "You're dead to me."

I shrugged and dropped a heaping spoonful of porridge into a bread bowl for him. "Cheers."

36

LOVELORN

It was up to me to handle the remainder of breakfast duty by myself. I tried to keep a cheery disposition toward each man I served.

"Good morning—There you are, mate—Yes, you're welcome—Nice to see you, gunny." Unfortunately, my enthusiasm came off as insincere, and my brothers just glowered and snatched up their bowls. By the end, I'd given up. "Morning, you—Yeah, sod off—Your mother made the same face last night."

When mealtime had ended, Dirk had everyone circle around him in the ballroom.

"Brothers, gentlemen, thank you for remaining beside me. You have shown inspiring allegiance. I have a secret, as all men have secrets, and I hid it because I, like many of you, had lost faith in this world. I was born a prince of the Luftburg bloodline."

A shiver of whispers echoed across the room, but a hush fell as he began to speak again.

"What happens next is your choice. If you don't care about politics and simply want to thieve and whore your way to an early grave, then you may abandon my cause. But this is the chance of a lifetime. I will retake my throne, and when I do, those who helped me will be rewarded beyond their wildest dreams. Gold. Pardons. Dukedoms. Lands. Marriages to wealthy and well-connected brides."

"Is that Miss Lily up for grabs?" someone shouted. The men laughed.

"Why, yes," he said. "*Lady* Belle is looking to marry. So be cordial." Their chuckling resounded throughout the room. "Our host Lord Belle is revitalizing a network of royalists who can help us. I know we just went through an ordeal. We lost a beautiful ship..."

As the men bowed their heads in a moment of silence, I slipped away to find Lily. It made sense to try her room, but she wasn't in there. Nor was she in my room. I did see the violin she had gifted me. The case lay on the bed. I thought I should play her a song when I found her, which might win me forgiveness for my unsavory remarks.

"You there," I said to a servant girl as she passed me going down the stairs. "I am looking for Lady Belle."

"She went with the young miss to see the chickens."

Down I went, toting my violin on my back. I followed a row of rosebushes around the vine-covered house. A dirt road wound into a wooded area. I trekked along the trail until I came to a shed, a workshop, and animal pens for goats and geese. Amidst them was a chicken coop, where Molly peered in, clucking at the hens.

"Molly!" I called. "Is Lily with you?"

Molly stood upright and came skipping over. "She's not feeling so well. She went to lie down in there." She pointed to the workshop.

I proceeded toward the log house. The door had no working knobs, only a twisted rag filling the hole where one should have been. I pushed it open and entered a studio rich with the aroma of tree sap and lumber. There were carvings all around, wind chimes of dragons and birds that hung from the ceiling. Their wood flutes jangled as I closed the door behind me.

"Lily?" I purveyed the rows of animal figurines perched on shelves and worktables. They all had the same signature carved into their hindquarters: LMB. "Are these yours?"

Lily sniffled somewhere in the shady heat of the shop. I discovered her behind a tall sculpture of a ship climbing a wave. "I would like to be alone," she said.

"Let me apologize."

"Please just go. You've done enough."

"No, I won't go. I'm sorry if I embarrassed you! It's hard to be sugary sweet when your whole world gets snatched out from under you!"

"I am sorry for your losses... your brothers... and the Wastrel."

"You think that's all I lost? They didn't know I was a woman, and now that they do, they think I'm supposed to act like one. They all treat me like I'm useless, like I should just look after children and turn invisible." My breath trembled as my emotions boiled over. I held fast to keep from bursting into tears.

Lily came around the sculpture, her eyes puffy and red.

"Have you been crying?" I asked.

"It's one of the few things we're allowed, isn't it?"

"No," I said. "It isn't, actually, or they'll never respect you."

She took me into her embrace. I resisted the urge to pull away. I let her hold me because I could tell it made her feel better. "I can't help it," she said. "I'm just so ashamed."

"I'm sorry."

"You were only doing me a kindness." She dabbed her eyes with her lace handkerchief. "I'm a daft ninny to encourage that man's attention. Nobody ever pays me any mind, and he saw that and tried to exploit it."

"He's not so wicked as that. He likely did take an interest. And much of what I said wasn't true."

"So then he doesn't lie with whores?"

I chuckled at her innocence. "Oh, Lily. All men lie with whores."

Her face went white with shock.

"Well, perhaps not all men." My voice quavered on the lie. "Certainly all the ones I've known, but they might fly straight for the right woman. The thing is, you should be courting with men of your own social class. If anything ever happened between you and Baker, it would not be secret long. Your father would find out, and the two of them might duel, and one or both of them would be dead."

"But I hate my suitors! They're stuffy and boring. They treat me like a child. Sandy says 'Good girl' to me like I'm some toy dog. And he buys me dolls. Dolls!"

"That's disturbing," I said, remembering the prince's chamber on the Crescendo.

"And Bartholomew is the worst. He comes just to smoke with Father and goes along with everything he has to say about art, no matter how subjective or inane. Then during the ten minutes he shares with me, no matter what I say, it's wrong. I'm just another silly girl to him."

"Huh," I said. "Compared to that lot, Baker sounds like a prize."

"He is. He truly is," insisted Lily, taking both my hands in hers as if we were about to frolic like maids around a maypole. My whole body clenched up, but I forced myself to look amicable. "There is something so gentle about him," she said fondly.

I remembered a time Baker skewered a man's neck with his dagger. The blade jutted out the front of the fellow's throat, squirting blood like geyser. "Hm," I said. "In his own way, perhaps."

Lily began to weep.

"Oh, no. Don't do that."

"I can't help it. My heart is in shambles."

"You barely know him."

She said through belligerent sobs, "All I know is what I feel."

At this point, I'd had enough of girls always crying in my ear. Molly, at least, had the excuse of having been cursed. "All right." I took the violin case off my back and readied the instrument. "A pity party then. Just for you." I played my mother's song for her. Not only did she stop crying, she actually began to laugh.

"I must seem perfectly ridiculous!"

Smirking, I nodded. Even after I stopped playing, her sorrows had fled. She dried her tears on a lace handkerchief and thanked me for cheering her. "I know it's silly. I became enraptured by this idea of us running off together, traveling the world."

"That I can understand," I said. "But you don't need him to travel the world. You could simply pawn some of your household's silver, pack a suitcase, and go!"

There was a knock on the door, and without waiting for an answer, Molly burst in. The wind chimes clonked together across the ceiling. "Clikk! Clikk!" she called. "I found some sticks for swordplay. Will you teach me?"

I grinned at the child. "You want to play choppy-stabby?"

"Yes! Please!"

"All right, Princess. Care to join us?" I asked Lily.

"I shouldn't," she said. "If you bruise me, Father will be furious."

"Everything fun makes fathers furious."

"Please, Lily," Molly squeaked.

"I suppose if we're careful…" Lily swept her hair back, weaving it into a long braid. "Just try not to hit me in the face."

37

MILLICENT

irk assembled the men on the lawn outside. The sun glared down on us, high and bright in a cloudless sky. Dirk had a special guest to introduce to everyone, a dapper blue-eyed gent stuffed straight in a brocade vest and a collar as crisp and as sharp as a dagger's edge. Everything about him had an angle, from his dress to his darted sideburns to the sideways glances he thrust in the direction of Lily Belle. When she met his gaze, she made a deliberate show of tossing her hair at him.

She marched in my direction and murmured in a low voice, "I put a basket together for us. Will you teach me some more swordplay today?"

"Certainly."

"Meet me up on that hill yonder."

With that, she gave Jon Arnault a look of loathing and stormed into the house. Old flame? I wondered.

"Let me introduce Mr. Jon Arnault," belted Dirk. "Philanthropist, duelist, inventor, and businessman, this most generous gentleman has volunteered his wealth and the arsenal of his small arms factory to aid the royalist cause."

Mr. Jon Arnault produced and twirled a pair of pocket automatics. The men offered up some applause, which amplified when Jon tossed his firearms behind his back and caught them again on either side.

"I'd be happy to give a demonstration!" said Jon.

This roused a slew of approbations from the crowd. Several men called out their wish to volunteer. I, on the other hand, had less interest in watching some fop show off his gun tricks.

I saw Lily climbing the hill with her basket and I sprinted to catch up to her. When I sighted my lady nearing the trees, I picked up a stray stick and chased her. Lily yelped and quickened her pace. She found her own stick and twirled to deflect my attack.

I beat the stick right out of her hands. "Ow!" she cried, grasping her wrist.

"Don't underestimate your opponent!" I gathered up her stick and handed it back to her. "Again!" I whipped my stick into hers, and this time it broke in half. "You see that? You're strong. You cannot doubt yourself. You cannot hesitate. When the Blue Dusk come, there will not be time to think or consider; you have to kill them straight away. A woman your height and weight already has a disadvantage. If you can't kill every last one, they'll…" I couldn't say it aloud, but I could see it in her eyes that she knew. I frowned, struck dumb by grief as I remembered the soldiers ransacking my childhood home.

"I'll kill them," Lily said firmly.

I nodded and dropped my broken end. "I cracked my sword."

"That's what you get for sparring with an expert like myself," Lily said, flourishing her stick like a baton.

I couldn't help but smile. I had come to like Lily. For a noble, she had a good sense of humor and knew how to handle a wretch like me. She put up with my berating her for backing away from me in battle. She never fussed over broken nails or torn stockings, and in spite of my low birth, she treated me as her equal.

We found another stick and started a lesson on blade work. I made her learn the response to every assault and perform the action over and over until it felt as natural as breathing. The breeze coming down from the hills smelled of lavender. It chilled the sweat on my clothing and infused me with the energy to keep practicing.

"Quite similar to ballet, isn't it?" she noted.

"I wouldn't know." I thrust at her. She countered and tapped my arm. "Good."

"Might we take a break?" she asked.

"We haven't even begun."

If I aimed to give this young woman a chance to protect herself in the coming war, I had to be hard on her. We continued to practice, shuffling in the dirt, jumping over roots, and sliding behind trees. Lily's dress was soaked with sweat and her hair became a tangled nest of black wisps.

She jabbed me hard in the ribs and shouted, "You're dead, Clikk! It's over, all right? You're dead!" We both laughed deliriously, catching our breaths. I sat down on an exposed root and she took a seat beside me, reclining against the trunk.

"Oh, my heavens," she gasped, "Corsets should be illegal."

"You've been wearing a corset this whole time?"

"My shackle." Cackling, she kicked off her pumps, which were sullied with earth. "I think they make us wear these to keep us from thinking clearly."

"Makes sense," I muttered. "Imagine what women might get up to if they could breathe."

"Why do you say 'they'?" asked Lily. "Aren't you one yourself?"

"Surely, I am, but I'd rather people think I wasn't."

"Why is that?"

"It gets in the way when you're trying to find work outside of whoring."

Lily nodded slowly, but she looked incredulous. "In the new kingdom," she said, "Women must have all the same rights as men.

We should be allowed to work in all trades. Of course, to achieve these rights, we will first need to establish a stable political system, one that can be managed without bloodshed."

"Nothing happens without bloodshed."

"That is what they would have us believe," she said. "If we stay quiet and subdued, we are already finished. We need to make our voices heard."

"And when they give us lashes?"

"A hundred lashes couldn't silence me."

"Have you ever been lashed?" I asked. "Each and every strike is a pain that bites you in half. A dozen is the standard, and such a beating puts a man out for weeks. A hundred, Lily? That is certain death. That would silence anyone."

Lily sat up straight. "Martyrdom only makes a message louder."

Her sheltered upbringing had made her naive. Too many martyrs had come and gone in the scattered rebellion against the Blue Dusk. This delicate girl knew nothing of how the system repeatedly crushed the men and women on the lowermost rung of society. She likely based all her knowledge on what she read in books, pretty stories about heroic uprisings. The real world entertained no such justice. Unsung soldiers like myself would pay with our lives to reestablish Dirk's reign, and we had only the inkling of hope that he would prove less corrupt than Perceval or Lucius before him. I asked her, "What made a girl like you care so much about politics?"

"What a terrible question," she remarked. "What do you mean by 'a girl like me'?"

"Beautiful, privileged, beloved—you would fare perfectly well without taking sides in the coming war."

"I have known too much injustice," she said indignantly. "My family lost everything to the Blue Dusk. We saw friends and relatives hanged like dogs and had to pledge fealty to their murderers, the stress of which claimed my mother's life. We lived in Locwyn when the royal family was deposed. I saw the turmoil in the streets, the sheer brutality. Many noble families were butchered."

"I did not know. Forgive my presumption that you had it easy."

"We relocated to this estate after Locwyn became too dangerous. And since then, I have never left. All my life, I've longed to return to Locwyn, to see the steelwork fountains and the museums that my mother loved, to visit the home I grew up in. But Father would never let me travel, especially with insurgency so rampant. I envy you, having gone with Derek and seen so many places. I will likely never board an airship."

"No, Lily. You must fly someday."

"What is it like?"

"Why, it's the greatest thing in the world, that rush of joy when your ears pop and your stomach's in your throat."

"Perhaps someday, you will take me."

Lily reached for her picnic basket. Today she had brought the usual baps and honey, but nestled between them was a six-chamber revolver with a pearl grip. These guns were expensive and owned primarily by upper-class men. Most people fought with swords or used crude firearms such as pistols or rifles.

Lily handed me the weapon. "This is Millicent," she said. Millicent, a firearm crafted to fit a lady's grip, impressed me with her lightweight feel.

"My," I said. "She's beautiful. Is this yours?"

"She's yours now, to pay you for the lessons."

"No payment necessary." I tried to give it back, but Lily folded her hands delicately in front of her.

"Please, take it. A former suitor gave her to me, but I'm no marksman."

"Which suitor was this? Dolly-boy or daddy-lover?"

"Neither," she said. "This one I liked. We were promised in secret, but he jilted me. He announced his engagement to someone else earlier this summer. They are to be married come Spring."

She stood and moved up the hillside. Across the meadow, we could see the men enjoying their demonstration of the weapons provided by Jon Arnault. They took turns using their pocket automatics to shred a scarecrow, casting hay fragments to the wind. Lily folded her arms over her chest and glared down at them.

"Is that him?" I asked. "The small arms manufacturer?"

"Am I so transparent?"

"What happened between you?"

She sighed, turning away from the sight of him. "I was foolish. My books on the art of courtship all told me a woman should engage in games of chase, but I failed to heed their advice. He said he was in love with me, sent me presents, and called on me constantly. Like a fool, I told him I loved him too. I wanted to be open and honest with him. I wanted to be myself."

"I do not see anything wrong in that, Lily."

"He lost interest because I gave my heart too easily."

"I think your open heart is one of your finest qualities. You are too good for him. You will find someone better."

She blushed, too embarrassed to respond at first. Finally, she said, "Please, take the revolver. It holds no sentiment to me now, and if I keep it, I will likely shoot him before the day is through."

I opened the chamber, which spun with ease and clicked back into place neatly. "Thank you, Lily. I will never forget your kindness. Not ever."

"Ho!" The call came from below as a bird erupted from an open trap. Jon Arnault took aim and fired, hitting his mark and causing it to burst into a spray of feathers. I noticed him look up the hill at us to see if Lily had been watching. She turned away.

"Why don't you go shoot with them?" she suggested.

"He'll see you gave his gun away."

Lily smiled wickedly. "Exactly. He wanted games. He can have them now. I think I will go in. I've had enough exertion for one day."

We bid farewell to each other, and that good lady started back toward the manor.

38

SHOOTING

I jogged down the hill to join the men below. Aside from Jon Arnault, they were all men I knew from our company, including Baker, Pierce, and Jasper. Baker sulked off to the far end of the crowd as I approached. Jon shifted his weight to one side and rested his pistol against his shoulder, his perfectly coiffed goatee pointing out as he leered at me.

"Did you see that shot, girl?" he boasted.

"I did. Very fine," I said.

"Care to match it?"

I shook my head. "I'm not proficient in firearms. My talents lie with the sword."

"I'd be happy to offer some pointers."

Jon Arnault sauntered over, offering me his rifle. I drew my revolver so he would see it as Lily had wanted. It surprised him at first, but whether or not it had irked him, he did not let on.

"Show me your stance," he said.

I stood tall, lifting the gun straight with both hands. Jon took my index finger and lined it up with the shaft. He had my left hand cradle my right, steadying it. Once he had corrected my hold, he came up behind me, squaring my shoulders. I lowered the gun and stepped away from him.

"Do you want to learn or not?" he said.

I looked down, nodded, and resumed the stance. Jon patted my hip and nudged my left foot back to ground me against the recoil. Then he held my arms again, having me bend my elbows slightly. His touch sent my skin crawling up my spine. I swallowed. I needed the lesson to survive the war. I needed to do a great many things I might not feel comfortable doing.

"Clikk don't like to be touched." Baker's voice carried over the general murmur of the group as he broke through the cluster.

"What lady does?" remarked Jon, his voice deep in my ear.

I shuddered, and before I realized what was happening, Baker was shoving Jon away from me. Our men burst out laughing and a few of them sang out an "ooh" of foreboding.

"Keep your hands to yourself, toff!"

"Forgive me, my good man!" cried Jon, chuckling nervously as he regained his balance. "Am I trespassing on your lady love?"

"Oh, that's bold of you!" spat Baker. "We ain't even friends. But you take advantage, sir. You can teach someone to shoot without wrapping 'em up in your lewd embrace."

"Where do you come from?"

"Where I come from ain't important."

"On the contrary, it is critical. For you see, in Shale, we are more accustomed to such embraces! I should hug you where you stand to prove my point." Jon opened his arms and Baker drew back like an adder. "Unless you object, good man."

Baker gave him his most formidable death stare.

Jon moved the conversation forward. "No? Very well. Rest assured, I am your friend! I want to help you form a Shalean resistance group to secure the countryside while you take the capital. We come from different places, but we have everything in common in regard to this revolution."

Baker put his face close to Jon's and took hold of his vest. "Listen, toff. We might be on the same side of a war, but that don't make us chums. And I'll have you know I've spoken to the lady of the house and know all about your broken engagement. So don't expect me to trust you so far as I could spit."

Jon's nervous smile dissipated. He smacked Baker's arms away and straightened his rumpled vest. "I doubt you know *everything*," he said. "First of all, we were never officially engaged. There was no ring. No date. No blasted proposal. I wanted to marry her, yes, but I never asked. Fact of the matter is, Lady Belle is off limits. Her father will not accept any son-in-law short of our long-lost king, your very own Prince Derek."

"She's to marry our prince?" I said.

"Ha!" cried Jon. "There's the hitch, young lady. The prince does not love her, nor does she love him. Why do you think you are all staying here in the manor and not in the village? It is a ploy to push Derek and Lily together. So, my good man," he said, turning at last to Baker. "I did nothing so dishonorable as break an engagement with the lady in question. I asked her father's permission, and he said no. I had to move on. And it pains me to learn that my lady hates me so fiercely, but she will do what she must to forget me."

The thought that Lily had once been enamored with this egomaniac made me ill. That girl could fall for any man if he were handsome and under thirty.

Jon approached a row of wooden pedals. He stomped one, activating a spring mechanism that opened a trap. A pigeon fluttered frantically skyward, knowing some seconds of freedom before Jon's rifled discharged and shot the poor thing out of the air.

"Who's going to Aixenport tomorrow?" he asked.

The men looked about, confused. "Some of us were assigned the task of digging trenches around the property, securing it against the coming war," one of them said.

"What's happening in Aixenport?" I asked.

"We're going to my factory to retrieve a stockpile of weapons," explained Jon. "Also, there is a resistance group there that simply must see Prince Derek is alive and well. I hope you'll join us, Miss..." He waited for me to fill in the pause, but I was still recovering from being called Miss. "What was it that young man called you? Cricket?"

"My name does not matter."

"Let me try and guess it."

"You never will. And by tomorrow, you'll have forgotten me."

He laughed robustly. "All right, Cricket. Now watch this shot."

He stomped a release peddle and shot three birds in a row as they tried to escape. As he murdered the poor things for sport, he sang a song about Aurora riding across the sky on a pearl-white horse. It was a Shalean folksong that I vaguely recalled my father singing to my mother when I was a girl.

For the rest of the afternoon, I said nothing and focused on studying his shooting technique.

39

AIXENPORT

Dirk armed me with an elegant cutlass to use should we be attacked on our way to Aixenport. The journey took six hours, all of it under heavy rain. I rode in the coach with Dirk, gripped by guilt every time I glanced out the rear and caught sight of our crewmen in tow. They were packed like cattle in the hay cart, mercilessly pulverized by the heavy deluge.

"Don't feel sorry for them," said Dirk. "They needed a bath."

"It don't feel right, us being dry while they suffer."

"Would you prefer your leader and future king arrive to meet the rebels soaked and shivering?"

"No," I said. "But what about Mr. Arnault in his fine coach with Lord Belle?" The pair of them rode ahead of us, leading the way through the storm's mist. Every now and then I could see the back of their heads through the rear window.

Dirk snorted and bent forward to pilfer the coach's cabinet of its amenities. "Well, considering that both coaches belong to them, nothing seems fairer in the world to me." Dirk found an amber bottle, which he promptly uncorked, sniffed, and knocked back.

"Is that liquor?" I asked.

Dirk's face crinkled up. He twisted, slid back the panel on his left, and spewed the draught out the window. After a nasty fit of coughing, he answered me. "Ammonia... with a dash of citrus.

Might consider trying it again if I get desperate enough. I hate ground transport."

"I hope to Throm you aren't serious."

"We could huff it."

"What is wrong with you? You need a clear head when you meet the rebel faction. Who are they anyhow? What do you know about them?"

He slumped in his seat, fingering a hole in the silk and making it bigger. "They're not what one would call perfect allies. They bombed a bridge to take out some Blue Dusk officers, killing twenty-eight civilians in the process. Brutal business."

"Then why are we meeting with them?"

"Jon says they are the largest faction of insurgents in Shale. If we get them, we can sway the others to help us form an army here."

"How have they grown so large without the Blue Dusk finding them?"

"They're very insular. They don't collaborate with other factions, but they are willing to make an exception if I can prove that I am who I say I am. Could get hairy, so I'd keep that cutlass at the ready."

I nodded, squeezing the cross guard. "I will stay on edge until we are returned safely to Nelise. I don't have the most faith in Jon Arnault's relations with such men."

"What do you mean by that?"

"He's a fop. If I were the Aix Resistance, I would not do any dealings with him."

Dirk laughed, patting my hand. "He might be pretty, Clikk, but don't forget he's an arms dealer. And this isn't his first time giving guns to insurgents."

"I don't like him."

"No?"

"Did you know he and Lily Belle were in love?"

"Really?" Dirk looked legitimately surprised, but he acquiesced with a nod. "That seems appropriate. They are well suited."

I scowled, clicking my tongue against the roof of my mouth. "There is something you should know," I said. "Can we keep this between us?"

"Funny, I asked you exactly the same thing before, and as I recall, you told Baker, then you told Fitz…"

"You're funny," I said flatly.

"Proceed."

"Lord Belle rejected Jon's request to marry her because he had someone else in mind already."

My story of everything I had observed occupied us for at least an hour of our journey. My prince could scarce believe that Dorian Belle was keeping Lily's hand for him.

"She'll end up a spinster," he said.

"Maybe she's better off."

"Let's be realistic, Clikk. Lily isn't you. She's Lily. I will speak with Lord Belle and clear up the matter. Jon and Lily are a fine match."

"Just one problem. He is engaged to a girl from Leridia."

"He'll drop her. No woman in the world could be as beautiful, as charitable, or as kind as Lily."

"Well, if you think so highly of her, maybe you should—"

"Lily is like a sister to me! I used to lock her in the outhouse when Molly and I lived with them. How would I ever explain that to our children?"

"How can you explain it now? You were an adult when you lived with them."

Dirk looked indignant. "She was a villain as a girl. You have no idea. She called Molly's red hair 'an unattractive color' and said that she would 'never be pretty.'"

"You locked a little girl in an outhouse," I said, shocked that he could not fathom how wrong he had been. If it had been me locking children in outhouses, I would have never told the story to anyone.

"I think I deserve some credit for Lily turning out to be the lovely girl she is today. Without me, she'd have gone on thinking herself better than everyone. I took her down from her high horse and placed her right in the piss pot!"

For the next several hours, Dirk and I spoke very little, using this time to nap so we would be well rested for our meeting. When I awoke, the arms factory loomed at the top of a cliff just beyond a road that wound through the moors. Rain trickled down my window, streaking the vista ahead.

Jon's building was nothing so memorable. A utilitarian construct, big and bleak, the factory's most interesting architectural detail was the tall iron gate surrounding it. The grounds had no trees or foliage, only long stretches of heather, characteristic of the heath it was built on.

We entered the factory and took a late lunch in the cafeteria. The dining table was on an upper level mezzanine that looked out over the factory floor. The staff provided us only gravy on bread, but we were happy to receive it after such a long journey. They also offered cider, which warmed our cold bones. My poor crewmen dripped rainwater everywhere. A janitor came by with a mop, cleaning underfoot as we ate.

I took notice of Jon's many employees assembling automatic rifles below us. They looked exhausted and hungry. The guns outnumbered them by the hundreds. Rifles and pocket automatics lay in racks running down the length of the warehouse. An inspector walked down the aisle, examining each and every one.

When Jon came to sit next to Dirk and across from me, I asked him, "So, Jon, how much you been working this sorry lot?"

"Excuse me?" he said. I realized he hadn't understood me because I'd been speaking while eating my sandwich. I swallowed and repeated myself. He nodded. "Ah, well I don't manage the factory schedule. That's done by the floor manager."

"You just rake in the profit, eh?"

Dirk gave me a subtle kick in the boot.

"What?" I whispered.

"Must you sow dissent everywhere you go?"

"S'pose it's in my nature."

Not long after we finished our meal, the rain stopped. Jon led us down to the factory floor to take a look at the weapons. The plan was to offer half of these to the Aix Resistance. Of course, on the books, we were transporting them to Locwyn to pad the Blue Dusk's arsenal.

Jon's employees helped us to load the many weapons into crates padded with hay. Before nightfall, we had stacked them on our cart and made off for our rendezvous with the rebels of Aixenport. I rode in the carriage with Dirk, escorting Jon Arnault, Dorian Belle, and our lethal cargo. The rest of our company travelled by a local omnibus.

We convened at a colorful establishment called the Hog's Dick Tavern. Four hours later, we were still waiting with no sign of the rebels. I had the privilege of joining Dirk's table with Mr. Pugg, Mr. Weston, and the much too self-confident Jon Arnault, who I tried exceedingly to ignore. I could have sworn that for every boastful statement he made about himself, the table where Pierce and Jasper were seated would erupt with laughter.

A young boy approached our table several times, asking to shine our boots. Dirk sent him away with some coppers under the condition that he get lost, a choice I deemed to be a wise one. The Kindred used children all the time to pickpocket throughout

Aixenport. Ordrick had called them his rats. You never wanted one crawling around by your feet.

"You know, I found Clikk not far from here," said Dirk. "It's a funny story. She was pretending to be a boy."

"Really?" said Jon. He smiled at me. "And what was it that drew you to the pirate captain Alexander Dirk?"

"I needed a job."

They both laughed. I found myself wearied and in no mood. I never felt right in Aixenport, always too worried some shadow of my past would crop up. Gods forbid I should see Mikhail lurking in the corner of this very tavern.

I would never forget the first time he had to kill for pay. When a Kindred turned sixteen, he graduated from rat to sellsword and was required to kill at Ordrick's behest. Mikhail's first hit was a shopkeeper who had fenced our stolen goods for years. The man wanted out of the business and had threatened to peach on us if we did not leave him alone. So Ordrick assigned young Mikhail to the task of tying up that loose end.

My lover did not return to the Thieves' Den until close to dawn. I waited up for him and kissed him when he came down into the lair, but his face was like a statue's cast in stone. I drew my hand back when I felt his sleeve was cold and wet. Blood stained my palm. A thick streak ran up his arm.

"Will you wash it?" he had asked. "I can't look at it."

I took the shirt and boiled it over the cookfire, pretending that I did not hear as Mikhail wept in our bed. He sniffled only once or twice. But I knew. He was never the same after that.

"My ring!" Dirk shouted, springing up from his seat. He searched beneath the table and stools. "I've been robbed!"

40

THEM RATS

Everyone but myself leapt from their chairs and searched the floor beneath their feet. They surely would not find the ring there. "It was that boy!" cried Dirk.

"Shh. Take your seats," I said. "Don't draw attention to yourself. Thieves seldom work alone."

Dirk nodded, and as he took his seat, so did the rest of the men at our table.

"He took it off your finger?" I asked.

"I wouldn't be so bold as to wear it in this part of town! It was inside my breast pocket! And I had it when we came in. The eel!"

People don't realize their innermost pockets are the easiest to pilfer. Fact is, the safer you think something is, the more likely it will be a pickpocket's prime target. I set my hand on Dirk's shoulder.

"Lower your voice. Is the ring important to you?"

"It's vitally important," he stressed.

"Then I will get it back. Stay here. Act like nothing's happened."

He did as I told him. The rest of the men at our table went silent and watched me as I crossed through the tavern. I searched the patrons for other children the same age as that boy. When I was Kindred, Ordrick often sent the rats out in groups.

I went outside, bumping Pierce who was coming back in. He reeked of tobacco and gin.

"Got a fag?" I asked.

"Not for you."

So much for looking like I had a reason to go out there. It was all very well. I could still pretend I'd gone to bum a smoke. The rain had started up again. Against the wall of the portico, a teenage boy was flicking a coin across his knuckles and back. I watched him and recognized the Kindred brand on his forearm.

"Lighter than air, unburned by fire," I said.

The boy looked up at the sound of my voice, and we finished our secret greeting in tandem, "We are the shadows."

A nostalgic smile crept over my lips. "How's Ordrick?"

"Who's asking?"

"Clikk Greyson." I looked around, and seeing we were quite alone, I lifted my shirt and showed him the brands on my ribcage.

"I heard of you."

"Yeah?"

"You're Mikhail's girl."

"My own girl now. You working the pub tonight?"

"Some of them rats were. I'm only here for the drinks."

"Where are them rats now?"

"They took off."

I chuckled, amused by the idea that my old crew had just stolen from my present crew. "Back to the nest, I gather. Gods keep you."

"Gods keep you."

When I returned to Dirk's table inside, I found the men still sitting in perfect stillness like mannequins made of wax. "I know where they've gone," I told them. "Could be dangerous us marching in there. These men are cold-blooded killers."

"All of us are cold-blooded killers," Dirk rejoined. "Except Jon, maybe."

"I shoot pigeons and cans," he said, his mustache tips curling as he laughed.

"These men aren't like us," I insisted. "They haven't any conscience. They'd kill your sweet sister for mere silver."

"How do you know so much about them?"

"It's the Kindred."

"Your old gang? What are the chances?"

"Quite good for us being in Aixenport. They used to say nothing stolen in this city got fenced without passing through Ordrick's hands first."

Without further delay, we gathered our men and headed out. As we were leaving the Hog's Dick Tavern, we saw our crated cargo rolling away, driven by cloaked figures.

"Earth and sky," cried Dirk. "Where are our men?"

On the distant corner away from their post, the men we had assigned to guard our weapons were talking to a group of painted harlots. I remembered Mikhail and myself using that exact ploy. Our men saw the cart taking off into the night, and they came running, drawing pistol and sword to no effect. They frowned, edging away from Dirk who was fuming.

"How are you this stupid?" he said to them.

"It's no matter," I chimed in. "I know where they're going."

"Take us while our goods are still hot!"

I led them through the night street market and deep into the slums. The rain and the dark and the uncertainty brought me back to that very first night Mikhail had carried me to the Thieves' Den.

As we reached the rusty old cellar door with smoke seeping out through the crack, a thousand butterflies flitted in my stomach. I kicked the door in a rhythmic pattern.

"That's the old passcode. Try again!" groused a voice from below. I recognized it as belonging to my old pal.

"Remi? That you?"

"Clikk?"

The doors swung wide open. Remi poked his head through, sucking on a pipe. When he saw my escort of nigh fifty men, he slammed the door shut.

"Did you come here to die, girl? Who have you brought with you?"

"The deadliest sky pirates in all of Elsace. Your lot stole my captain's ring and all our guns. Give them back, friend, or we'll raze this den to dust."

"Who's there?" I heard a deep voice ask.

"Clikk is with the sky pirates," said Remi.

"Clikk? Our Clikk?"

"The very same."

The whispers halted. The door reopened. And there was my old master Ordrick, squinting up at me, his nose crinkled in a discerning sneer.

"Good gods, it's really you. Come 'ere, my girl!" Ordrick beckoned for me to descend the steps, which I did. He gathered me up in his beastly arms and spun me about. Dirk drew his pistol and our men followed suit, all aiming down at the king of thieves.

"Easy, easy," Ordrick said, backing away with me, his human shield.

The spin had me all disoriented, but I pleaded with Dirk. "Don't shoot me."

"Put that shite away and come in!" cried Ordrick. He held up a hand for calm as he drew Dirk's signet ring from his top pocket. "This is yours, ain't it, Prince Derek von Luftburg?"

Dirk signaled for his men to holster their firearms. They came down single file and joined us in the underground den. Oil lanterns and tea candles illuminated the dwelling, a sea of lights reflecting off their grimy glass shades. I recognized many of my old friends and discovered a host of new faces as well.

"Sorry we stood you up," said Ordrick. He grinned, chewing a toothpick.

"You're the Aixenport resistance?" said Dirk.

"Forgive me. We had to make sure you were who you said. I planned to find you once my appraiser finished looking at that ring of yours. Here." Ordrick flicked the ring.

Dirk caught it midair. "I assume you were satisfied with your man's report."

"A white gold setting, a red diamond worth the city of Aixenport three times over, your mother and father's family sigil on each side. Yes. Yes, I am. I'd have kept the damn thing if you didn't need it to amass your army."

"Where are the guns?"

"Perfectly safe! Forgive me. I like to hold all the cards in my hand."

I interrupted with a bewildered snort. "Ordrick," I said. "What got you to care about politics?"

"Your Mikhail. He's a smart lad. Our operation ain't sustainable with half the city starving to death. When the middle class suffer, we all suffer, which is why we need to join forces against the Duskies. Am I right, my liege? Tell me, where are you staying tonight?"

"Jon here is putting us up in the low-income housing he provides for his factory workers. It's only a mile out of town," said Dirk.

"Bah! We've more than enough room here. I own every building on this block, every cellar connected by tunnels."

"I wouldn't want to trouble you."

"No trouble! It's the least I can do after making you wait hours in that tavern."

"Good man. That's kind of you, but we will have an easier journey tomorrow if we sleep outside of town."

"If you insist. Come, let us break bread and toast to our alliance!"

The notion agreed with Dirk, but he eyed Ordrick dubiously. "I've always said never trust a man who will not break bread with you."

Ordrick slung an arm around the pirate prince and led him through one of the man-made tunnels. As we followed them, Dirk continued to look over his shoulder, anticipating a trap at every turn.

"You all right?" said Ordrick. "You ain't quite sure about me, is you?"

"You can trust him," I said to Dirk. "This man is like blood to me."

Dirk nodded. "Forgive me. You have a reputation, Ordrick. It is jarring to meet you in the flesh like this."

"Relax, my prince. As Clikk said, I consider that girl my own blood and would never do nothing to harm her or her friends. Now come and sup with us. I want to know everything about my girl and your travels together."

We came into a massive dining hall. The space was part of the city's catacombs. Its walls still held rows of skulls crammed in along endless stacks of limbs. Three iron-wrought chandeliers hung from the stone ceiling at least twelve feet over our heads. Some children came through carrying candles. They climbed onto the long wooden table and fitted them into the fixtures. On the far end of the room, we saw our weapons crates.

"Ah, there they are," said Dirk.

Ordrick smiled, showing all his teeth, even the gold ones in the back. "Safe and sound, my prince."

We took our seats at the table's long benches, and our men discussed their displeasure that they could not spend the night here. The Kindred carried in an assortment of mismatched chairs and tucked in where they could. Everyone under sixteen had to serve and take what was left from the scraps.

They had prepared for us a meat and potato stew. The children brought each of us a bowl and set freshly baked bread upon the table. Our mandolin player William, who sat on my right, could not keep quiet about the meat. When I first joined the Kindred all those years ago, I had the lovely task of gutting and deboning rats for our suppers. Thereby, I told William not to pry into the story of the meat.

As we supped, Dirk and Ordrick discussed the notion of building an army in Shale. Money seemed to be Ordrick's first concern. He had the manpower, but he needed lots of coin if he was going to stretch a devalued currency to fund the liberation of Shale. Jon Arnault professed to know a vast network of royalists with the necessary wealth. These men knew a great deal of war strategy and would serve well as officers in Dirk's army.

"I don't see why your class should automatically be made officers," I said. "You think us riffraff know nothing of warfare? We been at war our entire lives. Why should we fall in the front lines while yours sit atop a hill sipping tea."

"Clikk has a point," said Dirk. "But so does Jon. I don't think the gentry boys would do so well in the front lines. Ultimately, we cannot be distrustful of one another. We need to unify as a single entity and find something that appeals to everyone. Do you understand what I'm saying?"

"You're saying we need a name," said Ordrick.

"We do need a name. We cannot be Kindred in one corner and Arnault Arms in the other. We need something to call ourselves."

"The New Dawn," suggested Jon.

"I do like the notion of a rising sun," mused Dirk.

I cut in, "It's too similar to the Blue Dusk. We need to be something different." I remembered what Baker had said to me back on the Wastrel. He expressed concern that Dirk would follow a pattern of autocracy. "Dirk is not just another king seizing power over the realm. He is a man of the people."

"The People's Army," said Ordrick, whacking the table so hard it made everyone sit up a little straighter.

"Too militant," said Dirk. "I want something that captures the spirit of how this revolution began. It was all put into motion by that young woman there."

He pointed at me. I lowered my eyes as Dirk went right into telling the story about his sister's curse, my magic song, the wedding, and about my fast and loose plan that resulted in the deaths of Perceval and Torrent.

Ordrick looked like he was getting all choked up. "My girl," he kept saying, which shocked me considering we had never been particularly close.

"We could call ourselves the chameleons," suggested Pierce. "Or Camilla's tail."

"The Risen." The answer came from behind me. I turned my head and saw the voice belonged to my old lover, Mikhail.

41

LÏTTLE MOUSE

The sound of goblets and silverware died down as everyone turned to see the young man standing at the mouth of the tunnel. Mikhail looked very much the same, only his hair had grown to the length of his shoulders, long and straight. It had been only a year and a half since I had seen him, but in that time, he had acquired a new scar. His frayed sleeveless jacket showed how the mark stretched over his deltoid muscle. Someone had sunk something deep there. I wondered how long he had been listening to us before making his presence known.

"The Risen," Dirk tried it out aloud. "I like it. The Risen Revolution."

"It has the essence of the rising sun without being obvious," explained Mikhail, nonchalant in his observance of me. "It is simple, easy to remember, inspiring. It is Clikk. She rose from the ashes of Shale, survived the cutting of her throat, and today she is right hand to a prince. For a girl born on a cruddy farm in Nelise, that is not so bad."

His accent that I had found so seductive had faded somewhat, giving way to a more Shalean dialect. But he was still an objectively beautiful man, one that I hated with the fire of the stars themselves.

"Mikhail, you're back," greeted Ordrick. "Were you successful?"

Mikhail shrugged, pouting his lip. "He begged like a dog for the life of his son."

"You didn't spare him, did you?"

Mikhail just stared at Ordrick as though he could not believe he had to ask.

"Have a seat, Mikhail."

"Is there wine?"

"Of course there's wine!" cried Ordrick, motioning for one of his rats to fetch another case. The boys were seated at the far end of the table. One of them stood and went running to the pantry. Mikhail grabbed a chair from the wall and squeezed in across from me.

"Clikk," he said, nodding to me. "At last, we meet again."

Ordrick belted out a hearty laugh. "Can you believe it? Our girl running with pirates! Killing the emperor!"

"Actually, a man named Nicolas Fitz killed the emperor," I corrected. "All I did was put a plan in motion and try not to get my head blown off."

"Don't be modest," said Mikhail. Coming from him it sounded like a threat.

Ordrick leaned to his side to tell Dirk, "We pilfered these crates from a vineyard in Gras. Very potent, very costly stuff. Aged to perfection. The winemaker and his family went on holiday, you see, leaving the property with his ninety-year-old groundskeeper. We swept right in and loaded up everything he had. Who was it brought us the tip?"

"I did, sir," said Remi.

"Remi always gets the best tips," said Ordrick.

After dinner, Dirk stood and gave a clap. "Thank you for this bountiful feast, Ordrick. You are a magnanimous host, truly. Now! Let us crack open some of these crates and show you the weapons we brought you, which you stole, but which were always intended for you." He laughed, evidently drunk on the Shalean wine.

The pirates opened one of the crates with a crowbar and started passing out firepower like candy. Ordrick's grin cut wide as he took hold of a state-of-the-art pocket automatic. He handed it to Mikhail. "Ain't she a beauty?" he said. "One for each of us. Even the rats."

Mikhail nodded, but there was something off about him. He did not look impressed at all. He placed the gun back in the crate with the sorry attitude one might expect from a pacifist. I wondered if Ordrick had lied when he said the revolution was Mikhail's idea, but I could not imagine why he would.

As the empty bottles of fortified wine accumulated on the table, I began to dread the end of our supper.

Mikhail's eyes were on me throughout the evening. He was waiting for his chance to get me alone and grill me on where I had been the last year and a half. When Dirk announced that we needed to depart before it got any later, Mikhail shot up and came around the table toward me. I felt like a mouse backed into a corner with the cat approaching.

Everyone stood up from the table and followed Remi, but Mikhail closed in on me. *Shite, shite, shite,* I thought. It was not that I feared my old lover. I knew Mikhail would never hurt me. What I dreaded was the chance of him asking why I left without a word. For if he had the nerve to think he could pass off some lie or make amends for his deceit, I would have to stab him where he stood, effectively burning our alliance with the Kindred.

I tried to move quickly on the edge of the group, but Mikhail, being so adept at slipping through crowds, reached me in seconds.

He caught me by the arm. "Wait."

"No," I said. "I did not come here for you. Had I know the Kindred were the Aix Resistance, I'd have stayed in Nelise."

"You run away from me. With pirates. Why?"

"I don't owe you anything. Now let go of me before I get angry."

Though we had been whispering, our conversation was observed by Jon Arnault. He broke off from the group and stopped to ask me, "Is everything all right?"

"Everything is fine, Mr. Arnault," said Mikhail. "Clikk and I have much to discuss."

"This dear girl has been travelling all day, lifting heavy crates, and waiting around in a tavern while your leader finished vetting ours. It is past midnight, and Dirk wants his crew ready to leave for Nelise at first light. We must bid you farewell before it gets any later." That chivalrous fool had no clue what he was getting himself into by challenging Mikhail.

"We're fine," I said. "I'll be only a few minutes." As generous as Jon was to worry about me, I found his fuss somewhat vexing. Had I been a man, he would have trusted me to handle this kind of situation myself.

"I don't mind waiting up for you," said Jon.

Mikhail looked close to decapitating him and starting a war between our factions.

"I said we're fine." I had to prod him. "Go on. Tell Dirk I will be there shortly."

Jon, with much reluctance, left me behind. Mikhail and I sat back down at the end of the table. The rats were still clearing plates, but most of the Kindred had retired for the night.

"All right. Say your piece, Mikhail." I crossed my ankle over my knee and slunk back in my chair, glaring at him.

Mikhail held his mouth, leaning into the table. "I hardly know what to say. You are very changed." He gestured to my short hair. "I like this."

"You've changed too. You never struck me as the revolutionary sort."

"Used to be I had more to lose." He gave me a look, implicating me. "Why did you leave?"

"Think very hard, Mikhail, about what you were doing on the day I vanished."

Mikhail sighed, picking up on the temper rising in my tone. "You saw me with Cora."

"Is that what her name was?"

His lips tightened. He nodded. He reached into his breast pocket and laid a block of rosin on the table between us.

"What is that?" I asked.

"Bow rosin."

"I know what it is. Why are you showing it to me?"

"When you ran away, this was all you left behind."

I snatched it up and threw it on the floor, my heart maddened. "You knew what it took for me to trust you, and still you betrayed me."

"I know."

"Listen. We both want this revolution to happen. So it's best we give each other some distance. These wounds are still too fresh."

"Clikk." He reached out and touched my knee. Unlike any other man in the world, when Mikhail touched me, I didn't shrink away from it. "Until an hour ago, I thought you were lost to me. I thought I would never hold my girl again. I made a mistake. And I would take it back if I could. Please. Can you forgive me?"

I stood, eager to flee before I lost my resolve. This was someone who had been the other half of my heart at one time. We were twin souls spawned from the same childhood of poverty and endless loss.

"I am trying to be better at forgiveness," I said, my voice frail for there was deep sorrow welling in me. "Give me time."

Mikhail stood and put his arms about me from behind. It was jarring to feel that powerful wave of rapture fall over me after having gone so long without it. I had consigned myself to the idea that I would never feel that way again with someone. He kissed my ear and whispered, "You will always be my little mouse."

I squeezed his wrist, wishing he would stop but finding myself unable to say anything but, "Mikha." It was the first time I had felt safe in someone's arms since the last time he held me.

It was already too late for me when I agreed to speak to him. I twisted around in his embrace, holding the back of his neck. As much as I hesitated, my desire won out. Our kiss was innocent at first, like a kiss between children, but as we loitered in its rapture, we found ourselves slipping into a more passionate congress. Mikhail hoisted me onto the table, sweeping the plates to the floor as he pushed me down on my back.

"Out, rats!" he snarled.

The children scurried off, giggling. I heard one of them say, "That's Mikhail's girl. She's a master picklock."

Once we were alone, Mikhail's kiss became more explorative, travelling down from my lips to my sternum.

I arched my back, hooking my knee over his shoulder as his mouth trailed down to my belly. All the fun was spoiled when I looked up and saw Jon standing in the steel arch of the tunnel.

"Ahem!" he cried. "Dirk told me to come and fetch you."

Mikhail glared at him, helping me to my feet. He clasped his hands on each side of my head, bringing our foreheads to touch. "Stay," he whispered.

"I can't."

"Sleep here tonight. I will ride you to Nelise myself."

I breathed deep, fighting my urge to be with him. It was futile. "Jon," I said. "Tell Dirk I will find my own way back to Nelise."

"I really don't think that's appropriate—"

"Gods keep you, Jon."

Jon looked positively shocked. "All right then," he said, throwing up his hands.

Mikhail led me out of the dining hall. We followed a tunnel to where he had his own room, a windowless cellar bordered with racks of unlabeled wine. I could see he had come up in the gang. It was a rare thing for Kindred to have private lodgings.

Mikhail struck a match and lit every candle he could find, tucking them in amongst the wine and eyeing me wickedly in the gold and burgundy light. I collapsed against his mattress on the floor, sighing to myself and wondering what all of this would amount to by morning.

Mikhail removed his jacket, tossing it to the floor. He grabbed me by the ankle and untied my bootlace. In my mind, it was like no time had passed. I had never left the warmth of my lover's bed, nor seen him with that other girl. I pretended I was dreaming of my past. It was just me and my Mikhail, a fleeting glimmer of joy in a dark and dreary world.

42

SAME OLD LIES

Beneath a coarse woven blanket, shirtless and slick with sweat, Mikhail and I were twisted up tighter than copper filament, kissing fiercely. He ran his fingertips up my jawline and along the shaved patch on the side of my head.

A stray fantasy drifted through my thoughts as I imagined it was Baker's rough hand caressing me. The thrill of that idea caught me by surprise, and a wave of confusion and anxiety rushed my brain. I tried to muddle through as I ran my nails down Mikhail's back, but suddenly I remembered Baker showing me the scratches he got from visiting one of his girls.

"I'm sorry. I need a second." I pushed Mikhail off, chasing those thoughts from my mind.

"What's wrong?"

"Nothing. I... um... my head's not in the right place." I sat up, facing away from him and put my fingers through my hair.

He sighed, and because he knew my past, he thought he understood. He placed his hand against my back. "You are safe here. This is your home, little mouse."

During our haze of clumsy foreplay, I had toyed with the idea of returning to the Kindred. I could still fight the revolution with the Aix Resistance. I could avenge my parents by liberating my homeland from the Blue Dusk. But then I would be abandoning my captain and crew. I would never make peace with my brothers nor prove myself to them in battle. I could not go backwards. If I returned to my life with the Kindred, I would never be anything more than a stunted weed growing in the shadows of the slums.

Still, I longed to partake in the release I had been without for over a year. I returned to Mikhail's embrace, tasting his mouth and slipping his belt through the loops.

Again, Baker stole into my mind. I remembered opening the belts on his grappling apparatus and stripping him of his shirt after a raid. I could still see the avian tattoos that mapped his bronze physique. The memory compelled me to draw back from Mikhail.

"What is it?" he asked.

I traced the new scar on his shoulder, pretending I had just noticed it. "What happened here?"

"Ordrick."

"What?"

"Remi got nabbed after breaking into a warehouse. We had to bribe the warden to get him out of lockup. As punishment, Ordrick told me to break his fingers. I said no—a thief needs his hands. Ordrick took up a machete, said he'd take my arm—Tch. He tried."

I kissed the mark. "I wish I had been there. I'd have killed him."

Mikhail held my chin, looking long and deep into my eyes. "If you had stayed, I would have deposed him long ago."

"Why don't you?"

"I don't want his job."

"You like yours that much, do you?" It was difficult to forget that earlier that evening Mikhail had carried out the assassination of a man and his son. "Why do you stay here, Mikhail? There's a whole world out there."

"It's my home, my kind." He placed his hand over my heart. "I was not made for anything noble or pure like you."

After saying this, he got quiet. Even after all this time, I could still read him. He was hiding something. He had that same countenance as when I saw him put the pocket automatic back in the crate.

A terrible thought dawned on me, striking my brain like a dart. Was it guilt in his eyes?

"No, you're not, are you?" I whispered, seeing the truth at last. "There's a double-cross in play."

"Clikk," he said in a pleading tone. "I would have never done it if I knew you were with the pirates—"

"What's the ploy?"

Mikhail closed his eyes and lay back into the pillows. "Promise me you will hold your temper."

"Tell me now and I might."

"We heard that Jon Arnault wanted to give weapons to the Resistance. So we impersonated them. It's all been a con for the guns."

The news of this caused a shock in me. I sat up, my hands shaking as I searched for my shirt. "Oh, fuck. Mikha. Tell me this is not happening. No. You're quite serious. I have to warn them."

"It's too late. They've gone. Ordrick has the guns, and he plans to keep them."

"You would have slept with me just now, knowing you had just betrayed me. Unbelievable!"

"I did not betray you. You are Kindred for life."

"I ain't been Kindred in ages! I have a new crew and we are going to war. If we're to stand a chance, we need the Aix Resistance! Fuck! Are they even real?"

"They are. But they'll never ally themselves with the gentry class."

"They have no choice. They'll never win on their own."

"Exactly why we must take advantage. This revolution will spread chaos throughout Shale, leaving her lands vulnerable. Ordrick wants to stake a claim."

"To what end?" I cried.

"Expanding our operation. We could be the next Brotherhood of Blight."

"You aspire to that? Being like the nastiest of the anarchists? They kill women and children. They raid villages and burn everything to the ground!"

"You forget what we are, mouse. I'm certain that if you weighed the wickedness of your heart against that of a Blighter, neither one would tip the scale."

I fastened my scabbard to my belt and started for the exit, turning in the threshold to say, "You've sabotaged our whole campaign. And for what? Your machete-wielding slum king?"

"Come back to bed. You have had a shock, but in time, you will understand why we do this."

"I will never understand why you do anything. Why you lie to me, why you call me 'mouse' and cling to the past." I took up his oil lantern.

Mikhail knew at once what I was thinking. "Clikk. Put it down."

"Tell me why, Mikhail."

"Because I was afraid. Because I love you. I don't want to lose you again."

"Liar." I smashed the lantern into the floor between us. A fire erupted across the oil. It spread like burning rivers over the concrete, flames moving in their dazzling crusade until they reached Mikhail's bed. Mikhail grabbed up his cloak and tried to subdue the flames, but they only grew, raging like the hot spears of hate that burned in my heart. I slipped out, leaving him to burn.

I followed the tunnels to the dining room where the crates had been stowed. They would not get away with this.

"Fire!" shouted Mikhail as he fought the growing conflagration. The air thickened and I felt it shredding my lungs. I coughed through the haze, fighting on. In the dining room, the weapons crates were still piled against the wall. I uncorked one of the barrels of gunpowder stacked beside them. I splashed black powder over each of the containers, connecting them with streams that mapped their destruction.

Meanwhile, the Kindred ran to help Mikhail. As they hurried down the halls, a mischief of actual rodents came rushing out, carrying a chorus of shrieks. An explosion of glass erupted from the wine cellar. The men screamed.

"Seal it off!" bellowed Ordrick.

I tried to strike a match, but my fingers shook so violently it never lit. I did another, and still quivering, pinched the flame. I might not make it out, but I accepted that. I would die before I let the Kindred sweep through Shale, terrorizing its people and recruiting their children into a turf war.

The match fell and ignited the trail of gunpowder, sizzling as it ran up the dust toward the first crate. I fled to the main entryway. My eardrums popped as a series of explosions decimated the dining hall. The last explosion was the most deafening. It had been the end of the gunpowder.

The rodents underfoot swarmed the exit through the cellar door. Oil lanterns and candles lit my way. I kicked as many of them over as I could without slowing my escape. I came out onto the street and sucked clean air into my lungs. The Thieves' Den burned behind me, spewing a pillar of smoke.

I watched and listened to the fire eating away at that subterranean world. Now I had to consider my next move. I had no money.

If I walked all night, I might reach Jon's factory before my crew left at sunrise.

Mikhail came up the steps, out of the fire and chaos below. The smoke had him wheezing severely. The air continued to thicken as Hell burned beneath our feet. Mikhail drew his sword, and I matched him, drawing my own. To his indignation, I also drew Millicent, my Ace in the hole revolver, which I aimed at his heart.

"You would shoot me?" he said.

"If I must."

"I should have left you in that alley to die."

He charged me, holding his sword outstretched behind him until he got close and struck. He was right; I could not shoot him. As we clashed, the smoke obscured everything but our steel. I had to listen to his breath to keep track of his position. He often exhaled hard right before he lunged. Each time his face pierced the thickening fog, I thought I saw my death.

Our two swords danced in the mist. Mikhail's sword, having trained mine, knew every maneuver I felt comfortable making. But he had not been my only tutor.

I used Baker's favorite evasion, which set Mikhail off balance as I came up behind him. Mikhail deflected me over his shoulder, escaping into the smoke. I tried another move I'd seen Dirk use when dueling, a tricky bit of footwork ending in a lunge that targeted the lower rib cage. Mikhail anticipated it and angled his body away just in time. He did not, however, anticipate the dagger I kept in my boot, which I drew whilst in my lunge and used to cut him across the chest.

"Agh!" he cried, his sword spinning out as he staggered backwards. I had cut him deep. Clutching his heart, Mikhail lost his balance and fell against the side of a brownstone. He gripped his blood-soaked shirt, groaning through gritted teeth.

I crouched over him, lowering my voice to a volume barely audible over the sound of his beloved Thieves' Den burning. "So you know, I would have survived just fine if you never found me under that cart. Pray we never meet again, Mikhail."

Mikhail glared up at me. "You will pay for this."

I knelt before him and aligned my dagger's edge with his throat. "If you dare come after me or any of my allies, I will finish what I started here…" I pointed the blade's tip at his chest. "…and I will feed your black heart to my king."

Mikhail bared his teeth, gasping through the pain of his wound. I had no pity left for him, after all that he had done. I fled through the alleys of Aixenport.

Had I really almost gone back to my life in that dark world of his? I did not think I would have ever stayed. I had to face the coming war as my own person, a separate, independent entity from the final set of hands that shaped me as a man.

43

DELAYED

After the hours of rain from the day before, the foliage had taken on a vibrant color. Greenery glittered all around me in the wild grass that stretched across the rolling hillsides. I rode a strong-willed horse along a dirt road, a gray mount with a pale splotch down his nose. His black mane tossed violently each time he fought my commands, but my determination won out. I would reach Nelise before nightfall.

The sun was still high in the sky as I cantered down the avenue. All day, I had been considering how I would deliver the bad news to Dirk. Part of me wished I could simply leave him a note as Maive had done. *Dearest Captain*, it would say, *we been buggered without a kiss. The guns are forfeit. Sorry. Gods keep you.*

Baker emerged from a forest trail, cradling a pair of bird's nests in the crook of his arm. I cast my gaze down modestly, as though I were afraid my indecent thoughts from the night before had somehow gone to him in a dream. I had a hard time deciding if he would laugh at me or cringe with disgust.

Regardless, I thought I should say hello to bridge the chasm that had formed between us. I slowed as I neared him and was about to speak when Lily leaned down from a nearby tree and handed him another bird's nest.

"Clikk!" she called, waving from the branches of that tree.

"Ya!" Smacking my legs against the horse's sides, I shifted my weight forward in the saddle and rode on as though I had not seen them.

I led the horse to the stable, a massive construct fit to house twelve or more of them, and removed his riding gear. Dirk came in as I was brushing the trail off his coat.

"Back already?" he said.

I sighed and went on brushing out the horse's mane, which the beast tossed defiantly.

"I take it your Mikhail has disappointed you."

"To say the least."

"Whose horse is this?" asked Dirk. "Did you steal a horse?"

"Borrowed... indefinitely."

"What happened?"

I leaned against the pen's wood siding. I was exhausted from the long ride. It had given me time to temper my rage, but now the heartbreak of it all was hitting me in full force. "I messed up. The Kindred were not to be trusted. I should have known it."

"Should I sit down?"

I nodded. Dirk pulled a mounting block from the corner and sat upon the highest step. From my learning the truth to burning down the Thieves' Den, I recounted the ugly tale.

Dirk seemed composed at first. The truth had not sunk in yet. He paced briefly and then kicked the mounting block into the wall. The horse reared and thrashed its front hooves. I held the beast's mane and stroked his neck, shushing him. He settled when Dirk began to shush him as well.

"Jon is going to shit himself when he finds out about this. It will be weeks before he can replace what was lost," said Dirk. "Did you have to blow the place to Hell? We could have taken the guns back."

"I didn't want us to suffer casualties fighting over what should have been ours already."

"On either side, I'm sure."

"No. The fire could have killed them for all I cared."

"Even your Mikhail?"

"Especially him. I hope the wound I gave him gets infected."

"All those guns... up in smoke."

"At least they can't use them against us."

"It would not have mattered. Once we make contact with the real Aix Resistance and unite the rebel factions, we will secure Shale in a matter of days."

"Mikhail said they would never fight alongside the gentry class."

"What does that cockroach know?"

"Enough to get the better of us. And your Jon Arnault let it happen."

"Don't put this on Jon," said Dirk. "Jon has a contact, man by the name of Stovel, who puts him in touch with buyers on the black market. Stovel is one of these types who knows everyone. Which was why Jon trusted him to find the Aix Resistance."

"Bastard probably sold Jon's name to the Kindred."

"Might have even helped them cook up the scheme. He's going to have a lot to answer for when we find him."

Together, we walked back to the manor. Dirk said, "Well, I hope you got your fiddle tuned, at least."

It took me a second to realize he was talking about sex. "No. I made the mistake of talking too much beforehand."

"Oh, Clikk," admonished Dirk, clicking his tongue at me. "You should never talk to a lover at all."

After that candid exchange, I was happy to return to living quarters with Molly. She seemed oblivious to the idea that anything untoward might have taken place during my little sleepover.

It stormed endlessly over the next two weeks at the manor. Despite the hopelessness of our rebellion, we had no more deserters. I stayed with Molly and Lily upstairs. Shut away from the men, I would entertain the girls with song or offer lessons in street savvy.

I taught them how to walk with their gaze straight ahead and their hand on their pocketbook. They laughed and teased me for purposefully trying to look unfriendly. I told them that was exactly how one should appear in the city, but those silly girls said I would never meet my true love that way. This led to me telling them about Mikhail and warning them not to give their hearts to a rogue.

"What if you yourself are a rogue?" asked Molly.

"Well, then, you must find a perfectly respectable person and ruin their life," I said.

Shut away on the manor's second story, we had to keep finding ways to entertain ourselves. I guided them through some simple hand to hand combat, but we had to stop when Lily accidentally gave Molly her first shiner.

During this time, Lily procured me a wardrobe of men's clothing more sensible than a footman's uniform. I had a cambric shirt that had been tailored in the village and fitted trousers with gold buttons alongside my calves. I had a dull, gray frock coat and a wine-colored vest, all of which did wonders to make me feel like myself again. She also procured some stovepipe top hats, and one day, all three of us dressed as men of the gentry class and strode about Lily's bedroom with an air of pomp and frivolity. Lily and Molly spoke in silly voices as they condescended to each other with claims of how rich they were and subtle digs about one another's flaccid coat tails. They so aptly satirized society's fops that I could not play along for I was laughing too hard.

Those days it seemed like the sky would never stop weeping for the war on the horizon. And yet it became a time I would treasure all my life. I knew now what it was like to have sisters. And though I would never admit it aloud, I favored them even higher than I had my brothers.

44

Witching Hour

I stood before a long mirror, combing back my hair. The shaved parts over my temples tingled where new growth had sprouted. If I squinted, I could almost look like a man.

I dipped my hands into a water basin, collecting water and splashing my face. When I rubbed my eyes dry and looked about, the guest bedroom had vanished.

Instead of a water basin before me, I discovered the helm of an airship. I glided alone through a cold, dark sky. A disembodied moan on the wind seemed to whisper, "Brace," as I soared into a cloud. I hunched behind the wheel, gripping its foundation. Black feathers scattered like rain across the deck. The howling of the wind rose to a screech. Trembling and creaking, the wood threatened to give out under the force of the mighty gale. I felt afraid. And then, I heard a voice.

"Little one, is that you?" The woman sounded gentle and sweet.

I looked down at myself and saw I was a child again. I wore a faded green farm dress and little ankle boots with heels.

Mother stood beside me, pristine with skin like marble. She knelt and brushed back my long yellow hair. "I'm sorry I wasn't there to protect you," she said.

"I never blamed you." My voice ringing clear surprised me. After years of rasping, I had forgotten the sound of it.

"No, but you throw hate at the world. This isn't what I wanted for you. This isn't what your father would have wanted." Thunder rolled, and my mother veered her head in its direction. "Remember our song, little one. It will protect you."

An orb of crackling light flickered behind the brew of rainclouds in the night sky. The storm overtook the skies around our ship.

"Remember the songs of the sky. You know them all. They are locked deep inside your heart."

"Songs? There were more than one?"

"Hundreds." Her whisper tickled my ear.

When I looked back at my mother, her hair was dark. She was Maive, the witch. Filaments of black smoke and feathers danced on the air around her. They shrouded her in an amorphous set of black wings and then dispersed on the wind. My mother was gone.

"Clikk?" Maive said. "Are you dreaming about your child-hood?"

"S'pose I am," I said, crossing my arms in front of myself.

"What a lovely little girl you were."

"I should cut you for them words." Without any coarseness to my voice, I sounded ridiculous.

The witch squealed with laughter. "You are adorable."

"Yea, all right. You've had your lark. How is the capital? Is Fitz still with you?"

"He is. After the first week, he wanted to return to your crew, but I had need of him. He is the only man here I can trust."

"How is he?"

"Quite well. He begged me to meddle with your dreams. I told him there was no time for that."

"Meddle how? By pretending to be my mother?"

"Your mother? No. We had some ideas. One involved you mar-rying Derek and becoming queen."

"Sounds like more of a nightmare."

Maive swallowed a chuckle. "Will you convey a message to him for me?"

"That's what I'm here for."

"Tell him I have successfully infiltrated Rex's inner circle."

"Rex?"

"General of War."

"I know who he is," I said. "Is he the one in power?"

"He assumed leadership after the emperor's death. Aside from Prince Torrent, there were no other heirs, and so the army of the Blue Dusk seized the palace and placed Locwyn under martial law. Rex intends to rule Elsace by force, crushing any who oppose him. But his opposition is growing. Rumors circulate that Prince Derek is still alive. Every day there are demonstrations in his name, effigies burned in the Old Square, Duskmen fired on in the streets. General Rex grows paranoid. He executes people for crimes as trivial as defacing the flag."

The airship pitched left. The smoky clouds in the distance took on the shape of a skull. That skull broke apart into hundreds of skulls, which broke down into thousands of smaller bones. Skeletal apparitions writhed in agony.

"He arrests people in droves, and then he executes them to clear out room in the dungeons for new offenders. Blue Dusk are permitted to exterminate any and all royalists on sight. No arrests and no trials necessary."

The skeletons ignited and lit up the sky with tongues of orange flame.

"We must act quickly while the Blue Dusk are weakened, while the people still doubt their might and faithfully await their true king. Travel to Windmark. It was the training grounds for Duskmen before a man called Gnash led insurgents in a takeover from within. He was a former knight under the old monarch, and if Derek can prove he is the Luftburg prince returned from the dead, they might be swayed to join our cause.

"The fortress of Windmark is inside a mountain where it snows all year round. It is accessible only by air and one must navigate a border of treacherous peaks to get inside. It would be the perfect site for building a rebel army. It is close to Locwyn. The Blue Dusk is currently too preoccupied with holding the capital to launch an air attack."

The fiery clouds cooled and took the form of a howling mountain the shape of a knight. The mountain wore a crown of jagged rock and spiked gauntlets wet with blood. He unsheathed his saber and tendrils of phantom mist curled about it as if soul-bound. As the smoke cleared, I saw his face, a visage deathly pale like snow, with eyes like frozen water. His smile gleamed in the shine of the moon. Seeing him made my stomach twist into knots.

"This is General Rex," said Maive. "Memorize his face. He must not escape the siege of Locwyn."

I clung to Maive's velvet skirt, hiding from the general's soul-singeing stare. I was still only a dream child, a form that saddled me with an overwhelming sense of vulnerability. "His is a face I shall never forget again," I told her. "He is the monster I have always dreaded, the demon watching me from the shadows. He is darkness itself. The Cerulean Knight."

I woke with a start, inhaling so sharply there came a little shriek in the back of my throat. My heart pounded in my chest. The Cerulean Knight's evil had touched my soul. I could feel his presence humming in my bones. I searched the corners of the room, sat up in bed, and hugged my knees. Molly slept soundly in her bed beside me. There was only us. I told myself not to be afraid and lay back down against the soft mattress. I was not a little girl anymore. And I had call to rejoice. The moment of vengeance was at hand.

My nerves went haywire once more as I heard a gunshot outside. I jumped out of bed and got fully dressed in my cambric shirt, my breeches, and boots.

"Clikk! What was that?" said Molly.

"I don't know." I climbed over her bed and drew the curtain.

Out on the green, we saw Jon Arnault had returned to Belle Manor with a man he held at gunpoint.

"I've brought you Stovel, the snake in the grass who gave my name to the Kindred!"

45

INFORMATION

S tovel was a wiry fellow with an awkward mustache that did not fully fit his upper lip. His hair hung like greasy oil rags on either side of his head. He kneeled before Jon, awaiting a swift execution. At first, he appeared to be praying, but when Molly opened the window, we could hear him plead his case.

"My lord, my good man, I beg you, do not turn me over to sky pirates. I really dislike sky pirates. And they dislike me."

My heart was in my throat when I saw Lily darting from the house in her nightdress and robe. She marched out to meet Jon Arnault and spoke to him in an admonishing tone. All I could make out came at the end, when she shouted, "Put that thing away this instant, or we shall never receive you here again!"

Lord Belle came out soon after that, taking his daughter by the shoulders and placing her behind himself. Jon had already holstered his gun by then. Now Dirk, Mr. Pugg, and Mr. Weston had gone out as well.

"On your feet, Stovel!" shouted Dirk. He took Stovel's collar in hand and shoved him indoors.

"Are they going to kill him?" Molly asked.

I shook my head. "Not here anyway."

The girl stared at me, wide-eyed.

"He'll be all right," I assured her, though in truth I had no idea. A few minutes later, we could hear the lad's interrogation muffled through the walls. Molly and I focused on deciphering pieces of the conversation, helping each other with whatever parts one of us missed.

"Who did you tell about Jon Arnault?" asked one of ours.

"Please, I'm so tired I can't think straight. Mr. Arnault made me ride all night to get here. Let me rest and tomorrow I swear I will explain all."

"Who did you tell about Jon Arnault?" our man repeated. I recognized that deep voice that had always carried so well. It was Baker.

"I told the Kindred. And I am sorry for it. There was no malicious intent. I sell information. It's what I do. I swear to you, though, on my mother's honor, I did tell the Resistance leader as Jon requested."

"The Resistance leader," Baker echoed. I heard Dirk laughing. "Whose name escapes you—"

"I cannot make the same mistake I did when I told the Kindred about Jon. It was a dire mistake, but I don't deserve to die for it."

"What makes you think we want to kill you?" said Baker amicably. "We're only going to inflict suffering on you, but once you tell us, we might very well become friends."

Stovel began to cackle hysterically. "Here's the thing, *friend*. I don't know where these people meet. I don't know what they're planning. All I have for you is a name. And even if I give you that name and you find this person, they might deny everything, and you will think I made it all up under duress. You will come and kill me anyway!"

"Then what do you have to lose?" asked Baker. "Give us the name and tell us where to find him."

Stovel kept laughing. It was a nervous, ongoing laughter that communicated only his fear.

"I'm going down," I said to Molly. "I won't let them kill him."

"Thank you," she said.

I passed Lily, Jon, and her father in the hall. The three of them argued in hushed voices. When they saw me, they all went silent. I followed the jarring sound of Stovel's laughter until I reached the door to the billiard room.

"The leader of the Aix Resistance is a woman," said Stovel.

"You are making this up," said Baker.

"I am not. She's the widow of one of their captains. She staged a coup, aided by her turncoat lover, came out the victim in all of it. But she protected the defectors and grew their operation. She used her survivor's pension to fund her efforts, making the Blue Dusk essentially pay for the revolution against them."

"Never trust a woman," said Baker.

I opened the door and went in. "Never trust anyone," I said from the threshold.

Stovel had been strapped like cargo to the billiard table. Baker was leaning over him, his dagger pointed at the bottom of the man's eye.

"Ah, Clikk," said Dirk. "I thought you'd be in bed."

"Not with your racket. Is this how we extract information? With fear?"

"Baker has a background in interrogation."

"Does he?"

"I'm standing right here," said Baker.

I continued to barely acknowledge him, which Dirk noticed and seemed to find somewhat disheartening. "Yes, Baker was a Blighter before he joined us."

I forgot to breathe when I heard that. The Blighters had a bad reputation throughout Elsace. They terrorized the small villages along the southern edge of the Wastes and dealt in the trafficking of humans and highly addictive substances. I thought I knew everything about Baker. Apparently, I did not. It all made sense now, the ease with which he killed men, the anarchic values he spouted.

"Fuck me," whimpered Stovel.

"Baker's methods aren't very effective," I said. "Stovel here's been selling you a dog."

"No, no, no, no," he stammered, pleading with his eyes. "I would not take that risk."

"But he would. He lives for taking risks." I thought it best that I explained myself. "I know this man from my youth. He frequently sold information to the Kindred in exchange for opium. He's dreadfully addicted. I could have told you not to trust him. For he's a very good storyteller. He'll walk you right into an ambush. Is that your plan, Stovel? Sell us a dog about some black widow and let us walk right into the enemy's clutches. You, sir, have not changed. This is your true king standing before you. And you would put his head on a pike."

"Funny thing," said Stovel, only looking at me momentarily before returning his gaze to the dagger and laughing again. "I remember everyone, Clikk. I know things about you that I could sell to these men right now."

"Go ahead. I have no secrets."

"Only the ones you keep from yourself, right? Mikhail talks when he drinks. He told me a heart-wrenching story once about a girl named Ramona."

"You should kill him, Dirk. He'll not give you anything you can use."

"But I wanted to take his eye out," said Baker. "Dirk said I could." Baker primed his dagger for gouging. The glint of it made Stovel's eyes pop.

"Wait!" he cried. "It's my older brother. The Aix Resistance, that's his project."

Baker laughed, sheathing his blade. "Now this is an interesting turn."

"It's true! His is the only name I swore I'd never sell. Now listen. If you harm me, he will never join you."

"Is he telling the truth?" Dirk asked, looking to me.

One could never really say with Stovel. I doubted he even knew what truth meant anymore. The Kindred always accepted his tips with caution.

"Why won't your brother accept our help?" I asked.

"He's a factory worker. He despises men like Mr. Arnault. He wants to overthrow it all, not just the government. He wants to rebuild the entire country from the ground up. He doesn't care if your man really is the dead prince. He fought in the people's rebellion to overthrow King Lucius and he doesn't want that same regime regaining power."

"I too had my doubts," said Baker. "Until I realized Dirk was different from his father and the kings before him. He ain't doing this for power. As a captain, that weren't how he run his ship neither. Every man got equal shares. Every man had the right to speak his mind and be heard. Dirk ain't no monarchist. He's fighting for a new Elsace, one that hears the people."

Stovel nodded, his breath shaky. "I'm not sure it's a pirate king who can save this country."

"Maybe not, but we can kill us some Duskies for the hell of it," said Baker.

Dirk stepped forward and loosened the belts securing Stovel to the table. "We never had any intention of taking your eye out."

"We didn't?" said Baker.

Dirk shook his head with disdain. "Ignore Baker here. He's skylarking."

Stovel rolled off the edge of the table, springing up with his fists in front of his face. He backed toward the door, glancing between us in a frenzy. He seemed not to believe this was happening. "I can leave?" he asked.

"Yeah, get on," said Baker. "We never get to take anyone's eyes out anymore."

Stovel chuckled hysterically. He sounded like he was about to cry. "I bet you're fun to get drunk with," he said.

"Why don't we have a drink right now?"

Stovel's laugh evaporated into a voiceless hiss in the back of his throat. "Yeah, all right," he said at last.

"The enemy of my enemy is my friend," said Dirk. "Your brother might not wish to ally with us, but we still want to help him in his battles against the Blue Dusk."

"I will remember the mercy you showed me. My brother will hear of it. You know, for pirates, your lot ain't half bad. Let's go have that drink. Oh, and fuck you, Clikk."

He and Baker went out together, laughing and discussing where they could pilfer some of Lord Belle's brandy. I stared at the door a moment, wishing I had said something back before they left.

"Is there something else, Clikk?" asked Dirk.

"Yes," I said, shrugging off the jab. "I had a dream about Maive."

46

PUBLIC SPEAKING

I removed my gloves and wiped my palms down the sides of my trousers. It was nerve-wracking enough speaking my mind to Dirk, and now he had brought me to stand beside him and address a ballroom full of men who distrusted me not only as a woman, not only as a witch, but also as a former member of the Kindred who had ripped them off.

"We have received word from Jon Arnault who says the real Aix Resistance has made contact and will ally with the gentry in the fight for Shale. We, however, will not be remaining in Shale much longer. Our prerogative is to retake the capital. Clikk will explain our next move."

All eyes fell on me. My body tightened, cinching up like a blasted corset. I projected my voice as best I could. Once or twice someone in the back hollered for me to speak up, but he shut his hole after Dirk told him to scrape the wax from his ears. I shared the details of my psychic link with Maive and the information conveyed to me through a dream. The men had questions, which I answered to the best of my ability. In the end, my point was made clear. We needed the rebels at Windmark to liberate the capital.

"Why should we trust these blasted witches?" asked Jasper. "The first witch set the very curse that destroyed the Wastrel."

Sweat slithered down the back of my neck. I curled my shoulders in, looking to Dirk for assistance. He was too busy telling a rowdy bunch on the end to pipe down.

"The witch served the emperor because she was bound to do so by law. Now the order is disrupted and she wants to restore peace under the rule of our true king. We must trust her for we have no better option if we are to take the capital."

"Why don't we take Shale first?" shouted Jasper, getting only more fired up. "We secure one region at a time and close in on the north."

"Do you not hail from Locwyn, Jasper? I know Baker does. Will you not fight for your people there? They are dying in droves under this cruel regime."

"Fuck that city!" exclaimed Jasper. "I left for a reason. So did Baker. Anyone who stayed was an idiot and deserves what he gets."

"Not everyone is free to move about," I said. "There are families there, children, elderly, people too sick to be carted off like… like…" I was so furious I could not articulate how wrong he was to forsake them. The men eyed me strangely, as if they wondered why I had been allowed to speak.

Dirk intervened with all the charisma of a prince and the men's attitude shifted dramatically, their skepticism giving way to utter enthrallment. "Every moment we waste, General Rex is growing his army and securing the capital against a siege. If we do not get to the North soon, the Blue Dusk will spread like a plague across the cities there, growing exponentially, pouring south until they've surrounded us here in Shale. We will be trapped in a battle we can't win. And when the Blue Dusk descends on us, they will crush the rebel factions and take us prisoner. We'll be executed for treason. And it won't just be the common hanging. No. We'll be boiled alive. Burned at the stake. Disemboweled in the old square. We must take our chances at Windmark, or we will never see victory. Clikk, are there any other details you remember about our General Rex?"

"Just one," I said, my voice fading. "He is called the Cerulean Knight." Baker's eyes met mine, and I felt as though the wind had been knocked out of me.

"How will we be rewarded after the siege?" a man asked. A clamor of approbations lifted off the crowd.

I stepped out into the hallway where Lily waited. "How did you do?" she asked.

"Just fine," I said. "Windmark awaits."

"You're going with them?"

"Of course I am."

There was a twinge of something sad in Lily's expression, a kind of misty yearning. "I will miss you," she said. For the past week, I had been grilling her on swordplay every hour of the day, teaching her how to parry, thrust, and sidestep. I was extremely proud of her progress and felt confident that she could take care of herself in the coming war.

She took hold of my hands and brought them to her lips. "I will pray to Throm endlessly for your protection."

"You are very kind, Lily," I said. "I must tell you, you have changed me. For much of my life, I have been distrustful of nobles like yourself. But the kindness you have shown me will never leave me. I will always regard you as a very dear friend."

"Oh, Clikk!" she cried, putting her arms about me. "Be safe, I beg you."

She excused herself for she was becoming emotional and did not want to be seen weeping over me. She went upstairs to wash her face. I was about to go outside for some air when Baker called to me.

"Clikk. Might we talk?"

"What is it you want?"

"To keep my word," he said. "Is Rex the man who killed your parents?"

I turned to face him, cutting through him with a sharp look. "It don't matter. You made that promise to someone else."

"Clikk, we need to talk." He moved out of earshot from the ballroom and motioned for me to follow.

"No, we don't. I'm not your brother anymore," I said, throwing his own words back at him. "Since you found out about me, you have shown yourself to be a petty, close-minded bastard."

"I'm trying to apologize."

"I don't want your apology. I don't want your help. For the first time, I see you clearly, and you disgust me."

Baker donned a mask of indifference as though nothing I said bothered him whatsoever. "Are you done?"

"No. When this war is through, I will be happy to forget your name. I will forget I ever called you friend."

"Strike me then for being the dog I am."

"I don't want to strike you."

"Come on, you ninny. I come from Locwyn's slums. A crack to my head is the only thing I understand."

"I don't want to strike you. It is against the house rules."

"So is shagging our host's daughter and that ain't stopped me."

"How dare you speak of her like that!" I cried in a hushed voice.

"Ain't stopped you neither, has it, brother starling?"

"Degenerate," I snarled. I fled upstairs where he was not permitted to go.

He called aloud, "Give our sweetheart a kiss for me!"

When I was in my room and had shut the door, I fell to my hands and knees, shaking so violently I thought I would explode. I would have never imagined I could hate Baker as much as I did at that moment. In my mind, he had placed an image of him and Lily Belle in the throes of passion. I could not purge that image once it was there. He had taken advantage of that sweet girl.

I ripped the quilts from the trundle bed and flung them into the vanity, knocking over a powder box and a bottle of perfume. This place, this girl, all of it had been a precious memory in the making, and now Thomas Baker had tarnished it.

47

THE ECLIPSE

We were bound for the treacherous mountains of Windmark. With an assortment of clean clothing stowed in my knapsack, my new violin on my back, and Millicent holstered under my arm, I felt restored in my sense of self. Perhaps I was not a man and would never hold my brothers' esteem in quite the same way again, but that seemed to matter less to me knowing I had found sisters in young Molly and dear Lily Belle.

Outside the men were loading weapon crates onto a caravan of carts and wagons. Pierce stood on one end of a cart, supervising—or rather, barking incoherent orders as to where the weapons should be placed.

"Oi!" I cried, running up and grabbing a corner of a crate as the men heaved it up. "Let me help," I said, trying not to grunt as I felt the true weight of the cargo.

"Don't get your knickers in a bunch," said Pierce. "You want to help, go get us some water."

"Yes, sir." I paid no heed to the slight for he still outranked me. Pirate no longer, I had to learn to be a soldier. As Dirk had said, this meant I would need to follow orders. With a rigid salute, I took off toward the well some distance from the house.

It was nearly dawn, and a veil of periwinkle sky stretched over the swaying fields of grass. Little bluebirds peppered the meadow, pulling worms from the earth. I thought to myself, as I trudged through the tall grass, that this morning had a distinct feeling of finality to it. It was an end of rest, an end of peace. War would soon be a permanent fixture in my life. And if I survived, it would be a permanent fixture in my soul as well.

I lowered one bucket after the other and carried each on the end of a long stick. My shoulders could bear the weight. I held back when, returning with the water, I saw Baker loading a crate. Why was he still here? He cared little for revolutionary ideals and even less for me. And yet here he was.

I hoisted my stick over my head and laid the buckets down gently. The men came with their tin cups, dipping them and rehydrating.

When our cargo was loaded, and it was time to set off for the Skyport tower in Aixenport, Dorian put us into a cart reeking of hay and animals. It might have offended anyone else to be carted around like pigs, but in truth, our company smelled fouler than any barnyard menagerie imaginable. The dunderheads had washed their clothes in a pond just several acres from the house and, not considering the shade of the woods, thought hanging them on trees should help them dry. Now they reeked of mildew and sweat.

Dirk sat in the driver's box beside Dorian, and the remaining twenty in our company climbed into the cart.

Pierce plopped down next to Baker, chewing a sprig of lavender. He had a discerning scowl on his face as he looked between us. "What's eating the two of you?"

Baker glared at his friend, and Pierce laughed.

"Sorry I asked."

I considered crawling up to the box seat to sit with Dirk, but there were already rumors about us, about why he allowed me on his ship in spite of knowing my secret, and what might have happened in the carriage on the road to Aixenport. I'd overheard Jasper telling some of the men that he didn't want Maive cursing us again if she found out.

Something white fluttered in the corner of my eye. Lily came running over from behind the house. She wore a light ruffled garment with a pristine apron, which she carried out in front of her, for it was full of apples.

Baker turned his back to her, idling himself with pulling strands of hay out from between the wood planks of the cart. I felt something twist in my heart. If he did lie with her, he was resolved to ignore her now.

Lily reached the edge of the cart and called to me. "Clikk! Oh, Clikk! Thank goodness I did not miss you!" She hopped up on the spokes of the wheel and spilled her apples onto a hay bale. "Please take these for your journey! And do be careful!"

"I will," I assured her. "Will Molly not come down to say goodbye?"

Lily exhaled a listless sigh, glancing over her shoulder toward the house. "She went out to take the air this morning and has not returned. I will tell her you asked after her."

"Thank you. Gods keep you, Lily."

She kissed both my cheeks. "Safe skies." Looking past me, she noticed Baker and called to him, "Mr. Baker! How dare you try to leave here without saying goodbye to me?"

Baker offered a reluctant smile, using Pierce's broad shoulder as a foundation as he stood and slung his body over the edge of the cart.

"Lady Belle," he said, bowing. "Gods keep you. I would kiss you for luck, but your father is watching."

Surely enough, Dorian craned his neck to observe his daughter's conduct.

Lily hopped down from the wheel, smiling. She folded her hands behind her back and meandered toward Baker. "I am glad to have known you, sir. It is an honorable and selfless thing you are doing."

Baker crossed his arms, the corner of his mouth pulling. "Careful," he said. "You might talk me out of it."

My heart pounded as the distance between them shrank. Some magnetic force of nature compelled the two closer. Dorian sat up a little straighter in the box. His knuckles tightened as he gripped the back of his seat.

"In that case," said Lily, "may this last farewell give you courage in the coming battles." She went up on her toes and kissed him pertly on the lips.

Pierce snickered in my ear. "Oh, I see. You let a woman come between you."

"Shut it." I looked to Dorian whose face now darkened to a vivid shade of chartreuse.

"Lily!" he shouted.

She seemed not to hear him over the riotous cheers of the men. Emboldened by the support of his brothers, Baker grasped Lily's hair and opened his mouth against hers, holding her waist and tipping her back a little.

"Unhand my daughter this instant!" bellowed her father.

Lily pulled away, spinning out of Baker's arms and giggling helplessly. "My!" she exclaimed, gasping for breath.

"I am much obliged, my lady," said Baker, winking as he climbed back into the cart.

Dorian fumed. "I should box your ears, you vile man!"

Derek patted the old man's shoulder and said, "Come now, Dorian. It's just a kiss."

"Just a kiss? *That*, I dare say, was hardly what any gentleman should consider 'just a kiss.' It is unbecoming of anyone to kiss

like *that*. We will talk about your behavior when I return, Lily!"
Dorian whipped the horses and gave a shout. The cart sprung forth
with a powerful thrust and off we went.

I bit into one of the sweet apples and gave another to Pierce
and one to Baker. They might have irked me, but I was not so bitter as to hoard the apples all to myself. No fruit was so fresh and
flavorful as those that came from Shale.

As we got farther and farther away from the house, all the men
prodded Baker for details, wondering how Lily's mouth had felt
and tasted.

"Her father's right there," answered Baker with an admonishing
shake of the head. "I'd like to at least make it to the Skyport alive."

"Soft, sweet girl like that," said Pierce, sucking spit through his
teeth. "We won't see a girl like that for a long time."

"At least we've got Clikk!" cheered Jasper, and I looked at him
with hate in my eyes. "She's a woman, and she knows how to fight,
fiddle, pick locks"—he counted my skills on his fingers—"fix our
junk when it breaks, clean a rifle—"

"Aye," chuckled Pierce. "She'll clean all our rifles, won't she?"

The men laughed and Pierce knocked my shoulder playfully.
Baker scowled at him but said nothing. He lay back in the hay,
closing his eyes.

"More like your pistol, Pierce," I bit back, and the men laughed
even harder at that.

For rest of our journey into town, I decided it best to keep quiet.
I lost myself watching the scenery of Shale. The calm sights of the
country soothed my indignation over Lily's involvement with Baker
in spite of all my warnings. I came to understand and accept how
important it might have been to her. Even though she would receive
her father's verbal lashing later, she had seized the pirate whoreson at
her pleasure. Everything fun made fathers furious, after all.

We reached Aixenport by noon. The shadows had receded and townsfolk took refuge in the pubs. I dabbed my sweaty forehead with the cuff of my sleeve, clenching my jaw as our cart rattled on the cobblestones.

We disembarked outside the Skyport, a series of stone towers flecked with airships of every sort, some with the standard balloon and gondola, some with propellers that sliced the air, and a few with membranous leather wings that caught the sun and showed spindly veins in their silhouettes.

"That one's yours, the Eclipse!" said Dorian, pointing to a great black beast of a ship. When I saw her, I could not help but whistle.

Her suspended gondola shined black like wet obsidian, sharp and menacing at the bow. Her oblong balloon shined silver, a third painted black and divided by a C-curve. Instead of being propped on the engines, the sleek turbines abided within a black steel cowling.

"She's beautiful," I whispered. I climbed out of the cart with the others and we followed the cobbled street to our ship's tower. Dorian shook each of our hands—all except Baker's—and gave each of us a folded piece of linen paper that listed the airship's amenities and unique features—except Baker, because Dorian said he should keep one for himself.

The Eclipse had earned her name after an older model was essentially eclipsed by superior technology. She was of the same generation as the Wastrel, but had been installed with electric engines, reserve gas cells, showers, heat, and plumbing. Another lovely upgrade was the helium element filling her balloon.

Stairwells unhinged and dropped open at the bottom of the gondola. Skyport personnel began loading our weapons into the cargo hold. I was next to board when I noticed something amiss on one of the gun crates: an open padlock. Had some of the deserters robbed our cache? I followed the loading crew up an incline into the back of the ship.

The hold was dim. I saw the shadows of two men as they slid the crate off a dolly and between another two boxes.

"Gods, that were an 'eavy one," exclaimed one of them. They chuckled and went out again, not seeing me crouched in the dark.

I approached the crate with as much caution as one approaching an engine taken by flames. I held my breath, removed the padlock from the latch, and lifted the lid to the crate.

Both of us screamed. There lay Molly amidst the hay and automatic weapons.

48

STOWAWAY

I pulled her out by the arm, whispering, "What are you thinking, child? Come with me now before we lift off."

"I will not stay in Shale while you go off to die!" she growled,
fighting my grasp.

"It is a selfish thing you've done, girl. You're our backup, and
we need you safe and hidden away. We must go and find your
brother."

"No!" Molly twisted her arm away and darted through the
hold.

"Molly!"

She reached a ladder and climbed up like a mad little monkey. I
tried for her ankle, but she had already opened the trapdoor above
and went through before I could get her. The engines came on and
began to shake the ship.

I climbed up into an engine room and caught sight of the girl's
pink skirt as she fled into the passageway. The compact passages
wound through the belly of the ship. Molly slipped into the mess
hall and made a sharp left, stumbling into one of the metallic tables
that were bolted against the wall. Baker and Pierce were seated at
one such table, and as we came in, their conversation evaporated,
and they stared at us as if we were a pair of unicorns prancing
through.

"Gentlemen," Molly greeted, bouncing in a slight curtsy.

I stood in the doorway, holding both sides as the ship lurched into motion. Molly lost her balance, and Pierce stood halfway to catch her.

"Ah. Thank you," she said, holding the back of a bench as she pulled away from him.

"You have to hold onto something at takeoff, pet," said Pierce, sitting back down. Molly sat down on the bench beside him and all three of them gripped the table. I held fast in the threshold, look-ing at Baker, noting his grim countenance. The windows went gray as we rose up in a dense mist. Molly squealed, and her effervescence put a smile on Pierce's face.

We floated like a bubble breaching the surface of water, rising higher than the birds in an instant. As my ears popped and that rush of adrenaline hit me, I could not resist the urge to grin a moment longer, but I soon noticed Baker was not smiling with the rest of us. A hard expression stole across his features.

A man is different when he doesn't smile, and while Baker was a good friend to have on a pirate ship, he made a terrible enemy. When I called him a petty, small-minded bastard, I had neglected to remember that he could snap my neck with his bare hands. He was a hardened criminal, a former Blighter. To him, stealing was the same as earning, and killing meant nothing because the whole world had been out to get him from the start.

"Come on, Molly," I said. "We are going to see your brother now." We left the mess hall and went to find the captain's quarters. We followed a narrow corridor to its end and took the stairwell to Level B. Dirk's chamber occupied this floor.

"Captain," I said, knocking on his vaulted door.

"Come in!" he called.

The door squealed as I pulled it open.

What this new ship lacked in adornment, it made up for in utility. The berth was above a row of wooden drawers and beneath a lofted storage closet. It had a rail that slid up and down to keep the sleeper from falling out.

Dirk was attaching his hammock to a hook on the wall. He did not look up. "I don't see why you should have to bunk with me. You must know your brothers would never harm you. Those who are still with us are the most honorable men I've ever known. But not to worry, Clikk. I want you to be comfortable. And so I will sleep in this hammock like a blasted swabbie."

"Would you trust these good-hearted pirates with your own sister?" I asked.

Dirk looked up from his work with the hammock clews, and when he saw Molly standing next to me, his levity was gone. "What are you doing here?"

"I will not be sent away again," she said. "From now on, wherever you go, I go as well."

"Have you taken a knock to the head, girl? It isn't safe."

"I am safer with you than I am amongst strangers."

"We are going to war, Molly! I cannot accommodate your needs. What are you to wear? Are you going to start dressing like Clikk and bathing once every other full moon?"

"I bathe more often than that, Captain," I murmured, though neither of them seemed to hear it.

Molly went to Dirk's luggage trunk. "I made preparations, brother." She opened it up, pulling out several of her dresses as well as a thick brown envelope. "I've brought my own clothes and my own entertainment."

"Was this your doing, Clikk? Have you already forgotten all that I said about following orders?"

"I'm the one who found her stowed away in a crate of firearms—"

"Molly, is this—what are you doing?" he cried.

I turned to discover Molly working on some messy project. Loose hair lay scattered like a fine mist across the metal floor. The child wove the strands into coils and was mounting it on cardstock.

"Is that?" I gasped. "Is that my hair? Or rather Fiona's hair?"

"Who?" Molly asked.

"For love of Throm, clean that up! This is a shared space!" barked Dirk.

"Sorry," she said, collecting the hair back into the envelope. "I just wanted something to keep busy."

"I'm sure Clikk will think of something appropriate," he said.

"Captain. I really am not fit to look after the girl."

There was a pinch of salt in his tone as he said, "No, and yet you continue to have such an influence on her. I am turning this ship around. Molly will be returned to Dorian Belle. And both of you will stay in here until we moor."

"If you send me back, I will run away," said Molly. "You cannot control me anymore, *Captain Dirk*. I will find my way to the capital and join you in the fight to retake our father's throne. You cannot stop me, for I too share the blood of conquerors."

"Molly, what is this about?" Dirk demanded.

"Our shared destiny, brother. I am not your rook to be tucked away on the fringes of the board. This is my battle too."

"Oh!" Dirk burst out laughing. "Do you want to lead the charge then?"

"I wish only to stay with you!"

"Why? Why must you be so difficult?"

Her eyes welled with tears, but she did not cry. She met his gaze and said calmly, "Because you are my brother. You are the only family I have left."

Derek was speechless. He looked at me, almost expectant that I should have something to add. I did not. All of it seemed too much for him.

"Fine. You can stay," he said. "Go on. Get settled." He went into his luggage trunk and retrieved a flask from one of the leather pockets. Then he left us, sealing the door behind him.

Molly's face blanched as white as a cloud. "Clikk," she said. "Does my brother hate me?"

"No. You know he doesn't."

"He has never wanted me around. First, he sent me away to school. Then, he tried marrying me off, and when that didn't work, he tried leaving me at the Belle Manor."

"It's not that he doesn't want you. I think it has more to do with a promise he made your mother many years ago when you were just a little girl."

She asked me what I meant. Perhaps it was not my place, but I told her what Dirk had said about their escape from the Black Spire and his promise to his mother to keep Molly safe. He might never have the courage to share the story himself.

This explanation worked only to upset her further, and I thought it best to distract her with an activity. I went into my own luggage sack that was hung from the metal bed frame. Inside was the Cecil Lariat Lily had gifted me.

"Let's write a song, something to motivate our men before the siege of Locwyn."

The task of writing a song with a thirteen-year-old girl proved a regrettable idea. Over the next twenty-four hours, I came to despise myself for suggesting it. Molly and I rewrote it over and over, loving it at times, hating it at others. Molly handled the lyrics while I composed a standard uplifting melody, but everything kept changing until we both arrived at the conclusion that we wanted it to be done. We played our final version for Dirk on the second night of our journey, Molly singing while I accompanied her.

Rebels of the rising sun,
Royalists assemble,
Unite and slay tyranny,
In our wake, they will tremble.

Arise and see the light that tears
Through the clouds of a midnight dark.
'Tis your King, 'tis the rising sun,
Resurrected and crowned by the gods.
Raise your sword at your captain's behest,
Run them through, disembowel the rest.
Arise, Elsace!
Arise.

"A bit macabre, don't you think?" commented Dirk.

"The old anthem had an entire verse about the entrails of corruption," Molly pointed out.

"I see. Well, you're entitled to your creative license, but we will not be using that for the anthem."

My stomach flipped when, for a moment, we lost altitude. Early signs of worry wrinkled Molly's brow.

"No worries, child. Only a bump on the air," I told her.

The ship rattled with such violence that put even me on edge. It tossed like a carriage speeding over cobblestones. Molly gasped and clung to the bedpost. "I don't want to go to Windmark anymore! Can I change my mind?" she cried.

"Molly. You needn't fret! It's only turbulence!"

"Aye," said Dirk. "No sister of mine is going to be afraid of a little rough air."

"The last time I was on an airship, it was blown to bits!" she cried.

"Shh, don't talk about such things," said Dirk in a low whisper.

"Why? Why not? Clikk?"

I tried to ease her concern with a gentle chuckle. "Airmen have silly superstitions. They believe that if you talk about... *such events...* they are likely to happen again."

"Are they?" she cried, her eyes going electric.

I scratched my throat and squinted at her sideways. "No, no, this is a very safe ship, and the journey only takes two nights."

"We could be attacked again! Has a ship been sighted? Is that why we're bouncing like this? We're fleeing?"

"Unlikely, and if we were, you're on a ship full of pirates. We'll keep you safe."

"Do you promise nothing bad will happen? Promise we will get there safely."

"I can't promise anything, but the likelihood of something happening is very small. And you've got only a few days ahead of you on this ship. I've spent weeks at a time in these old birds without incident. These ships are built to withstand all kinds of things, and this one is shiny and new—"

"Molly, you should sit down and hold onto something," interrupted Dirk.

As she and he went to the floor and held fast to the bedframe, I continued to saunter about, hoping it would put her at ease.

"Rough air is no big deal, my girl." We lurched, and I showed how easy it was for me to keep my balance.

Molly chuckled, though her eyes were damp and bloodshot. "Don't you ever get scared, Clikk?"

"Course I do! And sick to boot! But flying is too much fun to let that get in the way!"

There was suddenly a bone-shaking boom that rattled the cabin enough to knock me off my feet. The lights flickered out.

49

THE STORM

A red bulb came on in the corner of the room.

"Those bloody idiots!" Dirk snarled, jumping up and hastening into the passageway.

"Clikk!" Molly wailed, crawling to me and clasping my hand in hers.

"It's only a bit of lightning, my girl. You'd be surprised how common it is for lightning to strike the ship." I saw the terror flashing in her eyes. An imminent fall had already swept through her mind. "The reserve power will keep our engines serviced. Nothing to worry about. I'd best go help your brother." I put my violin and bow away in their case and strapped everything to my back. If we were going down, I wasn't losing my Cecil Lariat.

"Don't leave me here!" Molly cried as she chased me into the passageway.

I nodded, taking her arm. "Come on, then. Keep up."

We traveled down narrow hallways, following the rows of red lights along the runners. The ship slid on the wind, and we fell against the wall. Molly screamed, catching herself. I heard shouts overhead in the engine room. Something was not right in there, so up we went.

"Clikk! I'm scared!"

We came around the bend of the staircase. On the next level were some parachutes, so I ripped one off the wall and handed it to Molly.

"Take off your dress and put this on. Quickly." I helped her strip down to her chemise and bloomers; then she stepped into her harness, and we secured the belts. I went over the cords with her. "When the altimeter on your wrist reads a thousand feet, pull this. If that don't work—look at me now—if that don't work, pull this one immediately."

She sobbed uncontrollably. "I don't want to fall again. I don't want to. Please, Clikk."

"Why not? They say first time's the scariest. Second time's a blast!" I pulled the child along into the engine room. The men were shoving random debris into a furnace. I began to understand what was going on. Our electric engines were shot, and we were dead in the air.

The Eclipse's induction engines had been built right on top of its original steam engines, coils wrapped around the old form. The men gathered old maps, books, hammocks, and whatever else they could scrape together to shove on the flame. With good old steam heat and pistons, they fueled the antique engines to propel our ship.

"If it's not bolted down, burn it!" Dirk hollered over the rumble of the old engines breathing life. He labored alongside the men, breaking down any timber he could find to fuel the flames. "We're all dead if we can't get out of these winds!"

I could hear the riveted panels moaning beneath the howl of the storm. High enough wind speeds could rip us open bow to stern, and if we didn't get moving, it was only a question of when.

Lightning burst like a cannon blast, striking the ship again. A steel cable snapped outside. The engine room jerked, and we all took a spill.

"Oh, will you look at that!" Jasper growled, throwing his finger at Molly. "I knew a woman on a ship was bad luck! And our fool of a captain has two of 'em up here."

The wall sucked me up flat against it. Molly screamed and, as the wall pulled her in, she didn't stop. Her wail made my eardrums throb.

"Jaz! Climb up into the envelope and flood that balloon with helium!" Dirk shouted, crawling on the wall. He made it over to the lever that manually released ballast and gave it a hard yank. Jasper battled against gravity and climbed the central ladder. It traveled directly through the mast into the lower section of the balloon, where helium tanks could be manipulated directly. "Clikk!" shouted Dirk. "Take that sealant there and go patch the balloon!"

The pull eased up as Jasper filled the bird with lift. Our spinning sink was under control at least for now. I secured my footing. The wall with the tool fastener was closest to me, so I grabbed the sealant gun off its tether and dashed toward the stairwell. Molly came chasing after, pleading for me to stay with her. I could not. I had orders.

Rain pummeled the balloon like thousands of pins colliding with tin. Visibility came and went as black clouds drifted across the deck. We were caught in a swarm of darkness and danger so much greater than ourselves. The wind roared and tore several railing pegs out at their roots.

"Hold onto something, and if you must, jump!" I told Molly.

I could not know she had heard me over the wind until I saw her wrap her arms and legs around the center mast. A steel cable had come loose from the balloon. It undulated like a wild serpent, smacking the body of the gondola. I leapt onto the cable that ran alongside it and shimmied toward the envelope, sealant gun clenched between my teeth.

White light flickered. My heart skipped a beat as crackling thunder cried out for my body and soul. The pouring rain blinded me. The wind ripped off my flight cap. My hair, instantly drenched, clung to my face. Weather fabric rolled on the wind, rippling violently. I pulled it over a beam of the balloon's skeleton, took the sealant gun in hand, and aimed at the leak, squeezing the trigger hard. Silver gunk oozed out and bonded the gash.

A gust of wind lifted me off the cable and the sky swallowed my gun. I flew toward the stern, barely catching myself on the rail. My body flailed on the wind. Soon every muscle in my arms ached and began to tremble and burn against the force of the moving ship. The sky opened its ghastly maw to claim me.

"No!" Molly's strident screech tore through the wind roar.

I felt a pair of hands tighten around my wrists like hose clamps. I looked up, squinting through the dense rainfall. Molly reeled me in, emitting a fierce cry as she harnessed all her strength. She truly was her brother's sister.

I thought she might rip my arms right out of their sockets, but she succeeded in getting me over the rail. We collapsed against the deck, shivering, our clothes soaked through.

"Make it stop!" she cried.

"I can't!"

"Please!"

Hearing Molly weep broke my heart, but there was nothing I could do about the storm. Thunder ruptured a nearby cloud. A sea of rainfall surged on the wind, drowning us. I was reminded of the dream I had about my mother when the black feathers had overtaken the deck. I recalled my mother's last words to me.

"Remember our song, little one. It will protect you."

The siren song. I had to try it. If it could make a girl stop crying, perhaps it could have the same effect on the sky. I took my violin off my back, opening the case. I got up into a kneeling position, my instrument perched against my chest, and played my mother's siren song.

A flash of light danced across the storm curtain and a distant boom echoed through the skies. I focused my mind on each and every note, hearing my mother's voice singing it as clearly as she did the day before she died.

"How strong you are, Mona!" I could remember her saying to me once. I had carried a bag of animal feed as tall as me. I brought it to the barn all by myself without any wagon, and mother laughed and told me, "You'll be strong like your father."

The rain softened to a gentle hush, a sound like she used to make before singing me that lullaby. The clouds thinned. The winds quieted.

My music relieved Molly's distress as well. She caught her breath and exhaled mystified, silent laughter. "It's working!"

The ship stabilized and rode the air currents smoothly. The night sky cleared well enough that we could see the moon and its entourage of stars between patches of mist. Dirk and the rest of the crew came up. All stared in a state of wonder as the clouds dissipated and the air went still. I continued to play as a precaution against any more bad weather.

"So women are bad luck, hmm?" Molly snapped at the crew. "Was it not men who built those finicky engines? And did not a man fly us directly into the squall?"

"You are absolutely right," said Dirk. "Like I said, men, superstitions are only worth the theories behind them, and as long as everyone treats one another with respect, we shouldn't have any problems."

"I demand an apology!" said Molly. "Which one of you called my brother, your captain, a fool? Which one said I was bad luck?"

Jasper stepped forward, hanging his head. "I apologize, little miss," he said. "The storm had me panicked."

"I am no little miss," she corrected. She marched up to Jasper and glowered up at him. "I am one of the last two surviving heirs to the throne. I am the princess of pirates, and if anything happens to my brother, I will be your queen. If you follow him, then you follow me as well." Her fearless pride brought a smile to my face. I leaned into my violin to hide it.

I'd caught some men captivated with my song, staring at me as if I were communing with the gods. Their astonishment persisted. Their whispers filled the air but reduced to a hush as Jasper took a knee and kissed Molly's hand. "Forgive me, Princess."

50

WINDMARK

The mountain pass known as Windmark was intolerably cold. I had never before suffered so much during a mooring. People called this region the frozen tiara because it capped Elsace to the north. The landscape lived up to its moniker with icicles tapering down from the cliffs. The outpost lay high in the snow-peaked mountains. We soared through a collage of black and white on either side of us. The craggy surface came so close to our ship's flanks that I could have reached out and caught snow in my hands. A gale rushed over the deck, speckling beards with frost. My blue-lipped brothers smacked their numb fingers against themselves and huddled for warmth.

We were traveling in the midst of a mild blizzard. I was grateful to have Lily's velvet mantle as Windmark produced temperatures that tested my physical limits. The garment smelled of lavender and hay, of Shale itself. The scent took me back to the warmth of my native province. I could have never imagined how much I would be missing Lily Belle.

I was glad Molly had come along against her brother's wishes, but as we neared the rebel outpost and moved amidst the silence and stillness of the cliffs, the potential for danger became suddenly tangible, rendering her presence all the more agitating. She was, at least, safely stowed below in the Captain's Quarters.

"Eyes!" shouted Dirk. This command told us to watch for threats. I surveyed the floor of the crevice, as I imagined they might try shooting us down. We were invading their airspace without warning.

"Mountain wall, port side!" called out a crewman.

"Mountain wall, starboard!" called out another.

I examined the mountain wall on my left and saw one of them. The Windmark rebels wore grey spotted furs that camouflaged them against the snow. Once I realized this, I could see all of them clearly, hanging off the cliffside from hooks and rappelling rope. They thronged against the rock wall, more and more emerging from concealment. They were everywhere.

Twenty or more of them boarded us, jumping down from the looming cliffsides and landing with heavy thuds. They were the most emaciated warriors I had ever seen, but they were vicious, wielding bastard swords longer than my torso. A haggard man who stood a full foot taller than me landed nearby. His long grey hair and beard were thick with frost, his eyes harsh and full of hate. He swung his hefty blade at my neck. The steel sang as it sliced the air. I leaned back, just barely avoiding decapitation. I didn't need any more scars on my throat.

On his next incoming blow, I drew my short sword and deflected; the impact between our blades knocked me right off my feet and sent my sword flying. Down came his mighty weapon, about to cleave me in half. I rolled out of the way; I could hardly breathe.

"Stand down!" bellowed Dirk over the clinking fury of battle. "We surrender!"

I put my hands on top of my hood. The ogre of a man who had nearly killed me sheathed his blade and marched directly toward Captain Dirk. "State your purpose here," he growled.

"We seek the rebels of Windmark. Having just slain the emperor and his son, we believe we share similar goals."

"So it's true?" the man grunted. "The emperor is dead?"

"Oh, yes. After a few minutes of carefully aimed burst fire, there was hardly anything left of him." Dirk's tense mouth gradually eased into a smile. It was a smile posed as a question. Was the stranger pleased to imagine the emperor obliterated by machine guns? His beard was too thick for us to read his expression.

"I am Gnash," said the man, offering his arm. "Commander of the rebel cause here."

"Dirk, former captain of the Wastrel." They shook hands.

"I've heard of you," said Gnash, "They say those who forgo surrender to Alexander Dirk meet the clouds. I'm flattered you should yield to us so quickly."

"I cannot afford any loss of life. I seek an alliance against our true enemy."

"We are always taking in new recruits. Currently, we are sending ships to raid the supply chain to Locwyn. You would be a prime candidate for this kind of work. If you are ready to kill Blue Dusk, we are ready to house your men and share what resources we have."

"I don't just want to kill Blue Dusk," said Dirk. "I want to eradicate the order. I aim to sack Locwyn and retake what is rightfully mine by birth." Dirk reached into his breast pocket and presented his golden signet ring. Commander Gnash took one look at it and fell speechless. "I was born Prince Derek Alexander Xavier von Luftburg. I became a pirate after Perceval killed my family. Having lived the life I've lived, I want to change this nation forever. No more Blue Dusk. No more haughty royals. A king who respects the needs of the many. You served my father once. I know your loyalties may have changed, but I swear to you, I am the man who will save Elsace."

Gnash nodded slowly. He turned to his crew. "People have likely told you that Lucius von Luftburg was not a great king, and maybe that's true, but when I served him, I knew him to be a man of honor, a man who truly wanted a better world for his people. But a king cannot will the rains to come any better than a farmer. He cannot always see or stop the corruption festering amidst court officials.

"I was there the day Blue Dusk took the castle. We led our king through a secret passage. We made it into the great library and took to the city streets. It was then we saw Perceval push Prince Derek, his mother, and siblings out onto the balcony that overlooked the mob. Duskmen put steel at their necks and the people screamed for blood.

"Perceval proclaimed the king a coward and said he would kill one member of the royal family each hour until he gave himself up. Lucius did not hesitate. He told me he had a duty to his children and before I could stop him, went running into the square."

Dirk nodded. "A day I'll never forget. The mob surrounded him. Like animals, they tore away his clothes, beat him to death with stones and clubs, and mutilated his body, taking his head and lifting it on a spike."

"Ever since that day, I've longed to make it right," said Gnash. He addressed all of us. "The people paraded the king's head in front of the castle, in front of his wife and children. That was the day the riots broke out and the shell blotted out the sun."

There was a murmur of disgust and anger.

"I was born in Locwyn and I'll be damned if I can't die there too!" shouted Dirk. He brought his sword high overhead. "The usurper is dead! Follow my lead and we shall take back Elsace!"

"Elsace!" Gnash roared, raising his sword. The men cried out and thrust their blades toward the sky. Their echo exploded through the mountains.

Gnash rode at the bow of the ship, one foot firmly planted upon the bowsprit. He signaled for his men to stand down and give us passage. We descended into a vast plain of snow sheltered by tall rock walls and a flat overhang of stone.

Rebels came out to greet us, at least three hundred men. They stood in rows, formidable as stone in spite of the cold. We tossed ladders over the rails of the Eclipse, and our men began to disembark, either climbing down or going through the belly of the ship to take the hatch access stairwell.

I strapped my violin on my back and was starting toward the rail when a huge snowball hit me in the side of the face. I brushed the frost off my shoulder and turned, ready to chastise Molly.

I was taken aback to see Baker standing a ways off with his hands plunged deep in his pockets. He stared over the edge of the stern, humming a sky shanty to himself, then he looked at me and smiled.

51

―

NOT ONE TEAR

More men arrived each day, and within the fortnight, we were a thousand strong. Dirk used the rebel unit's airships to visit the villages surrounding Locwyn. Every few days, a shipload of new recruits would fly in. The wan, malnourished creatures with cheerless faces would queue up at the mouth of the cavern and sign their names in the roster.

They didn't speak much, but when they did, they spoke of the devastation across Elsace, how the city economies had collapsed, how quickly everything they owned was gone. While the army and government officials received daily rations, the rest of society had to fend for itself. Many found themselves left with no choice but to either pick up arms as Duskmen or live outside the law.

Unfortunately, with our diminished supplies, we had little more to offer save a bowl of oily slop and a mug of our rotgut brew. Without the means to rehabilitate these soldiers, we had to make our last stand as soon as possible.

We slept underground. Our cots were buried in the mountain caverns, arranged in rows. Dirk and Molly had their own tent, a more private dwelling where he could keep a close eye on his sister. I wanted to live amongst our men. I felt it would bring us closer together in the coming battle. Though it was often dark and there were people I did not know, I felt confident in my role here as a faceless soldier. The low light aided my masquerade. While officers kept oil lanterns, the rest of us had to make our way by the light of campfires littered throughout the hall.

I believed this to be the reason the men didn't notice me much. Many of them only knew the passing rumor that a female soldier lived amongst them. Occasionally some fool would walk by my cot and request I perform some vulgar act, and I would bite my thumb at him or walk away if I had to.

I was leery of walking anywhere alone. I tried to tag along with members of my original crew as often as I could. There were many new strangers in our company, and while we all fought for the same cause, we didn't have to trust one another wholeheartedly until battle.

Our first night there, I visited with Baker to put our bad blood to bed. Funny to think something as silly as him throwing a snowball at me had been enough to redeem our friendship. The sleeping cots were arranged head to foot going around the fire. I did not feel comfortable sitting down on the same cot as Baker, so I borrowed the one next to his. He did not look up at first. I saw he was staring at his broken pocket watch.

"Do you still want me to fix that jerry?" I asked.

He shrugged and put it away in his pocket. "I feel wretched, Clikk."

I hardly knew what to say. The words did not come easily to him. "I'm sorry for the way I treated you before I knew you were… you know. I'm sorry for all them games of Mercy when I hit your shoulder and you cried—"

"I never cried."

"Yeah, you did, Clikk. I heard you in the privy sniffling like a babe."

"Must have took a chill is all."

"What I mean to say is… I'm sorry for saying women was bad luck, and for giving you all them explicit details about what Mathilde and I got up to."

"Relax, mate," I said. "No hard feelings."

"Most of all, I'm sorry for how I treated you when I found out."

"No hard feelings. Really." Listening to Baker apologize was about as pleasant as watching a man fumble for a tourniquet while bleeding out. I knew he was sincere, and I had no intention of drawing this out.

He sighed, but he didn't look any better. "Clikk. I need to know… is Rex the same knight who killed your parents?"

Just the sound of his name scraped at something deep inside me. Without a word, I nodded.

"I thought about your story of what he done to your mother, and it troubles me even more than it used to. I understand why you would hide as a man, how you must have felt to be exposed, and I hate myself for how I acted once I knew, how I pulled away in Nelise. I know what it's like to be abandoned. It ain't enough to say that I'm sorry."

"Baker…"

"I'm with you 'til the end of this. I hope you know that."

"I appreciate your apology, friend, but really I should be apologizing to you."

Baker scratched his stubbly neck, frowning. "For what?"

"I should not have tried to come between you and Lily."

Baker turned his head, squinting at me sideways. "There weren't nothing to come between. The girl was a noble."

"I thought I was protecting her, but maybe I was only treating her the way everyone else does. She understood what she was doing—"

"Clikk," he interrupted me. "I never took a turn with her. When I said I done that, I was only trying to goad you into hitting me."

"What?"

"To be perfectly honest here, I thought you was the one winding her up."

I scoffed. "You just wanted to think that."

"I do have some sense of self-preservation, you know. I made a similar mistake once before and learned my lesson. Dueled three men, the father, the brother, and the betrothed, all for a girl too proper to be any fun. Never again."

"Yes, but Lily is anything but boring... not to mention beautiful."

"Perhaps," he mused. "I may have enjoyed her attention or her pretty stories of Shale, but she was not a wench worth dying for."

"If she did not matter, why did you say I was dead to you?"

Baker only laughed at me. "That was the thirst speaking. A few days without Skye made a grouse of me. You don't have to take everything personally simply because you're a woman now. I took no offense that you thought I had the clap."

"That was uncalled for on my part. I am sorry."

"It's all right. I'm sure that corset they made you wear dislodged your womb and gave you the hysteria."

I grinned and gave him a playful shove. "Shut it, you knob."

Over the course of the next few days, we shared our evenings just as we had done on the Wastrel. During the day, we trained our bodies and built war machines to be mounted on airships.

I was put in charge of the men too weak for the intense training regimen. Dirk said I had a gentle way about me, a comment I forgave only because I knew he meant well. One night, after training a group of bone-thin farm boys to use their swords, I headed back to my cot to grab my violin. The soldiers had gone to dinner, and I wanted to play some music to lift their spirits.

"That's her," I heard someone say. It sounded far away, so much so that I barely took notice.

I walked along the edge of the shadows and was nearing my camp when a man wearing a bandana over his mouth punched me in the eye. I corkscrewed in a bewildered state, and another man grabbed my jacket from behind and pushed me down on all fours.

"Keep quiet, or you're dead," he hissed, his shank already cutting into the flesh at my side.

I could never have expected that I would find myself hunted and cornered. Screaming would not have helped me, my voice being damaged as it was. I tried for my sword but there were others with him. Two of them grabbed my arms, while one stole my weapons. The one at my back snared my hair in his grip and bore down on me.

"We'll set you right, girl. Remind you what you're missing." He reached around the front of my belt, struggling to open the buckle.

I could not see their faces. I imagined myself on the battlefield weeks from now, not knowing if the man at my side was someone who would have hurt me like this. Too much in shock, I found myself immobilized. I had always thought that if something like this happened, I would have the skills and the strength to fight back. But my extremities froze up. The men got me flat against the cold ground, my cheek pressed hard to the stone.

Left with no choice but to submit, I closed my eyes. My one resolve, as I remembered Mr. Greyson's last words, was that I would not shed one tear. I kept repeating that thought in my mind. It became my mantra, consuming everything around me until none of it seemed to be happening. I was in the abyss of a black ocean, so deep underwater that nothing but white noise filled my ears. They couldn't touch me here.

Then the sound of a bone-crunching crack broke through my cocoon. The weight bearing down on me was flung away. I crawled toward the cave wall, returning to the world and trying to get my bearings.

To my amazement and morbid delight, Baker and Pierce appeared to be beating the living daylights out of my attackers.

At once, I memorized their faces. I had never seen them before this day. I believed them to be former Duskmen who defected, for they had more meat on their bones than the average Resistance fighter.

Two of the four assailants escaped. My crewmen homed in on the chief offender and his accomplice who had punched me. As much as I wanted to fight beside them, my body was still shaking. I felt like a child again, watching the Cerulean Knight hurl my father to his knees and run him through.

Each time I tried to stand, my vision became dark and spotty. I cowered in darkness, watching as Pierce kicked his target in the ribs while he was down. Meanwhile, Baker went on repeatedly striking the bloodied face of the man who had nearly been inside me.

"I'm sorry," said the devil. "Have mercy."

Baker lifted the man's head by the hair. "That's the extent of my mercy."

"I'm sorry. I don't know what come over me. It's this mountain. We been here so long."

"Let him go, Baker. We'll let everyone know he's a sodomite," said Pierce.

They released them, and as the last of my assailants fled, I too tried to get up and run. And still, my legs betrayed me.

Baker beheld me in my ruined state. A world of hurt struck as I realized how I must look. There I was on my knees, paralyzed by the fear I claimed did not exist in me. The shame of being so degraded made me want to turn my back on this entire enterprise, return to Nelise, and hide in Lily's attic until the war was over.

"You're all right," said Baker.

I shook my head, hugging myself. "I'm not."

"Come on." Baker offered his hand. "Get up."

"I can't."

"You're not a little girl. You're the bloody Falcon. Now get the fuck up."

I forced myself to let go of the shame that clung about me like a burning cloak. It was a useless feeling. I clasped his hand in mine, and he helped me to stand tall beside him. I looked past him, my eyes trained on my assailants as they returned to their camp.

52

FRIENDSHIP

After the assault, Baker had me bring my cot beside his. For days, I feared some violent retribution from my attackers or their friends. Each night, as I tucked in, I slipped a knife under my pillow, holding its hilt as I slept.

One night, I was tuning my violin by ear when Baker asked, "How you do that? How can you pull a note out of thin air?"

The question made me smile. "I just make up daft little songs to help me remember. Here's one." Alternating between the G and the D strings, I sang, "Baker eats mud. And he looks like crud."

"Tosser."

Plucking my A and E string, I sang, "Baker's queer, Baker's queer, likes a finger in his rear."

"You're a tosser. I fuckin' hate you," said Baker.

A soldier passing through the cots slowed to ask, "Are you cold, sweetheart?"

I had been too dizzy with an all too familiar hunger to realize I was shivering. I shook my head and refused to look at him.

"I'd be happy to keep you warm," he said.

Baker, who was cleaning his nails with the tip of his dagger, made his presence known when he said, "If you like the skin on your face, I suggest you keep walking."

The soldier quickened his pace to a hustle. Oh, how I had missed my tall, terrifying friend.

"Thanks," I said after the man had gone.

"No trouble." Baker reached over to my cot and cloaked me with my blanket.

He got quiet after that, and to break through the silence, I said, "So, you used to be a Blighter, right?"

That caught him off guard. He shrugged. "Ain't something I'm proud of."

"How did you go from being a Locwyn brat to running with anarchists in the Wastes?"

Baker shrugged. "I got caught in their webs as a hijacker. I would take small ships right off the mooring towers outside of Locwyn and fly them to the Wastes to be scrapped. I was young, stupid, my head full of ether."

"Ether?" I whistled. "I would not have taken you for a rag sniffer."

"Got my first taste at fifteen. Kicked the practice, fortunately."

"And you left the Blighters."

"I did, though not for the right reasons. I crashed a stolen bird into the Wastrel. That's how I met Dirk. I thought I was a dead man, but instead of killing me, he had me join his crew to work off my debt. I would have been pilot, but after the crash, my hands shook every time I took the helm. So he made me latrine swabbie, and everyone treated me like shite. Had no respect."

It was a scenario I could hardly imagine, knowing Baker as he was today. "How did you become a Hawk after that?"

"Over the years, we got more people on the ship, and much of the old crew went their own way. In battle, I showed no fear, no hesitation, which made Dirk notice me. Once he made me a Hawk, the men acted like they'd never known me as anything less. Someday they'll look at you with the same esteem as before. They'll remember the Falcon leaping into an open sky, not that day in the woods when they seen you in your skivvies."

"I don't think they'll ever forget I'm a girl," I said. "As it turns out, the legend of the Falcon is a farce."

Baker shrugged and pulled his blanket tighter around his shoulders. "Not to me, it ain't."

"Be that as it may, our brothers aren't ready to accept someone like me."

"They'll distrust you a while yet. Let them. When we take Locwyn and shed our blood together in the city streets, our brotherhood will be restored."

His counsel almost made me feel warm in the freezing cavern, but I noticed him suppress a shiver.

"Here," I said, setting my violin aside and moving to sit next to him so I could share my warmth. I layered my blanket over his and joined him beneath the cloak, our shoulders touching through the layers of wool.

Perhaps it was cruel, but I leaned against him. His dreadlocks scratched my cheek, but I didn't care. He smelled like campfire and tobacco. A blush warmed my face, and I could feel my blood pounding in my chest. Had he put his arm around me, I would have squirmed to get away, but I trusted him not to ruin this.

Baker stared into the flame. His shaking subsided, but his body language was closed off. After a minute, he said, "It's hard for me to pretend you're not a woman."

A nervous tremor struck me, but I hid it well. "Why do you have to pretend?"

He smiled like one who figures out the punch line to a joke before everyone else. The way his dark eyes caught the firelight made them look like shards of amber.

As I studied them, I realized I was holding my breath. My throat was dry. I got up and returned to my own cot. Taking up my violin, I ran my bow over my strings and played the first phrase of a song. "Shall I play 'Wench of Amaranthia'? That's your favorite, ain't it?"

Baker shook his head. "Something soft and slow, I think."

"Hm. There is something I've been working on." I held my violin propped just below my collarbone and played him the anthem Molly and I had composed.

As I held the last high note with long sweeping strokes, I noticed Baker looking at me in the strangest way. It was a knowing sort of look that made me self-conscious. I placed my violin in my lap and frowned.

"Why'd you stop?" he asked.

"My fingers are cold."

"Ah."

"Can I tell you something?"

"Yeah."

"I'm scared. I admit it. I don't know how things will go when we lay siege on Locwyn. Baker, I must confess, I have never killed a man before."

"You never—? That's impossible. You been in raids nigh a year."

"No doubt I've come close to killing. I've put men through worlds of pain, sure. But never have I gone for a mortal blow."

"I saw you fire on Duskies the day you saved my life."

"Over their heads, Bakes. My guts ain't rusty enough to kill. What kind of soldier that make me?"

"So you're green. Most soldiers is green, Clikk. You'll be all right out there. The first kill's the hardest. It gets easier."

I remembered getting sick the time I stabbed a man for Ordrick. I'd already made an attempt at killing. But could I do so again knowing that most of the men on the field were just fighting to feed and protect their families? I was older now. I knew more than I had as an orphan under the influence of the Kindred.

"Nobody's forcing you to go," added Baker. "You could stay back to protect the princess."

"No. I must see this through. Besides, I would not leave you to fight this war without me at your side. Why is it you've stayed?"

"I don't know."

"You must have a reason. Your mum?"

"She'll land on her feet. Truth is, I look at my life and all that I done with it, and I think it ain't worth much. I never done nothing worth shite, never had a girl I loved, never owned nothing. I might as well keep a promise to a friend, help her gut the devil that killed her parents, and do something meaningful along the way."

"You're better than you think, Baker."

"Right," he said, but he didn't sound conciliated. Perhaps it was the cold, but I had never seen Baker so down on himself. "Will you play it again?" he asked.

I did, and this time, some soldiers joined us around the fire to listen. About halfway through the song, I noticed our pirate princess had emerged out of hiding. She stood at the edge of our circle, wary of stepping in until I beckoned.

"Molly," I said. "Does Dirk know you're here?"

She pressed her lips together and shook her head. "He's asleep."

"You should get back."

"I heard you playing our song."

"Yes. For my friend here."

"Your friend?"

"Baker," said he, nodding to Molly. "It's a fine tune."

"Did she sing the lyrics I wrote?" Molly asked.

"No. Clikk won't sing for no one unless she's blitzed."

Molly smirked at him. "Clikk has sung for me."

"Course she done," Baker said. "You're a princess, after all."

Molly rocked on the soles of her shoes, giggling.

"Molly," I said, "Would you be so kind as to sing for Baker here?"

She nodded. "I would."

I played close to the fingerboard. We tried to keep our volume low, but as more men gathered and listened, we were less reserved. They had a sober air about them. They watched in a state of silence and awe, stagnant as the stalactite hanging over our heads. A few of them brought crates over and sat down beside the warmth of our fire.

I followed Molly's high soprano, trying to accentuate rather than lead. She sang without any vibrato or flourish, and I played long, languid notes. Our music echoed throughout the cavern, taking on an unearthly sound, a somber, haunting intonation, like the whisper of the wind through a ghost town.

53

HYDROGEN

I awoke to an empty sleeping hall. Hundreds of cots surrounded me, not one of them occupied. Absolute silence throughout the cave was an anomaly. At any given moment, one could usually hear people murmuring in the surrounding tunnels, but tonight the hollow dark was perfectly serene. I threw on my mantle and gloves, donning the hood. The winding caverns had no sound except my footsteps and the occasional water droplet. I ducked under toothy stalactites overhead, making my way to the mouth of the cave. Maive waited on the snowy cliff edge, silhouetted by a harvest moon. She smiled when she saw me.

"I'm dreaming, ain't I?"

"Yes," Maive affirmed.

"You have more intelligence?"

"I do, but first, I must tell you something. I did some research on that melody your mother taught you, and I discovered something of interest. The school of witches that practiced siren song has been thought extinct for decades now. Their exceptional gift takes a toll on their constitution, and many of them are infertile or die young before rearing any offspring. You might be one of the last."

"Mother was always frail," I conceded. "Does this mean I too will grow weak?"

"I'm afraid it would seem so," said Maive. "Though historically, one of these siren witches was recorded as living to be as old as sixty. She was so feeble, she could not leave her tower. People traveled from all over the world seeking her aid until the day she finally passed into the World After."

"It's no matter," I said. "I never pictured myself as having a long life anyway."

"You are a soldier," said Maive, nodding. "I would offer you my help in awakening your abilities. You will be affected by them either way, and it would be a shame to squander such a gift."

I was reluctant to give an answer.

Maive took notice and said, "You may think on it. Nothing can be done until after Locwyn is liberated."

"Do you have intelligence for me to pass on to Dirk?"

"The capital is encased in an exoskeleton, historically impregnable from the outside. All successful takeovers have happened from within, but you will find the people there are too debilitated to be of any help." On the mist behind her, I could see droves of starved apparitions struggling against an iron gate.

"How do we get in?" I asked.

"A hero must be willing to die to blow open the mechanical shell that protects the city. As the gate opens, there is an opportunity to damage it so that it cannot close. A hydrogen airship rigged with explosives could create enough energy to do just that. In theory, your hero could put the ship on autopilot and base jump before the ship detonates. We have an ally here who would be willing to collect your man."

"Or woman," I said. "If there is no one else, I will do it."

"Very well, Clikk. Tell Dirk he must take the city on the night of the summer solstice, and whoever flies the hydrogen ship can expect to see a green stagecoach with speckled grey horses waiting beneath the clock tower."

"Maive, Gnash told us of a secret passage that runs between the library and the palace. Once we're in, we can use it to get directly to Rex."

Maive nodded. "Then we will all convene at the library. Have Dirk send his army to wage a frontal assault while he joins us in this covert approach." She held up her magnifying glass pendant, twisting it to reflect moonlight in a specific rhythm. "The one who flies the hydrogen ship will need to know a passcode to get beyond the first gate. They use code to identify supply ships," she explained. "Memorize this sequence now and share it with Dirk when you awaken."

As she finished flashing the pattern, she began again. I committed the dots and dashes to memory. My vision grew blurry as the shadows amalgamated into a pool of darkness over her face. I fought to keep the dots and dashes straight in my head, whispering them aloud. I awoke with the sequence on my lips.

"Dot, dot, dot." I opened my eyes. I was on my cot, the nearby fire warming my face. It was crucial I remember the code, so I continued to repeat it out loud as I searched frantically through my knapsack for a piece of charcoal.

"You all right?" asked Baker, stirring to what admittedly sounded like a feverish delusion.

"Dash, dot, dot, dot," I went on.

I found no quills. I went to the fire and fished out an ember with my dagger, repeating the phrase. I pulled on a thick glove and used the blackened wood to scrawl the pattern of dots and dashes onto the cavern floor.

"Clikk?"

I stared at my markings and memorized the pattern.

"Clikk!" cried Baker.

"Hm?"

"What are you doing?"

"I have to go." I pulled my mantle on over my layers of wool and tweed.

"Now? How will you see where you're going?"

"With this." I had a candle I had made from a shoelace and a can of sardines. After eating the fish, I had not let the oil go to waste. It wasn't the safest of torches, but with limited resources, it was effective. Now I had occasion for my creation.

"Are you sure that's a good idea?" said Baker, flinching when I lit the thing. "It looks really unsafe."

"Your mum's really unsafe."

"Don't make me haul your ashes."

I juggled the unstable flame as clipped my sword to my hip and headed away from camp.

54

A Ship-Shape Captain

The edges of the cavern hall were pitch black. I carefully moved between the cots until I found my way to the open aisle. All the officer tents were made of the same weathered canvas, but Dirk's I knew had a spray of pink roses embroidered along the edge of the entrance. Molly's doing. I held up my little tin candle until I found it.

"Psst. Dirk."

"Clikk?" The voice was Molly's. The glow of her lantern fluctuated behind the canvas as its flame came to life. She pulled the tent flaps apart and beckoned me inside. Both of their cots were empty. Some tiny blonde braids from Molly's hair project lay in coils on a little table. The floor was littered with Dirk's personal effects: pomade tins, a comb, some scarves.

"Where is Dirk?" I asked.

"We had an argument," Molly whispered. She twisted the wick's regulator to dim her lantern. "It was a very ugly one. I was asking about our parents, and he wouldn't tell me about them. I said he was selfish. He called me spoiled. I called him a drunk. And I said I wished he had left me to die in the Locwyn dungeon. Then he walked out."

"I'll find him."

"Thank you, Clikk."

She gave me her lantern, which I used to make my way to the nearest opening of the cavern. My gut seemed to be telling me Dirk would have gone outside. He would want to be somewhere he could see the sky.

The snowfall was thick, but it fell as softly as the footsteps of thieves. It got in through the tops of my boots for the snow on the ground was as high as my knees. The path's edge extended only six or seven feet out, and I walked with my gloved hand against the frozen side of the mountain. I saw a man's silhouette at the far end of the path. He was standing before a full harvest moon, holding the neck of a bottle.

My approach was noticed for I was breathing very hard from the cold. Dirk craned his neck and gave me a nod of acknowledgment.

"You'll freeze to death out here," I said.

"Leave me. I don't want your company." He spat the words out in a belligerent jumble and sucked down some more of his gin.

"I have a report from Maive."

"I don't need to hear it now."

"It's a plan for infiltration."

"I'm in no condition for it now. Tomorrow. Tell it me tomorrow. Go back to bed."

"Sir—"

"That's an order."

A freezing gale blew over us. I gritted my teeth and squeezed myself until it let up. As much as I wanted to return to my fire and heavy quilts, my conscience would not let me.

"If you are unfit to hear my report, you are unfit to give orders, sir."

Dirk faced me. "What?"

"Look at you, moping over your dead parents like it happened only yesterday. I've known little children made of stronger stuff."

"You don't get it," he growled. "Their bodies were mutilated, robbed of all dignity."

"Death mutilates all. There is no dignity for any corpse. We all rot or burn or get eaten. Everybody is defiled in the end."

"My little siblings—" he stifled a sob with another gulp of his gin. "All those weeks in the dungeon—knowing they would die there."

"Does drinking quiet these thoughts of yours?"

"Sometimes. Or it makes them louder. Helps with the cold of this place, at least."

I snatched his bottle, reeled my arm back, and tossed it over the edge of the cliff. We watched it vanish into the pale mist of the snowstorm.

"Well, that was a waste of good gin," said Dirk. "Are you pleased with yourself?"

"Your drinking is a problem. It might have been acceptable for a pirate captain of a ship called the Wastrel, but it will not suit for a king."

"I'm a pirate king! The king you said you wanted!"

Child, I thought. *Belligerent, idiotic child*. I thought he needed a good smacking and I might have given him a clout had I not been hugging myself to keep warm. Anyway, because a drunk often acts like a child, he needs to be treated like one. And having been struck many times when I was small and wandering the streets, I knew it did little more than build resentment and distrust. So instead of hitting him, I pulled him into a sudden embrace. That surprised him. It surprised me as well for it was not as awkward as I had expected. In fact, his warmth gave me comfort. Feeling his arms about me reminded me of when I used to hug my father.

"I have seen only glimpses of the man who will save Elsace. You are so close. If you would give up the drink—"

Dirk drew back from me. "How? I cannot even look upon my sister's face when I am sober. I see only her disappointment. Or I see my mother."

"Have you not seen how she adores you? You are the greatest man she has ever known. Her rescuer. Her hero. Father and brother all in one flesh."

"Perhaps. But she sees the drunk as well."

"Then change it. The next drink you take must come from the bottle of gin at the foot of this mountain. Do you hear me? If you cannot quit your vice, it is better that you freeze to death and leave Molly to rule. A man who is not in command of his vices cannot lead a country."

The wind blew hard again, cutting through me. Dirk gazed out over the rolling plains of white snow.

He unbuttoned his wool coat. It billowed viciously as the gales surged once more. From his breast pocket, he withdrew his flask. He grasped his old friend firmly, holding it out in front of him like a man might hold a demon by the throat. Shouting, he brought it over and behind his head. He thrust it with all his might into oblivion.

55

RALLY

We needed a symbol to identify ourselves as the Risen on the battlefield. It was decided our bandanas would be the things to help us differentiate between allies, enemies, and civilians. Each had a round red sun contrasted against a vivid morning sky.

Many of the weakening soldiers in my charge could no longer train. I led these feeble creatures in the task of dying bandanas and hanging them to dry. We strung lines across the crystal-studded walls; we had so many, the display looked like spider webs dripping with blood.

Whenever she could, Molly would sneak away from her brother's surveillance to help us. She liked to mix the red dye. She said it reminded her of making fruit punch for the winter solstice party at boarding school. Of course, then she would prattle on about her old chums. Sometimes, if she were tired of talking, she would ask the men for their stories, where they came from, if they had loved ones, and what they planned to do after we sacked Locwyn. Dirk figured out where she was going quickly enough, for upon her return, her fingers would be stained with dye. But he did not put a stop to it. He was learning to allow her more freedoms and to see her more as an equal.

The evening before the siege, the army congregated in a contained arena within the caverns of the mountain. Hundreds of whispering voices resounded off the high ceilings with a sound like snow blowing over a heath. A fire blazed in a pit at the central stage, eating away at old logs. I went up and down the aisles until I found Baker sitting alone.

"Oi, there!" I used his shoulder as a prop as I hurtled myself over the bench and plopped down beside him. "The battle for Locwyn is finally here. Can you believe it?"

"You sound far too cheery, Clikk."

"Why shouldn't I? Survive this and you'll be a decorated hero, one of the fearless few from the Wastrel. Think of the songs they'll sing!"

"There won't be songs for a man called Baker. That's no name for a hero. Too occupational."

"They'll call you something else."

"Thomas ain't any better. Let's be honest. Even if I kill a thousand men tomorrow, I'll be forgot. No matter. It don't bother me." He offered me his leather flask. I took a swig of what I discovered was spiced whiskey.

"At least you'll be paid," I said. "You can have your whores and your fancy parties."

"That's the whole reason I'm here."

"The *whole* reason?"

"Well, besides loving subzero temperatures and a diet of firewater and gruel."

"Oh, you are a droll one. Surely you fight because you believe in a better Elsace."

"Not really. No."

"In some way, you must."

"I don't. I think this revolution, like all revolutions, will only result in greater civil strife. But it's happening with or without me, so I might as well get rich off it."

"That's ridiculous. Dirk will do good work for the poor when he is in power."

"I doubt it very much. Kings never follow through on that."

"Aren't we cynical," I said. "If you get killed, I'd like to think you died fighting for something you believed in."

"You don't have to believe in a war to fight in one."

Outrageous. I looked straight ahead. I did not want to speak to him anymore about it, for I was perilously close to losing my temper.

"What?" he said, prodding me. "What's the matter, Clikk?"

"Leave it."

"No. What's it matter to you whether or not I die in vain?" He surveyed my face in a way I found very irritating; it was as though he was trying to look inside my head and read my thoughts.

"You shouldn't have come."

"Little late for that now, ain't it?"

The assembly fell quiet as Captain Dirk entered. I almost did not recognize him. The nature of his entire bearing had shifted. He stood straighter and did not sway so much as before when he walked. Molly arrived in tow and stood beside him in the central pit. Her posture was even more emphatically regal, with her shoulders pulled back and her head held high.

Dirk threw a nest of dried moss on the fire, and the flame licked vertically at the air. Dirk needed no stage or megaphone to capture the attention of his army. Even dressed in a common flight suit and a wool-lined trench coat, he had all the presence of a king.

"Risen!" he roared.

"Rise!" answered the army.

The firelight glimmered on his face, and he circled it as he spoke. "Some of you have flown with me before and know I am a capable leader. Others have only heard the stories, and only imagined the horror I've wrought on wealthy men. I come to you today, not as a pirate, not as a king, but as your equal. Too long these lands have been ruled by tyrants, the people ever on the brink of starvation with no recourse but thievery. I also have felt the sting of shame in not being able to earn a wage or care for my own. I have seen my entire family murdered, watched my infant sister waste away from hunger, and been powerless in the face of it all.

"I have been to several dungeons and would not send any man to this dark hole for a crime as small as desperation. I should pardon every one of you this very night, and future repercussions would be repaid with rehabilitation! Not extermination! My family brought the revolution on themselves. I admit this freely. My father was isolated from the reality of the world he governed, which was why he did not see it coming when Perceval usurped him. We learned that trading a king for an emperor solves nothing, and so I do not want to be your king. I want to be your captain. I will not have subjects, but brothers and sisters whose interests are my interests.

"Many of us will not live to see the new dawn, but the capital is our battlefield, and the souls who perish will forever be laid to rest in her wreckage, which we will rebuild upon so that the bones of these brave revolutionaries are forever entombed in the greatest city of mankind. And every year, for a thousand years or more, people will take their children beneath the new city to see the ruins of old Locwyn. They will show them the stones and tell them of the day when pirates and peasants became patriots and made Elsace free!"

The arena resounded with a great roar of triumph. Baker and I stood like all the rest, raising our fists and crying out with the red lust for battle. Captain Dirk glowed with pride in all of us. He began to speak again, and everyone was seated, hanging on his every word.

"Now, soldiers, we have an airship rigged to blow the face of that city to smithereens. What we need now is the right man to operate it. He has to impersonate a trade ship, so he isn't shot down before reaching the gate. There will be a chance to evacuate just before the hydrogen explodes, but this man must ride the wind and touch down beside a green stagecoach. This carriage will take him to the library where he will wait to join our infiltration team."

Baker stood tall amidst the rows of seated men. I reached for his arm, but he slipped my grasp.

"I'll do it," he called down to Dirk. "Sounds fun."

Dirk shook his head. "Your nerves are shot."

"All the more reason to use me as cannon fodder!"

Dirk stroked his chin with his thumb. "How inspiring, Baker. You are the last man I'd have expected to be vying for a suicide mission. Of course, if anyone can ride the wind, it's you."

"He can't!" I shouted, standing up beside him. "There is a signal code used by the transport ships. I won't tell it to anyone. For it must be me who flies the ship." Some of the men laughed. I didn't care. I said it again. "It must be me."

Molly looked horrified. She whispered something to Dirk and he made a flippant gesture with his hand as he rolled his eyes.

"Well, Baker, seeing as Clikk feels so strongly about this…"

Baker shot me a vexed sneer. "What are you? My wife?"

"I did not save your life so you could throw it away opening a bloody gate."

Baker raised his voice to address Dirk once more. "The difference between me and any other man is that I will survive! If Clikk won't give me the code, then let her tag along. I will see that both of us escape the blast."

Molly was shaking her head before he even finished his sentence. She whispered to Dirk again. He gave her a dismissive pat on the wrist and said, "All right. Baker and Clikk will fly the ship and meet our contact on the ground. Now, our forces will be divided into three different groups: combat troops on the ground, an air fleet providing cover fire, and a stealth unit moving silently through the city. Within these groups, specific teams will have distinct objectives."

For the rest of the assembly, Dirk went over the battle plan. I would have liked to be more involved with the stealth unit from the beginning, dismantling enemy guard posts and sniping from the shadows. My skills were wasted on that hydrogen ship.

"What's wrong?" asked Baker, noticing my melancholic disposition. "You got what you wanted."

"Why would I want this? Why would you? You know that leaping from that ship as it explodes will be like falling through a sky of fire."

"Don't be a mollycoddle," he said. "This will be the greatest thrill of our lives."

56

THE SIEGE

Flying a ship was nothing at all like I had imagined. Baker did his best to guide me along, but I felt overwhelmed by the numerous details requiring my attention. We had radar flashing on a dim, amber screen. Our radio spewed endless static, stopping only when it decided to hum the most ear-splitting frequency imaginable. The capacitors were shot. Switches glowed red beside flickering dials, and every time a light started blinking, I thought I had done something terribly wrong.

"What's that?" I asked Baker, frantically tapping a red light that had come on.

He chuckled at what he saw there. "You don't want to know." He twisted a valve, and I watched the needle on the pressure gauge return to center as the light turned off.

"Baker," I said in a severe tone. "What was that?"

"Hydrogen expands as the air outside gets thinner. So if you don't vent or recompress as you ascend…" He made an explosion sound in the back of his throat.

"Thank you for that."

Remembering those cracks in the Wastrel's balloon made me wonder how we had survived to see this day at all. I tried not to think about it.

While Baker took care of controlling ballast and hydrogen distribution, I handled the propellers, the thrust, and the overall trajectory, which was controlled by a left-hand apparatus that fit like a set of knuckledusters.

Our ship's gondola was small, airtight, and freezing. Equipped in our flak jackets, parachute packs, goggles, and Risen bandanas, we were ready to blow open the gates of Locwyn.

Through the windows, we had visibility of everything in front of and beneath us. In the distance, the vane atop the communications tower winked at us as stars sometimes do in the mist. I glanced down at the dots and dashes scrawled on my wrist in black ink. I had the access code. I told myself over and over this would work. It had to.

Built like a lock, the city had a circular border encased in a steel dome. Mechanical moving walls decked with seven spires, the shell was tallest near the center where its features became sharp and dreary. This city had always been on the brink of starvation, its people controlled with fear and propaganda. It had never known fair rule; it had never known peace.

The wind got the better of me and bounced us furiously on its air currents. We sloped and heaved.

"I'm going to kill us before we even get there!" I cried. "You should take over!"

Baker laughed at me. "You're fine."

"It feels as though we're about to capsize."

"We're in a balloon. She can't capsize. Just relax and keep her steady." Baker stood and came behind me, leaning in and placing his left hand over mine on the apparatus. "Easy," he said. "Think of the air as a glass of Skye, bubbles rising to the top, up into the atmosphere. These bubbles are constantly bumping into each other, knocking about. So when we shake like this, it's really not your fault. It's just the sky." He knew how to ride the wind, and the bucking of the ship ended almost as instantly as he took hold.

I felt my blood warming my cheeks. His voice tickled my ear. "Are you blushing?"

"Don't be ridiculous."

He was deliberate in his torture of me, found some amusement in it. He returned to his seat to read the gauges. "I hope we live to see this crazy firework."

"We will," I said. "I brought your lucky ring." I pulled the chain out from my collar where the steel dangled.

"You still got it!" Baker laughed and shook his head. "I found that in Amaranthia. There's a smith who makes them."

"It is lucky though, ain't it?"

"So says the smith. The day I bought it were the same day I chipped my tooth in that brawl. I thought the man a charlatan… until you saved my life. S'pose the ring had some luck in it after all, for the day I bought it was the same day we became friends."

The mooring tower signaled to us. I pressed a switch to flicker the ship's lamps, hoping I had the correct code. If I had misremembered even just one dot or dash, all our efforts would be wasted. Our balloon full of hydrogen would be fired on and we would make one hell of an explosion just a few minutes too early.

To my relief, I heard the gears grinding behind the city's façade. The towers pivoted, and the walls slowly diverged, unveiling a cavity populated by a thousand lights. The arched windows sparkled like diamonds in the deep of a cavern.

"Clikk. Should we not make it—"

"The more you say goodbye, the stupider you'll feel when we're blitzed as bats at the victory party."

I engaged our initial descent. We moored at a checkpoint on the outermost wall. The trade officers boarded us and asked to be shown to our cargo. Baker did the talking. His Locwyn accent put them men at ease. He showed them the canisters labeled as pow-

dered oats, handing them the only one actually containing something edible. The rest had been packed with gunpowder.

The men found nothing out of the ordinary. They said only,
"He's not much of a talker, your friend."

Baker chuckled amicably. I feared my profuse sweating would
give us away. "He's my half-brother. Bit touched in the head, you
understand. I brung him along to see the city lights."

The men blessed him. I wanted to smack him but decided he
had made the right choice when the trade officers granted us permission to proceed through the gate.

Baker walked me through the steps once more of engaging the
engines.

"Touched in the head?" I muttered.

"First thing that came to mind."

"Prig."

A row of spotlights lit up the gate panels as we closed in. My
shoulders had been like rocks throughout all of this. They would be
sore tomorrow, if we lived to see tomorrow.

The gate bore adornments reminiscent of a pipe organ. Its
many rods lined the bleak steel panels. These enormous panels
were stacked, and the rods like teeth, stretched across the lower lip,
creating the impression of a ghoulish frown. We heard a bubbling
pressure accumulate behind the façade and steam began to shriek
through small openings in the rods. The white mist came rushing
from every opening and crack in the door. There came a roar of
metal scraping as the gate receded into the connected panels.

I pushed hard on the thrust. The ship reeled, and a rush of
blood flooded my heart as Locwyn opened its mechanical mouth
and received our deadly aircraft. The lights grew bigger fast. Soon I
could see silhouettes of armed Duskmen against that backdrop of
windows.

I turned on the autopilot mechanic. "Now," I said. We abandoned our station.

Baker tugged the chain that opened the hatch. We slid onto the air.

With a forward roll, I gave my body up to gravity. Time compressed. I was a shadow, invisible in the darkness. Suspended in air, I surveyed the world beneath me, searching for the horses and green stagecoach that were to be our drop point. Cobblestone alleys wove between towering buildings made of steel. I leveled out and pulled the ripcord. My parachute wrenched my whole body as it burst overhead. I used the handles to change course to be as far from the airship as possible. As I came around the bend of a massive building, the sabotaged ship exploded with an ear-splitting boom.

The force shoved me, and my nostrils filled with the scent of charred air. I heard the vague sound of Baker's shouts on the wind and looked over my shoulder. His parachute had caught fire, and a mountain of black smoke enveloped him. He cut himself free, fell out of the cloud, and released his reserve. There was a series of booms and implosions, which I felt in my bones as the façade of Locwyn crumbled. Men on the city streets went running, swinging lanterns and shouting.

I tried to see how Baker was faring, but when I looked again, he had vanished. Below me, a red flare burned at the back of a green carriage. The ground got closer and closer until it was right beneath my feet.

57

THE FALLEN

I set down half a city block from the coach and ran for it. A man in a duster and top hat jumped out and helped me slip my harness. We scooped up the many armfuls of my parachute and climbed into the carriage.

"Wait!" I cried. "Baker hasn't landed."

"We have to go!" The man slammed the doors shut and banged on the partition. The driver whipped the horses. We flew down the bumpy street.

The mustached stranger had familiar eyes behind his round black spectacles. I was still trembling from a rush of adrenaline and shock. I pulled my goggles down around my neck and nearly screamed when I recognized the person sitting across from me.

"Fitz?"

"The one and only," he answered.

"Where's Lord Terrence?"

"He was called away this morning and never returned. Maive sent me instead." He started to explain what happened. His words spilled out into the air between us, but I couldn't focus. A shrill frequency pierced my head. Baker had tried to say goodbye and I had cut him short. I longed to go back to that moment. Something pulled within, a dark chasm opening up in my chest. I couldn't breathe.

"Stay firm! You're across enemy lines!" Fitz said, patting my shoulder. "Clikk, our big bad Hawk brother is going to be fine. He pulled his reserve, and it carried him off course, but he has made it out of worse situations."

"I hear you," I said, sniffing air down into my lungs. "I just... I didn't see myself doing this without him."

"I take it the two of you are on better terms than you were the last time I saw you."

I gave a nod, breathless and weary. My fingers clenched up into pincers. I shook them out. "Sorry, I don't know what's wrong with me."

"You're hyperventilating."

"What do I do?"

"Breathe normally. Or scream. I used to hyperventilate all the time when I first started drinking Skye. Screaming helps."

"Screaming hurts my voice," I whispered as my vision blurred.

"Well, if you pass out, your breathing will correct itself. We should arrive at the library soon. Maybe Maive knows a spell that can help you."

I popped the knuckles in my left hand, counting out every breath until my head became clearer. We kept the carriage dark inside to maintain our anonymity through the slums of Locwyn.

I peeked through the curtain and saw humans in agony, men with bony arms and legs hunched in on themselves, bodies wrapped in rags and shoved behind waste compartments. As the poor never got any sunlight, rickets was a common affliction. The wealthy could afford to take supplements and sunny excursions, but everyone else had no choice but to grow weak.

A woman of the night walked down the street, her breasts bulging out of the top of her corset. Her skin was covered in filth, and her hair was matted into a dry braid. She pulled an even sadder creature behind her, a little boy with a distended belly. This glimpse at what might have been Baker's childhood filled me with voyeuristic shame and compelled me to close the curtain.

The carriage came to a halt. I saw Duskmen form a semi-circle around the front of our coach. The driver spoke to them in a low murmur; I couldn't make out any of the words. It sounded like a simple misunderstanding. Then I heard the breeching fall and clatter as they cut the horses free. A gunshot tore through the air. The driver's shadow fell across the partition window briefly as he fell from his box.

Fitz cursed under his breath. He lifted a carpet from the middle of the carriage and opened a trapdoor. Before I could ask what we were doing, he shoved me through and closed it. I hit the cobblestones and went flat.

"For the men of the Wastrel!" shouted Fitz. Loud automatic fire erupted from the coach. Two of the Duskmen fell, and the one that didn't die right away could see me there on the ground. He tried to alert the others, but when he opened his mouth to speak, nothing but blood came pouring out. Fitz's weapon clicked three times as he reached the end of the clip.

Craning my neck, I could see the officers' boots moving past our driver's lifeless corpse. His top hat was on its side several strides away from him. One of the Duskmen picked it up. The other two opened the carriage door.

"Your uniforms suck—" was all Fitz managed to say before his choked agony sounded overhead. Fitz joined the other men on the ground, bleeding out from a wide gash in his neck. I hated to watch anyone die that way, but I had a duty to Fitz not to close my eyes this time. He looked at me and I at him, and as much as I wanted to reach out and take his hand, I couldn't. His suffering quieted as he accepted his death and went still.

"That's the last of the spies," said one of the officers.

"Lord Terrance said he was tasked with collecting one of their agents. Where is he?" asked their commanding officer.

"The radio tower reported a man leaping from the hydrogen ship. They say he burned alive before hitting the ground."

"Good. Get this cart out of here and prepare the ambush. The imposter prince is still on his way."

"Yes, sir."

I kept my breath slow and silent, trying not to whimper aloud for poor Thomas Baker. The blood of my allies wound down the cracks in the cobblestones until it found me, staining my sleeve. I gazed into Fitz's glassy dead boy eyes and swore to never forget him, this creature of such bewildering altruism.

58

CARNAGE

The battle raged in the distance. A mortar round landed nearby and smashed the awning of a bakery. Every second I spent waiting beneath that carriage made me feel like more of a coward. The sounds of cannon fire and screeching babes echoed in the distance. The rational part of my mind knew I had to wait here for Dirk so I could warn him of the ambush in the library, but the more I stared at the bodies of Fitz and our driver, the more I wanted to head in there and take vengeance myself.

When the Duskmen finished dragging the bodies away, they pulled the carriage around the corner and left it in an alley. I was exposed. A Duskman saw me lying there, but he must have been influenced by all of Fitz's blood on me, for he didn't see me as a threat until after I had already fired Millicent three times into his chest. My rage fortified me as I watched the life slip from his eyes. I had killed a man, somebody's child, somebody's husband or father perhaps. And now I had to kill more, for the gunshots had been loud. Waves of adrenalin coursed through me like streams of pure electricity. I rolled behind a stoop and reloaded my revolver.

The library doors burst open and some men came running out, raising lanterns and inspecting the scene. There were three men. I took aim from the shadows and fired shots at each. I felled two of them, but the third I missed entirely. I fled down an alley. His footfalls grew louder as he gained on me.

"Your arse is mine!" he shouted.

I went around the bend and drew the dagger from my boot. As he came around, I tried stabbing him in the gut, but he sidestepped and disarmed me. His pocket automatic screeched as he pulled the trigger. He was young, had clearly never discharged his weapon outside of training. The weapon's recoil knocked his wrist back, and bullets sprayed the alley wall, breaking off small clouds of cement debris. When the clip was empty, he drew his short sword and tackled me. We grappled on the hard ground. I tried to wrestle his sword's tip away from my throat, but it was a losing battle. I closed my eyes and fought with all the energy I had left, which wasn't enough. He was too strong.

The Duskman drooled down my shoulder, and his body suddenly went limp. I opened my eyes and saw a dark figure standing over us. It was Baker. He yanked his dagger from out the man's back and wiped it clean on his pant leg. He helped me to stand up, but my legs shook so fiercely I had to lean against the brick wall. "You gave me a scare," I said. "I feared the worst."

"Lost control of my reserve, but I sorted it out."

"We've been betrayed. They killed Fitz."

Baker flinched, knitting his brow as he closed his eyes. He took the Duskman's pocket automatic and reloaded the clip.

"I killed three of them, Bakes." I hadn't noticed until now, as I tried to speak, that I was completely out of breath, and I didn't think I would be catching it anytime soon.

Baker held my shoulder firm. "Stay in your skin," he said. "Let's push on. I need to kill Duskies before I go ballistic."

I led him back through the alley. I knew he wanted justice as badly as I did, but we could not take the library without help.

As we came out onto the street, I realized we wouldn't have to. A barrage of footsteps sounded nearby as a mob approached. Dirk was leading the front lines. The dense rows of men resembled an army of the dead, for all were war-painted, their tunics and yellow bandanas covered in blood.

"Captain!" I cried, running toward him. "An ambush lies in wait in the library!"

Dirk signaled for one of his units to follow him and for the others to begin the onslaught of the palace. Fifty men advanced toward the castle gate and climbed the stone. Gunfire rained down upon them, but where one man fell, another would soon take up his place.

"Ned!" Dirk shouted. "Toss a boomstick in there." He pointed at the library.

Ned lit the fuse on a stick of dynamite and sent it twirling through a window on the ground floor.

The Blue Dusk cried out within. "Take cover!" The blast shattered the rest of the library's windows. We heard shelves collapsing. The front doors flung open, and a thick, white cloud came rushing out. A couple uniforms tried to flee, only to meet our swords as we advanced. We brought our bandanas up to cover our noses, the red suns vibrant and gaping like the mouths of beasts. Risen at my side, I held my breath and ran in. The explosion had set fire to the bookshelves, and it was spreading at a speed that would devour every scrap of paper in minutes.

Coughing fits hindered the Duskmen. They could hardly fight back as we gutted them.

"Put out those fires!" Dirk shouted once we had subdued the opposition. "Clikk, Ned, on me!"

We matched Dirk's pace as he dashed upstairs. The upper level was an ocean of smoke.

Dirk touched a marble bust, and one of the bookshelves spun, revealing a secret passage that descended underground. Our footsteps echoed on stone as we traversed the long dark hall. The other men in Dirk's infiltration team caught up to us. They used matches to light torches, passing one up for Dirk as he led the charge.

"There is a chance Maive hid in this tunnel," said Dirk.

I didn't want to tell him that it wasn't likely, so I kept my mouth shut. At the end of the tunnel, we came up some stairs and reached an opening and what appeared to be the back of an armoire with light peeking out beneath it. It was solid wood, but Baker and No-Nose Ned helped Dirk to topple it. We came out into the king's suite, a room that had fallen into disuse. The furniture was covered in white sheets, and the grand mirrors adorning the walls were grey with dust and age.

"Maive?" whispered Dirk. "Maive?" He peered under the bed. He opened the armoire and inspected the corner behind a large gilded mirror. The witch was not there.

"Captain," I said.

Dirk offered an admission of understanding. "Yes. We'll advance to the war room. That's where we'll likely find General Rex."

"Do you know where it is?"

"Of course I do. I grew up here. West wing, lower level."

We moved on, entering a regal hallway. A Duskman saw us and started to run, but Dirk grabbed him and ran his sword across the man's throat. These men weren't armed, which suggested that even if Lord Terrence had given up my landing point, he might not have known about the hydrogen airship or our plan to take an arterial tunnel into the heart of the castle. It made sense that Maive would provide him the minimal amount of information in case he was ever compromised. He knew about the green stagecoach that was to bring a rebel hero to the library at a specific time, and that was all. This boded well for Maive. If Rex didn't have her knowledge, she might not have been captured.

We continued on foot, slashing down anyone we met on our way through the palace. Some of them shouted, "Breach!" but did not manage to alert their allies before we cut them down.

A door flew open as a behemoth Duskman burst into the corridor, firing a mini-gun. He stood almost seven feet tall, his body solid with muscle. I leapt behind a stone column. One of the men jumped in front of Dirk, acting as a human shield for his prince. He died honorably. The bullet spray killed five more of our men, including Ned and our only medic.

A mist of blood lifted on the air, spraying our faces. I whipped around the other side of the column and came up behind the brute, driving my dagger between his ribs. I usually struck the heart with this attack, killing my target in an instant, but I had not accounted for the man's size. He swung around to hit me, and I ducked.

Baker came out from behind cover. He fired his filched automatic into the man's shoulder. Squinting through the flash of his fire, I finished the brute with Millicent, landing a shot between his eyes. The gun smoke dispersed. I dived for that fine weapon of his.

The mini-gun had a temperature gauge and a ribbon of ammunition that hung down like a bicycle chain. Lifting it took all my strength, but I propped it up against my hip and aimed low down the hall.

Duskmen exploded out of the war room, wielding ornamental rapiers. I squeezed hard on the trigger. The six barrels spun like a beast inhaling. Then a noise like a hundred rattlesnakes blitzed on Skye shredded the air.

The gun felt like it might fly right out of my grasp. An onslaught of bullets burst forth, decimating the officers. The corridor filled with quivering gore and the Blue Dusk uniforms turned violet as men collapsed into a heap. The wand on the temperature gauge went all the way into the red until the glass shattered. The metal scalded my hands, and I dropped the gun, cracking the marble floor. Blue Dusk assistance arrived with pocket automatics.

"Get down!" Baker shouted. Our men ducked behind columns and used the mound of dead as a barricade whenever they fired at the opposition. The stench of gunpowder, blood, and excrement filled the air. Just when I thought that vile scent couldn't be worse, it would amplify as more shots were fired and more men went down.

"Stand down! I have the witch!" bellowed a voice from within the war room, deep and gravelly. Dirk lowered his rifle. He had gone pale as a ghost. It was in this moment I realized I had lost him. I tried to tackle him, but he was already moving toward the sound of Maive's muffled cries.

"Captain! Don't!" I cried, inaudible against the gunfire rising from the enemy.

Dirk flung himself over the heap of corpses, and by some miracle, he dodged the sea of bullets that sought to drown him. On their next reload, I chased after him. A lone gunman tried to shoot me. His bullets only sprayed the wall at my heels.

59

STALEMATE

Someone needed to protect the true king of Elsace. Our brothers threw down cover fire as Dirk and I stormed the war room. Rex had retreated into a deeper station. Dirk rushed the inner haven, kicking open the double doors. General Rex sat behind an ivory desk with Maive on his lap. She was muted by the iron apparatus affixed to her jaw. Further down was an even grislier sight. Bandages covered her arms from her elbows down to the stumps where her hands should have been. Her hands had been amputated.

Rex held his rifle aimed at the door and shot Dirk in the stomach.

"Captain!" I cried, clasping him in my arms. His legs twitched beneath him, and we crumbled to the floor together. My heartbeat pounded in my ears.

General Rex lifted his sword from off the desk—that same curved sword with the sapphire tears along the hilt—and in one swift movement, cut open Maive's throat. Her blood trickled down the hilt, down the sapphires, and down around his pale fingers. She trembled against the iron jaw brace and her eyes went wide. Rex discarded her to the floor, pointing his rifle at me.

Dirk's wail of immense sorrow tore at my heart. He wept her name as he shook.

"If I'd known you would make it so easy, I'd have killed her sooner," said Rex, coming toward us. "Never trust a witch, and if you realize one is working against you, be sure to bind and gag her to prevent her casting. I may have taken it to the extreme, but I am a careful man, even when I snuff out causes that are damned from the start."

He stuck the tip of his rifle flat against the side of my head. I tasted vomit in the back of my throat. I swallowed it hard and readied for death, berating myself for my every mistake I'd made along the way.

"You are the one who is damned," I whispered. "Regardless of how this battle ends, your Blue Dusk will fall. We still have the princess. The people will never lose hope so long as she lives!"

Rex pressed his rifle tip harder against my skull. "You think I'm afraid of some little girl? I will find her, and when I do, I will have her drawn and quartered in the old square."

All these years yearning for justice, I was to be shot down by the demon who set me on my course in the first place. I had failed my parents, my king, and my country. I mouthed the words, "I'm sorry," just before Rex pulled the trigger.

His gun jammed. The instant I heard that click in my ear, I grabbed the shaft and pulled him down to the floor. We grappled for the firearm, but it was I who succeeded in elbowing him in the nose, stunning him long enough to steal the rifle and crack him over the skull with the stock.

A savage force consumed my soul. I aimed Millicent at his head and shrieked, already imagining the act of blowing out his brains. I wanted so desperately to pull the trigger, but I could not do it. Not yet. For to save my captain's life, we had to get a medic into the castle at once.

"Tell your men to open the gates and stand down!" I said, cocking the revolver.

Rex nodded. "I will," he said.

As more Risen were entering the command post. I issued the next order to them. "Take Rex to the gates and complete the surrender! Get a medic in here as soon as possible! That's the priority! If Rex tries anything, shoot his cock off."

Our boys marched Rex out at gunpoint.

"It's over, Duskies! The true king has captured your leader!" they shouted.

"Stand down!" Rex kept repeating it through the shouting and intermittent gunfire as the Risen moved him down the hall.

"How could you, Clikk?" said Dirk. I held him, compressing his wound with his Risen bandana. The red rising sun expanded like a supernova as his blood rushed out. So much blood. My knees were getting soaked. "How could you let him live?"

"I'm saving you."

"He killed Maive."

"You think I didn't want to do him in right there? He murdered my parents. I've spent the last five years wanting to kill him, but instead, I'm saving you. Your life isn't your own anymore. You see that, don't you? You're to be our king."

Dirk seemed to understand me, or at least, was too weak to argue. He shuddered and nestled close, tucking his chin. "You'll take care of Molly for me, won't you?"

"You're going to live."

He coughed. "Dammit, Clikk, just promise me."

"I will," I said. "You know I will."

"I need to tell you..."

"Shh, save your strength."

"If I'm... gonna die," he sucked up a deep breath and laughed off the pain, "I want to impart some wisdom 'fore I go."

"Shh."

"I loved her." His extremities trembled and his muscles clenched. "I never told her more than once or twice. Not sure why it's always been so hard for me." He clutched my sleeve, his face turning white. "I never had the gift of foresight. I thought we had time, thought…someday I would wake up as a better man, and everything would settle, but that isn't how it works, Clikk. You have to seize the day." With those final words, he fell unconscious. I detected a faint pulse in his throat, growing fainter. I screamed "medic" until the word sounded unreal to me. I screamed it until it shredded my throat.

Men arrived with a surgeon. They carried Dirk into the war room, cleared off the table and laid him down.

"Do any of you have medical experience?" asked the surgeon.

Nobody offered themselves up.

"Anyone good with their hands?"

"The musicians," proposed one of our men. "Clikk and William."

"You, kindle a fire," the surgeon told me. I went to work, fumbling with matches in the hearth. I found a page of schematics for a war machine on the floor and crumpled it up to use as fodder. Then I placed a wooden chair on its side and stomped the thing down into lumber for burning.

"You." He pointed to William. "Fetch water. Put it on to boil. You two. Hold him down in case he wakes up. There's time for dulling the pain." Two of our men placed a hand on each of Dirk's shoulders, expecting the worst. As much as I wanted to watch over my captain, I trained my eyes on my fire. I had to make sure it transferred to the wood.

William, our mandolin player, appeared at my side holding a saucepan filled to the brim with water. We worked together to keep it over the flame until it boiled. What they say about watched pots had never been so true as it was that day. The minutes dragged on.

The surgeon handed me a bayonet and told me to heat it over the embers. As I did, all I thought about was that it would soon pierce my captain's flesh.

Some of the Risen came to us from the infirmary, carting in supplies they had discovered there, including an oxygen tank with a respirator.

"Thank the gods. He needs it," said the surgeon. The life-giving machine hissed softly, and they placed a rubber face mask over Dirk's nose and mouth. Tiny bubbles appeared at the bottom of the pan.

"Yes," I whispered. "Come on."

"Put the tools in and wash your hands," said the surgeon.

We boiled the surgeon's tools for five minutes. I removed my jacket and unzipped my flight suit, tying the sleeves around my waist. The shame of showing my sleeveless undershirt did not even occur to me. All that mattered was preventing an infection. William and I washed our hands up to our elbows. When all was heated and boiled and as sterile as it could be, we assisted the surgeon at his operating table.

"Scalpel."

That first cut into Dirk's belly prompted a twinge in my entrails.

"Tongs," said the surgeon. William presented them.

"Grab that bayonet," he told me as he began to dig for the bullet.

I did so and held it at the ready.

"Come to daddy. There you are," he whispered, sliding the bullet from the gaping flesh. "Now!" the surgeon shouted as blood gushed like a bubbling brook. I pressed the hot blade where I remembered the wound being. It was lost now beneath the swells of crimson. Dirk's face appeared to be turning gray. I thought he might already be dead when I saw that.

"Oh, fuck." I choked, vomit rising in my esophagus. "Take it, take it, take it!" I cried to William. "I'm going to be sick!" He took the cauterizer as I staggered into the corner and held back from getting sick all over the floor. This was all too much for me to bear. I felt too accountable for his getting shot.

"All right! Get out before you contaminate the room!" shouted the surgeon.

60

Dawn Comes

I walked aimlessly past the bodies in the hall, hardly able to see through my tears. I lamented that moment I let my captain—my prince—rush the war room. This fight would be a waste if he did not survive. Molly was stronger now than ever before, but I could not help but doubt her in her youth. If one of her advisors manipulated her into marrying a tyrant, Elsace would fall back into chaos.

The men were clearing out the carnage, lifting the last of the bodies onto a cart to clear a path through the hall. I overheard some of them whispering about Dirk and theorizing what might be done if he didn't make it. The battle was won, and we had taken the palace, but nothing felt finished as we waited for news on our leader's state.

Baker stood amongst a few others who sought medical attention. He was a little battered and bruised, clutching a bundle of gauze against his forehead, but his bleeding was not profuse. My heart trilled in my chest. I marched toward him, path unbroken.

"Look who's still alive," he said as he shot me a subtle salute. His smirk softened as I grabbed a handful of his dreadlocks and kissed him, nearly knocking him over. He held the back of my head as his other arm locked around my waist. The thrill was exhilarating. I could actually lose myself in it and forget everything else, at least until I heard the hollers of encouragement from our fellow soldiers.

I pulled back, not entirely sure what had come over me.

Baker guided me away from the men who were gawking. We found a deserted corner, and he took me into his embrace. I rested my face against his collar and could feel my own tears drenching his jacket.

"Clikk?" he asked.

I couldn't explain myself, but I didn't want to apologize either. "I'm just so glad you're alive," I said. "I couldn't stop him in time…" My voice became too hoarse to make words anymore.

Baker kissed the crown of my head. "Dirk's tough. Have faith." He touched my face, catching my tears with his thumb. "Is my friend Clikk actually crying? Never thought I'd see the day. No tears, Clikk. We're alive. And you just kissed me."

"I might do so again."

"I won't argue," he said, and so I looked up from my sorrows and kissed him once more.

The doors to the war room burst open. Everyone turned to see the surgeon coming out covered in Dirk's blood. He removed his gloves and pulled down his face mask, so it hung from one ear.

My entire life, I'd been unlucky. We orphans tend to believe our existences are inherently cursed. We feel unwanted, undeserving, unhappy and, above all un's, unlucky. I'd known loneliness, bed bugs, food shortages; I'd been robbed, beaten, humiliated, and hungry all my life. Perhaps the steel ring was lucky, perhaps not. But on this day of the battle for Locwyn, the fates looked down and took pity on us.

"I've removed the bullet, cauterized the wound, and sewn him up," announced the surgeon. "His internal organs are intact. He has a good chance of surviving!"

All those years of ill luck had led to a series of miracles this day. Every last one of us in that hallway applauded the doctor. Someone began the chant of, "Long live the King!" and I grinned until it hurt, shouting along with the others who had fought for Dirk's return to power. It was victory, true victory over the Blue Dusk.

"Let's open the shell!" I cried.

For five years under a tyrannical reign, only the elite who lived in one of the seven spires had any view of the sky. I aimed to change that forever.

I darted down the hall and followed metallic sign markers until I found my way into the central control room. Baker and several other Risen came running after me. We examined a panel of switches and levers. One of the switches was larger than the rest, so I flipped it, and a light came on in an adjacent room. What had been a mirror was now a window, and it revealed a chamber with a scale model of Locwyn mounted on a platform. I twisted a knob on the panel and on the other side of the plated glass, a tower on that model shifted. Overhead, the castle rumbled and shook, and that was when I knew that whatever I did to the miniature would affect the actual city.

It was no different from any puzzle. The model through the observation window moved, and we heard machinery cranking as the very bones of Locwyn shifted. I fiddled with the controls until I opened the replica like a flower. It was the best lock I'd ever cracked, for when we went outside, we could see the sky overhead. The sun emerged over the horizon, burning like ruby fire.

Throughout the old square, the rebels began a chant of "Rise! Rise! Rise!" The citizens of Locwyn joined in, banging, clapping, and stomping in rhythmic accord that erupted into a mighty cheer. History would record Prince Derek as the savior of our nation, but in truth, he was only an intrepid leader of people who had saved themselves.

61

SAPPHİRES

I followed Dirk into the candlelit belly of the castle. This was the first place he wanted to go upon regaining consciousness, and though the surgeon objected to his traveling, Dirk grabbed a rifle off the wall and went hobbling away on it until one of the Risen brought him a cane.

I'd never been particularly fond of dungeons. This one was miserable, with not a single window or place for ventilation. The air was thick with mold spores and I had to cover my mouth with a rag.

Dirk carried a torch and bid the warden to give us the keys to the cells and the sword confiscated from the Cerulean Knight. We navigated the dark tunnels, Dirk's cane echoing each time it rapped against the stone. We came to a door with a tiny slot in the bottom of it. I unlocked it, and Dirk fixed the torch into a holster in the corner of the room. Rex was inside. His uniform was rumpled and stank of piss. Someone had already given him a beating. One of his eyes was swollen shut, the socket dislocated.

Dirk had the curved saber on his belt. He unsheathed it and handed it to me. Gazing upon the tear-shaped sapphires, my heart filled with fire.

I never thought this moment would be laid at my feet in such a way. I sometimes fantasized about seeing that sword in battle and going after the man. I'd chase him down and tell him why I had come to kill him. This wasn't anything like what I'd pictured. The Cerulean Knight was now shackled to a wall, degraded, abused, and no longer a threat to anyone.

"You orphaned me," I said to him, hoping the words might inspire my hate to flurry. All it did was remind me that killing him would not bring anybody back.

Rex spoke to me in a dry, tired voice. "Every warrior has orphaned a child at some point in his career."

"Quiet, maggot," said Dirk, striking him with his cane. "Take your vengeance as you please, Clikk. Do not kill him. He is to be tried for his crimes, and I need time with him as well. I'll be just outside." He handed me the saber and left, closing the iron door behind him.

Rex laughed weakly, his voice like a scythe scraping against a brick. His face was vague in the torchlight, but he had the same pale skin and blue eyes of the knight who cut my throat.

"Do you remember me?" I asked.

"Oh, aye," he said. "You're that pretty thing from the prince's wedding."

"We met long before that." I lifted the torch from its holster and held it so he could see my scar.

"I see. Cut your throat, did I?"

"You did. Five years ago in Lavender Country. I was just a child. You left me for dead on the floor of the kitchen."

Rex laughed, but this time it sounded like he was crying too. "Oh, my stars," he whispered, gasping. "I do remember you. Oh... oh what was your name? What did they call you? Little Rowena? Rosana?"

This vengeance was hardly a gift. "So, you do remember?"

"Many prizes of war blur together, but I took you just after we killed the king. How could I forget my little blondie girl in Shale?

Hadn't seen a blonde for months until you came running out of that farmhouse."

I told a specific narrative to Baker, the same narrative I repeated to myself until I believed it, but in truth, my mother had died of illness during the drought. The crimes committed that day were the same, but the victim of outrage had been none other than a child called Ramona. I cut Rex's cheek with the tip of his own sword. It was sharp. And it hurt him. He tried to hide it, but I could hear his teeth grit at the sting.

"Ramona!" he exclaimed with sudden laughter that reverberated in the cell. "Your name is Ramona. I remember it now for it was the last thing your father cried before I ran him through."

"A name you will never forget again, I assure you." I crouched before him. "Now I've had a long time to think about what I should do if I ever found you. I decided I should try and share with you the full torment of being forced. I could sodomize you, of course, leave you bleeding and humiliated, but your days are numbered, and I shouldn't want to rob you of the full experience.

"So I should gouge out your eyes with a hot spoon, cast you into darkness to show you what it is to never feel safe again in your own skin. I should fill your cell with rats, so they dig away at you in the night, burrow holes in your gut as you think of me, as you wonder if I'll return, if I'll kill you, or if I'm watching you from the shadows, dreaming up new tortures to inflict in the morning.

"And you shall think of me until it drives you mad, for that solitary image of my face shall be seared into your mind's eye and shall not cease to haunt you until you are dead in your grave."

Rex closed his eyes. "Do it then," he said. "Do to me what you think is just."

I wanted to kill him, bestow my justice on his head for what he had done. It would be so easy. The trial didn't matter. The public face of evil belonged to the emperor, and he was already gone.

Let Dirk despise me for losing control and damn the consequences. Killing Rex might not bring anybody back, but at least it would satisfy the agony festering in my soul.

I sheathed the saber. "What does it matter?" I spat. "All these tortures combined cannot amount to my suffering, and frankly, it would give me no joy. I think I will leave you in this cell, let you feel the sting of being sentenced to death at your trial. Know this: I will see your sword dismantled. I will see you buried with no headstone and the world will forget you ever existed. In time, I will forget you too."

I banged on the door, and Dirk opened it for me.

"Oh, Ramona," whispered Rex. "A girl never forgets her first."

We sealed the prisoner back in darkness. Dirk's eyes met mine in the firelight.

"Clikk," he said gently.

Had he heard the conversation between us? I remembered the slot in the bottom of the door.

"I'm done with him," I said.

I followed the corridor to the stairwell. I didn't want to talk. I didn't want to think about Rex ever again. I would leave him, and all the memories associated with him, down in that dank, dark hole.

62

HONESTY

Having taken back his palace, Derek promised all his men a warm bed and a living wage in his military for as long as we liked. Taking the castle as our prize was surreal. As much as I knew that Dirk was now my country's monarch, I would never be able to stomach calling him King Derek, much less Your Grace. He would always be Captain Dirk.

I lay on my bed, tuning my new violin, and the sun outside my window filled my chamber with an orange glow. I had my own quarters in the palace, as well as a butler to bring me tea and greet my guests at the door. It surprised me when my door flew open, and Baker entered unannounced; my butler came in behind him, sputtering his profound apologies.

"It's no trouble, Mr. Peake," I said, setting down my violin. "Leave us."

My butler nodded and excused himself, closing the door behind him as he left.

Baker stared at my outfit, from my ruffled poet shirt down to my laced britches. "You're still dressing like a man," he said.

"And you as well." I nodded at the same dirty duster he always wore in the cities. Baker hadn't embraced the fashionable attire of court, but he did have a clean shave. "Truth is, I feel quite silly in a dress," I said. "Are you here about your watch?"

"No," he said. "I won't ask you to fix it until I can pay you back your two silver. I'm turning over a new leaf."

"Ah, well, in the interest of new beginnings, consider the debt forgiven." I paused, waiting for him to state his purpose, but he just stood there. "If you're not here about the watch, why are you here?"

"I...well..." Baker crossed his arms and shrugged, smiling as if he knew exactly why but couldn't verbalize it. "It turns out, I don't much care for nobles or their parties. I thought I might head out with a crew bound for Amaranthia, but I couldn't. Something was holding me back. Someone, rather."

I felt a nervous flutter in my chest. "How now?" I avoided making eye contact and stared at a porcelain water pitcher resting on a marble end table. "I know your type. I'm nothing like it."

"I didn't think I had a type," he said, encroaching until I could smell the subtle fragrance of his aftershave. "All my life, women were either whores or wives. My mum was a whore until I was fourteen, and then the wife to a devil who beat us both. I never had anyone—never wanted anyone. I'd leap from an airship and ride the wind. But love? That's for madmen. You'd have to hold me at gunpoint."

I snickered into my fist. Baker smiled, but there was pain in his eyes.

"Except you wouldn't, Clikk. And that's why I haven't left. I would follow you anywhere, into mutiny, war, into an airship rigged with hydrogen and explosives... because I'm in love with you."

I had never heard him speak this way before and couldn't begin to accept there was any truth to his words. When I didn't say anything, he meandered toward the window and gazed out like some tragic figure. I joined him, leaning against the encasement on the other side. Beyond the glass, a courtyard of metal-forged fountains glistened like liquid steel.

"Baker in love?" I said. "I don't know what to say to that, friend. If you're only after a jolly, I'd rather you be honest about it."

"It isn't that simple."

A smirk pulled at the corner of my mouth. "Is seduction simple for you?"

"Like you and your watches."

Narrowing my eyes, I muttered, "Bloody rake" under my breath. "I swore off rogues long ago. Men like you cannot be trusted."

"I'm not perfect. I might tease you or steal a sip of your Skye while your back is turned, but I would never betray you." He took my hand and my heart trembled. "Not for anyone."

I shook my head, swallowing a lump in my throat. He was beginning to sway me, which scared me. It was already terrifying how I craved him like Skye. "I can't be something I'm not, and if you're with me, there are people who will whisper and point, who might even call you deviant," I said.

"I don't care." He came closer still, pressing his forehead against mine. "I love you, Clikk."

"You're really serious, aren't you?"

"I've known it since Windmark, but I never thought I had a chance until you kissed me."

His words and his touch made me ache for him. "Why not?"

"You know the worst parts of me—"

"—And yet I trust you with my life. Why shouldn't I trust you with my heart?" I wound my fingers into the laces of his tunic and tilted my face up to kiss his lips.

A flood of emotion charged my body. I let his tongue slide gently against my own. His taste was like ambrosia, like something I couldn't have enough of no matter how long I lingered in the kiss. The floor beneath my feet shifted as if we were back on the Wastrel, taking flight.

We fell upon the bed in each other's arms, hands groping at every tie that could be opened and every bit of fabric that could be pulled away. Baker unrolled the binding from my chest.

As his fingers trailed down the fire poker brands over my ribs, I flinched.

"Sorry—I'm so jittery. It's just... if you've opened more women than I've done watches..." I trailed off.

Baker laughed softly under his breath. "I haven't done."

"How many?"

I would not have believed it, but he appeared to color. "I don't know." He took a moment to think about it.

"Can you estimate?"

"Maybe fifty."

"Fifteen?"

His color darkened. "Fifty," he repeated. "Maybe less. I don't know. They weren't all at the same time."

I didn't quite know quite what to say, except, "One good night in Amaranthia, I suppose?"

"Some of them I actually cared about." He untied the laces at my hips. "What about you?"

"Women? None. I loved a bloke once. Didn't last."

Baker laughed wickedly. "No wonder you think I'm a rake."

He hooked me under both my knees and pulled me to the edge of the bed. The bed frame creaked under his weight as he climbed over me. Each kiss he placed on my neck and beneath my ear roused a shiver in me. His stubble scratched, his rough hands maneuvered my legs on either side of his torso. I closed my eyes, tensing up.

He must have noticed, for he stopped to ask, "Are you all right?"

I didn't want to explain. My eyes remained closed. I was holding my breath.

"Clikk?"

"We need to stop," I said, sitting up as I gathered the sheets around myself. "I can't. I'm sorry."

He allowed me some space as I tried not to weep in front of him.

I found my shirt and covered myself. Laughing through tears, I said, "This is mortifying."

"We don't have to rush into anything."

I looked at him a moment, watching him get dressed, and remembering that this was my dearest friend. I could tell him anything, anything in the world, even if it made me look weak.

"I had so many chances to kill the Cerulean Knight. And this last time, I held the very sword that slayed my parents. Still, I couldn't..." My voice gave way to a rising sob, which I swallowed hard. "Baker, I lied to you about my mother. It was not her that was defiled and shamed."

I didn't have to say another word. By his somber reaction, I thought part of him might have suspected it already. I told him everything from the beginning, letting the nightmare spill out of me without restraint. I spared no horrible detail. I did not pause to let him process, did not soften any of the terror.

Baker listened, and many times he closed his eyes in disgust or put his hand to his lips as though he would be sick. After I finished telling him the truth about the Cerulean Knight, he frowned intensely.

In all the time that I had known him, I had never seen him cry. But he cried then. It broke my heart to have that hardened man shed tears for me.

"His execution is tomorrow morning," I choked. "I'm not going. I wish only to forget him. This morning, I went to a black-smith and had his saber dismantled. I kept the sapphires from the hilt and gave all of them to the street urchins I passed on my way back to the palace." Hugging myself, I paused. "All but one. Gods forgive me, I could not part with it."

Baker nodded slowly. After a long silence, he said, "You've hated him for half a decade. How could you not keep some reminder?"

"It was my destiny to kill him. That much is clear. I was meant to find him and to kill him, but when I saw him lying pitifully in his own filth, I could only think of my mother and father watching from heaven, seeing the thing I've become. And what would be the point in killing him? I want to forget, but I cannot. I want him to suffer. He has. I thought my longing for vengeance would be sated, but it haunts me still, and now I will never have it."

"Let me ask you… how did it feel," he murmured in a careful broach of the subject, "when you got your first kill during the siege?"

"I don't know," I answered, caught off guard by the question. "Like nothing at first. It was survival."

"It's one of them things… hard to describe. Did you feel powerful in the moment?"

"S'pose I did."

"And how do feel about it now?"

"Awful. I feel sick when I think about it. And not just him. I feel sick thinking about all the men I killed that day."

"Wish I could say it gets better," said Baker. "But I never stopped killing long enough to find out. Point is, murder is an intimate act. You don't need to stain your soul for that devil. You keep your sapphire, Clikk. Fix it to an earring. You might never forget what happened, but you defy him. Defy him to your dying breath. Every day you are alive, every day you draw breath… that's defiance."

I went to him. I held the curve in the back of his neck. "Thomas," I said his name with care. "My real name is Ramona, and if you like, you may call me that when we are alone." Telling him my name took more courage than it might have taken to say that I loved him. And I did love him.

I had loved him since the day he chipped his tooth in Amaranthia. I loved him when we sat up late drinking together, when I played him songs, when I jumped into the sky for him. Even in the forest and in Nelise—when I hated him—I loved him.

"Ramona of Shale." He brushed my hair behind my ear.

A heightening sense of exhilaration filled my head as he put his lips to mine. I could see the earth below me in my mind's eye, as though my heart soared in tandem with his. Our rapture propelled us like a pair of untethered kites, climbing the atmosphere, touching the surface of the freezing moon, and tasting the fire of the planets and stars.

In his arms, the world and all its perils faded away. I was home.

63

ANOTHER WEDDING

Months passed. During this time, I reconnected with Lily through a letter exchange. I shared with her the news that Baker and I had survived the battle for Locwyn and that our prince would soon have his coronation. I was hesitant to admit to her certain developments, but before the end of that first letter, I did confess that Baker and I had become an item.

I told her everything, filled pages with the story of how we became friends under a false pretense, how I had saved his life, and how I had suffered the indignity of being exposed to him during the wedding on the Crescendo.

When we stayed with Lily's family in Nelise, I had not known how I felt about him, not completely. I confessed to having been jealous of Lily and, at the time, not understanding why. I was sorry if it appeared that I had kept them apart only to take him myself. It was never my intention to manipulate the situation.

To my surprise, Lily wrote back expressing her happiest blessings. Part of her had always suspected I harbored feelings for Baker. Anyway, she was excited to announce her recent engagement to Jon Arnault. She asked if I remembered the suitor of whom she had professed a desire to kill in cold blood.

Of course, I remembered him. Lily explained how he had made a name for himself in the rebellion. Jon helped organize a Shalean resistance that played a significant role in chasing the Blue Dusk from the region. He united the gentry and the Aix Resistance and led several successful onslaughts against Blue Dusk encampments. During all this, Lily and her father had transformed their home into a hospital for the resistance militia. Jon was injured by a piece of metal debris in his leg, and he ended up coming under Lily's care.

Over the weeks he spent recovering, they rekindled their love. Jon broke off his other engagement and pleaded for Lily to have him whether her father liked it or not. Her father, in the end, accepted him as his future son-in-law. It had been a whirlwind romance, she said, and she asked if I would be so kind as to return her revolver if I no longer needed it. She also required a favor. If I would only wear a dress one last time, she would love for me to stand beside her on her wedding day.

As traumatic as my most recent wedding experience had been, I had to oblige my friend. I sent her my measurements and agreed to attend a fitting in Nelise.

In time, I would learn that everyone I knew was attending the affair, including Molly, Baker, and the whole of Dirk's inner circle. This, of course, meant my favorite louts Pierce and Jasper would be there. Though I was mortified to appear in a dress before them, it was the celebration of love and life we all needed.

We arrived by airship, setting down in front of the Belle residence. Many of our company remained on the ship, but Lily gave me my own room in the house, that same little bedroom with the slanted ceiling and the trundle bed.

At some late hour of the night, there came a tapping on my window.

I lunged for my revolver. With what little light there was from the moon, I could see the silhouette of a man cast against the ivory curtain. I whipped it back as I primed the gun.

It was Baker. By some kind of magic of his own, he had discovered my room and climbed the delicate, wood lattice without breaking it.

I unlatched the window and helped him climb in. "What on earth are you thinking? You've brought muck in all over the bedspread."

"Shh," he chuckled, taking my gun from me and seizing my lips as his prize. He removed my weapon's bullets and let them fall to the floor.

The next morning at dawn, I could hear the servants setting up in the garden. Pale light shone in through the window, and just outside, the pigeons perched in huddles on the flower box. The calming roll of their voices made me want to sleep more, but I knew that if I did, I would be missing these minutes of perfect happiness. My beloved lay at my side, awake and pretending not to be, and for a while, I pretended not to be as well, and we stayed like this, cherishing our dream of love.

I traced the sparrow tattoos flitting down his forearm until I reached the little green chameleon curling like a leaf above his wrist. It still had a border of blushed, irritated skin.

"Fresh ink?" I asked.

"Yeah," he said. "I got it to remind me I should pay closer attention to what's right in front of me." I caressed the hawk on his pectoral muscle and groped the swirl of black clouds on his opposing shoulder. I could have remained there a fortnight, learning every line of ink on him. "Why don't you have any?" he asked.

"I don't know. Nothing in my life has ever been permanent."

His fingertips glided across my shoulder blades. "You should get a falcon with its wingspan stretching from your one lovely shoulder to the next."

I chuckled, rolling my eyes at him. "That sounds expensive... and needlessly painful."

There came a gentle knock from outside.

"Shite," I blurted as I snatched my nightshirt from the foot-board and threw it over my head.

"I've come to dress you, ma'am," said the lady's maid on the other side of the door.

I threw Baker's clothes at him. "Off with you!"

"What? You'll make me go out the window?"

"You're a hawk, ain't you? Now fly!"

I sent him down the lattice before I saw the servants arranging garlands around an altar below.

They cupped their mouths when they saw the half-naked man climbing down from a bedroom window. Baker gave a salute, donning his shirt as he trudged across the green.

When I was dressed in my blue taffeta gown with my hair slicked back, I reported to the bridal dressing room.

Lily looked like fairy royalty in her billowy white gown. I was pleased to see she had forgone the corset. Both her floral crown and bouquet had lilies intermingled with irises and baby's breath. The only thing lacking was her smile. She dried her tears with a lace handkerchief, explaining she felt overwhelmed by the magnitude of this day.

During the ceremony, the officiant made a speech about finding love in times of war. Jon appeared very changed since I had last seen him, owning something more severe in his countenance. He was no longer the frivolous rich boy eager to play with guns. It was clear from the way he looked at his bride that he adored her. The dart of love had claimed his heart.

At the garden reception, the strings swelled to welcome the new couple. Baker approached me with several sprigs of lavender bound up in silk ribbon, fasting them to my wrist in a perfect butterfly bend knot.

"I'm sorry," whispered Baker. "I would ask you to dance, but I don't know what it is they're all doing."

"That's the waltz. Can't you hear the triple meter?"

"I have no idea what that is," he said. "I dance to a rowdier jig. Next time we're in Amaranthia, I'll take you to the dance halls."

"Aren't they full of prossies?"

"Nothing wrong with prossies. Which reminds me, my mum will want to meet you when I tell her I belong to somebody."

"I look forward to it."

"You shouldn't. You'll see why. And then you won't fault me for wanting to leave Locwyn behind."

"You want to leave Locwyn?"

"I hate that city. And I ain't thrilled about the Watch neither."

"The Watch pays brilliantly, and it's honest work."

"Yeah, if you want to live your life out as a fucking guard." What was this shadow rising in his voice?

The garden went silent as the conversations within earshot halted. I felt everyone's eyes scrutinizing us; I curled forward, itching the skin on my neck below my ear.

"Would you rather... return to piracy?" I could barely whisper it. The words clung to the air between us like brambles.

"If it got me out of Locwyn, sure."

"Then go. This thing between us could be over in a week or a month or a year, but I think we both know that sooner than later, it will be over."

I stood up from the table and took off into the open meadow away from the reception. Beneath the shade of an ivy-covered oak, I found a sanctuary from the party's spectators.

Birds flitted amidst the twisted branches, roused by my approach. Sunlight spilled through the leaves, casting an emerald tint over everything beneath the canopy. Around the base of the tree, purple tufts of spiderwort flourished. Baker followed me, and for a moment we just stood in silence, both of us staring at the vines that climbed the ridges of the mighty tree.

"I cannot go back to who I was," I said.

"You don't have to. We can find a way to be together. Even if at times, we must be apart."

The muscles in my face tensed. I had endured enough uncertainty and loneliness for a lifetime. I didn't need a ring, or a vow, or any other contract of commitment, but I would not settle for a man who was still married to the sky.

"I knew two lovers once who like majestic oaks needed room to thrive. For years, they lived their own lives, pursued their own ambitions, and all this time they loved only each other. As great as they became, as magnanimous and powerful, they did not share their mornings waking in each other's arms. I want us to be like those twisting vines there, relying on each other as we climb out of the shadows. If you still crave adventure, I will not hold you back."

He took my hand in his and held it to his chest. "This is the adventure," he said.

We came out from our shady sanctuary toward the rows of tables. Amidst the guests, Lily walked all alone, curtseying as she received compliments and good wishes. Her new husband had become engaged in a conversation with her father.

I hoped she would be happy. She seemed so in her letters, but since my being there, she had barely uttered more than a few words to me. I thought it a shame she had married and done everything expected of her. Now she would need her husband's permission if she wished to visit the metalwork gardens of Locwyn.

Lily wandered back to her table. She opened a lace parasol and leaned with her chin in her hand. Her eyes went blank as she stared off into space. So much can be concealed in a letter between friends. Watching Lily now, I realized this marriage might not have been the blessing she described.

Jon returned from his discussion with Lord Belle. Lily smiled at him, but it was the cold, unfeeling smile one offers an acquaintance or a servant.

Baker bore a grave expression. Curiosity bore into me as I noticed the way he looked at her with a watery sheen over his eyes. For the rest of the day, he seemed distant and distracted. I understood she had meant a great deal to him. Her innocence made her see the best in us. When she looked at Baker, she never saw the whoremonger, or the bastard, or even the pirate. Through her gaze, he was a charmer, an adventurer, and a paragon of courage.

"Clikk!" cried Molly, running toward me. In her right hand, she held what appeared to be my violin. "The bride has requested that you play for the reception."

"Well, I can't rightly refuse a bride's request on her wedding day," I said and smiled to the girl. The strings went still as I approached the quartet. Molly introduced me to some scattered applause. Many of the guests barely noticed a change in the entertainment, but all were hushed upon the sound of my first note.

Beneath an open sky full of the softest, puffiest clouds I'd ever seen, I played everything that had been on my mind that day. I knew in my heart of hearts that Baker would never abandon me, but lovers sometimes change in the night, reveal some shadow that was so clearly there all along. Baker's shadow was an entity I thought I understood. He might not know how to be in a relationship, but surely, he would not run from it. It was everything he craved in this world.

Thinking on this, I played a melody that moved like the drifting clouds at dawn. It came to me from some invisible muse as ancient as the sky. Unlike the sea, the atmosphere gives back what it takes. Birds nest in the spring. Gravity pulls us home. Even the clouds return to earth in the form of rain. If I ever did wake to find Baker had gone away, I knew I would be all right.

There was great uncertainty in love, like that in a bout of turbulence, in which one yields control to the wind and to the ship herself. I marveled at the thought of love and how people called it falling, for to fall was something else entirely, and love had little to do with it. Love was more like flying.

64

SONG OF RAMONA

S hortly after my return to Locwyn Palace, Molly summoned me. The princess resided in her mother's old room atop a tower of iron stairs. Obeying her summons proved quite the trial. Each step stung more than the last, which helped me understand why her guards had not escorted me on the climb. As I neared, I heard the child singing, her voice echoing through the metallic casing of the stairwell.

The doors and windows to her room hung open, spilling sun throughout. Saturated in light, Molly looked radiant in her lavender dress. She stopped singing and smiled.

"Hello, Clikk."

"Oh, heavens," I said, noticing the wall behind her. I laughed outright. She had finished her hair work, and Fiona's blonde locks were configured into the image of a falcon taking flight, pressed in glass within a cherry wood frame. "Molly, you didn't."

"Do you like it?" I could hardly breathe, much less answer her. "Don't laugh at me, Clikk! I have had nothing to do since becoming a princess!"

"I'm sorry," I said, clearing my throat to resist chuckling. "It's lovely. Truly."

"You don't have to humor me, Clikk. You're different these days, you know. All smiles. How is that beau of yours?"

"Molly!" I chided, and then softening, added, "It's not so serious as that. We're seeing how it goes."

"I see," she said. "He'd better not try and take you away from me. I've already lost Lily to matrimony."

I stumbled over my own words as I murmured, "Oh, no, no, no. You have no need to worry about that."

"Not the marrying sort?"

"I would have to suffer a serious head injury to even consider marrying Baker. Are you dizzy, princess? Until recently, he was lord of the rovers, prince of prossies, king of concubines! About ten years of fidelity is what it would take for me to trust him not to sink back into old habits."

Molly said, "I hope I never marry. Men are such tyrants. I can barely suffer my own brother telling me what to do."

"Neither should you. Listen, Molly. I am not planning to leave any time soon. Eventually, though, I will set off. Baker isn't thrilled about the Watch. And I don't think I could ever feel at home in a palace."

Molly's eyes flared. "I knew it!" she cried. "He is trying to take you away! You would choose a life with that incorrigible reprobate over one as the king's favorite? You mustn't! Dirk needs you. He has a council made up only of men, men like Dorian Belle and Jon Arnault. How long before they try to barter me away again?"

"Dirk won't make that mistake again."

"How can you be so sure? Our nation needs international aid to feed its people. What better way to get it than to form an alliance through marriage?"

"As princess, you belong to the state, just as I did as a soldier. But now that I've done my service to the crown, I'm ready to pursue my own dreams."

"He's going to knight you, you know. Don't tell him I told you. Try to look surprised. Memorize this face you're making now."

"Knight me?" I could only mouth the words for my voice was completely lost. "I could never."

"Don't you want to be a knight?"

"I'm not sure what I want, Molly. I'm not much older than you, you know? Some days I think I want to work the land and settle down, and other times I think I want to bounce around with scrappers for a year. Anyway, do I look like a knight to you?"

"No," she sighed, dreary sorrow asphyxiating her glow. "You look... like a sky pirate."

I gave her shoulder a tender squeeze. "I don't plan to return to that brutality, but I should never stay grounded long. Whatever happens, remember that you and I will always remain friends."

"What if..." She trailed off, looking up. "What if I asked my brother to make you his emissary? You could travel all over the world as a representative of the king you put into power."

Her proposition appealed to me. Almost instinctively, I was about to say no, but I could not help but think of the opportunities I would be missing if I did. I imagined myself seeing the world, my adventures just beginning. "I might consider that."

"Consider it! Do! Can you imagine?" She tittered into her palm. Suddenly, her merriment was halted by a thought. "There is one condition," she said, swaying nervously.

"And what is that?"

"It is only that... on occasion... you take me with you."

"I suppose it's only fair. Does this mean you're not afraid of flying anymore?"

"Well, I won't have to worry about storms with you around, and should we encounter sky pirates, I'm certain they'll let us go once they recognize you."

"Oh, most definitely," I said. "We're all chums in Amaranthia."

"Good. There is just one last thing I must request of you." She went to a rocking chair next to her bed and retrieved two needle-point hoops fitted with linen.

"Oh no," I said. "No, Molly."

"I am going to teach you some proper needlepoint."

"I told you I already know needlepoint."

"Prove it then."

I could not say which would be more demoralizing, the project of needlework or the circumstance of having needlework extorted from me by a little girl.

Molly handed me a loop holding a blank square of linen. "Come, let me help you," she said, her tone suddenly harmonious and kind. "Do sit. Take this to mark your linen. You can stitch your initials. It's called a monogram."

I narrowed my gaze. "I know what a monogram is."

"Good! Let's begin."

Molly's own handkerchief already had green leaves stitched into the fabric. She went straight to work at it.

"Perhaps you could do needlework while I play something on my violin?" I suggested.

"You're wasting precious embroidery time," answered Molly.

I consigned myself to my fate and took a moment to consider what I should stitch and embellish. Most people chose flowers or initials. I knew I should preserve some memory to keep in my pocket, some ideal to uphold in my conduct. I made a choice and executed the design, stitching with care.

Molly's elaborate tree sprawled in coils of bronze and green. Her stitches lined up in neat succession and every root and branch had perfect form. She said the tree commemorated our adventure in the forest and would remind her of the day she came to know how much her brother loved her.

She looked over my shoulder to see what I had done. Having completed my piece, I proved I knew needlepoint after all. A name adorned the handkerchief in gold thread.

Ramona.

She was no ghost and never had been. She was the bravest sky pirate who ever lived.

AUTHOR Bio

Meg Merriet is a medievalist working toward her PhD in Literature at Louisiana State University. Obsessed with medievalisms of the Nineteenth Century, she enjoys writing Steampunk fiction with a fantasy twist. Her short stories have been published in *The Antigonish Review, Mad Scientist Journal,* and the *Brave New Girls Anthology.* These feature unconventional female protagonists cast into fantastical worlds full of masks, machines, and unearthly perils. Meg lives in New Orleans with her gentleman robot husband and their young steam-powered son. Her favorite writing haunts include Crescent Park, St. Vincent's Guest House, and the levy at World's End. *Song of Ramona* her debut novel.

www.ingramcontent.com/pod-product-compliance
Lightning Source LLC
Chambersburg PA
CBHW022204030726
47494CB00019B/241